PRAISE FOR ENOK

This is no light fantasy. The deep, thought provoking side of the book touches on high intelligence, spirituality, and prejudices. Enok is a book that will envelop you ... and leave you deeply touched.

— *BookReview.com: Excellent*

A remarkable origin story unlike any other ... A magical mixture of history and mythology ... Masterfully penned.

— *The Independent Review of Books*

Solid entertainment. An impressive re-imagining of Biblical myth.

— *Blue Ink Reviews*

Immensely satisfying in its endeavor to put a spotlight on such intriguing mythical beings ... the Nephilim, the Watchers, and the Serpent of Eden ... [a] unique and thoughtfully conceived saga.

— *Self-Publishing Review:* ★ ★ ★ ★ ★

Action-packed and well written ... As cerebral as it is beautiful ... An excellent read for anyone interested in reading a fast-paced Christian fantasy with wonderfully crafted characters.

— *BookReview.com: Excellent*

A richly woven fantasy. Will appeal to fantasy lovers and ... those who may have speculated about a pre-Biblical time-frame.

— *Self-Publishing Review:* ★ ★ ★ ★ ★

Brings into brilliant focus the harmony of science and theology with lyrical power and simplicity. Highly entertaining and at the same time affirms the strength of the classical past.

— *Readers' Favorite:* ★ ★ ★ ★ ★

ENOK
AND THE
WOMB
OF
GODS

A. SkoroBogáty

First Edition, published in 2020 by Lost World Tributes.
www.lostworldtributes.media

Text and illustrations copyright © 2020 by André SkoroBogáty.

ISBN 978-0-6487703-0-5 (Trade paperback)
ISBN 978-0-6487703-1-2 (Trade hardback)
ISBN 978-0-6487703-5-0 (EPUB eBook)

A catalogue record for this work is available from the National Library of Australia.

Cover, James T. Egan, Bookfly Design LLC, *bookflydesign.com*
Print interior styling, Graeme Jones, KirbyJones, *kirbyjones.com.au*
Artwork, Hilman Hamidi, *99designs.com/profiles/hilmanham*

Typeset in *Bembo,* SHANGO, and Century Gothic.

For high school friends of old, and other migratory animals.

How I loved your mothers' sandwiches.

CONTENTS

Online glossary: *www.lostworldtributes.media/universe*

AUTHOR'S NOTES

OPTIONAL READING

Sagas of the ancient Zmee and Elim were often episodic and were enjoyed in either short or nested longer forms. Likewise here, for an abridged experience, begin at Episode 3 and skip the overarching storyteller's timeline labeled with the ‡ superscript. I recommend this approach for all but fans of complex fantasy or for those unfamiliar with Biblical mythos.

Now, while few may ever re-read a book, this story was designed so that it could be read twice: the short way first and the long way later, where the overarching layer makes new of something old.

STYLE

Many ancient idioms have no modern equivalent; however, I have done my best to convey this saga in vernacular English while retaining some sense of the archaic original.

GENDERLESS PRONOUNS

Imperial English has long accepted the plurals *they/them/their* as epicene singulars. However, due to rising dissatisfaction over this, and over gendered third-person pronouns generally, I have coined the near homophonic *dey/dem/deir* to represent the equivalent epicene singulars for creatures of unknowable or non-existent sexual specie. For transcendent deity, however, I have retained the plural forms of *They* & etc.

LINGUISTICS

The guillemet symbol pair « » are used as quotation markers for the non-verbal sign language of Zmee facial tendrils, one that has no grammatical rules despite my representing it so. General expressions of surprise/disbelief or uncertainty/curiosity might well be rendered wordlessly by «!» and «?» respectively in much the same way as do human facial expressions.

The language of the yeti-like Wahoona relies heavily on non-pulmonic sounds such as clicks of the tongue, in-breaths, and on various coughs. For readability's sake, such in-breathed clicks are prefixed with an "implomation" mark *¡* and are always italicized.

Thus, dental clicks similar to the American "tut-tut" of dis-approval (or the sucking English "tsk-tsk") are rendered as *¡ts*. Similarly, lateral clicks like the "Tchick! Tchick!" used to urge a horse, are rendered as *¡tk*.

Crisp alveolar clicks of the tongue on the back of the gum ridge, a cork-popping sound, are rendered by *¡tkl*. For example, *¡tkla* and *¡tklo* are the onomatopoeic sounds children use to imitate the clopping of a horse; and in this vein, *¡mpwa* would approximate the sound of a kiss.

Glottal stops (coughs) are indicated with the usual apostrophe, thus 'Ugh and 'Agh are pronounced like coughs.

While such unusual sounds could have been rendered by IPA symbols, they are alien to most readers and the consensus has been to avoid them as they detract from the reading experience.

THOUGHT BUBBLES

Where supported by the reading medium or platform, internal dialogues, or thoughts projected from one person to another, are portrayed using a small-cap font to better distinguish these from standard italicized emphases of speech. Additionally, telepathically received thoughts are highlighted bold.

Finally, all these unorthodox devices have been used as sparingly as possible. Yes, they're experiments, but clarity has always been the objective here, and I beg the reader's indulgence.

EXORDIUM

Man, cursed is the earth because of you ...
Serpent, henceforth on your belly shall you crawl ...

— GENESIS 3

The Nephilim were on the earth in those days ... when the Sons of
God went in to the daughters of men ... These offspring were the
mighty ones, the great heroes of old.

— GENESIS 6

This story reflects upon the myriad sorrows of all that followed
after. This is a tale of the Woebegin.

VIEWPOINT CHARACTERS

EYDA, an aging widow once known as Deina, and the teller of the Enok saga. (PRESENT)

ELISHAN, an ethereal Watcher. (PRESENT)

ENOK, a young Elim enslaved by the Zmee. The story's main protagonist and eventual husband of Eyda. (PAST)

ZAKON, a crimson Zmee bull. Enok's nemesis. (PAST)

HATAN, a powerful aquatic yeti-like Wahoona. The young Enok's guardian. (PAST)

PUZO, a yashurakh (or yash'kh), a great marine dragon friendly to Enok. (PAST)

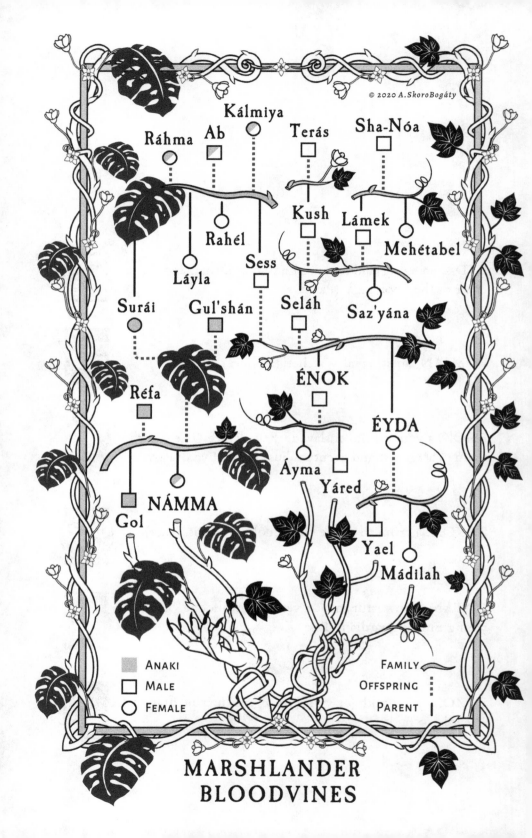

© 2020 A.SkoroBogáty

Ráhma   Ab   Kálmiya   Terás   Sha-Nóa

Rahél

Kush   Lámek

Láyla   Sess   Mehétabel

Surái   Gul'shán   Seláh   Saz'yána

ÉNOK

Réfa   ÉYDA

Áyma

Yáred

NÁMMA

Gol   Yael

Mádilah

ANAKI
MALE
FEMALE

FAMILY
OFFSPRING
PARENT

MARSHLANDER
BLOODVINES

OLD MAA ‡

The return of a long-lost son upends the daily routines of an aging recluse. Confronted by the discovery of grandchildren who know nothing of their heritage, she relents to a saga of bygone days.

"MA'NUNA! MA'NUNA! MA'NUNA!"

The chanting was now a frenzied chorus. The climax was near. It could end only one way now, and the worshipers were eager for it, needing it. Plumes of incense clouded the torch-lit cavern, draping horror in mystery and magnifying the terror.

Splayed across a sacrificial slab before a towering robed statue of the Twain Goddess, a young Deina thrashed helplessly. Hoarse impotent barks were all that remained of her screams. Her numb tongue and parched mouth refused to make a sound. They had slipped her yahl root to make her compliant. They must have. And though her head swam weakening against the intoxicating torrent, her spirit held defiant of any submission by the flesh.

"Ma'nuna: thou womb of the gods, thou weaver of souls, she and he, two in one, both and neither. Ma'nuna!" cried a priestess ecstatically.

"Hearken thy heart to the swiftening drums!" howled a priest. "Ma'nuna! Ma'nuna! Come forth!"

The bindings about Deina's wrists and ankles had cut deeply where her own blood had lubricated the struggle. Her anguished digits had long since welded into fists.

"I will not submit," Deina kept telling herself. "Burn you, Ma'nuna. Burn you!"

The wide-eyed statue leered grotesquely as the robe fell from its shoulders. Great static fingers of wood clasping the smoldering votive bowl twitched. Then came the sound of a great hiss as the flung bowl splashed into the temple laver. All hope now fell prostrate to terror.

The great effigy had come to life!

None had ever survived the bloodlust of this deity. No one ever would.

THIS IS NOT A DREAM, NOT A DREAM, whimpered Deina inwardly as she struggled vainly against the towering avatar with her teeth clenched against the pain.

Then fingers like wooden claws forced her jaws open, gagging her with a soppy yahl-soaked cloth.

Unable to flee, or breathe, or scream —

"Argh!"

Eyda woke suddenly, panting, ripping the blanket as she flung it from the bed.

It had only been a dream, only a dream, a nightmare from a distant life. A hundred years of nights had passed without such troubling memories, and at least fifty since she had even spared a thought for that hideous deity. Ma'nuna: a name so loathed it was never uttered. Left unspoken it should have stayed forgotten. And it was, or it had been, until today.

Her stone-and-timber bed was a luxury in these parts. She fell from it naked, and dried herself of terror's sweat with a scrap of blanket. There was no going back to sleep now. A crack of gray light around the door curtain told that night had ended. The reveille of nearby frogs amidst the dawn songs of the scores of marshland creatures were all part of that great awakening where returning to sleep was impossible.

And they all seemed to mock her:

Ma-aa — nuna! Ma-aa — nuna!

Her kissed fingers signed the traditional blessing over the life-tapestry that hung outside the entrance of her hut. So many different kinds of tokens emblazoned it: some of festivals, others of grand adventures, or births. Each was an emblem of mercy; indeed, the tapestry itself meant a life of mercies. Twenty-four twenties and five and two, the year-tokens declared: its owner had witnessed four hundred and eighty seven New Years, more than had any other marshlander.[i][ii]

The wall hanging was now so large it had acquired a fame of its own. It wrapped halfway round her dwelling — too grand by far for a humble reed hut — and with each passing festival, there never yet failed someone keen to embellish it for its own sake. But for the rebel who had been Deina, these tokens counted more than years. They were markers of a liberty whose price much blood had paid.

Draped in a coarse sarong and with her prayer mat in hand, Eyda hobbled towards the riverbank where water lilies framed a hallowed space. There she removed a slipper, and gingerly tested the shallows. GO EASY, she thought, favoring Old Stubby with a kiss. NOW FOR THE LEFT FOOT.[iii]

On her knees, and with palms to the great rising light, opened in petition like the lilies themselves, the ablutions of her morning ritual began in earnest. However, nightmare's grip still held her, and it told in the trembling of her hands.

"Let my hands do no wrong." She cupped them for water and drank. "Let no dark word pass my lips." A second cupping washed eye-sleep away. Then she faltered, more hopeful than believing, "Let my eyes behold no ... evil."

Her lips then loosed a stream of gratitude as gentle as the tranquil river before her, to The El, creator of the Greater and the Lesser Lights,[iv] and great keeper of her soul. Silent prayers were for heedless Deina, and timeworn chants, her thankless past. With so

---

i   Marshlanders typically count by twenties, using their fingers and toes.

ii Lifespans are rumored to exceed 700 years, though few survive long enough to prove it. Puberty usually strikes around sixty years of age.

iii *Old Stubby*. Eyda's right foot has a missing hallux, or big toe.

iv Names for the sun and moon, which in the marshlands are usually only observable as indistinct hazes.

much to be grateful for, she was not ashamed to express it, but it was old Eyda who prayed now, not the headstrong Deina of her youth. That restive girl had died a dozen times at Ma'nuna's feet; it was Eyda who had risen from the sacrifice reborn.

Hers was now a mostly solitary life on the edge of The Moud, a thousand islets of mud and reeds that had once been mere eyots in the shallows of a broad river delta. It was fear that had driven Eyda and the first families to the remoteness of this place. That very same fear that had extended these eyots into a network of islands now bursting with people and industry.

The Gihon delta seemed boundless, swallowing the horizon on every side. And here, nestled against the Crooked Thumb of its Six Fingers, her descendants were as far from centers of wealth, power and intrigue as it was possible to be, as far from the world of giant beasts and giant men as one could go. This was quite literally the end of the earth, and the very blessing she held most dear.

"For this haven and the peace we enjoy, I give thee thanks." With concluding obeisance, the aging woman rose, whispering, "Deina, I died: Eyda, I live."[v]

Stands of jute had grown up to curtain her river oasis against unsympathetic eyes. True, most of the passers-by were her descendants; however, recent generations held an almost alien array of faces that offered little reward of recognition or smile. With the passage of years, Eyda's celebrity had waned as her grandchildren's grandchildren wrought fame for themselves. She had been venerated once, touted the model of the virtuous widow. As clan mother, she had presided over disputes and auspicious occasions.

Later, as a great-great-great-grandmother, she had been highly valued as a midwife and healer, but after a series of nearby stillbirths some mothers-to-be considered the merest sight of her an omen and her very name had slipped into a byword. So preempting that final decline of regard, Eyda had exiled herself to a remote hut at the end of a narrow sodden track, at the edge of the edge of the edge of the world.

---

v   A common custom in Eyda's day was the taking a new identity when embracing a new belief or tribe. In young Deina's case, a crisis moment precipitated faith.

Honk. Ha-Honk!

A noisy marshland fang-swan sprang from between rushes onto the silted bank with a bobbing head and clattering beak. It had come begging for food.

Just as suddenly came a tap on her shoulder as a youngster gleefully declared, "And seventy six!"

"Oh, Sha!" exclaimed Eyda with startled hand on heart. "You'll scare the life out of me, sneaking up like that!"

"Sorry, Old Maa. I hope you live forever."

Eyda was touched by his naïveté, and gave the youngster a welcoming slap. "What are you counting this time?"

The lad was Sha-Noa, her great-grandson, almost forty now, and one of countless great- and great-great-grandchildren of similar age scattered across the everglades. He was by far her most frequent visitor and he loved to hear the old stories. To him, the natural world was captivating. He was a boy of a thousand questions and he had, despite his youth, a profound grasp of the most peculiar things yet with a strangely unchanging innocence — just like her long-lost husband Enok had been.

Sha-Noa was special and she loved him like a son. And why not? With his midnight skin and thick unruly hair, he was more a semblance of her than any image of his parents.

"Look what I have," he said, flourishing a great prickly orb from his sling-pouch. "A pine cone!"

"Where did you get it?"

"A long-boat pulled in last night. You should see the size of it! Anyway, I heard someone talking with father about herds of long-necks migrating upriver, and needing safe haven from the leaping great-fish."

Eyda wondered. The Gihon's Six Fingers were guessed at being about seven leagues wide. Their shallowness is what protected them all from the leaping great-fish. And the upriver neck beyond Log Jam was far too deep and swift-flowing for the lumbering long-necks. The story did not quite ring true.

"I traded my whistle with a boy called Ab. And guess where he found it. Way upriver, in the deep waters beyond Zakon's Reach." Then he whispered eerily, "Beyond even that — in the deep, dark gowfer forest."

"Tonight's meal, is it? It's not enough for two, you know." Roasted over embers, the great cone's seeds made quite a treat.

"By Baba's beard, Old Maa! About dinner in the morning, and breakfast in the evening: you're always thinking about food. No, these aren't for eating at all."

"No? Oh." She never managed to voice, EATING IS ONE OF THE FEW PLEASURES LEFT TO ME, or even PERHAPS YOU'LL UNDERSTAND SOMEDAY, for at the very mention of that dragon Zakon, she sank into remembrance like rock into river.

The boy too was pondering, studying a patch of bare earth while absently tossing loosened seeds to the fang-swan, and it snapped them up greedily.

Eyda sighed, foreseeing the inevitable regret.

"If I buried this here," Sha-Noa considered aloud, "will it root?"

"I suppose so. I have never really tried."

"When it's full grown, I'll build a house atop it, just like in your stories. Maybe I could catch some of the eight winds of the world from up there!"

Eyda applauded his imagination but winced at the thought of having such a towering tree laden with hundreds of these heavy cones overshadowing her home. Gowfer trees grew tall and straight, even taller than the long-necks reaching on their hindquarters, but thankfully they grew rather slowly — so, no danger for now.

Sha-Noa buried the cone under a mound and eyed his handiwork as though half-expecting it to sprout. "Old Maa," he wondered, without losing sight of his plot, "Will I have adventures too some day? Like Ava-Baba? Like Enok?"

Adventures? Eyda frowned. 'MIND WHAT YOU WISH FOR,' her mother's words echoed. How strange that she should hear them so clearly now.

Honk! Ha-onk!

The fang-swan was hungry and begging for more.

"Shoo! Clear off!"

"I almost forgot," Sha-Noa added, wiping grimy hands against his breeches. "Father says we're having a fire-feast today, and he said to bring river-yams. We can cook broth in the clamshell. Bye!"

As swiftly as he had come, the boy disappeared into the rushes, leaving his great-grandmother to her thoughts. Memories: the clangor of metallic weapons, the echo of distant joys and peals of terror, the voices of those long gone, faces both hideous and handsome all swirled unbidden about her.

MA'NUNA, NAAMA, ZAKON, HATAN.

The past, it seemed, would not give her up.

At the breaking of day, the new crescent of the Lesser Light hung yet high and pale above the western marshes, a reminder she hadn't toured the villages since its fullness. Actually, it had been at least two moons now. [vi] Old Stubby was becoming increasingly less fond of walking, and keeping one's balance while paddling a round-boat erect had grown more difficult of late.

Well, that was her excuse. She was safe here and independent in her private little hideaway. Though, if there was ever an inducement to join the thronging world again, a feast was surely it.

A string of hamlets surrounded by endless rows of skeins of drying jute marked Eyda's passage to Lamek's island. Here the cluster of domed huts by the riverbank was already abuzz with activity. In the clearing before the central longhouse, Sha-Noa's father, Lamek himself, a prosperous, driven man was stoking coals in an earthen cook-trough.

"Old Maa." Lamek bowed with proper respect. "Finally come to join the mayhem, eh? What a day for a fire-feast when fuel is so scarce!"

"The feast, yes. Your 'fourteenth' told me."

His vapid stare became a knowing chuckle. "Ah. Who else but Sha! So it's numbers now, is it?"

"Or big things."

"Him and his counting reed! Three thousand, seven hundred and something paces to your house. Did you know?"

"Hmmm, something like that."

As Eyda and her grandson bantered, another man emerged from behind the longhouse burdened with a basket of food. She gasped as recognition dawned for both of them.

---

vi   Marshlanders reckon years by autumnal changes and lunar cycles, or 'moons.' The fullness of the moon (the *Lesser Light*) marks a day of special worship known as Temple Day.

"Sess!" With arms flung wide, she hobbled to embrace him. "Oh, my darling boy! What a happy surprise!"

Basket on a hip, he merely nodded politely, and stooped awkwardly for a kiss to his forehead. As tears welled in his mother's eyes, "Hello," was all he managed to say, and shrugged weakly in response to the quizzical fondling of his smooth-shaven face. "Surai detests whiskers."

Oh. Eyda wondered whom he meant. Shurai? Sarai? She hadn't heard a name like that for centuries. If that was his wife, she was clearly no local. Anyhow, it seemed only proper that the head of his house sport a decent beard, but Eyda knew better than to make an issue of it. She slapped his arms, feeling the tension in them.

"My, how you've grown! So handsome, my youngest."

"Lamek, help me with this, will you?"

Older nephew and younger uncle grunted in unison over a giant clamshell, then over flagstones for the fire. "*Oi-oi,* that's heavy. I'm here to trade, Mother. Not to stay."

"You're not leaving straight away, though, are you?"

"My plans aren't settled yet."

"Won't you stay at least until the Lesser Light is full again, till Temple Day perhaps?"

He responded with talk of Lamek needing pitch for his boats and wanting to barter for flax rope and oil, yet essentially avoiding her question and the longing in her eyes.

In the seventy years of praying for the runaway's return, the imagined reunions were nothing like this. In the awkwardness of the moment, her gaze wandered about the yard to the far-flung buildings of Lamek's village and beyond.

What caught her eye next was a real surprise. Beyond the outlying huts, by the distant riverbank lay moored the largest long-ship of reeds she had ever seen. Cabins astern and abaft were easily the size of houses. Ropes she judged as thick as a wrist tied each of its upturned ends to a central mast cluttered with rigging and shrouds. A ribbed sail hung loosely, half furled from a great horizontal spar high above the deck. Garments for hundreds from a single cloth, so great was the size of it!

With this, and the sight of a similar vessel beyond it, a happy thought came bubbling up. HE'S RICH. It quickly burst, however, as other details sent shivers down her spine. Shields of electrum and animal skins, great gilded horns prized from beasts of impossible size, spiked clubs and serrated pikes adorned the cabin abaft.

"Ah, is that your ... home?" she asked, shuddering at the notion of living under such grisly instruments of war.

"Hmmm, not exactly." The reply was hesitant, eyes on his boats. "But mostly."

"I've missed you," voiced Eyda softly to Sess, while Lamek busied himself with the work of oiling the flagstones, and feigning deaf ears at the awkward reunion of grandmother and uncle.

"Mother, you've had thirty-seven other children," Sess countered with an audible sigh. "And how many of your daughters here have surpassed even that? Between the Moud and the Soud, it strains imagining how many tens of thousands of descendants you have scattered across the marshlands. You can't be that lonely, surely?"

For the first time in so many empty moons their eyes met and she wanted to let this handsome son of hers know all that was in her heart, yet the words remained unspoken. In all but the grin and the hair he was the very image of Enok — OH, EL! — even to the sound of his voice, yet the embarrassed silence made her realize once again that his were not the eyes of his father, or of the last fruit of her womb, but of a familiar stranger.

Upon this fatherless son, she had once lavished every affection. Yet the more she had loved him, the more he had spurned her. Had it all been her fault? Had she driven him away? Now suppressed memories, emotions and the solid image of him collided. The source of old hurts stood before her, unblinking, unfeeling, behind darksome eyes; and yet there was a pleading in them.

"It must take quite a few hands to move these lummoxes, eh?"

"If it's my sons you're referring to, they're out are trading for food," he informed in his classic taciturn manner.

"Sons?"

"Thirteen of them. My eldest is nearly sixty now," he explained, straining under the weight of another large stone. "You'll meet them soon enough, I guess." And before she could utter another word, he added, "Don't even think of suggesting a bride. It cost a fortune in silks and rare ointments to secure him a ... an *Isha* any merchant would envy."

Isha? Strange that he should use the archaic form of 'woman.' Anyhow, the edge to his tone meant the subject was closed, and the reunion over.

AFTER SEVENTY YEARS, NOT EVEN A HUG FOR HIS MOTHER! she kept thinking. Marriage and time had little improved him, and she pondered on his choice of wife. She, at least, might have better manners.

As others arrived to barter, Eyda slipped away before bitter words cut deep regrets, and now across the clearing by his vessel, she spun to seek consent upon his face, but Sess was engaged with friends of old, freely granting others the very warmth he had denied her.

Now standing by the river's edge, the craft completely filled her view. Stars above! It was easily thirty cubits long, and the trading barge beyond was even larger. Its rope ladder smacked of invitation, and she climbed aboard. Two boys were huddled by the dragon-head prow with an obvious air of mischief. A stranger with a tattooed cheek kept glancing over his shoulder, while his partner kept bobbing guiltily, a lad with wild ebony hair like bulrushes gone seedy. It was Sha-Noa with a large figurine.

"Old Maa," he whispered nervously. "This is some boat, isn't it? The wind blows and it moves! Just like in your stories!"

But his Old Maa was focused instead on the cabin astern. Parted curtains revealed two infants, a pink newborn and an olive-skinned toddler suckled by a shaven-headed maid who seemed barely out of childhood herself, and an older wet-nurse. And snooping eyes discerned a third and very large someone sleeping curled at the rear. A brother-in-law perhaps?

A tug on the frock distracted her. "Look, Old Maa." It was Sha-Noa. "I made a trade of my own!"

The tattooed boy kept glancing furtively at the cabin, while Sha-Noa rubbed his hands with a flourish, wondering aloud, "What were the magic words again? *Hallel nefesh talah talah,*" he eerily intoned.

The presumed toy was heavy and more than half his size, a statuette with great brooding eyes, a grotesque caricature of the female form clasping an empty hollowed gourd on one side, and a male figure proudly sporting its exaggerated member on the other. The mere sight of it left Eyda open-mouthed and speechless.

It was the goddess-god Ma'nuna in miniature!

A younger self had survived this incantation before, and the terror of that distant day at the feet of its towering lookalike came again in full force.

MA'NUNA! MA'NUNA! MA'NUNA!

If not for the daring of a strange young man, Eyda would never have lived to marry her savior. The girl taken into slavery would have become just another plaything for the gods, a pillow wailing beneath an outpouring of lust so monstrous that for many death was its consummation. Indeed, death would have been preferable to being crippled by its memory.

ENOK, SAVE ME!

A dozen heartbeats passed. Trembling from the crippling torrent of long-suppressed memories and a hundred-hundred tortured dreams of drums, blood, and the stench of burning flesh, summoning all her strength, she flung the fertility idol overboard, wailing, "Burn you, Ma'nuna! Burn you!"

"What'd you do that for?" the tattooed boy cried, mystified. "It was an honest trade!"

ENOUGH OF IDOLS AND GODS! AND BOATS! AND LIFE!

Sha-Noa protested loudly as she began to drag him by his breeches. Kneeling beside the boy and reasoning with him proved ineffective. Though he kept saying, "You don't understand," she refused to release her grip, and he would not be consoled until he beheld the idol bobbing in the river alongside the boat.

"See," he declared triumphantly, "it does have magic."

The woven headdress of an elder's wife bobbed briefly as its owner climbed clumsily aboard. It was Sha-Noa's mother Mehet'abel, with one hand cradling the bulging life within.

"Look, mommy!" Sha-Noa beckoned. "Did you see it float?"

"I'm sure it did, dear. Now, why don't you boys go retrieve it?"

The tattooed boy dived into the river. Sha-Noa, however, was content to study it bob on the waves of the splash.

"Maa, you're causing a scene." The younger woman gestured discretely towards the ladder. "Please, these are our guests."

"No! The sacrifices! It's a fertility idol!" Eyda exploded. "You have no idea of what I endured ... what it represents ... or of the monsters who worship —"

"It's alright," Mehet'abel soothed. "Surely you don't take so-called magic seriously, do you?" she said taking Eyda's hand, and was startled at the ancient grip that crushed her fingers gravely.

"Oh, but I do," returned Eyda. "More than you know."

"How did they manage to get hold of the idol?"

"The other boy claimed they traded for it."

"*That* boy?" The younger woman rolled her eyes. "There will doubtless be trouble when his mother finds out."

Lacking gold, gemstones, or scented rosins in its votive bowl, the idol had little worth. What mischief were the boys then up to?

A baby cried and the women in the cabin began to stir.

"All I know is," Mehet'abel continued, "Sha was out to prove someone wrong. He has a new fascination."

"In addition to counting everything?"

"Trees, I think. He has some seeds, you know."

Eyda knew only too well how nebulous Sha's ideas could be, yet a cord of reason always bound the train. Then came understanding. "And the idol ... is carved ... of wood," she chimed to the rhythm of his mother's nods.

"Look! Come see, Old Maa!" Sha-Noa beckoned, anger all forgotten. "Is it really magic?" He was clearly intrigued by some new phenomenon.

"So, have the ghosts of old departed?" asked Mehet'abel in that disarming fashion Eyda so loved in her, but her Old Maa shook her head, frustrated that the right words, which were ever her defense and her weapon, were all suddenly eluding her.

"I'm disappointed that my very own blood would receive such an abhorrence into his home! You cannot go swimming —"

"— without getting wet," Mehet'abel finished.

Eyda was dismissive. "You're nearly full term. You shouldn't be wandering about."

"Have you no desire to meet your son's family? Come, I'm sure that you do."

Eyda stroked the dragon figurehead absently, sparing a sidelong glance at her new kin at the rear of the enormous floating house. She pondered Sess's loveless greeting, and the meaning of the trophies adorning the cabin. "Perhaps, for today, I have family enough."

*

It was a fragile Eyda who stood on the lonely side of her grandson Lamek's yard, watching the throng of traders and children growing to rival the bazaars she had known of old. Dozens of little round-boats were sculling towards the flat and featureless trading barge beyond the houseboat, all laden with goods for barter: rope, pitch, river-pearls, or grains. Beyond the daily toil, festivals, and match-making gossip, local life offered few diversions. It was no surprise then that many youngsters too had been drawn by the novelty of boats so impossibly large.

"Maa! You're alive!" The cheerful voice and the sight of the lanky, slightly stooping figure never failed to comfort her. It was Mati, her firstborn, accompanied by wife Saz'yana and Kush the scribe.

"Alive? That's hardly funny. I just prefer my own company. Is that so hard to understand?"

"Hmmm." Recognizing the scowl on her face, a finger touched her lips. "Tut! Not a word! I already know what's on the tip of that tongue about goddesses and such. I'll have private words with Sess before tonight's fire-feast."

Eyda humphed, then, "You'll be wanting barley bread."

Saz'yana reached out, nodding admiringly at the strand of lilies Eyda had woven into her hair. "Yours were always the best, you know, and I could always use some help. Besides," she winked, "our youngest has a suitor."

"Ha'leya?"

"No doubt you women will have much to discuss before the boy's aunts," Mati and the scribe were grinning widely, "formalize the arrangements." [vii]

Sha-Noa ran past them with a pretty dark-skinned girl who could easily have been his twin. Both were dripping wet. "Baba Mati! Wood floats like reeds. It's magic!"

Mati stopped him in his tracks. "Well, of course it does, and I daresay the whole village now knows it too. Listen, Sha, there are far too many young folk here. Why don't you lead them to, say, Temple Island? Storytellers will be along shortly. Later, your Baba

---

vii   Nuptial bargaining rituals were primarily matriarchal affairs involving aunts and older sisters. They sought to equitably establish the betrothed with their own dwelling and means of support.

Sess will happily let you all explore his long-ships — when the Greater Light crosses the river, perhaps after fourth shadow."[viii]

"Promise?" Sha-Noa and the girl shared a look, then shrugged an acceptance. "It's magic!" he sounded again, trotting off hand-in-hand to spread the news. "Magic!"

Mati chuckled. "To keep the child alive in ourselves would really be something, wouldn't it?" A single eyebrow rose, challenging his mother's frown. "That was Raama, by the way. Sess's daughter. Dark as an Ember Night,[ix] and with that same raven mop of hair, she's the image of Sha-Noa, the very image of *you*."

Eyda could tell where this conversation was heading but was determined to focus it elsewhere. "Look, Priest and Elder you may be, but I'm still your mother and I don't want the children infected with all this talk of magic. You only have to see how quickly young Sha-Noa has been —"

"Mother. *Eyda!*" Mati interjected. The informal address breached all etiquette, and by its tone it wasn't just her son now speaking but the High Priest of the Gihon. "All of life is filled with magic: the way of birds in the sky, the way of youths with maidens, the cycles of the wind and the heavens, that something should sink but does not. Sha-Noa is still very young and cannot yet distinguish between the beauty and the mystery of the natural world and the darker forces you fear."

"But the idol —"

A reassuring hand gripped her shoulder. "You worry needlessly, Eyda. He will not fall. The breath of The El stirs his soul."

Her firstborn towered over her; she retreated to look her Mati in the eye. "And yours too, my son."

Upon a whispered nod from Mati, Saz'yana and the scribe moved on, affording mother and son some privacy. "Do you remember when Sess was a boy, when we lived on the prairies? His greatest fear was of being trodden-on by long-horns in the dark."

---

viii   While marshlanders can mark time by a series of sun-stick shadows equivalent to two daylight hours, they generally just eye-ball the Greater Light's (sun's) position. Third shadow would thus be midday.

ix   *Ember Night.* The monthly moonless night when torches pepper islet shores to guide river-craft home. The river can be deadly in the dark.

Eyda remembered all too well. "Particularly when the Lesser Light was full, when the herds would march."

"And so we moved into the woodlands and he would sleep high in the trees?"

"Yes, but what …?" His point eluded her.

"It was always Lamek and his sons who joined him for the night. Lamek is *my* son and Sess's nephew, but Sess being so much younger —"

"— looked up to him like a father." Yes, Mati was right. Sess was only a child when Enok vanished.

"So, were there really long-necks crossing upriver that caused him to beat a retreat here? And of all the myriad of islets along the Crooked Thumb, to navigate The Moud in the dark, right here to Lamek's very feet? Or has Sess stumbled into trouble again and needs his adopted father?"

"He always was an adventurer." Eyda winced at the memory of Sess atop a fledgling, big-headed, scavenging dragon, reflexively rubbing Old Stubby, her bad leg — a leg robbed of its hallux that day. "Remember him riding that young trr-bahal?"

Mati chuckled. "He kept to his tree house for days because he thought its mother would eat him. Stars above! That was a massive tree. He has boldness aplenty, but …"

The pause invited conclusion. "He's feeling vulnerable?"

Mati's nod confirmed it. "Trust me, it's not trade that drives one to brave the rivers on an Ember Night, it's desperation."

"And I'm not being very helpful." Her shuddering hands clenched into balls as she faltered, "It's just … I had a terrifying dream last night. *That* dream."

"The Twain Goddess? She woke me too," echoed Mati ominously before burying concerns with a smile. "Anyhow, what feast doesn't loosen tongues, eh? Failing that, the maidens' dancing surely will. He'll tell all soon enough. Meanwhile, let's not be so quick to censure our visitors, alright?"

Eyda smarted, and was about to conjure some defense, but which her son quelled with a look.

"And I perceive something else, something our canny Old Maa will sense soon enough for herself. Sess's children are like empty vessels waiting to be filled. And they *will* be filled," Mati paused for effect, "but whether by someone with firsthand knowledge of the sacred stories or by some lesser person, that I leave to you."

"There are so many younger tellers now. My time for such has long been over."

"There's no deception like self-deception, right? Eyda, your very skin is made of stories."

"Sha-Noa always manages to wheedle one out of me. The others, well, let's just say I've feasted long enough on ridicule."

"Still dining on ashes, eh? Eyda, love makes of fools of everyone. And it's no less true of faith. If you don't stand for something, they," he waved a finger at the marshlands entire, "could almost fall for anything."

"You're preaching."

"Well, that's what High Priests do," Mati grinned. "Besides, they were father's words to me ... before he went ..."

A tear welled in his eye. Then just as quickly, one in hers. Both dried their cheeks and left their loss unspoken.

Eyda knew his every expression, so despite his winning smile, Mati the ever-serene was clearly unnerved, and it puzzled her.

"Rest assured, Mother, you'll be saved a place at the feast. Meanwhile, Sess has children who know little of who they really are." Teeth gleamed in entreaty. "There's just no one else I can rely upon today. Don't do this for me, Mother," he implored as children ran past merrily. "Do it for Enok. It's what father would have wanted."

Oh, Mati was such a diplomat. And that perpetual smile he wore was quite disarming, just like his father. No wonder everyone liked him.

"Here, give these to the women." Eyda unslung her pouch and passed on the vegetables intended for soup. "I suppose I'm off to the teaching circle." She slapped his arm reassuringly before leaving. "There's no escaping my own skin, now, is there?"

A succession of crude flagstone bridges over sluices formed a causeway into Temple Island, and they seemed altogether more erratic and treacherous than ever. Great stands of rushes and wild jute bordering the retting ponds arched over Eyda like some winding organic tunnel. Together, they served only to funnel the most bone-chilling breeze, and she clutched all the more tightly at her jute-silk shawl.

She paused between islands where a bridge had subsided, as much to marshal her balance as to ponder the strangeness of Sess's return. His hideous instruments of war, the Akadian fertility idol, Lamek's usual jocularity swamped by Sess's cheerless mood, and the worried look spied briefly on Mati's face, though quickly masked, told much to those who knew him well. These were all connected somehow, and all screaming at the hearing ear.

And that both she and Mati had relived old nightmares about Ma'nuna was a sign too ominous to ignore.

Her stomach rumbled. In all the tumult of the morning, she had completely forgotten breakfast. Though was it hunger gnawing at her now, or premonition?

© 2020 A.SkoroBogáty

THE SIX FINGERS
IN EYDA'S DAY

Gowfer
Forest

Longnecks'
Trample

Swan
Lynns

The
Soud

Zakon's
Reach

Log
Jam

Tidal
Lake

The
Moud

Grand
Banks

Grain
Lands

Temple Is.

Lamek's Is.

Eyda's
Is.

The
Shallows

Grain
Lands

Crooked
Thumb

Great
Salty
Sea

2 LEAGUES

~ 6 miles or 10 km

THE GIHON DELTA

THE HEAVEN BELOW ‡

In the invisible realms, beings guarding the marshland tribe are
startled by a strange device and an emissary for whom Eyda's
storytelling seems key ... The Old Maa of the marshlands begins
her tale of Enok's time among the serpents of Zoar.

THE MUTED ECHO, THE FLEETING SHADOW, the sudden chill
might well give cave dwellers cause for wonder, to ponder
worlds beyond their burrow; but sounds and shadows,
however wondrous, make feeble emissaries and demit to eternal
puzzlement a far greater, richer reality.

So great the gulf between all they have known and the vastness
beyond! Only revelation could bridge it.

This was hardly the first time Elishan mused upon present
parallels, recalling those eons long past in a distant heaven when
his people were the watched, and their own transfiguration a future
glory that few had suspected. And now the principal difference
between his 'ascended' kind and Eyda's was that he could traverse
some realities without physically moving, like ascending a musical
scale. At a higher frequency, a higher energy level, one became a
whisper and a shade, a thing beyond the apprehension of Eyda's
'cave dwellers;' but in the ascending, colors waned as the thought-

forms of living things hued the ether, and sentient spirits glowed incandescent, outshining all natural light.

Eyda's was the world of mere matter; this was the world between the worlds, this was the realm of the spirit.

It was at once bewildering, overwhelming, and intoxicating.

These levels of reality, these ethereal 'octaves' that his people called Harmonics, formed not merely a universe but the layered heavens of the multi-verse. Perhaps a better analogy was —

"Here's our storyteller," Helon announced, interrupting Elishan's thoughts.

Invisible atop the schoolhouse roof in their fatigues of khaki tunics over indigo leggings, the two colleagues followed Eyda with their eyes as she wound her way through retting ponds and their whispering forests of jute.

The streaks of gray through her once ebony hair, the way she kept clutching at her shawl for warmth, how she tread unsteadily along the flagstone causeway to a gathering crowd of youngsters — they were telltale signs all of the Woebegin, the curse that was slowly enveloping this world:

MUTATION, DECAY, INSUFFICIENCY, DESPAIR.

Elishan knew her intimate details: those loves, those hopes, those joys dissolved. The once athletic daughter of Seer and Healer had challenged every custom of the world that had birthed her, rebelling against such village binaries of leaper-youths and sweeper-maidens, yet all the while clinging vainly to the hope of a love requited. But that same world had buffeted her, humbled her, and robbed her in her prime of the love that had saved her. It was only herself that had changed, and she hobbled now with the gait of defeat.

One couldn't help but to watch and be saddened.

Watching is what he and Helon did. They were Watchers.

To keep eyes peeled for local trouble was a Watcher's role, protecting both adult villagers and others of angelic kind. Just 'below' them on a lower harmonic were the Guardians in their white-and-creams, bolstering children's welfare and of others particularly vulnerable. The Elim, Eyda's marshlanders who were so much like themselves in miniature, were the 'cave dwellers' of the lowest harmonic, and only dimly aware of the hostile forces loosed upon their world.

There had been a rebellion against the governance of The El, that great emperor of all the worlds beyond.[x] The rebels, the enemy — sometime colleagues, elders, even intimates — had brought havoc to countless civilizations in their bid not just for independence but dominion. Somehow, the peopling of this refurbished world had triggered the insurrection. It would all become clear someday, Elishan hoped.

Meanwhile, this was a world under enemy control. El'A they called it, and it was a dangerous place to be — on any level of reality — and if not for the presence of he and his kind, the little beings of Eyda's race would have been utterly defenseless.

In the higher harmonics, Starion was on patrol with his warriors, there where most of the real conflict occurred. Not that Elishan was unhappy with the quiet, but there was nothing like some action to keep one peppy.

"It's been years since she laughed," Helon noted. "I mean *really* laughed."

Elishan nodded, studying Eyda's careworn features. "Sess always was a magnet for trouble. His return now only puckers her brow."

"Not just hers," said Helon tapping his breast, and his freckled face came alive when he added, "His boats brought more than eyes discern, at least on this harmonic."

Elishan shook his head knowingly at Helon. Wisdom advised waiting for Starion's return, for dealing with Sess had never been easy. Unpredictable as a child, the runaway youth had returned now a man, and capable of who knew what mischief. However, Helon had been an engineer before the war, and he had that indifference to deportment that the best of his kind displayed. He could scarce help fingering things, seeing how they worked or what they contained, even if the enticements were merely primitive reed boats.

His expression suddenly soured, prompting an inquiry.

"Those riverboats are Akadian," Helon responded. "I'm sure of it now."

Elishan shuddered. "The upturned ends, and the dragon-head prow ..." The Akadian Reavers were mercantile explorers, true,

---

x   *The El.* That mystery of mysteries, the Eternal Creator Spirit. Known by some as the First Cause.

but their commerce gorged upon extortion and enslavement. Their tactics lacked all morality.

"I'm not sure I understand," he eventually said. "The Akadians and their Anaki lords are hundreds of leagues away on a completely different river system. And I doubt such flimsy vessels could ever have survived an ocean voyage. Besides, how did Sess manage to navigate the shoals at the mouth of the Gihon, and against the currents without Starion noticing? Especially since most of the craft is submerged: it would have failed to make it through."

An engineer's conviction etched his partner's face. Helon already had a theory and was merely waiting for the catch-up.

"Elishan, you're no technician but you understand just fine. I stand by my words, though. Look harder. They're Akadian for sure."

"Ah," Elishan countered, "but the vessels are tarred, and pine tar is a local invention." Gowfer pines were common upriver, he continued to explain, beyond Zakon's Reach. Sess had probably made the pitch himself from their over-boiled sap.

"Yes, but the boats look too new," countered Helon. "Besides, the mast tackles are of iron — spotless, not a trace of rust. Doesn't that surprise you?"

Well, Elishan thought, perhaps Sess has been among the Akadians long enough to acquire some useful technology. After all, they were rather good metal smiths, they and their godling lords, and he had barely uttered words to that effect when it all made sense.

"My point exactly!" exclaimed Helon. "It's not the boat that's traveled, but the culture."

Elishan's brow creased at the implication. "And smithing is a collective effort."

"Indeed. Sess hardly built such vessels by himself," Helon ventured, "and I have an uneasy feeling that whatever the Akadian connection, the Reavers themselves won't be too far behind."

For over two centuries, Elishan and his colleagues had done their utmost to keep Eyda's people from Akadian attention. His little charge, she who had once been feared as Deina, had a past that had vowed to obliterate her very name, and humble her every descendant until they had naught but dust for food and their hearths were but a boneyard. Elishan knew this enemy well, and their mad implacable hatred; this was no idle threat. So, if Sess were in league with the Akadians, the very right hand of the enemy, then the dark sands of time were already flowing.

"This mission might be compromised," Elishan reflected, adding, "We may have to prevent Sess from leaving."

Helon thinned his lips, considering a reply. "Remember when you were Deina's Guardian, when she as Eyda was but a girl? It may be too late already."

Elishan scowled. "No need to remind me. Eyda's, rather, Deina's life, was turned upside down in a night."

"And today could be just like that."

Silence ruled as each beheld fear being birthed in the other's eyes. Here they had long been beyond the furthest reaches of corrupting civilization and, thankfully, the enemy's attention. However, what was war if not a convolution of paradoxes and oxymorons? In fighting for peace, one had to expect the unexpected.

Then — a faint whistling, a tremor in the ether.

Instinctively, Elishan leapt to earth in a crouch. "That sound, did you hear that?"

"Eh? I didn't mean to spook you."

Louder now.

"There, by the temple across the clearing." With war-staff at the ready, Elishan flung himself over the school ground towards the disturbance.

Beside the grand temple of reeds, the telltale pattern of an inter-harmonic jump took shape. The air shimmered as ripples in the ether traveled backwards in time from an imminent future event. Its sheer size betrayed a descent not just down local harmonics but across whole 'octaves,' from another heaven entirely.

Helon voiced the obvious. "Military!" This could only be the result of highly restricted transportation, and indeed of unimaginable power.

Children in the clearing laughed untroubled. The eyes of their Guardians however, searched skyward as ripples in time brought a sense of *déjà vu* or just ringing ears to the marshlanders.

With a rush of wind and a blast of light that only the Watchers could apprehend, an orb began to materialize, crackling the air with electric discharge. This thing appeared crystalline, and as it solidified, perpendicular wheels of light were to be seen rotating within. Behind it, a magnificent being took form, suspended midair, frozen in a running position.

Both Elishan and Helon were Melakh. At five imperial cubits they loomed over the tallest of Eyda's people, but this newcomer was positively huge — nearly two cubits taller than they, and easily a cubit taller than even Adjutant Starion. Eyda would appear as a child by comparison.

The classic white-and-gold uniform, the long-sword, the deeply bronzed skin and positively enormous size gave dem[xi] away as an El-Benei, of the warrior race like Starion — though the ginger shoulder-length hair was at odds with the usual bleach of deir kind. And the archaic lace sandals, ornate golden breastplate, the elaborate sword hilt, the epaulets and rank embellishments of the cloak's collar meant this was no ordinary soldier.

Elishan's attempt at lightening the mood with, "More humorless flag," evoked a frown from Helon. "What? At least dey're ours."

But the concern on his partner's face was plain: since when did flag officers travel alone, and if the giant really had leapt across the gulf between one heaven and another, how had dey managed it without a vessel?

"I've never seen an orb like that beyond the court of The El," said Helon wagging his head. "This is either very, very good ..."

"Or?" Elishan prompted.

For long moments, the sphere hung suspended, and the huge unblinking eyes of the hoar-coated newcomer gave no sign of recognition. Such large, deep-set, bottomless pools of green tinged gold they were, bespeaking an age beyond reckoning and intelligence of rare proportion. In an instant, time unfroze. The flame-colored hair and the white and gold cape rustled in the invisible wind of other-dimensional ether. As they straightened, the giant's chest heaved in an urgent grab for air.

The crystal machine fell to earth and almost rolled into the river; however, it suddenly arrested its momentum, and continued to roll and rock indecisively at right angles. It finally came to rest by the newcomer's feet. Like some strange inverting lens, the image of

---

xi   See the preface on Genderless Pronouns: *dey/dem/deir* are the genderless
      equivalents of the singulars *they/them/their.*

nearby objects shrunk as it passed them, and now the image of a giant with scrawny legs seemed too comical to be menacing.

Their leader Starion was an El-Benei too. His ungainly bulk, lack of emotion, great strength, radiance, and body heat (that Starion had learned all too slowly to cloak) had all taken some getting used to. But this new being's emanations were beyond even Starion's and a retreat seemed prudent.

The emissary rounded on Helon in an irresistible baritone command. "You: advance, and speak."

Helon responded immediately. "Helon, engineer from the Dominion of Melakh-Anan, assigned as Watcher over then marshlander Guardians." After a backwards step and a chest-salute, he added, "Sir!"

WHY NOT COMMAND A PROPER SUMMARY? puzzled Elishan. With but a wave of the hand, a holographic scroll would have told more than words. The El-Benei was likely a male despite deir epicene looks, and dey were after something more than information. Blame fancy, but those great eyes now seemed to pierce his very soul.

"Elishan," he stammered, finally stepping forward. "An historian from ... on the world of ..."

So many the intervening years, yet even now his tongue could scarce acknowledge what helpless eyes had seen. Orbiting a distant luminary in another heaven, rings of debris and ice were all that remained of his world.

"I was from Melakh-Anan too," he continued. "Also assigned as a marshlands Watcher, especially over Eyda and her son Mati's immediate family." He thought this would be sufficient, but the great being's stare demanded more.

"This is my second assignment away from home," Elishan explained. "And you are?" No reply filled the void, and he squirmed under the increasing intensity of those fathomless beryl eyes before finally snapping to a salute. "Sir!"

The giant stood mute, just staring, then: "A tragedy indeed. I am sorry about Melakh-Anan," dey delivered in the richest of timbres. "You have my deepest sympathies. More than you can know."

Another long pause heightened the tension.

"Relax, I know all about you," dey finally said. "I've not come unprepared. An engineer and an historian: an odd pairing for volunteers, but kinsmen, I judge by appearances. And the braided hair was once the fashion of imperial clerics, Elishan. Was it not? But that's all in the past. That you are Watchers now is what should define you. So, where is your Princeps?"

"Princeps? *Adjutant* Starion patrols the higher harmonics, sir," Elishan replied. "He'll return soon. And the children's Guardians —"

"Later. They are not my priority, and we are in no hurry." The giant stiffened, enacting some military ritual before ending with a quirk of the head. "Yuriyel, erstwhile Legate of the Seventh Legion in the service of The El."

"In the service of The El," they replied, exchanging somewhat baffled looks.

Here was a flag officer, alone and unescorted, that must have voyaged straight from the imperial court. Thoughts ran tangent to panic. Were they in imminent danger?

"Curious. Danger, adventure: only attitude divides them," the Legate mused.

Deir ethereal shine was hard on the eye, and the notion of he or she reading minds was unsettling.

"Be assured, little Watcher," the giant added, "I'm not a mind reader, exactly. And being gendered is no longer a gift I possess."

The Legate cleared deir shoulders of hoarfrost, all the while staring at the ground until a single eyebrow rose and the corner of deir mouth spread slightly in the merest suggestion of smile. "You have a shadow."

"Illumination is rather feeble here," replied Elishan, bemused by the observation.

Deir great eyes were still fascinated by shadows when the Legate observed, "Everything seems so frail compared to my own heaven. Entropy isn't the same. Light itself is subtly different."

"Sir, you *are* going to brief —"

"Apologies. I hope my arrival did not startle you too much. It was a fly-by drop into the seventh harmonic from across the first Great Divide into Second Heaven, and then into this heaven with a jump across multiple harmonics. Quite a ride, I assure you; a trip which neither of you would have survived."

This was no idle boast. To leap the gulf separating one series of harmonics from the next, the two heavens would have had to intersect each other for the briefest of moments in time, space, and ether. Lacking a chariot's protection, the naked forces ought to have utterly sundered even the most powerful of beings. Clearly, the Legate was far more than appearance suggested.

Many races already served in defense of the Elim. The newcomer was not a skin-walker, a Shinarn, a black-eyed changeling who could access the patterns of life from the Gayan, what some called the Wisdom or the World Soul. These could infiltrate enemy strongholds with whatever form that suited. And the being's great size outclassed any Melakh like themselves, who generally took less combative posts such as Emissaries, Watchers, and Guardians.

And this Yuriyel had come without a complement of troops even though the flame-haired, square-jawed giant had all the makings of an El-Benei, one of the so-called warrior races. Without a chariot, however, none of these races would have survived what this being had just lived through. And like themselves, the El-Benei were gendered. So what exactly was this Legate, and why were dey here?

Helon voiced his concern. "Are we surrounded?"

"Nothing we can't handle." Yuriyel partook of another deep breath then continued. "For the present, I'm merely here to record and assess. As you can imagine, there are multiplied legions across countless worlds whose prime thought is to know how this campaign is progressing." There was a strained silence until dey added softly, "And it's important that they *do* know."

Elishan frowned quizzically. "This insignificant campaign? Why send a Legate? Are things set to worsen?"

"Possibly, as there have been some rather disturbing reports from The El. I suspect we are about to find out." A great, clawed finger marked Elishan out. "Mission status. Historian, you first."

"Sir, are we being reassigned?"

"If so, we will learn of it together." It almost seemed like a wink when the Legate added, "Probably when your 'Adjutant' returns."

Silence.

Yuriyel raised an eyebrow suggestively, frozen like it could arc forever.

Elishan looked to Helon for reassurance, who nodded slightly.

"Well, that older female," he indicated Eyda, "is pivotal to all that's happened here."

Legate Yuriyel leaned forward, assessing the Isha. "Is it ... I mean, is the *she* still bearing young?"

Elishan shook his head. "No, not since her spouse went up ... Anyway, she's alone now, but continues in the ancient traditions and encourages reverence for The El — well, at least she used to."

"Except for her being so tiny, and having such a rounded little head, she has all the looks of a Melakh Seer — the unruly hair and the ebony complexion. Anyhow, let's go see," Yuriyel decided, and surged ahead to the schoolhouse. Dey overshot to land in a clump of reeds. To Eyda's people of the first harmonic, the reeds rustled but slightly. The Legate righted demself with no trace of embarrassment. "This heaven will take some getting used to."

Now standing within earshot of Eyda and the scribe, Yuriyel was oblivious to the face-splitting grins of the Watchers. The crystal machine followed the Legate closely, glowing in hues of emerald green.

"Aura. Yes," the Legate noted. "She bears the mark of The El very clearly, though I see an embryonic darkness there."

To what insight was the Legate privy? "Aura?" Elishan wondered aloud before gasping as the Legate unsheathed a long-sword that squealed melodiously when plunged into earth as a prop.

Yuriyel was kneeling now on one knee, hands in communion with hilt and pommel, chin reposed upon them, and rapt with Eyda's every word as she shared a joke with the scribe.

"Humor. It is a difficult concept for my people."

Eyda paused, her expression sobering, though the scribe continued to laugh.

"She's more sensitive than you think," Elishan whispered. "Sir, you in particular should keep your distance."

The children's Guardians now sensed Yuriyel's presence, or perhaps that of the long-sword, for it wailed intermittently in haunting metallic tones. Without official warning from 'above,' it was wise to be cautious, and their hands spread wide in a shielding dome about the youngsters.

"I am well aware of the regulations," came Yuriyel's rejoinder. "The sword was a test."

A release of the pommel is all it took, as though sword and orb were of equal mind, for the crystal machine blushed coral bright, then with a faint whir came rolling, summoned by the sword, turning at right angles only, the internal wheels of its etheric machinery remaining unwaveringly steady. A slight quiver, a single faint ripple in the air preceded a transition to a lower level of reality, and the Guardians relaxed almost immediately as both the machine-being and the attendant sword conveyed Yuriyel's message.

Yuriyel rose, resuming deir study, and with piercing eyes squint to slits. "The aura is fading, slowly but surely."

Ever the analyst, Helon had a different perspective. "Or perhaps, Legate, it's your perception that's fading."

From a Watcher's viewpoint, Eyda's material world seemed comparatively dull, for as one ascended the ethereal realms, more was perceived than mere flesh and bone: superimposed on the fabric of ordinary matter were the wondrous colors of mind, soul, and the outlines of spirit that shone ever more glorious in the higher harmonics. The little Elim were amazingly complex beings housed in a fragile shell. With so much already manifest, what gift had this Legate that left them so blind?

No answer came. Elishan's race, the Melakh, were now creatures of eternity: they could wait indefinitely for the towering Legate to voice deir thoughts. However, they were also eternally curious; nothing tantalized quite like a mystery.

Long moments passed as the Legate was lost in contemplation. Elishan had bivouacked with militia before, so the notion of a deep-thinking warrior surprised him. After all, it was their supernal strength for which the El-Benei were renown.

Drawn by silence, the two Watchers came kneeling by the stolid giant, their auburn crowns level with Yuriyel's shoulders, and so close as to become uncomfortably warm. The beautiful gossamer thing that was Eyda's spirit now sparkled iridescently.

Suddenly, Elishan understood. It was Legate Yuriyel's aura that was fading, not Eyda's. And while the scribe laughed nervously at a wedding joke, oblivious to it all, little Eyda sought the sky quizzically as Yuriyel's empyreal radiance illumined the depths of her spirit as nothing prior ever had.

Elishan gasped. He had been Eyda's direct Guardian once, her Watcher now, but never before had the sanctum of her being become so unmasked to his eyes. Growing within the decaying vessel of her flesh, despite the splendor of its form, her spirit was internally misshapen, and several dark lesions where prominent where it and flesh had disconnected. He'd have wept, if such had been the gift of his race, for the very core of her eternal potential seemed hideously impaired. Moreover, as the Legate had already perceived, there truly was a darkness in Eyda, and left unchecked it would in time consume her every joy.

Indeed, it already was.

Eyda, his little Deina of old whom he had protected and nurtured for over five hundred years, had a birthright and a destiny beyond glorious conception. How was such damage to be ever repaired?

Nigh unbearable heat flushed Elishan as the Legate stooped cheek-by-jowl at his side. "Remarkable. What do you make of it, Historian?" the Legate inquired with an almost patronizing air.

Elishan was as much absorbed as confused. What exactly was he supposed to be seeing? The sight of Eyda's core was mesmerizing, even vaguely familiar, but for the present the allusion escaped him, and sadness moved him to say so.

Helon instinctively brandished his staff, but there was no enemy here, only their legacy. "Not only have the Elim had their world stolen from them, but they have to live as cripples under the Woebegin's curse. We serve to protect them, save them if we can."

Fury sparked in the Legate's eyes. "If?"

A wave of uneasiness washed over Elishan. Helon shrugged in return to his gaze. If this were a test, neither had scored very well.

With a quiver, the crystal orb, that spirit-machine, and the Legate's long-sword reappeared in the local harmonic.

"I have a mission, Watchers," the giant explained without any trace emotion. "I need to hear the account from the Isha herself; however, until thoughts find their voice there can be no recording."

On cue to the snap of Yuriyel's fingers, the wheels-within-wheels of the translucent orb began to whir like the rustle of insects' wings and it sprang to float above Eyda. And the sword leapt back with metallic song into Yuriyel's hand it, leaving the impression that it too was alive.

"So, let the story begin."

With a hand to her brow, Eyda again searched the sky.

Having armed himself with a disciplining reed, the young scribe led her to a circle of rapt children where a boy with a tattooed cheek was describing a scene of horrific carnage.

An iron-fingered tap on the shoulder and the baritone voice of the Legate inquired in unison, "I am curious, Elishan of Melakh-Anan. What, in all the heavens, is a maggot?"

A TOWERING, TRIPLE-DOMED TEMPLE of timber, thatch, and bamboo was the focus of Temple Island. Ringing it were monumental story-poles whose intricate carvings rivaled the structure's imposing threshold, and cross-legged about them, cohorts of young scribes from across the everglades droned in groups of threes and fours with their cantor, committing to memory the prayers or sagas their poles particular represented.

Elsewhere, clusters of maidens rehearsed their Temple Day dances. The festive attire of bracelets and anklets of jade and shells, and hair coiffed high with pearls and long arching feathers had changed little since Eyda's day.

On the far side of the island, by the largest of the school's open-walled huts, Eyda caught the laughter of delight. Someone was already regaling with stories amidst a cluster of children. Though not a school day, a zealous scribe was busy mending a story tapestry by the carved timber arch of its great-room. He was skinny and smooth-faced, with ebony hair woven in a bun at the rear after the fashion of younger scribes. And with so much emphasis on coiffures these days, she wondered if her grandson Sha-Noa could ever be a scribe having the messy tangles that he did.

"Oh!" The scribe rose in greeting with a bow. It was Teras, one of Kush's boys. "Old M-maa! It's been ages. W-what an honor!"

"Yes, I'm still alive, as everyone here seems intent on reminding me." She recognized with a grin and a nod the sedating power of busy hands. "Dowry jitters?"

His face reddened. "Y-you heard?"

"Stop worrying. The way your father and Baba Mati were beaming this morning, the bargaining is as good as done. 'Handy to have a scribe in the family,' I'm sure the aunts will say."

"M-my words exactly!" the young man stammered. "A-a-are you the storyteller Sha-Noa m-mentioned?"

"There's no one else, apparently. But with all this ruckus here, it seems I've come too late."

"Some n-new boy impresses with f-faraway tales."

She had rarely seen a groom-to-be so badly affected, and attempted to lift his spirits with a few bride-bargaining jokes as both made their way to a clearing beyond the school. Clustered there in a teaching circle, a number of youngsters seemed already to be enjoying a show-and-tell.

"Slime oozed from the dead great-fish's eyes. Even a stinking trr-bahal was loath to eat it." The crowd shuddered at the mention of that great-headed near-mythical scavenger. "You could only guess the shape of the carcass by the blob of wriggling maggots — each twice the size of your mammy's thumb," avowed a tattooed boy with proof.

"Bit me here," he added. A red swelling behind the knee clearly impressed. "In my armpit too." A lifted arm revealed a festering sore to a chorus of *oohs* and *ahs*. Then peering down his loosened skirt, he exclaimed, "Argh! And there's one still —"

"Oh, enough of that!" Eyda clapped for attention, happily killing his punch line. "Gather round, children. Take your places."

A bale of reeds proved as good as any stool, and with her bad leg stretched out, her gaze was fixed on the new boy as Sha-Noa and the others formed two naturally separate groups, crossing their legs with enviable flexibility. As malcontents hung at the rear, this newcomer made his way forward to sit by her feet, chewing a stick of some aromatic bark and with a grandiose show to whit.

"You ruined my story," he glowered.

Eyda glared in response, "Boys! That gag is older than I am."

"Hey, is that Old Maa?" a boy called out before the newcomer ribbed him. "Ow! I bet she knows more about the talking dragons than you do!"

"My mother told me everything," declared the newcomer in a know-it-all manner. "All dragons are nasty."

"They are not!" Sha-Noa exclaimed. "Old Maa, can I hear about the Zmee boat?"

At his side a girl who looked remarkably like a twin sister asked innocently, "Why would dragons need a boat?"

Ah, Sess's daughter.

The young scribe kept hovering, quelling rowdiness with the poke of his reed. "Q-quiet, you," he growled at the troublemakers. "N-not all Zmee were evil, were they Old Maa?"

Eyda sighed. Perhaps there were mothers nearby. The younger ones in particular had trouble believing in anything not seen in the everglades. To them, the Zmee were just a myth, the villains of endless morality tales. Their doubts echoing in the mouths of innocents had angered Eyda to silence.

But these children were still quite young. Perhaps their ears were still open.

"Now, children, there are no such things as talking serpents," she whined cynically. Then leaning forward, fingers clawing the air, she asked in a lowered voice, "So, who wants to hear of Ava-Baba Enok's escape from the isle of the Zmee?"

Little hands shot up like a sea of bulrushes. "Old Maa, was there fighting, with Zmee gizzards spilling everywhere?"

"How did Zmee build boats of wood? Were they bigger than Baba Sess's?" Of course, Sha-Noa would have to ask *that* question.

"How about the Burning Waters story," cried another, "though mammy says it isn't true. Did you *really* see a whole lake on fire?"

"Forget fighting. How about the romance? Is it true you were married to Ava-Baba? Just exactly how *did* you get fated?" the older girls begged, clasping each other's hands and fluttering their eyes.

"Aw, keep your boring sissy stuff! Besides, Sha-Noa knows all about the Zmee, don't you Sha?" The boys sniggered while girls responded with poking tongues.

"Children, I haven't seen a Zmee since your grandparents were babies. Back in those days, they were highly cultured and lived in great settlements of their own."

The tattooed newcomer, a boy somewhat older than Sha-Noa, was still chewing noisily on his stick. "Prove it," he demanded. "Preeminent Mother says you embroider stories like a wedding veil."

Eyda considered the trouble before her. "Whose are you, boy?"

Stick in mouth, he replied, "I'm Ab, son of Sess."

"Sess with the long-boat?"

"The very same," the boy responded with pride.

AH YES, THE TATTOOED IDOL STEALER. "And your mother?"

He shrugged, "I have three mothers."

The comment perplexed her. EITHER WAY, HE'S ONE OF MINE, she thought.

"Here," she teased, throwing a tooth the length of her hand. "It's a bull Zmee's fang."

The tattooed boy turned, pulling faces. "*Huh*. It's not *that* big. Probably from a dead marsh hog." He laughed and hoped the rest would too.

Eyda grinned mischievously, knowing he'd misread the sea of grimaces, and into his lap fell a desiccated toe kept for such moments as this.

"Great goddess!" Ab curled his nose. "And where'd that come from? Zmee vomit?"

Eyda's ire rose at Ma'nuna's mention. "From this, you skeptic."

His raised eyes met her outstretched foot barely a thumb's length from his nose. It was a sight the equal of his 'flyblown carcass,' and he recoiled, gagging.

The scribe and his poking reed struggled to control the explosion of laughter. "Shush. Q-quiet now. Settle down, or Old Maa won't t-tell any story today!"

Boys elbowed each other, mocking Ab with belching sounds. "Did you see his face? Ha-ha!"

"*Blergh*." Even the girls lampooned him. "Upriver twerp!"

Eyda re-slippered Old Stubby, waiting for the hubbub to subside, yet with eyes following the tattooed boy who had slid away.

FELL THE GODDESS! HE NEEDS TO KNOW ABOUT HIS ANCESTORS.

When eager eyes were upon her, Eyda began. "So be it: Ava-Baba's escape from Zoar." She winked at the boys to a chorus of muffled hurrahs when Sha explained there would be fighting aplenty.

"And the Pyramid of Stars?" Sha-Noa begged.

"The Zmee Reliquary? That's too familiar, I think."

Of all the tales of Zoar's serpents, it was both the strangest and yet the most familiar, for it paralleled the creation dances that even now the maidens were practicing. Even so, was it fact or fancy, or some sublime allegory destined for greater minds than hers to unravel? Anyhow, the capacity of marshlanders for doubt was legendary, so who else but a child could believe it? But under the boy's pleading looks, she relented.

"Alright. If time permits."

"Yes!"

Mindful of Mati's counsel, she called after her grandson Ab, now refreshing himself by the river.

"The story of my missing toes — well, I'm saving that one especially for you!"

Children never truly settled until the story began, so she began.

"Far beyond the Great Salty Sea was once an island called Zoar. Unlike our river islands, it was utterly solitary, and grander by far than the Moud and Soud combined. Imagine: hills and mountains, impenetrable forests and dune lands, winding rivers and stretching beaches of colored sands, and cities of reaching spires and elegant elevated gardens and watercourses.

"A long time past, before old Baba Mati was even a bump in my belly, a young man called Enok once lived there but was the only one of our kind. Now, you have to remember, the island teemed with giant serpents called Zmee. They kept him there against his will, and though many were kindly, most were otherwise."

"Oh, sure. And there were *thousands* of dragons, and he wasn't killed? Or eaten?" Ab, now at the rear with the mischief-makers, chuckled smugly — "Ow!" — before wincing from a jab from the scribe.

"I-it is customary here to raise your hand a-and await recognition," voiced Teras officiously. "Please be seated, or I will be forced to remove you."

"Fire and ashes! When Preeminent Mother hears of this, then we'll see who gets their bum poked." Ab seemed sure of scoring a chorus of giggles but was crestfallen by the opposite.

Sha-Noa's 'twin,' the new girl Raama, rounded on her brother Ab, and with empathic hand gestures silently mouthed "Sit!" and then "Down!"

Ab harrumphed and made a great show of seating himself, scattering a flock of little scoop-billed dragons that dashed for the river's edge.

"The Zmee were more serpent than dragon," Eyda corrected. "Dragons have hind legs, and Zmee do not."

She was about to add "Not any more," but that particular curse of the Woebegin was best told another day. In so many of her travels, she had seen habitats and species change to almost beyond recognition, and beloved creatures turn unspeakably violent. It was as if the very soul of the world had a canker that was slowly spreading to affect all creation. But here in the Six Fingers, she continued to pray, things would remain happily stable.

"Now, does anyone have any questions?"

A distant hand raised itself gingerly. It was Ab again.

"Good. Stories are for more than just entertainment, you know. And sometimes," she winked at the scribe, "they may not be *entirely* true. But they challenge us to wonder — 'What if?' — for 'It's only in questioning that we ever truly learn.'"

That was Teras' saying, and he was beaming from the flattery.

Ab's hand was still raised.

"Boy, if you can keep that query on the tip of your tongue, I will answer it at the end of the story."

The hand came down with a grunt.

"Perhaps you would like to sit a little closer?" Eyda gestured to a place at the very front.

Ab looked stricken.

"The foot will stay in its slipper," she promised playfully.

Ab declined.

Teras returned Eyda's wink, announcing, "For those who have a *lot* of questions, our Old Maa is always happy to receive visitors a-afterwards, right? Sha-Noa can show you the way."

EMBROIDER STORIES, DO I? A chagrined Eyda could scarce forgive Ab's earlier pronouncement. And how would his mother know anyway? *WEDDING VEILS INDEED!* [xii]

She hadn't come to Temple Island in at least three moons, and had forsworn storytelling for as many years before that. But was this then her legacy, being remembered as little more than an inventor of lies?

But she had a promise to keep. So how should she 'embroider' today those faces and places that had nigh vanished from history?

----

xii   Wedding veils, though meant as keepsakes, were laborious, competitive undertakings designed to out-do other weddings. Ab's aspersion is to both unnecessary length and embellishment purely to laud oneself — that is, Eyda's stories are untrue.

She would tell it straight. Let these younglings appreciate how gnawing was the emptiness of growing up without parents, peers, or love. Only someone who has known fellowship without intimacy, rejection, and a life of despair could even begin to recount such a tale. But such was her lot now, and maybe that's what qualified her. The voice of her beloved still echoed:

'BE THE SICKLE THAT HARVESTS SOULS, MY LOVE. IT'S A SACRED STEWARDSHIP, A PRECIOUS GIFT. TRUTHS BECOME LEGENDS, LEGENDS BECOME MYTHS, AND MYTHS BECOME FICTION. SO TEACH THE CHILDREN, TEACH THEM FROM YOUR HEART, FOR WITHOUT HEART, EVEN TRUTH ITSELF WILL BE FORGOTTEN. SEE HOW MUCH WE HAVE FORGOTTEN ALREADY!'

"For you, Enok," she sighed, and gave the children her heart.

HOLLOW VICTORY

Alone of all his kind on an island of the Zmee, a captive young Elim ponders a lonely future as a slave now that his only friend could be leaving forever. A simple strategy game with an unexpected visitor, however, becomes the catalyst for a very different destiny.

IT WAS A NEW SENSATION, this tickling. The flimsy first whiskers of his nascent beard stirred in the easterly zephyrs. Land's Breath, they called it, that gentle summer force that nudged the mists of yesternight. It came moist and sweet, and laced as much with imagination as the aromas of far-flung shores.

Dawn was the time to savor it, for by mid-morning the stronger and drier mistrals of Sea Broom would sweep away all redolence of anything exotic. By evening, the cycle would complete as low-lying mists rolled in from the sea, enshrouding the island in a two-fold darkness, leaving only some summits exposed to the stars. Such was Enok's world: Zoar Island, home of the Zmee.

Breaking dawn was Enok's favorite time of day, and on a bluff with arcing vistas of endless ocean, he welcomed anew that gladdening orb. Lids closed, and with hands for wings and fingers for feathers, he partook of that gentle breeze while soaring with his mind's eye across the foaming blue desert towards the face of those exhilarating dreams — dreams that woke him now, and with such clammy consequences. Those tender almond eyes kept beckoning to a world so inconsolably distant, to a mainland no longer remembered.

"Ouch!" A sharp nip to the ankle and all dreams of freedom collapsed. It was the half-bird Jin-jin: pet, confidant, and constant glutton.

"Nothing to eat?"

The leathery vermilion head with its fleshy golden wattles squawked an affirmative before pecking his pouch for food.

In his need for a sympathetic ear, a special relationship had developed between them, and although he had once regarded Jin-jin as merely a superb mimic, that the turkey-lizard could really talk was now abundantly clear: it wasn't just what the bird said but when dey[xiii] said it. While their mutual vocabulary was limited, there was no doubting Jin-jin's comprehension.

One word especially was sure to excite even at death's very door.

At the mere mention of food, Jin-jin alighted on an outstretched arm, and balancing with a flap of deir blue-and-gold wings, took the proffered insect in a wing-claw. There was a loud crackling as the carapace fell victim to a toothy beak. The morsel was gone in an eye-blink — *tsum, tsum, tsum* — and the beak smacked happily in the afterglow of the treat.

Nose-to-beak, Enok inquired, "Fess up. Have you been eating my grapes?"

"Zhuk!" came the denial, yet a suspicious master found himself wondering whether birds could lie, for something had been eating his most treasured crop, and if not Jin-jin, then who? Or what?

Perhaps the bird was right. Maybe it really had been a swarm of zhuk, those shiny black beetles the size of warbler's eggs that sometimes blew in from the mainland. Or maybe the culprits were the giant dragonflies from the island's inner swamps. Anyhow, whoever they were, the robbers were taking whole stems, leaving nothing to seed the arbor he'd planned for the butterfly house. This was more than theft, it was vandalism, pure and simple.

---

xiii   See the preface on Genderless Pronouns: *dey /dem /deir* are the genderless equivalents of the singulars *they /them /their.*

Now Enok's new windmill began spinning wildly, rattling a tune from its bamboo xylophone. *Rik tik tak tok. Rik tik tak tok.* Its crescendos rose and fell in great whims: the morning's zephyr was fast becoming a breeze. And khrii, those leathery acrobats of the ocean airs, were flapping their wings by the edge of the cliff, preparing to take to the skies.

"Ssla's holy light! Yet another contraption!" The sibilant voice was Hrazul's.

Enok bowed a servant's greeting. "Interesting *music*, eh?"

The serpent's tendrils twitched disapprovingly. «Noise! Noise! Noise!» "Drums, wind-powered flutes, now this. It's becoming an obsession. What sort of a word is 'music,' anyway?"

"One I recall," he replied, "from long, long ago." So many things from childhood, things in the head, were now dim or erased, all victims of time; whereas memories of music were heart-felt, untouched, and alive. But all recollecting ended as the music died abruptly with a hollow *thunk* and muffled cries from Jin-jin. Chasing beetles had trapped dem inside a bamboo tube, and deir legs were twitching wildly from its end.

Enok sighed. "Jin-jin! Honestly!"

Hrazul was a Zmee, and Enok's only friend. To familiars she was Wise-eye, though privately her name was Hrazul. Outsiders, of course, would address her by title: First Disciple for short, or First Disciple of the Prime Mapmaker. Etiquette demanded no less.

Like all the adults of her kind, she was easily five times his height in length, and her clawed, six-fingered hands were nearly twice the size of his own. Her gecko-like head, with its large eyes, tapered snout and thick shiny tendrils, seemed oversized for her leaf-colored body. And her four wings — for want of a better term — were like collapsible sails, veined and translucent extensions of ribs. She may have looked like some weird serpent, but Hrazul was no mere reptile. More so than the expressive tendrils of her snout, her eyes would give her away. They were large and forward facing, intense, and questioning. And now her great green head filled his view.

Enok scowled, "You're blocking my sunrise."

"I thought you were concentrating on — what's that noise called again? — *music*."

"There's a certain pleasure from both together," he sighed. "A feast for the senses you'll never appreciate."

"You have strange senses, Enokhi. Truly," she noted with a quick flick of her tail. Her words conveyed one message, the tendrils on her snout another: «Glad to see you.»

"Me too. It's been over a six-day.[xiv] Hey, mind that tail! Last time it sent one of my drums over the bluff."

«Beauty in silence!» "Flying drums: no drums," Hrazul said flatly.

He had known this enigmatic Zmee for nearly twelve years now, and had learned to read the many subtle elements of her body language: the tension in the tail, the arch of the neck and the great head's slant, the squint in her eyes — those beautiful golden eyes, when had they colored? — the aperture of her mouth, the various hissing sounds that defied translation, and too the secondary language of her facial tendrils. And, oh, she could be a tease! The rhythmic flicking of the tail-tip meant she was toying with him.

And how curious that so many instruments should become airborne during her visits!

A strange race indeed! Rejoicing through music and song seemed a concept forever beyond them.

The khrii by the cliff's edge were now lining up in ranks. At the rear, hopping on their wing knuckles, squabbling and jostling for position, were the younger members of the flock, while those with the bony-crested heads took pride of place at the very edge of the bluff, their huge leathery wings outstretched both to mount rising Sea Broom and assert their dominance in the hierarchy. On land, they were clumsy, vulgar creatures, but in the sky khrii were masterful fliers, unrivaled lords of the ocean airs.

Hrazul and her kind, however, could but soar on wings of imagination. Sure, they could launch from a height, but staying aloft wasn't easy. To fly was the pursuit of enthusiasts, though eventually all fell to earth, and more rapidly than pride would allow. It was ironic, he thought, for creatures so well endowed with aerial membranes to be consigned forever to envy. For the ungifted, flying was a touchy subject indeed.

---

xiv Annual administrative cycles include sixty-one six-days, with the final period being adjusted at the end of the solar year in the intercalary period.

Enok queried slyly, "Don't you just wish you could take off into the sunrise?"

"Ssss," hissed Hrazul as she parried the gibe with her tendrils blushing darkly. "Our Oracle has commandeered your afternoon, I hear." «True?»

Mistress Zoia was the Prime Oracle of Maps and Enok had been her slave, a prisoner for nigh on twenty-four years, but the aging serpent and her close associates treated him kindly, addressing him simply as 'Servant' and taking turns in harrowing him with chores.

And Hrazul was Zoia's disciple. After six years, she ought to have graduated as a Venerable and joined the elite of Zmee society. However, Hrazul had been invited to understudy a further six and become an Oracle herself. Here talent succeeded over discipline. Now her years were at an end; she would soon be among those august teachers, thinkers, and leaders who were so revered that their every word was unquestionable truth. And if Venerables were society's backbone, then truly Oracles were its brain.

"At least I have the morning to myself," Enok sighed. "After noon, it's the butterfly house, then I'm back in the library for the whole evening!"

Life could have been infinitely worse than being a Mapmaker's servant but his heart just wasn't in it today. This was meant to be his day off.

"Apparently my little hands will be sewing maps onto a great sphere — some pet project of hers with the High Wisdom. Somehow even that *rakh*-Xira's involved, so nothing good will ever come of it. You'll see if it doesn't."

Mispronouncing that nasty Zmee's name allayed the seething emotions the very thought of her evoked, and it balmed in successive little triumphs a wound that time had never truly healed.

"Xira, you mean," Hrazul corrected. «No need for rudeness.» "She's being made an honorary Venerable."

"Because of the wandering stars?"

"Her achievements are many." «Yes.»

"Though it's hardly a new idea, is it?" Enok scoffed, knowing full well that old arguments just weren't worth rekindling.

In his zeal to be useful, Enok had shared his knowledge of the wandering stars with Xira long before she had 'discovered' them.

The bright morning star she had called Zeruha after some long-dead Ish-hating snake. The naming right should have been his, and it hurt that his only friend was indifferent. Like others of her generation, Hrazul was so in awe of Xira's genius, they overlooked her darker side.

"A new Venerable of a whole new science." «So exciting!»

While she wondered admiringly, Enok let a putrid sound escape, one a serpent could neither make nor comprehend; and he grinned mischievously: such rudeness was indeed revenge.

Enok was familiar with Xira's work, for she too had once been a student of Oracle Zoia.

When Zoia had been away on expedition, Xira had twice beaten him to within scant grip of life for who knew what indiscretion. Surely that was reason enough to loathe her; however, it wasn't the beatings that pained him now but humiliation's scars.

His mistress Zoia was renowned for the invention of the Map-maker's spyglass, and her young disciple Xira, focusing this new invention on the heavens, had devised balloon-like sky-boats as her means to rise above the incessant evening mists. It was all done in secret and no one really knew how. Nevertheless, she had unintentionally gifted her race with a means to take to the skies like in the legends of old.

The tang of the balsam air, the chill of the copper cupola beneath him, the memory of those long-gone nights of Xira theorizing with her mentor on the library rooftop had lost none of their potency. Zoia was an austere but well-meaning Zmee; however, Xira had been a rude introduction to the wider world. She was arrogant and she lacked — no Zmee word expressed it — *compassion* for those she considered beneath her. And him, she simply hated.

He relived afresh every nuance of that clear night in the dry season when he and Zoia were the first to peer through heaven's veil with Xira's special spyglass. Her contraption, however, had revealed little beyond what he'd already gleaned from countless star-whorled nights atop Mount Oush's barren flanks. There he had marveled at the myriad gems in the Backbone of the Night with no device but the gifts of birth.

It was a defining moment; it had left its mark. He had been

humiliated that night, and even at such remove, his cheeks still
flushed at the memory:

"The signs in the heavens mark seasons. Some seem to be wanderers,"
he had shared of the constellations and the faster-moving solitaries.

And ineradicable was the memory of Xira's distinctive chuckle,
monumental both for its arrogance and denigration of his most
prized childhood memory.

"How quaint this superstition of the primitives. Great Zhmee!
Having messages in the sky presupposes an intelligent origin, but
any meaning is purely what the beholder ascribes, thus there can
be no 'meaning' that 'proves' design. That's circular logic. Are you
hoping to make a theist of me too?" she growled to a rejoinder.
"Not by the Twelve Pillars! I expected better of you, Oracle."

Yes, she had wounded him, and the scar in his soul throbbed
at the mere recollecting. It wasn't just that she had flaunted his
observations as her own, but that she had impudently dismissed his
people's belief that the constellations were signs, heralds of the ages
of grace yet to come.

The *malad*— The *maran*— Or something like that. Sadly, their
names eluded him now.

Why, even the sky-boats had been his idea, sparked as it had been
by the bloating entrails of a rotting yashurakh rising in the heat of
the day. And later that night when they had slid down to the upper
balcony, bitter words had sundered student from mentor. Foremost
among the acerbity had been the mention of his name, and it had
pricked his ears awake.

"A vain hope in an extraordinary fool!" Xira had spat. "So *this* is
what you believe? I'm soiled if I continue here." With her parting
words she proclaimed herself a stargazer, *the* Stargazer — after the
mythical sky-watcher Aghz — and leapt from the balcony vowing
a glorious return, but return she never did.

Though neither an Oracle nor a Venerable, in less than a year she
had become a celebrity up north as one after another her amazing
discoveries had earned her the highest praises of Zoar. 'Stargazer'
stuck as her moniker and she reveled in the fame. All the hallmarks
of genius were hers, true, as was her equally prodigious pride.

*

Life was quieter in the years that followed. Visitors would come and go, discussing the latest science, talk of dredging the Susyaan canal, seeking Oracle Zoia's advice, or coiled beneath a water-fire lantern late into the night, reliving the glories of past expeditions. The life of a Mapmaker's servant knew little of drudgery. While feigning preoccupation with menial things, a humble Enok served attentively, committing to memory more than anyone could ever have guessed.

A recent event was a late night conversation deep in the bowels of the library between mistress Zoia and Ukhaz, the black-feathered Chief Oracle of Law. The Oracle had journeyed from afar for an audience with Zoia, burdened with weighty questions. Weighty indeed! Behind a tower of parchments for cover, and catching fragments of some proposal to honor Xira, the shocking discovery was that he, Enok, was the primary subject of the evening:

"Is that slave you harbor as docile as they say? There are many who doubt it," Ukhaz had asked.

"By 'many,' I presume you mean Stargazer," went mistress Zoia's retort. "The creature was barely ten when we snared it — the age when younglings prepare for discipleship, and there was really no comparison. Even at eighteen, when they graduate, the little Ish was more like a clumsy hatchling. I shouldn't be too concerned."

"Your last such experiment failed, admit it. I daresay its offspring will fare no better. What did become of Enokhi's sire, that furry monster? Great Zhmee! Violent and untrainable!"

"Died in the swamplands, as best we can tell. But the violence you speak of was purely defensive, the way you all provoked it. My Ish is far better trained."

"All the same," Ukhaz added gravely, "I would like to see the High Wisdom's records of this beast for myself. These arrangements were meant to be temporary, and a final decision is long overdue. After all, even The Fear were a novelty once — that is, until they swarmed feral. And how about those 'charming' green ants some Biotist brought for their butterfly house? Oh, my! They multiplied so profusely, that we had to burn the entire pavilion just to be rid of them! So we need to be doubly careful these days, Mapmaker, with all the exotics you keep importing."

And as his mistress was replying with "I agree, and that's what the promontory of Sha-Noa is for," Enok remembered getting excited by the prospect that something of his stolen past might yet remain.

Surely, if they were here in the library, wouldn't he have come across these parchments already?

Anyhow, the whole tone of Ukhaz's inquiry became increasingly ominous. Luckily, mistress Zoia had placated the other's fears that night; however, she had always replied with a much younger Enok in mind. She was such a disciplinarian, forcing an extraordinary workload of him, and force-feeding him loathsome herbal 'tonics' when he wasn't even ill. And in times of private banter, when he'd been silly enough to express an opinion, she was keener than a coral reef in shredding it.

That she was utterly humorless, none could deny, smiling only at graduations, so the rumors went. Though in the butterfly house, he'd stolen glimpses of a beaming wide-eyed youngling when her prized butterflies emerged. Anyhow, in her uncharacteristic dissembling that night, he'd seen a glimmer of something reserved only for disciples. It was an Oracle's fidelity.

Was he mistaken?

Upon the Lawmaker's departure, he gasped at fear of discovery as the High Wisdom emerged from a hidden cavity! She then chanted some invocation and produced a sparkling emerald from under her bonnet as Zoia protested, "Surely, it cannot be yet!"

"Thus we break the chrysalis," the High Wisdom intoned as Zoia wept, conceding, "and may the First Cause preserve us all."

"Hello?" *Snort.* "A challenge to zhakh while Ssla hangs low?" *Snort.* Hrazul broke his reverie with unusual intimacy. Her breath fogged his vision.

'THESE ARRANGEMENTS WERE MEANT TO BE TEMPORARY. A FINAL DECISION IS LONG OVERDUE.'

"Eh? Sorry," Enok replied sheepishly, clearing his eyes. To explain daydreaming was pointless, for Zmee never dreamed, not even in sleep. "Hey, are you growing *another* pair of snakes?"

Hrazul's great orbs were golden, and her pupils unusually dilated. The tendrils of her snout were velvety and engorged, almost masking the sprouts behind them. Soon there would be four.[xv] At his stroke, her hide rippled and her eyelids shuddered.

"Why, even your eyes are changing," Enok observed. "They're as beautiful as Ssla herself."[xvi]

Her great orbs narrowed as she pulled suddenly away. "On the subject of eyes, are you still woken by those leaky visions? Still haunted by those sinister 'almonds in the night'?"

If the experience of an imaginary world while fast asleep seemed a laughable notion, how much more so were caressing, disembodied eyes that filled you to ecstasy?

"I never said they were sinister. And how do you know about the leaking?"

«I know everything.» "Don't my eyes look like almonds?"

"Didn't you come for a game?" said Enok flatly.

«I came to play.» "I'll forfeit the Prefects and shorten the game. You seem out of sorts."

"Actually," he eyed her quizzically, "it's *you* who seem odd today."

Silently, and without reply, Hrazul set up the double game board with her tail. She had begun teaching him zhakh's strategies after meeting twelve years ago, and they were now almost evenly matched. But lately Enok had been having a losing streak and maybe the offer of an easy rematch was Hrazul's way of caring.

"Knowing my luck, you'll get posted up north near the badlands, at Zu'u-Susyaan." WHICH MIGHT AS WELL BE THE EDGE OF THE WORLD, he wanted to add, but he found his throat thickening and the words died unborn.

"All of life is coming-and-going, little Ish, but you and I will always be close." There was no Zmee word to describe their friendship, and 'egg-sister,' used of colleagues or hatchlings raised together, hardly seemed appropriate.

As if privy to his thoughts, she raised his downcast face with the tip of her tail, to display an iridescent blue butterfly in the palm of her six-fingered hand. Years ago, they had met in the butterfly house

---

xv   Like Enok, Hrazul is 'pubescing.' Adult females only achieve estrus every sixth year, and depart for the Great Pilgrimage, the *j'Athra-Ya*.

xvi   *Ssla* is the poetic Zmee name for the sun, otherwise known as the *Greater Light* — just as the moon is termed the *Lesser Light*.

over just such an event. And now, as before, the Grand Enokhi had only recently emerged and was lazily testing its wings. Even after a good shake, it remained strangely fast.

"Maybe it's time to end your confinement to the peninsula."

Propelled by a puff and a flick of the finger, the butterfly finally took flight.

"Hrazul, I've been thinking: if I could present my case to the Shav'yat, convince them —"

«No! No!» Hrazul became suddenly animated. "Leave the Council of Oracles to me. Nothing rash, alright? Promise me, Enokhi-noki." «Promise me!»

When she called him by his pet name, he knew there was no denying her, but his tongue would not comply. "Rash? You've got the wrong Enokhi, mistress."

She held his gaze with those pleading golden orbs, waiting for an agreement that never came. "Anyhow, let's not dwell on it. I don't feel much like chitchat."

Just as he was thinking that she had never been much of a talker anyway, the whinnying of a nearby khwatl signaled mild alarm. The towering terror bird peered briefly through the shrubbery, snapping its beak in agitated bursts, then scampered away when it spied Hrazul. It was only Chiruk, and Chiruk didn't like strangers. Maybe Gray-face was coming.

However, Hrazul was oblivious to all but her favorite pastime, clearing out the forfeit pits and fussing over the debris that had littered the two game boards. In hardly any time at all, she had readied her ranks for battle. Hers were the red pieces, Enok's the black. Only to the wielding player knew their identity, that is, until it vanquished a lower-ranking enemy — and then the opponent had to remember that for the remainder of the game. Zhakh was as much about memory as deception.

The challenge "Ho-Za!" began the game in earnest, and Hrazul accepted with "Zha-a-Kha!" and an opening move on the 'lose' board rather than the 'win,' which wasn't her usual gambit.

Enok considered his response, fingering a Deceiver. He had barely uttered, "How will I play without you, Wise-eye?" when she swept all melancholy aside with a spray of blue-and-gold feathers. "What? Jin-jin!" he gasped. "I can't believe you plucked my bird!"

"I will be needing a graduation necklace," she wheedled with voice and eyes. "These are my favorites."

Cries from the xylophone meant Jin-jin was caught in the wind-mill's gears (again!) and was squealing comically for rescue.

"That's hardly enough. I'd have to pluck Jin-jin bare! What about pearl-snails? When they desert their shells for mating —"

«N-no! The Fear!» her tendrils shuddered. "I'm not letting you anywhere near the thaakh plantations!" From the pouch of her wrist-wrap, she produced a larger assortment of feathers. "You needn't worry about your bird. I have been collecting for years."

"The Fear are just insects, aren't they? If I could show Jin-jin —"

«No! The swarm! No!» "The Fear can overpower you in a heartbeat. I absolutely forbid it!"

Another cry from the khwatl and the rustle of its departure were all that announced the most annoying of youngsters, Sneak-tail Snei, Hrazul's junior.

"I thought you were Gray-face," Enok muttered. "So much for a secret hideaway."

«Secret?» "Our Oracle knows. Gray-face too," Snei shot back, freeing Jin-jin in passing and now dangling dem by the tail. "Why, even Kitemaker knows. It was she who gave me directions. Besides, between the wailing of that clumsy bird and the racket of those wind-things, blind Zmee could find their way here."

Suddenly released, Jin-jin bounced off a great drum, and with deir characteristic waddle disappeared through a thicket.

"That strange little red-head lacks all sense of fear," the youngster observed. "An ideal fetcher for shells." «Eh?»

Hrazul's tendrils curled angrily. "You were eavesdropping!"

«Orders.» "I was paying attention."

Hrazul hissed, "To a private conversation." «Private!»

«What?» "With Little Animal?" «Not a person.»

It sounded insulting, but young Zmee were plain-spoken like that, without intending to offend. However, Snei had always been particularly tactless, and if anyone could vex him, it was she.

The elder glowered at the younger. «Be gone!»

«No!»

"I was merely demonstrating the game. Enokhi, help me pack."

Confused, he watched helplessly as they battled with nothing but stares, snout tendrils throbbing rhythmically and both of them hissing. Was Snei being scolded or threatened?

The younger broke off towards him. "Little Animal plays zhakh?" «Disbelieving.»

"Believe, or be thrashed," Enok crowed.

Hrazul now confronted the youngster forcefully, and was poised to strike. «Leave! Now!»

«Cannot!» "And we all thought you were flying with Gray-face." «Not? We?» demanded Hrazul.

«Eww!» Snei signed, diverting the topic. "Now that it's domesticated, are you trying to civilize it as well? The Zeruhawi say — *zoiks!*" she yelped. Hrazul must have struck her.

"Disciples! Please! I have a game to win."

Snei snorted. «Pah!» That he had the wits to play two games at once was clearly preposterous, where you sought to win in one but lose in the other.

A final attempt by Hrazul to arrest the play he challenged with angry words. Their effect was immediate, as was his regret, for Hrazul slumped and sank away to the bluff's edge, unfurling her membranes with a sudden snarl and scattering the posturing khrii.

The disciple took over from her elder and within a dozen moves apiece was badly losing the 'win' game, and winning the 'lose.'

"I should claim this bluff for myself," voiced Snei casually, "with Wise-eye now leaving for the Temple."

"To Zul-Al-Kahhri. On the Great Pilgrimage. *I know,*" Enok growled. He ought not have lost his temper with Hrazul. With her upper wings splayed, she was rocking in the breeze by the precipice.

"Those toxic jellyfish are already in the Pilgrim's Channel," «And sooner by a whole moon!» "Such a pity," Snei sighed. "I was so hoping for an invite to the pilgrims' chechi feast."

> "O sweet chechi!
> Desire of pilgrims.
> A curse."

The Chechi Archipelago was a bounty of the most prized of Zmee delicacies, chechi, that carmine sea lettuce reserved for pilgrims and special celebrations. And though a single jellyfish wasn't lethal, a swarm with their sticky dangling tendrils would stop any heart but a yashurakh's, those great dragons of the reefs. And if there were to be no feast, then the ever-practical Zmee would simply leave early.

Is that what Snei was jabbering about?

Enok's thoughts fell to the logic of an early departure when its implications struck. "Then Hrazul, I mean Wise-eye, leaves just after graduating!"

Snei never responded, and instead began wondering aloud about a graver matter entirely. "Why would a Mapmaker's student keep having midnight meetings with the Chief Oracle of Law?" She chuckled privately. "None can hide secrets from Sneak-tail Snei!"

The revelation was startling, particularly in light of the exchange a few nights ago between mistress Zoia and Ukhaz, that very same Oracle. And how could Snei have possibly been privy to them? Her self-talk paused as she sweated a few turns, though silence could never reign long over younglings, and especially chatterers like Snei. She so loved the sound of her own voice!

"But then, if she barely speaks to me, I doubt she would confide anything to a servant — especially Little Animal."

"Actually, in her own way," Enok ruminated, "I think she was trying to."

Hrazul was poised to embark on adventures forever denied to him. *Forever:* such a gloomy, terminal notion.

"And it's a good thing the pilgrims are leaving early. The wetness of her tendrils, the gold in her eyes," «How vulgar!» "Wise-eye is so ready for mating, she'd be entwining with anything before long."

"*Bulls:*
But one on Zoar.
Saved!"

True, Hrazul had new snout-tendrils emerging, but so did he, and he was proud of it too. He arched his chin for Snei to see.

"Look. It's a sign of adulthood too, I think."

Till now, she hadn't even locked eyes with him, but Snei leaned forward, examining. "Fur on the face! How hideous! The Upholder is the only bull on Zoar, and *he* doesn't have fur." She sought her elder's agreement, but Hrazul was still at the precipice, riling the last of the khrii into flight.

Having privately sign-signaled «Meet Alazar» and «Breakfast Island,» Hrazul, with outstretched wings, dove into the swirling currents below.

Within moments, one of Snei's Prefects acquired Enok's most valuable piece, an Adji, thereby winning the 'lose' game.

"Khozaa!" he reveled in the triumph. "Winner me, loser you."

«Disbelieving.» "It cannot be 'khozaa'." Snei surveyed the remaining pieces, with her tail twitching irritably. "How can an inferior —"

"I did warn you."

«Deception!» her tendrils bristled. "The Upholder will certainly not be happy about *this*."

"Oh? I don't see why not. The 'lose' game is all about deception."

Jin-jin seized the prized Adji from the forfeit pit only to drop it in Enok's lap with a squawk. "Khozaa!"

Snei uncoiled, rearing high, toppled the remaining pieces with an angry flap of her neck-wings, filling his eyes with dust and sending Jin-jin scurrying.

"That wasn't deception at all, but cheating!"

Enok rose with the customary bow but met and held her glare. "Second Disciple, you and I will be spending a lot more time together now that ..." He sought composure through a slow deep breath before delivering emphatically, "Look, *'To believe what you see, stop seeing what you believe.'* [xvii] Someone wise taught me that. Perhaps it's time you learned that too."

Snei snorted. «Impertinent animal!» "Someone wise? Who?"

A flung Adji whizzed past her in Hrazul's direction. "She did."

Her hiss then distilled an entire spectrum of outcry as her tail scattered the game pieces angrily; and when she kept regarding him bleakly, clenching her fists and toying with a Deceiver, Enok honestly thought she would slap him. Instead, her eyes narrowed to slits at the end, and she simply departed with her souvenir.

*

---

xvii A quote from the *Aphorisms*, the Zmee Wisdom Literature penned primarily by Zulyi but includes the life's lessons of many philosophers.

It was mid morning now. The seas were blue and sparking, and the crisper airs of Sea Broom were refreshing. The commanding height of the bluff afforded views rivaled only by the lofty balds of Mount Oush to the rear. The distant eastern beaches were clear of yashurakh, those powerful reef dragons that tolerated Zmee even less than did the khwatl.

The great horned tortoises too had long since laid their eggs and departed. Even the blood-red tree crabs were notably absent. They trekked by their thousands into the forest each year before suddenly reappearing in the Shine Water, that one night of the newborn year when the reefs came alive with a spectral glory to outshine the Lesser Light. That knowledge had almost cost him his life.

Anyhow, the beaches were his. Such was the season.

Yashurakh, tortoises, tree crabs, khrii, and even the zhrat knew these seasons, these beginnings and endings. All creatures did, Enok reflected, and reflecting on the strangeness of the day, so many things seemed suddenly inverted, as though there had been some kind of ending and a beginning. But what kind of season awaited him now?

Snei had never visited before, so why today? And frankly, why would she have wanted to? The promontory was a long way from town, and supposedly off-limits to all but certain Oracles and their students. Moreover, only Hrazul Wise-eye and Alazar Gray-face had ever known of his private hideaway. That Snei had discovered it from Hozny Kitemaker was troubling, but at least his winning drought was broken thanks to her.

And as for shy and gentle Hrazul, why had she been acting so peculiarly? As her senior, she was Snei's secondary mentor, but the happy relationship between the two — one that was supposed to last a lifetime — seemed to have suddenly soured and he was at a complete loss as to why.

AN ENDING, AND A BEGINNING.

"Enokhi!" squawked Jin-jin, breaking his thoughts and arching deir head for a scratch. The little bald vermilion head was a comfort in the light of what Sneak-tail Snei had just let slip.

What should he make of Hrazul's clandestine meetings with that nasty Oracle of Law — as well as her almost irrational anxiety over a simple game of zhakh with Snei? Anyhow, why should that bull

Upholder care whether a slave won or lost a simple game? Snei had been so badly in need of a lesson in humility, and today's victory had been long awaited. It had been an easy win over Sneak-tail — in fact, way too easy — and he should have been euphoric.

And, if anything, Hrazul should have been pleased for him too, right? So why then did such a glorious victory suddenly feel so hollow?

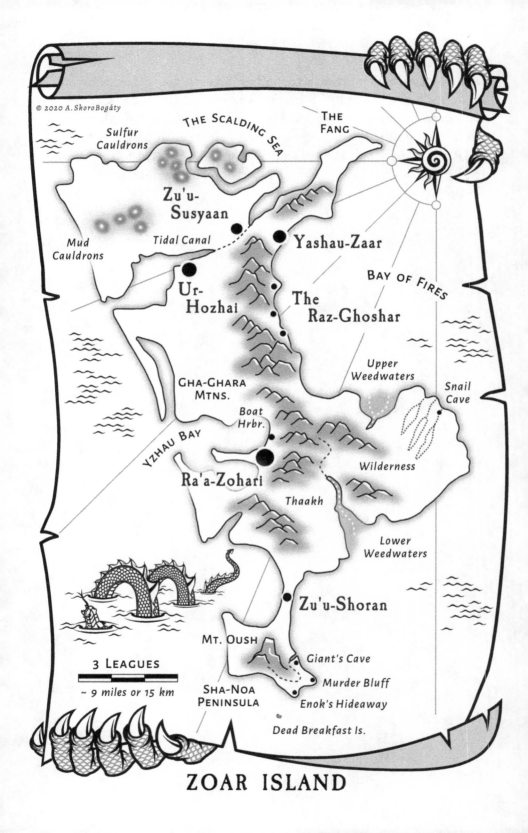

ZOAR ISLAND

EPISODE 4

ENMITY ETERNAL

An old enemy thrashes Enok. The painful lesson is that not just his peaceful existence but his very life is in jeopardy, and he becomes resigned to the fact that his only hope for survival is not in escape but in universal acceptance.

BRIGHTLY HUED MAZES OF CORAL ringed Zoar Island like a barricade, forming a refuge for myriads of dazzling fish, nudibranchs, turtles and lesser dragons — a cordon that neither the great lumbering terrors of the deep or the swifter long-necked porpoises could penetrate.

Between the reef and distant shore of this haven floated a series of captive islets that drifted endlessly with the tide, colliding and recombining, separating and dissolving. These breakaway growths of the eastern weedwaters were the Breakfast Islands. The largest of these was now to be found near the tip of the southern peninsula that Enok called home.

A densely tangled network of a licorice weed called khasha buoyed the islet from below, while verdant tubular leaves of ghaazli carpeted it above. The Breakfast Islands were the result of two very different plants thriving only in each other's company, creating an edible habitat studded with pools of a nectar that allowed coastal succulents and berry bush to colonize these roving shores.

That nectar now coming cupped to Enok's lips was sweet potable water. For Zmee and Ish alike, the Breakfast Islands were aptly named, larders of the sea.

Hrazul was half-down a water hole harvesting the bitter licorice, while her confidant, Alazar Gray-face was across the islet demonstrating its sponginess to her young co-disciple Yuni. The senior was visible in the distance by her tawny helm and phylacteries[xviii] bobbing over a rise, but the emerald hide and smooth crown of little Yuni made her almost invisible.[xix] And Jin-jin had tired of chasing those posturing dragon-gulls and was now splashing noisily in a sweet-water pool, toying with sea turtle hatchlings.

By contrast, Enok was content to simply recline against his outrigger with his face in the sunshine and nibble idly on ghaazli. It was almost like working on gourd seeds to get to its sweet inner core. And it was a little peculiar that only Zmee and yash'kh found the outer flesh bitter, and lead to death if they ate it.

With slaps to her tail, he signaled Hrazul. Bulbous objects that glinted sporadically were heading straight for the islet.

The tip of her tail disappeared just as her great head emerged with a mouthful of weed. «What?»

"Wise-eye, we're about to have company, and I don't recognize the helm."

«Students?»

He had barely uttered, "Not unless they've stolen shiny head-gear," when that connection to metal unnerved him.

With their heads above water, and propelled by their sinuously curving tails, Zmee in a wedge shaped formation seemed to be towing some lumbering barge. At the crest shone the buffed ornaments of a distinctive brass helmet. Its two backward-facing horns like windswept metal tendrils shone like gold in the midday sun. Despite the passage of years, the mere thought of it was loath-

---

xviii Phylacteries are large amulets containing scriptures from the Aphorisms that have special meaning for the disciple. The way they are worn depends on seniority. Primarily a Southern tradition.

xix Unlike snout tendrils, those of the crown are a source of pudency for adults in much the same way as exposed genitals are for humans. Only younglings, who lack these, ever show a naked head in public.

some, and truthfully, Enok had never dreamed its owner would dare to venture so far south again.

"Oh, ruin the day!"

«Eh?»

"It's *rakh*-Xira,[xx] your celebrated Stargazer from the north. I'm not sure of the others."

«You're being impertinent.» "But Stargazer! In person!" The words came thickly through a mouthful of weed. «What an honor!» "She rarely grants an audience and her public appearances have become even rarer. Quickly, fetch Gray-face!"

"I think you will find the public and the private Stargazer to be very different indeed."

Hrazul looked at him incredulously. «Really!»

Enok sighed, "Just wait and see."

Red-on-black collars were clearly discerned as the party approached. Hrazul dropped her head, gulping loudly, tendrils drained of color. «Low! Stay low!» "We had hoped to spare you this."

WE? THIS? Her blanched expression was baffling.

Her tendrils shuddered, «Danger!»

"I can't read you. Xira hates me. Jin-jin and I hate her. But me afraid of that conniving snake? Never!"

"j'Na-Zeru, Enokhi!" «Fearful!» "These aren't Reef Scouts or Forest Spotters, little one, but Zeruhawi fanatics, the Upholder's elite guard. We must get to Gray-face." «Quickly!»

As an Oracle's servant, Enok had had may encounters with Northerners over the years, and had listened carefully behind partitions and parchments to half-whispered commentary on the growing social rift between the greater North and the smaller South, between the Zeruhawi and the Azhakh-Na.

What little else he knew came gleaned of hushed fragments in the library — not happy gleanings, to be sure — but nothing was ever discussed openly, and never in his presence. While it was increasingly true that the Zeruhawi worldview differed from that of the contemplative Azhakh-Na who had raised him, Hrazul's

---

xx   The prefix *rakh-* forms a mild Zmee curse, as does the suffix — whence the Zmee name *yashurakh* for the reef dragons.

alarm was surprising. And who or what were these j'Na-Zeru? The name suggested a ritual burial, or an ancient sarcophagus he had once read about, and the prefix '*je-*' stood for religious duty, or if '*j-*' then possibly fanaticism. Clearly, something new and dangerous was brewing up north.

The celebrated Stargazer, Xira herself, had come ashore barely thirty cubits away. Her tendrils lazily tasted the air and her jaw yawned open as it ever did when catching whiff of him. He was upwind and with no means of masking his scent.

Enok began a suggestion when Hrazul knocked him flat with her tail. «Quickly!» "Keep behind the mound," she whispered. "My poor Enokhi, there is much you don't understand. The j'Na-Zeru are dead to every living pleasure — save one. If we bolt for Grayface now, they would surely intercept you." «Keep low!»

Enok scowled. Understand? How could he? He was a lowly servant; questions were the prerogative of superiors. "My outrigger: it's too late to hide it."

Hrazul had barely whispered, "They'll see your fire-bird anyway," when Jin-jin leapt upon the knoll, posturing noisily.

"Khaa! Xiwa!"

Then it hissed across the glade, that sharp intake of breath as Xira's head swung their way. His old enemy slithered along the islet's banks towards them, while three guards dragged the barge ashore.

Hiding was useless now. Hrazul emerged from cover and bowed open-palmed like a servant, though with eyes fixed on the remaining guards quickly cutting off their rear.

Water trickled from Xira's tendrils as she removed her verdigrised trademark. After a quick, drying whisk, she greeted Hrazul with a civility only Enok knew as forced.

"Ah, my old Oracle's First! Who else would keep such a slave!"

Hrazul remained genuflected, signing «Bow, bow» to Enok, but all he could do was gag. The stench of rotting yash'kh clung to her like flies.[xxi]

"Nigh unbeatable at zhakh, I hear," Xira pronounced for all.

---

xxi   *Yash'kh* is a politer form of *yashurakh* — particularly since the prefix *rakh* forms a curse word.

"What a tournament of minds we'd have! You must come and stay at my private compound for a while. I rarely extend such invitations, but in your case, I insist."

Eyes rose to meet their idol. "We are honored."

"Ssss, but that animal!" Xira's tendrils made an obscene gesture. "Long I loathed it under Zoia's tutelage, as any patriot should. Leave it behind when you come, though. One can't be too careful, you know — diseases and so forth. Animals are so," her fingers signed disgust, which made the guards chuckle, "unsanitary."

Hrazul's membranes bristled. Her hero's true nature soured all expectation. Perhaps it was the obvious shock on her face, of worship betrayed; perhaps it was the fault of his sprouting whiskers; maybe even the culmination of the years of belittlement under student Xira, catering to her every whim no matter how cruel or taxing the cause; maybe it was due to all these things: he exploded with reciprocal insult.

"This is *our* island, *rakh*-Xira, you ... you arrogant worm. Have you soiled all the others, that you drag your stench here?"

«Please!» Hrazul signaled to Enok. «Silence!»

Xira's pupils dilated eagerly. "First Disciple," she addressed Hrazul, "Zmee have names, Zmee have rights. By definition beasts have none. That you treat this slave as an equal affronts not only me, but all Zoar, and every member of our race whose hide now clothes the loins of that perfidious species."

A copper barb gloved the tip of her tail and it hung menacingly in the air, ready to strike at the circling fire-bird. Jin-jin had no more love for Xira than had he.

"This is all the fault of your limp-tendriled Oracle, the sad old fool." Xira continued to regard him bleakly, while signaling the remaining guards to surround them more tightly. "It has been indulged for too long. And it's high time, I daresay, it showed proper respect for its betters. It will bow, now."

Enok spat, "You? My better? Strip away the title and what remains? Nothing but a pustulant dung-worm."

"You've lost control of your slave, First Disciple, but these j'Na-Zeru here have a remedy," she chuckled. "A solid chastening will surely beat the insolence from its hide."

A guard snickered, "Why not dispatch it to its god?"

"I am Stargazer, god of sky!" proclaimed Xira, gesturing grandly. "And what need have gods of filth?"

Hrazul positioned herself between Xira and her prey.

"Come now, disciple. A mantle of petulance ill befits you. Besides, there's no need for hostility between *us*," voiced Xira in her silken manner. "I need talented people, and there's no doubting your abilities. Imagine ships of the air traversing dozens of leagues in a single watch, let alone a day! And Zoar as the hub of a legion of colonies" — her hands spread nebulously — "spanning sky and sea and land, connected by aerial thoroughfares beyond all barbarian reach. Join me, and together we will forge it. And be true gods, all of us!"

Hrazul kept steadfastly silent.

"Actually, I'm glad our paths have finally crossed. The Chief Oracle of Law speaks very highly of you, thus rendering me all the more concerned for your future."

«My future?»

«Yes.» "Can you not see the shadows lengthening? Twilight falls swiftly upon Zu'u-Shoran. Your dour little city of philosophers will soon just be margin scribble in the scrolls of Zoar's history. You know this. Ooh, I discern that you do. Close your eyes with me. Feel now both the power of my logic and the sheer momentum of that clamor for change. Now open them to apprehend a glorious Zeruhawi dawn! It is *we* who will rule Zoar, not your backward-looking —"

Hrazul was coiling herself into a living shield about him and not all being said was clear. Anyhow, the words matter little. He had known Xira well enough in the past to realize she was merely stalling for an opportunity. Keep the eyes averted, and then strike from behind. Her tactics hadn't changed. The guards had completely encircled them now, blocking any hope of escape; though one had made after Alazar, who had promptly fled, trailing little Yuni's dash to the sea.

"Nothing to say? Frankly, I'm a little disappointed."

Hrazul continued in a silence that bespoke an ineffable distaste for Xira's true character, a silence that partook of the green heaving surface of the island as the force of waves traveled through it, of the susurration of leaves in the salty breeze, of a hope that Stargazer would tire of this bantering, and simply load-up her barge with whatever she'd come for, and go.

"You forget," Xira continued, "that I too once made your city my home. I know your thoughts, young disciple. You want to understand the world? So do we. And you believe there's no enlightenment without self-discipline? We do too. We're both Zmee, after all. Are we not?"

"I am of the Azhakh-Na, as is my Oracle and the Oracles before her! We have very different philosophies," came Hrazul's muffled proclamation through the coils of her body.

"Philosophy, eh? 'We Azhakh-Na strive to understand the world; the Zeruhawi want but to subdue it,' your Oracle once argued." Her voice the texture of down, Xira looked smug and predatory as she eyed her encircling guards. "Surely *you* don't think so poorly of us Zeruhawi, do you?"

His protector's coils were now squeezing uncomfortably tight, and for the first time ever, Enok sensed real fear in her.

Xira continued in a slow arc, locking gazes with Hrazul. "Well, it's an argument she'll acknowledge as lost when a Zeruhawi sky-boat rests proudly in Zu'u-Shoran's common! And sooner than you think. You Azhakh-Na believe eternal truths are apprehended by reason's force alone: a cracked egg's thoughts for sure.[xxii] You see, to fully understand something, you poke, you prod, you test. And in the process of understanding something changes, either the subject or yourself. Indeed, and usually both!

"Methodics teaches that there can be no real insight without," she paused, making a dramatic gesture, "*transformation*. We Zeruhawi acknowledge that. Change is inevitable, progress unstoppable. We are the bright morning star that every eye will follow, and the four-legged wheel that crushes all opponents.[xxiii]

"The Ish, you see, *they* are the bitter spring in every font of woe. Once the Shav'yat is disbanded,[xxiv] and the High Wisdom deposed,

---

xxii   *Cracked egg.* A mild Zmee profanity with a meaning equivalent to *fool* or *dimwit*.

xxiii   *Four-legged wheel.* A reference to the Zeruhawi emblem.

xxiv   *Shav'yat.* The permanent governing council of Oracles headed by Enok's former mistress, the Grand Oracle (High Wisdom) herself.

I will show my egg-sisters the true meaning of progress — which is dominion! — and with my flotilla of sky-boats, rid the world of every last barbarian."

Enok was astonished at the pronouncement. "You're insane!"

Xira squealed as Jin-jin attacked the nape of her neck. Without her helmet, that sensitive area was vulnerable, and the clever little turkey-lizard knew it. In the confusion, the rear guards leapt on Hrazul, nearly crushing Enok in the scuffle. She squealed as they overpowered her and tore him away.

Blue — green — blue — green — blue!

The world flew past at dizzying speed as the j'Na-Zeru tossed him about like a melon.

Whump!

The fall to earth winded him. Water stoppered his mouth and nose as his face lay submerged in a pool. Before he could react, a heavy weight forced him underwater. And panic gripped him when yet another power sucked him deeper into the water hole.

THEY'RE DROWNING ME!

Breathless below the buoyant world, he struggled frantically towards the light, to air; however, the mystery power kept dragging him down, so effortlessly down, down into a darkening shaft of russet and licorice, down until nothing of hope remained. With equal suddenness, an upwards thrust propelled him to strike the ceiling of an air-filled chamber. In that numb and desperate moment, spluttering and gasping for sweet life in the blackness, an alien thought formed in his mind, vital and insistent:

LIVE!

ON THE GENTLED WAVES OF this reef-bound sea loomed the largest and most ignominious of the algal flotsams. Rumor had it that more yashurakh had perished feasting on its ghaazli than on any other of the Breakfast Islands. *Dead Breakfast Island* Zakon dubbed it with amusement. Those irksome sea dragons had no fear of Zmee and could attack without provocation. Frankly, Zoar was better off without them.

He had been scouting the southern perimeter of the barrier reef. Debris had been sighted there recently, artifacts of alien origin.

Simple things really: a piece of rope, a sheaf of creosoted reeds, a crudely graven image — of themselves, 'Nothing to worry about,' his Reef Scouts assured.

The latter jetsam, however, was some kind of barbarian art, a grotesquely proportioned statuette with protruding chest mounds, an impossibly wide pelvis, and with great ebony eyes that seemed designed to threaten.

And that *did* worry him.

Ish and Isha were bloodthirsty savages who killed Zmee for sport. When he was but a mainland sprat, they had decimated his all-male tribe and very nearly skinned him too — not the slough, but his living crimson hide, mutilating beyond all hope of repair not just his flesh but his very identity. Well, some memories were best savored with a twisting lance in the enemy's back. There was no understanding the primitive darkness of their minds. The Ish were beasts of instinct, randomly blessed with excursions into reason just long enough to twine rope, tar a sheaf, even whittle some crude semblance of themselves.

Perhaps the Zeruhawi were right: exterminate the lot. Better still, he should do to them as they had done unto him. An eye for an eye, a fang for a fang, and — ah, he liked the symmetry of it — male-hood for male-hood.

He was the Upholder, chief sheriff of the law, keeper of the peace, and defender of this community from any threat, whether internal or external. Zoar Isle was the last known female colony. The alpine lakes and the cascading overflows of Sha'an-Ghor, the fissure caves and geysers of Zhatli, the gold-topped spires amidst the swamps of Jokol-Hra — all ruins now, ruins, stripped bare with not so much as a skeleton remaining.

His was the burden of the race entire, and he bore his office with all the gravity of extinction. If the flotsam brought hither by impudent currents was of Ish manufacture, then this sanctuary was gravely at risk. He was the Upholder, a bull in his prime, and given the weight of his office, any risk was an enemy.

The Shav'yat, that noble Council of Oracles — pah! — invested all their faith in hiding as defense. On the contrary, Zeruhawi doctrines promoted attack: strike first, strike hard and decisively. *Total War* they called it: total death, no survivors.

Each strategy had its merits. Unfortunately, the Shav'yat was, for the most part, anti-Zeruhawi, bolstered by support from the ancient and inscrutable matriarch, the High Wisdom herself. However, should her health suddenly fail then the remaining council members might easily be pressured —

No! he decided emphatically, and for the second time in as many moons. Politics was for green-skins; he would not meddle. Oh, burn the temptation! A red-skin's time was better spent on practical matters. Besides, why did opposites appeal above combination? Instead of just *or*, why not a spectrum of this *and* that? Polarization fomented trouble, he sighed, and that was yet another kind risk.

The spongy surface of the islet tickled the delicate underside of his jowls as he slithered ashore. Not until he raised his torso high and drained his helm did the merriment across the islet catch his eye. The ocean and the island's verdure shimmered blindingly by midday. Under day-goggles, the details became lamentably clearer. Guards where flinging an Ish between them like ball sport, despite a senior disciple making every attempt for its rescue.

Meanwhile, Xira the Stargazer was lashing defensively with her tail-barb at some avian attacker; however, all she had managed was to blood her naked crown. Flagrant nudity gave poor rewards, he observed with a scowl.

And these weren't just militia, that is, Civils, but his personal elite: j'Na-Zeru, sworn to die for the Zeruhawi cause, a kind of living dead who obeyed his every order without question. Their assignment here was to harvest ghaazli for Xira's manufactory, not this … this foolery!

Approaching a-rears with his notorious stealth, Zakon boomed, "This is hardly the most productive use of time. What say you?"

Startled, the guards stiffened and the beleaguered Ish crashed by a water hole.

"Lord Upholder!" Deep bows from all masked guilt ridden tendrils before a final shove from an eager guard sank the Ish from sight.

With a startled cry, the marauding bird made straight for the Ish, followed by the frantic disciple.

"Ah, Zakon!" exclaimed Xira smarmily, with a sideways glance at the pool.

"These are death-hardened j'Na-Zeru, Stargazer! A security detail against those beastly yash'kh, not a troupe of entertainers!"

"I'm dispensing a lesson in manners. You needn't concern yourself with the chattel." Xira began to grow witty about torment by juggling when Zakon cut her short.

She had used his intimate address in public, and in front of his own subordinates, though he and she were hardly confidants. That and her public nudity raised his ire. And there was an odor about her he couldn't quite define. It wasn't unpleasant: more chemical than natural, but even so, a Zmee's personal hygiene should never permit any smell at all.

"Not much of a lesson, was it?" Zakon said finally. "And it seems your own tail-barb was getting the better of you. You're bleeding from crown to ear."

«Oh?» Xira smiled crookedly and gave a deferential bow. "As you say, Lord Upholder."

Meanwhile, the disciple had emerged coiling tail-first from the pool dragging the coughing and spluttering Ish to the surface while Xira spat an invidious remark against the youngster's Oracle.

The student ought to have fulminated, especially against Xira's slight to her teacher. *I WOULD HAVE,* Zakon admitted. Besides, honor demanded no less. Instead, she was remarkably self-composed and merely glowered briefly at Xira.

"You're from Zu'u-Shoran, right? The Prime Mapmaker's firstling?" «Aren't you?» Her lack of response compounded his growing annoyance. A mere disciple was ignoring the Upholder. More than one here needed upbraiding!

"Enok. Enokhi. *Enokhi!*"

She kept shaking the creature, desperate for signs of life — but how it burned his tendrils to behold such an elevated scholar openly distraught over some half-dead barbarian!

The creature coughed a little before responding in quaintly accented speech. "Hrazul, I'm fine. Really. Nothing broken."

«Up! Get up!» "Little Enokhi, we cannot afford to lose you!"

The Ish rose tall before squeaking, "I'd love to see these brainless barbarians toss Stargazer around."

Zakon was incensed. Had the beast just sputtered that Zmee were barbarians? Had he heard true? Had it also just called Wise-eye by her intimate name, and in public? Xira was right. It did indeed need a solid lesson in manners.

She had begun to suggest something along these very lines, when he was forced to reprimand her. "Stargazer, this isn't your slave."

"But, Upholder!"

«No!» "I must enforce the law. It may be just a chattel, but it isn't yours to punish." «Hear me?»

«I hear.» "But are you always so joyless? Can't you at least send the thing away? Its sickly sweet smell attracts the yashurakh."

There was a hardly a tendril without surprise when Hrazul whispered to the slave, then challenged Xira to a game of z'hadai while the slave flashed its teeth in defiance. It was quite juvenile really, a simple game of chance, of pea-under-the-shell.

"Three shells, ten games," she proposed. "Win more than five, and we depart. Win less, and *you* do."

Xira gasped. «What?» "How dare you!"

Zakon chuckled privately. The j'Na-Zeru too thought the wager amusing. This Hrazul was bold and the Ish had no fear of him either. IT SHOULD, he thought. IT REALLY SHOULD.

Anyhow, if Xira lost, it might teach her a little humility. After all, she had nearly killed someone else's slave, even if it was only an animal, and a hated barbarian at that! Anyhow, it was far more fun to even the odds.

"Let me change the rules: two shells only, all else as before," Zakon proposed. "If Stargazer wins, your slave gets its 'lesson,' then you both go free. However, if she loses —"

Xira was signing furiously at him, «Stay! Stay!» But why was she so desperate to remain? There was no shortage of Breakfast Islands this time of year, even in the north.

"If she loses," he continued, "then you both leave immediately, with the slave spared another beating."

Xira smiled. «Good!»

The disciple was as stony-faced as ever. The Ish, however, was perching the bird on an outstretched arm and baring its puny fangs more widely than before.

And was it his imagination, or had that bird just squawked "Khozaa!" the victory cry?

*

The lots of z'hadai had not fallen to Xira, and her countenance burned like Ssla's midday flame. With only two shells and a single pea, the little nimble-handed primitive had shuffled quickly and repeatedly until its hands were a blur. Xira's guessing proved poor. She won on the first turn, only four times in all, and the slave skipped happily free of another of her 'etiquette lessons.'

Xira scowled privately, "You thin-tendriled bull, you ought to have made sure I won!"

She was neither an Oracle nor a Venerable,[xxv] not even a Prominent, merely a failed disciple turned upstart celebrity with powerful allies. And with poor manners to boot. He was comfortable enough with his authority, though, to allow her the illusion of equality. He found it faintly amusing.

«I got rid of them,» he signed casually, stifling a smile. "That *was* your original request, wasn't it? And it clearly needed doing if we're to make anything of today." To the guards he growled, "Load the barge with ghaazli, double time! The day's half over already and we're a long way from home."

Xira had donned her helmet and was staring out to sea after the Ish and its primitive craft as they disappeared behind the headlands. "These will all be Zeruhawi waters soon. My waters. And our standard will fly high above the Isthmus Gates."

«Curious.» "You regard Southerners so poorly," Zakon noted, "yet you're a Southerner yourself, right? Didn't you apprentice in Zu'u-Shoran?"

"We had our disagreements. Their bloated toad of a matriarch treats us all like younglings. Sooner she croaks, the better for Zoar."

"I'll pretend I didn't hear that. Just focus on what you came to do, Stargazer: to harvest ghaazli, to make your stink, to inflate a sky-boat, so we can all fly."

Xira's gaze was still on the horizon. "That cowering Ish-licker. Because of her and her kind, the pride of our race has bitten the dust. Weaklings without vision. They know nothing of the power —"

Zakon cut her short with a gesture. «Ignorance!» "More than you, I daresay."

---

xxv *Oracle, Venerable, Prominent.* In descending order, the three strata of Zmee public office. Only Oracles can take posts on the ruling Shav'yat.

«Not so!»

"Power is merely a tool and it has limitations, but the very Grand Oracle you keep deriding wields it consummately, I'd say."

«Doubtful.»

"The sarcophagi of the first Warrior Oracles, for example. She knows how you Zeruhawi want to venerate them, so she sealed them in the Reliquary, that great vault to which she alone has the key. And no one's sighted the key in — what? — fifty years now?"

«More or less.»

"That single act underscored who's in charge and quelled unrest among the Zeruhawi. See, *that* is power — a single act whose effects yet remain. The ultimate power is to control *this*," he propounded, a claw nail clacking against the brass of his helmet. "Control what people think, their perception of their own limitations, and you control how they behave —"

«Yes, yes.» "Her Azhakh-Na believers are beginning to spread along the grand canal of Zu'u-Susyaan. Among the mine pits of the Raz-Ghoshar and even in the underground forges of Yashau-Zaar itself I hear of 'cells.' This has not escaped your attention, I'm sure. If we Zeruhawi don't act soon, their loopy philosophy may soon begin to affect the north beyond all repair." [xxvi]

Xira spun towards him with as earnest an expression as he had ever seen on her, and with eyes that almost shone. "But if we could somehow unseal the Reliquary," she added with a spreading grin, "display the relics — that would certainly change their 'perception,' and thereby weakening this so-called power, eh? Just think, it would rally Zeruhawi everywhere."

"You're positively dangerous! Don't think it hasn't been tried, though — long before your time. Nothing seems to cleave that stone. Oh, you can mark it unintentionally, but once you try in earnest ..." Zakon's voice trailed away. "It's like it refuses to be cut."

HOW MUCH HAVE WE FORGOTTEN THAT WE NO LONGER EVEN REMEMBER THE FORGETTING?

"It's time we simply took that key. She has it; I know where."

---

xxvi   By legend, Zoar was settled by a militaristic cabal that dissipated as civilization prospered, or so the Zeruhawi lament. Only the influence of the Azhakh-Na has kept their war-like tendencies in check.

"How?" Zakon queried cautiously. "What knowledge do you possess that my spies and I do not?"

"Aren't you for us?" she pleaded, sensing his lack of enthusiasm. "For the Zeruhawi cause?"

«No,» he signed slowly and emphatically. "I'm for Zoar. North *and* South."

"How easily Zeruhawi artisans could be charmed to build you a sky-boat of your own, if there was, ah, sufficient inducement." Xira let the offer tantalize the Upholder's tendrils, but the bribe was lost on him and it told in trail of her voice. "I understand the ancient tablets of wisdom, the Aphorisms of Zulyi, the original etchings, are locked away in the Reliquary too. Wouldn't you agree, Upholder, that having them accessible is in everyone's interests? Wouldn't they unite rather than divide?"

"What a silken serpent you are!"

"Upholder!" A guard seemed suddenly excited.

«What!» signed Zakon.

"There are no peas under the shells!"

Xira grew livid in spasms, her tendrils blaspheming. "That dung eater! I knew it!" In her rage, she beheaded a nearby tortoise and flung its carcass into the sea.

No peas. Had the Ish hoodwinked her? *She* seemed to think so.

Impossible. It was only a savage and probably ate the pea.

It probably meant nothing.

Right?

THE GREATER LIGHT WAS LONG past its zenith. Enok had returned to his bluff to lounge on his favorite overlook. He stared absently out to sea, being diverted occasionally as his eyes followed somersaulting khrii glide elegantly along breaking waves in a taunt.

Every muscle in his body groaned for mercy. The slightest movement pained him, and it kept forcing him to relive today's encounter with Stargazer Xira and that muscled red bull, Zakon. Perhaps calling her a 'pustulant dung-worm' had been a tad unhelpful, but she had provoked the tirade, hadn't she? It was amazing, he concluded, what the tongue could dredge forth with so little provocation. How effortlessly it mined a sordid repertoire he never even knew it had! But then, he had merely been returning insults in defense of those he esteemed. Honor demanded no less, right? That was fair, wasn't it?

As an inner voice was whispering *no*, he began to wonder if Zmee too suffered from these internal dialogues.

It was between diversions that he noticed that Jin-jin was perched on the largest of his drums with wings aquiver and squawking angrily. An assortment of the bird's own feathers had once been arranged in a pattern before Jin-jin ruined it. Hrazul was too punctilious to have left them behind accidentally.

Was it a clue? A plea?

Her odd behavior this morning had nearly led to blows. Were her golden eyes and sprouting tendrils at fault, making her more emotional, more explosive? And under nose and chin, he was now sprouting fine tendrils of his own. Would that explain his sharp-tongued outburst? With her new additions, Hrazul had would soon have four adult tendrils, but if he could count his own, how many would there be? Easily more than thirty. Did these betoken, then, a darker temper and a rogue tongue?

And what of his haunting dreams of a shadowy but beautiful face, with wild darksome tresses, the complexion of midnight, with beckoning, tapered eyes; gentle, touching, the smell of ... of ... flowers — a face to fill the hollow within yet make him all the hungrier? Were these new whiskers behind it all?

Hrazul was changing. He was changing.

Maybe everything was.

Maybe everything should.

He had missed his appointment at the butterfly house with Zoia. A rebuke and chastisement would surely follow, yet something in him refused to budge, and aught from any sprain. Why the endless chores anyway? Oracle Zoia taxed him harder than she did her own disciples. Khrii obeyed no one, so why should he? And why couldn't he just lounge melding with the overlook, if he wanted, and mark time by nothing more than birdcall and the darkening sea?

A glance at the copper manacle around his ankle ended the argument. "Because you're a lowly slave, Two-legs," said Enok to himself. "That's why."

On the beach below, yash'kh, enormous marine dragons with towering spiny dorsal fins, were posturing aggressively. Having spent the morning feeding at the tidal seaweed plains of the Chechi Archipelago in the southeast, they now began to arrive and bask in the warmth of the afternoon heat. At the edge of the all-male pod lay Puzo, the battle-weary old bull recently ousted by a younger rival. His great collapsible sailfin, normally stalwart, hung limp whilst younger males, eager for recognition, jostled for the prime waterside positions free of any shadows from contenders.

In a way, Enok pitied old Puzo. In another, he envied the great dragon's sense of belonging. Puzo knew his place in his world, and could leave at a whim. Enok's melancholy thought was that he had no peers, and whatever the freedoms in his head, there was never the freedom to leave. Or the means.

The most bitter of today's truths was that after almost fifty years on this island, many familiars still remained wary, and even strangers were turning hostile. Witness the incident at Breakfast Island: Xira had always loathed him, but why the guards? What crime had he committed? And why had Alazar Gray-face so thoroughly abandoned him in his most desperate watch? Perhaps in defense of little Yuni? It was justifiable, he thought, but still completely cowardly.

And there were stories, just whispers and fragments really, of brutal slayings, of Zmee being captured and tortured, even eaten! Polite conversation avoided it, and neither Hrazul, nor mistress Zoia, nor the High Wisdom herself ever permitted any probing. To question was not a servant's privilege, let alone a slave's, and so his chief query remained unanswered: what had his people done to the Zmee that had spawned this cycle of hatred?

If he had won any lesson from today's events, it was that he had none but Hrazul for protection. In a crunch, he had no friend but her. He shifted rear-sore on the outlook, despondently fondling the blue-and-gold feathers she had left as a hint, taking in the beach below, the gulf beyond, and following a solitary khrii as it soared on motionless wings towards a blue horizon.

Flying. Freedom. They were not for him.

Time and again, in years gone by, he had tried to flee the island, but every attempt had nearly cost him his life. Escape was clearly impossible. He had to resign himself to that. 'Only fools desire the unobtainable,' mistress Zoia often said.

He was an Ish, a male of the Elim, human; and to Zmee eyes, the eternally inferior savage.

The echo of Xira's words tormented him: 'ZMEE HAVE NAMES, ZMEE HAVE RIGHTS ... BEASTS HAVE NONE.'

Inferior perhaps, but irredeemably so?

Today's brutal encounter underscored the library whispers. With the Zeruhawi ascendant, there was little hope of surviving much longer unless he could convince the Zmee, even the Zeruhawi, that he was every bit their equal.

As a servant to one of the island's leading Oracles, he knew better than most how Zmee accounted intellect and knowledge above almost everything else. But they were obsessed with flying, and passionate about flowers and butterflies too. Zu'u-Shoran's butterfly house was magnificent, the talk of Zoar. Both the High Wisdom and mistress Zoia were avid collectors and breeders. How unsightly the caterpillar to all but its keepers, but oh the public delight when from the chrysalis emerges a butterfly! It was curious, wasn't it? They were both the same creature, yet how much more acceptable was the one form over the other!

And so, in a frisson of dread and the hope of success, Enok formulated his plan. If being Ish was so problematic, and escape impossible, then only one option remained.

Just as caterpillars became butterflies, he must become Zmee.

THE INERTIA OF HOPE

Zakon presents an old historian with an opportunity the cult of the Zeruhawi has long desired ... At the New Year's Eve ceremony, Enok nervously awaits the moment to consummate his daring plan for acceptance.

BESIDE THE TAPERED SPIRES OF Ur-Hozhai in the north, or the coppered cupolas of Zu'u-Shoran in the south, Ra'a-Zohari's jagged, angular architecture seemed utterly alien. However, lawns of flowering mosses, russet and ocher lichens creeping up the flanks of its towers, and traceries of pea-vines about its aqueducts, all softened its outlines so completely as to effect an image of some ancient and crumbling complex. And that soaring organic temple of the nearby thaakh forests further humbled any notion of industry defiant.

But what really set this prefecture apart was its luxuriant hinterland swamps. So although the drier north abounded with flowers, perfumes, and modernity, here the cool peaty air came thick and sensual on the tendrils, and was truly a joy to breathe.

Zakon had much business here lately. Ukhaz, the Chief Oracle of Law resided here, and there were always issues of legal interpretation to discuss, particularly when a life was at stake; for he would rather redeem a sloth through civic service than feed her flesh to the crabs.

However, Ukhaz was adamant that dissipated souls would always endanger the colony.

'Social fungus,' as she called it, 'begets after its kind. And doesn't such risk weigh upon *you* most of all?'

Yes, he was the Upholder; and if the colony was indeed at risk, he was duty-bound to act swiftly, however irksome the task.

Stargazer's manufactory was also nearby, which was his chief reason for coming. Xira's flying apparatus intrigued him. By his hand, her giant balloons might find employment for something more practical than stargazing.

Presently, however, he had business of an altogether different sort. Waiting patiently for entry into the upper-level office of this city's historian gave him time for reflection. The incident with the Enokhi creature on Breakfast Island was both worrying and amusing.

Aghz, so the occupant of this office had once told him, in the long-lost ancestral land of Zoriyan, was so preoccupied with everything above her — the clouds, the flying creatures, and especially the stars — that she was oblivious to the devastation being wrought by her ever expanding observatory. Beneath it lived a colony of fang-moles, and they were losing both home and life.

One night, Aghz, so heavenly minded and blinded to all earthly effect, was attacked in revenge for all the misery she had caused. Dismissing their assault with her usual impunity, but now with infected, swollen limbs and tendrils, Aghz accidentally set her own parapet alight, and the secrets of all she had learned burned with her. Such was the legend of glorious Aghz.

And the moral of the story? Never trust a mammal!

That morning on Breakfast Island, Stargazer had won the z'hadai guessing game four times only: the first, third, fifth and seventh — spelling AGHZ in the Mapmaker's alphabet.

The toothy little beast had indeed hoodwinked Xira: it had deliberately manipulated the outcome of every game. Indeed, as Xira had surmised, there never had been a pea under the shells, except when the Ish's nimble little digits had produced one. Hoodwinkery, however, requires intelligence and the slave had alluded to the legend of Aghz. It was smarter than Xira credited, and cleverer than any of its mainland kindred.

How *that* had escaped the official reports of his spies, Zakon wondered, was a curious question indeed. Moreover, the creature didn't just understand Zmee culture but could read as well! An Ish with such wit and intimate knowledge of Zoar was unsettling, for here was another 'fang-mole,' a shifty little mammal that could easily compromise this colony's safety. If the law was harsh on reprobates, how much more so upon enemies!

Zakon was the Upholder, the defender of Zoar, and tireless enemy of threat and foe. But what a to-do! For the greatest risk to Zoar had long been lying beneath the High Wisdom's very snout!

It must have been sheer kismet that he had crossed paths with her here in Ra'a-Zohari yesterday, and he had leveraged his observation of the Ish to 'persuade' the ageless matriarch to part with something she ought never have taken to bosom. In exchange for his silence and a pledge for the creature's continued safety within the confines of the Sha-Noa promontory, she had yielded the long-concealed green hexagon.

Though generations of Zeruhawi spies had failed to uncover its whereabouts, a young mole amidst the Azhakh-Na had learned it had always been under her very bonnet! It was a kind of crystal talisman, the key to the Reliquary, though what ancient science powered it was anyone's guess. No one really knew, not even its keeper.

It was a fool's deal really, for after Breakfast Island the creature was certainly doomed — perhaps not at his bidding, but certainly at Xira's. Something of his respect for the High Wisdom should have died then, but her final pronouncement intrigued him:

'You open the door to the whirlwind.'

Was it a warning or a threat? In any event, she had absolved herself, and weighted him alone with all the liability.

But where could risk be lurking here?

Before her cryptic prophecy, she had given some simple instructions regarding the object's use. He could scarcely breath for triumph when he had left her alone in that heavy silence that was, he first thought, her mantle of remorse; but the image of her piercing eyes, with jaws tensed in self-counsel, owned more of entrapment than defeat, and it hollowed his victory. And, oddly, she had returned home to Zu'u-Shoran almost as soon as she'd come.

In this deal of fools, however, who of the two was the fool?

He now held the object, the talisman, the key, and was about to make a gift of it.

A croaky voice beckoned, "Enter!"

Zakon peered gingerly inside the vacuous chamber. From the rectangular threshold to its sharp-cornered ceiling, every dimension was alien. The timber door creaked in its frame. It was heavy, and heavily carved. Despite its shape, at least its sinuous ornaments were familiar.

At the rear of the chamber, an oversized red-and-black Zeruhawi pennant dominated the room. Red was for victory, Zmee supremacy; black was for death, the end of the Ish. On an adjacent wall hung a graven Na-Zeru standard: a vermilion serpent coiled as a wheel, yet with arms and legs of grotesque size, one for each of the four winds. It was a cultic icon, a reminder that the Zmee once had more limbs than at present, but like the wheel, they would roll and crush their enemies. There was no doubting the occupant's extremist sympathies.

Hunched over an expansive crescent-shaped desk with mythological creatures in heavy relief on its rim, and littered with curled dusty parchments, was ancient Skazaar herself, the Oracle of Chronicles. Great age had rendered her virtually genderless. Now, neither green nor red, her once renowned lime hide had faded to a dappled gray.

"I have the key," he reported flatly.

Quill fell, and all calligraphy was abandoned as the tendrils of the hoary Zmee were reduced to amazement, and her widened eyes partook of the emerald now dangling pendulous from his hand.

«My!» "That was no mundane accomplishment, Upholder! Your persuasiveness exceeds all acclaim!"

He shrugged coyly, his tendrils expressionless.

"Lo, these fifty years I schemed and labored. We tried drilling, tunneling, all with nary a scratch on those blessed stones! But you made good a lifetime in day!"

While her eyes continued to swing as if entranced by the pendulum, Zakon regarded with renewed awe the sight through her window of the massive gleaming pyramid across the common. It was the Reliquary. Only now could he appreciate the frustration of living the bulk of one's years in sight of an enigma that mocked both the encroaching forest and every serious inquiry.

"Never underestimate the importance of espionage."

«Or you!» Skazaar tipped her crown deferentially. "You cannot know what this means, Upholder, to hide and bones as old as mine. The High Wisdom has had her way for too long. Fancy keeping the archives locked away for almost an entire lifetime. Reprehensible." Her tendrils quivered in censure. «Criminal!»

"I suppose she had her reasons, Chronicler, but they too are now the stuff of history, eh?" Zakon laughed at his own wit, fingering the talisman on proffer. "Now, let's consider *your* reasons," he added, indicating the Na-Zeru standard behind her with an obvious tilt of the head.

He gauged her eagerly outstretched hand. As an historian, she was excited by the prospect of ancient texts awaiting rediscovery. As a Zeruhawi, she was drawn to the relics of legendary warriors. Which was the stronger desire, Zakon cared little. The less he meddled in green-skin politics, the better.

Tendrils flopped and her hand withdrew a little. "Not much escapes you, O Invisible One."

«Indeed not.»

She fidgeted briefly with a parchment, recovering her aplomb. "Gratitude can be expressed in many ways, Upholder; many ways indeed." As she reached for the crystal, Zakon snatched it away.

"Shall we do this publicly, Chronicler, or privately?"

Old Skazaar uncoiled herself and bowed deeply. "Privately, Upholder, if that is your wish." «Grateful. Grateful.» "Now, by your leave, I will summon the sisters."

At the edge of the expansive ellipse of the central common lay the circular platform simply called 'the dais.' Stone fairer than sea foam shaped a broad three-stepped architecture in perfect alignment with Calendar Avenue.

The steps were an odd construction for serpents needless of such devices, thought Zakon.

From the pyramid's entry ramp, down through its two guardian obelisks, down again across the center of the dais and reaching to the wide green sea, the avenue formed a line straight to the setting of

Ssla's New Year's orb beyond the sands of Yzhau Bay. It was as if the entire common, and indeed the rest of the city, were afterthoughts to some ancient celestial geometry.

Clustered on the inner lip of the dais, and tangential to that sacred line, four stone sentinels with polished faces leaned inwards as if drawn together by some invisible force. There Zakon removed the translucent emerald hexagon from its makeshift wrapping. It hung gummed to a silver chain, sparkling with an inner sunshine. Ancient and mystical symbols like flecks of transparent gold floated endlessly within. The key was alive somehow, older than time. It was living stone.

'YOU OPEN THE DOOR TO THE WHIRLWIND.'

Zakon swept the unbidden thought aside as he wormed between the columns to the polished face of a stone sentinel, and there, detaching the chain, placed the flat hexagonal *thing* into a matching depression. Almost immediately, a rumbling and the sound of grinding stone evoked exultant whoops from old Skazaar and her coterie, for across the common, a great trapezoidal entrance into the Reliquary had been exposed at the head of ramp.

ANOTHER ALIEN SHAPE, thought Zakon, and he also pondered the fact that for fifty years, nearly three reproductive generations, no one had ventured inside that ancient monument. Only old-timers like the historian here, with a half a tail in the tomb, held any memory of its treasures.

Skazaar and her troupe bowed lowly, with palms extended and supine like the humblest of servants. "Peace upon you, O Venerable Upholder. You have rendered the Cause a great service. Won't you join —"

«No!» Zakon signed emphatically. "I have obsession with neither the relics and politics of the Zeruhawi, nor the arcane creed of those First Causers that you so love to hate. The archives are what matter, and they belong to all Zmee, Zeruhawi and Azhakh-Na alike. Now, however, I make south for Zu'u-Shoran. Enjoy the morrow's New Year, Chronicler. Prosper, all of you."

«My lord!» The entourage genuflected again with cries of reciprocal blessing.

"You're coming with us to honor Stargazer?" inquired hoary Skazaar. «How exciting!» "She heads an entirely new science."

«Not exactly.» "Something peculiar there does, however, demand my personal attention." And departing, Zakon added with his tail barb jabbing emphatically, "I have merely done my duty. Make certain now that you do yours."

STRADDLING THE NARROW NECK OF the island's southern peninsula was Zu'u-Shoran, the most leisurely and least populated of Zoar's cities, one where scribes, philosophers, artists and poets found a haven from industry's din.

Though Zmee settlements were largely underground, the increasingly restless north, he'd heard, loved soaring, provocative architecture. To their eyes, Zu'u-Shoran's coppered domes and broad conical structures seemed too squat, too humble; but here was Zoar's greatest cathedra, here the High Wisdom's archives housed the sum of all knowledge.

Enok's childhood memories were of local sandstone and northern pumice giving form to this city of columned rotundas and winding porticoes. From the sea, its curvy, organic style and earthen hues made it almost invisible. And many a weary soul hailed its unpretentious elegance a balm.

As thoughts shifted northwards, Enok could only imagine what lay beyond the Isthmus Gates. The vast edges of Zoar teemed with cities and marvels he could apprehend only from maps and tales. South of the isthmus, in tranquil paddies, scribes grew papyrus for parchment. Here too from renowned stands of balsa, artisans crafted colorful lacquer-ware: red from the cactus mite, purple from oyster shells, gamboge from monk-wood, brown from nut hulls, and green from the viridian bush.

And furthest south, beyond the city's limits, stretched the promontory of Sha-Noa, a preserve exalted by long tongues of sand, squeaky, and immaculately white. Winding groves of frangipani, gardenia, and hibiscus adorned the flanks of its central mountain like a pilgrim's garland. In Sha-Noa, generations of inquisitive Mapmakers and Biotists had been cultivating exotic flora and fauna to live peacefully there under their ever-cataloging eyes.

On a hillock cresting an amphitheater, and with views of the neck entire, two of these mainland aliens now stood admiring a younger Enok's handiwork. As masons had leveled a stony ridge into a plateau, and crafted a trio of amphitheater, common, and rotunda, he had chiseled a monument right here of his own.

Brushing aside the succulent creepers that had grown around his handiwork, Enok was elated to find it as solid as the day he had made it, and as private. Pumice itself seemed to last forever,[xxvii] but the broad weather-beaten bench, was now patchy with lichen and moss, and looked every bit forgotten. The prized seats were down the front; the elevated rear was for servants. And so, in a strange reversal, his was the grandest view of all, for etiquette had rendered this height off-limits to any self-respecting Zmee.

MY BENCH, he thought, *AND MY HILL,* for in all the intervening years, the views from his bench had delighted no other.

With darkness for cover, Enok planned to enjoy the coming pageant by the light of its festive lanterns until the evening mists rolled in — and unseen. Indeed, he winced at the memories. Only twice before had he and Jin-jin sat visibly in public, and both occasions had ended terribly; however, 'Third time, lucky' went the popular maxim, right?

Surely, nothing could tarnish *this* night.

The distant seas of the east were now gray and foamy. Across the isthmus, the great hazy light of day had grown slowly into a magnificent red orb against a coral sky, firing the western sea. Its setting ended the calendar, and sanctioned the Amok, those intercalary watches renown for their mayhem.[xxviii]

To that end, Oracle Zoia had been wise to command of him 'minimal mischief,' instead of banning it altogether. But he had to make good on his promise about Jin-jin, so dey were spooled off an unbreakable lead, leaving the bird free to chase the occasional insect.

Thoughts now fell to what tonight would bring, what it must

---

xxvii   Zoar island is a remnant caldera. Pumice and scoria are plentiful, especially in the geothermally active north, and are widely used in Zmee megalithic structures.

xxviii   The Zmee liturgical calendar is lunar, having twelve months. The administrative is solar. The difference of eleven days between these two systems forms the intercalary period. Unlike the North, the Amok of the South is tolerated only for the first evening, if at all.

bring, and he shifted nervously in anticipation of the single outcome that embodied all his hopes. Ominously, two six-days had passed without sight of his beloved Hrazul. She had been busy with exams, and in a manner of speaking so had he. And his actions could never *ever* be undone.

A head thrown back on its shoulders saw the glory of day replaced by another. The glory of the night belonged to the myriad lesser lights, and these began to lace the heavens, flickering like distant lanterns. What were those lights in the sky? That need to know had always defined him. Even hills were of no account at a distance. So, of what dimension were these lanterns? Tree-big? City-large? Zoar-great? He had never ceased believing in their higher purpose, but what was their message? Of course, the bigger question was, if there was indeed a message, then who or what was its author.

But his was the lot of the lowly, and the humbling truth was that there was more to be known than could ever be learned as a slave. But after tonight, it would all start to change.

THIS VERY NIGHT.

Serried ranks of locals and visitors now began to fill the amphitheater, while carefully preserving the distinctions of class. As the rows filled, all eyes fell upon the rotunda across the common. Its vaulted copper dome atop a circular veranda of a dozen double-caryatids of red and green stone formed a truly imposing structure. These pillars were the Twain Serpents, symbolic of renewing body and soul. A pair twisted conversely in a circle spoke of procreation. A pair entwined vertically meant healing. Twelve of such enshrined the hope of continuity, of eternal life itself.

The burnished cupola began to mirror the dying light, and the reflection struck him squarely. Memory thus served where eyes now failed. At the shrine's heart stood a great ebony obelisk spiraling into a well at least a dozen fathoms deep. It was the Pillar of Zmee, the history of this people in bas-relief, a hallowed stone, and off-limits to all but the Oracles and students now gathering there.

With the common emptied, prominent now was the dais, a wide-stepped circular platform of gleaming quartzite with a pyramid to one side that towered over the panoply of dignitaries before it. And at its heart, a soaring intercalary torch shaped as hands supplicating the heavens awaited the ritual spark.

Positioned about both shrine and dais were countless stone lanterns doubling as thuribles, and a procession of chanting stiff-collared acolytes were using their censers to light them. Thankfully, instead of rising high, the bluish fumes of the incense lingered stubbornly fog-like on the ground. For Zmee there was no holier fragrance, but oh what horrid stuff it was! To sit beyond its reach, therefore, was hardly some misfortune.

A cautionary cackle from Jin-jin and a rustling in the low growth alerted his ears to an approaching Zmee. Thoughts first fell to Alazar, Hrazul's egg-sister, whom she had promised to dispatch. Instead, a familiar hiss from Jin-jin confirmed it was that nuisance Snei. She was edging her way towards them with a water-fire lantern, a glass vessel of cultivated fungi and glow-bug innards.

"Ah, Little Animal. I bear a gift," the young disciple announced, awaiting his obeisance. Only after he bowed a servant's bow and resumed his seat did she coil herself on a bed of succulents and make a show of delivering a cylinder.

"I hope there's food. I'm hungry."

«Open and see.»

Its narrow strip of parchment hosted the florid calligraphy of intimate communication, and leading them was a pictogram of a butterfly, his symbolic cipher.

"A message?" Snei seemed almost surprised by the contents.

"To me from Hrazul," he replied while straining under lantern's light. "It ends with her mark."

«How rude!» "Servant! The proper address would be 'The First Disciple of the Prime Oracle of Maps.'"

"Easy for Zmee to say! All that hissing tolls my tongue. I'll stick with just 'Wise-eye,' thanks."

Typically curious, Snei arced to read the message. Annoyed by this lack of privacy, Enok spun away, but she quickly snatched the parchment from behind.

"I have better night eyes. Her mark is clear, but this," she pronounced with a flourish, "is clearly gibberish."

Enok held out a hand in gesture none could misread.

The message was returned with a snort. «Foolery!»

It was a scytale of course, though clearly something new for her. Spiraled about the cylinder, the rows of characters made sense:

Enokhi − Feathers − Necklace − Joy − Thank you − Hrazul [xxix]
«Beasts? Read? What nonsense!» signed Snei before mocking him lyrically.

"An animal.
A parchment.
The writing reads itself."

"And animals can't play zhakh either," went Enok's retort. "Please, challenge me to a rematch." His dry humor was probably beyond her. "I can't believe Wise-eye entrusted you with this."

Her negative reply made little sense, and the ensuing silence was short; Snei still possessed a youngling's impatience. "They call this Luckless Loft. I know how irrational this sounds, but *misfortune* plagues anyone who lingers here," she whispered as if merely saying so summoned it.

"Why the babble if words are wasted on 'animals'?" Enok exploded. "You might as well chat up Jin-jin." As he called, "Bird! Here!" the lizard-bird flew to his outstretched arm.

«Little Animal!» "Such violent swings of temperament! Small wonder the Ish are so brutish!"

Enok wagged his head in exasperation. "Imagine others treating you the way that you treat me."

"I ... I am a disciple! Of a first-ranked Oracle! Not some lowly slave consigned up the hill. First Disciple was right," she gabbed of Hrazul. "Little Animal *does* get moody."

"But you *are* up the hill with the slaves," sighed Enok loudly and praying she wouldn't break into verse again.

Silence. AH, GOOD.

Then, "Anyway, such is my task: 'Keep Servant to the hilltop and the lizard-bird from trouble.'"

"We like trouble," Enok muttered. "Besides, I was expecting Gray-face." He hadn't seen Alazar since Breakfast Island, and was on the verge of adding, "That coward," but the less said the better when dealing with Sneak-tail Snei.

---

xxix   *Scytale (ski–ta–li).* A simple tubular cryptographic device. The decrypting cylinder is not normally delivered with the message.

«Bad. Bad.» "Gray-face has the good sense to avoid trouble. And everyone knows about that time when the little Ish set fire to the grandstand."

Enok was taken aback. "That was thirty years ago! And gross fabulation, all of it!"

«Confusion.»

"Really, disciples can be so gullible. If some Oracle preached the sky was falling, you'd believe it." He slid away on the bench.

"And what can there be to believe, Little Animal?"

"You really don't understand, do you? Any creature uttering 'I' is no longer any-*thing* but any-*one*."

«Truly?» "I, I," she slowly mouthed with her head queerly tilted. "That never occurred to me."

"Well, there's your challenge. And you so go on about names and titles, all blind to the inconsistency! If I'm just an animal, then why does everyone summon me by title as if I really were a Zmee? *Servant* this, *Servant* that. Besides, do any other 'animals' speak?"

Snei rocked introspectively, her facial tendrils wandering lazily. Maybe, just maybe, she was beginning to see beyond her prejudice, and perhaps even to accept him. If he could win *her* over, then —

"The servant *didn't* torch the grandstand, is that what it says? I overheard a reading of the records. Amazing how so great a disaster sprung from one so tiny!"

"I was only a youngling then."

"At thirty?" «Hardly!»

"Sure, for a Zmee. I would love to know where these so-called records are." If they were in the library, then he could destroy them.

"The Chief Chronicler. No, perhaps I shouldn't say."

"Look, both of us have been banned from *any* kind of public gathering since before you or Wise-eye were eggs. Even your Oracle was still a disciple back then. Want to know why? Jin-jin."

The bird squawked inquiringly.

«Disbelieving.» "The fire-bird?"

"We were on this very bench when the fire started. In those days, only the Pillar of Zmee was standing — no grand cupola then, or amphitheater, just a razed plateau. The thuribles were just bowls of smoldering rosins on pedestals. Likewise the torches lining the avenues. Their fuel was some sort of oil, I think. Anyhow, a three-tiered grandstand had been hastily assembled over quarry rubble. My guess is that a youngling toppled either one of the censers or the torches during the dancing, setting the grandstand's timbers alight. As you know, Jin-jin so loves a flame."

"The bird flew into the fire?" «Not surprised.» "Idiot creature."

Jin-jin sparked at Snei with a nip to the hand.

«Be gone!» "Bald ugly bird!"

At a word from deir master, the bird desisted, and flew off in response to a hand sign. "Tie rope now, Jin-jin. Tie rope," he instructed in the half-remembered tongue of his kind.

«Not understanding.» "What language is that?"

"Anyhow," continued Enok, "I leapt to save him, but when I realized the speed with which the blaze was spreading in the panic, as other torches spilled over —"

«Not so!» "Zmee never panic."

"You weren't there!"

«So?»

"Honestly! I was trying to douse the flames and save the Oracles, not incinerate them!"

«Uncertain.» "The record read otherwise."

"You can guess who caught me."

«My Oracle?»

"No, Old Black Feathers. Ukhaz."

«Who is that?» signed Snei, baulking at his impropriety.

"You know, the now Chief Oracle of Law."

"Why is that wretched bird circling me?"

"In her younger days, she was the Upholder," he said of Ukhaz. "They say the then Oracle of Law died from her burns. She wasn't that old really, but of the Azhakh-Na, a Southerner. The inquiring mind might ask why a Methodic Northerner succeeded her instead of one of her own school, as is customary. I called it 'murder,' so they censured me and have called me an 'animal' ever since. Perhaps," Enok shook his head in a sigh, half-resigned and half-angry, "perhaps I was naïve. But me? Malicious? Never. And the poor bird still has a limp. It was years before Jin-jin recovered."

Snei regarded him curiously, head atilt. "But it seems our servant has not."

Silence again.

Now it was his turn to be impatient. After graduation, Hrazul would be leaving him, assigned to who knew where, and this youngster would become the elder disciple. As of tonight, his life would never be the same. As she swayed gently in self-deliberation, he wondered if there would ever be, or even if there ever *could* be, another wise-eyed Hrazul.

It was now completely dark. Neither the eastern nor western horizons held anything of interest, and the dais began to shine like an enormous pearl as the great intercalary torch roared to life with jubilant peals from below. The old year had officially ended. Tonight the Lesser Light would rise high and bountiful and smile upon the Amok, that intercalary period before the next eve when rank meant little and youngling pranksters (especially up north) lampooned officials and plastered each other with chalks.

"There is another reason for my presence," said Snei.

"Oh? Astonish me." Frankly, he needed to focus on tonight's mission. Enok was in no mood for banter.

"'Explain the proceedings,' my Oracle told me. Oh, look — the little ones."

Now a dozen criers, who echoed every word of the dais, took positions on its broad ringing steps. Thereupon, two groups of younglings streamed single file into the plaza from opposite ends. Each bore a colossal paper lantern suspended from a reedy pole, and shaped as giant butterflies, the Great Zhmee, sky-dragons, or other aerial creatures. The larger groups' glowed green; the smaller, red. And instead of colliding, the two interwove like serpents entwining.

"There are fewer males than before," Snei hissed sadly. And truly, there were fewer reds than in childhood memory.

Two dressy officials ahead of the dignitaries coiled on the dais unfurled their neck membranes and made a show of their festive mallets. One struck her great gong:

Gong! Gong!

And then her accomplice, her cymbals with equivalent rhythm:

Tsang! Tsang!

The dancers then sped to a quickening tempo, all darting with amazing accuracy.

Gong!
Tsang!
Gong!
Tsang!

"You can thank the High Wisdom for that — those instruments, I mean," Snei explained.

"Sure. Great," replied Enok sardonically. This was as musical as the Zmee had ever been. Ironically, they were only now beginning to grasp the concept, and with instruments once improvised of scraps by a lonely Elim captive some twenty years ago.

The tempo rose feverishly like a racing heart.

Gong–tsang! Gong–tsang! Gong–tsang! Gong!

The sight of the now motionless greens and the ducking and weaving reds was reminiscent of the mating frenzy of pearl-snails. The music ended in a sharp cadence; the dancers suddenly froze.

"It's the Chief Chronicler who strikes the gong this year," Snei commented, identifying the Convener of Ceremonies. "She and the High Wisdom have partnered on a major new project."

The news was surprising. "Project?" He had never crossed paths with that particular Oracle, and glad of it too, panached as she was in Zeruhawi red-and-blacks. What had driven the High Wisdom to an alliance with the likes of her was beyond imagining.

"Duplicating the archives," Snei supplied, piquing his interest.

"From the library, I suppose."

"The long-lost key has opened the Reliquary. I spied the crystal myself." «No. No!» her tendrils recanted.

"You mean the library, of course."

Silence.

Library? Reliquary? Were they not the same? Excepting the butterfly house, more of the workdays of his life were lived in the library than almost anywhere else. He knew it well: the totems and myriad scrolls in the basements, the map rooms of the second floor, the meeting chambers in the domed vault of the third, and all the other places that defined his days with Zoia.

If this northern historian had been working in his own city he would surely have noticed. So what and where was the Reliquary? It was not on any map he knew of. Perhaps she meant the feretory, the sealed labyrinth of the library's bowels. But it was sacrosanct, and off limits to all but Oracles.

The aging Convener with the Zeruhawi panache announced the new trainees in as hoary a voice as Enok had ever heard. These entered the rotunda to meet their Oracle, the preceptor with whom they would live for the next six or possibly twelve years and share their most intimate thoughts. The bond between student and teacher began here. It was the strongest of all social cords, eclipsing that between the egg and its bearer, and even that between egg-sisters.[xxx] However, whatever was transpiring behind the colonnade, only eyes of fire could penetrate.

"They go to embrace the Pillar of Zmee and recite their preceptor's pedigree," Snei explained, "which they take for their own now in the oath of dedication."

PEDIGREE? "I didn't know."

Unlike most of the green, the sanguine younglings stayed put.

"The new disciples," she explained, tapping the little cylinder on the upper arm, "receive phylacteries like mine. See? They house sacred texts from the Aphorisms."[xxxi]

"Except for the first year, when it's a pendant. I'm hardly ignorant."

«Oh.» "I was led to believe otherwise."

Enok muttered something in response, which the youngling mistook for a question.

"The life of discipline is for females alone, and only for those, well, special."

---

xxx   Unlike the Elim, who reckon pedigree paternally (for the Ish), and in some tribes maternally (for the Isha), the only formal Zmee equivalent has long been this scholastic thread, though the South has begun to adopt the matrilineal custom.

xxxi   Each of the three scriptures in a phylactery have special meaning or life-lesson for the disciple. The way phylacteries are worn depends on seniority. Primarily a Southern tradition.

"'Those like me,' you wanted to say. *Huh*. So you utterly ignore the males."

«Eh?» "No need. The reds depart for the pilgrimage," she told a little somberly, "and freed. Why is that bird still circling me?"

"Well, lucky them. They're bound for the mainland." He was about to add 'and adventure' but the sentiment would have been wasted on her. "So you just abandon them. No wonder males are becoming scarce!"

«Misunderstanding.» "They join the clans of their sires."

"Sires?" That each Zmee had a father was a novel thought indeed.

Zoar only had females and younglings, and he voiced his thoughts about possible mainland cities of bulls.

«Cannot say.»

"You mean, you *won't* tell me."

«Honest!» "I have never yet been a pilgrim, so I truly do not know. But I hear that fewer and fewer bulls survive the Temple journey."

"Oh."

«Yes! Oh!» "Cause for worry indeed. However, if neither my Oracle nor First Disciple have loosened their tongues, then neither shall I."

Enok pondered this strained conversation. The stodgy student had illumined more about the private life of Zmee than the last dozen years combined. And the subject of lineage struck a melancholy chord with unexpected power.

Something deep and nameless stirred.

Sires. Parents.

Once the younglings had settled in the front rows, the Convener of Ceremonies, that old Zeruhawi, began summoning the graduates.

"There are five this year," chirped Snei after a spell. "Six, if we include Stargazer's special ceremony."

"Khaa! Xiwa!" Jin-jin hissed.

Enok too squirmed at the mention. He had completely forgotten about Xira's graduation. "And there will be a seventh."

«Impossible.»

When the gong resounded to the cry of "Firstling of Prime Mapmaker! Egg of Steam-maker!" summoning Hrazul, she paused before the Convener to visibly fondle the feathered necklace he'd made for her, and spare a glance at the hillock with a juvenile wave of the hand.

For twelve years she had lived intimately with Zoar's Prime Mapmaker, poured endlessly over ancient texts, and ultimately birthed revelations of her own. It was Hrazul who had charted fjords in the uttermost north where ocean turned to stone from the cold, and then proven those bergs were of water. They were the water-stone of legend! [xxxii]

Though it had surely fueled a plethora of questions about this colony's genesis, she had shied from any celebrity and insisted the discovery was an allied effort. But now her many labors were being recognized. She would be hereafter the student of none, no longer the taught, but the teacher.

Hail the new Oracle of Maps!

The audience rose high, fluttering their membranous wings in the Zmee equivalent of riotous applause as she was stripped of her helm-borne phylacteries, the symbols of senior discipleship.

Enok dried a forming tear as he smiled. Both smile and tear were fleeting, however, for his next actions weighed heavily upon him. Like her, he would no longer be subject to others. A bright new future dawned tonight for him as well.

Jin-jin returned to the bench with an exultant squawk.

When the last of the five had graduated, the Zeruhawi Convener huddled urgently in conference with her peers and the High Wisdom.

"It seems we have another aspirant tonight — but, by Zulyi, we cannot ascertain who. Can the 'Firstling of Self, the Egg of None,' come forward?" Her thoughts were there for the taking:

THE AMOK HOURS! WAS THIS SOME YOUNGLING'S PRANK?

A cheer rose from certain quarters, when she added, booming: "'Firstling of Self,' you know who you are! Come, seize your moment!" The jubilant thought she meant Xira.

Enok's already high anxiety turned to outright fear at the sight of the transverse black-feathered miter that was doubly dark in its distinctiveness, for scaling the dais now was Ukhaz, the Chief Oracle of Law from the north. Then it struck him:

[xxxii] Zmee legends say they hail from a colder environment, one quite unlike the tropical Zoar. Mapmakers still search for it.

NORTHERNERS!

Suffering under Snei's banter, he had overlooked the obvious. Far more were assembled here than merely the local populace. And though all adults were helmed in some way, only northern guards seemed to wear copper or bronze. Glints of metallic headgear peppering the audience, plus the ubiquity of the red-and-black panache, only confirmed his misgivings. The throng was swollen by a third with Zeruhawi, and so many of them were militia!

Xira was being inducted tonight — perhaps as a Venerable, maybe even an Oracle — but here, *here* so she could gloat in the presence of both enemies and cadres.

The memory of Breakfast Island stabbed like a blade.

Enok plumbed a tremulous breath, and it startled young Snei when he leapt from the bench. "Whatever happens, happens."

"By the stones of the Great Temple! Stay put! I command —" However, her admonition died as he bolted downhill, and she cried out instead at the revelation that Jin-jin had wound her fast to the bench, and never hearing what Enok had muttered in parting.

"Die if I must, but tonight I am servant no more."

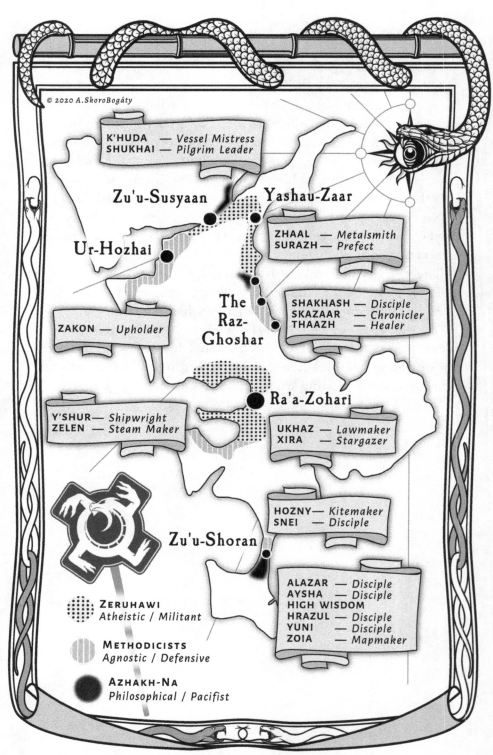

© 2020 A.SkoroBogáty

K'HUDA — *Vessel Mistress*
SHUKHAI — *Pilgrim Leader*

Zu'u-Susyaan   Yashau-Zaar

ZHAAL — *Metalsmith*
SURAZH — *Prefect*

Ur-Hozhai

The
Raz-
Ghoshar

SHAKHASH — *Disciple*
SKAZAAR — *Chronicler*
THAAZH — *Healer*

ZAKON — *Upholder*

Ra'a-Zohari

Y'SHUR — *Shipwright*
ZELEN — *Steam Maker*

UKHAZ — *Lawmaker*
XIRA — *Stargazer*

HOZNY — *Kitemaker*
SNEI — *Disciple*

Zu'u-Shoran

ALAZAR — *Disciple*
AYSHA — *Disciple*
HIGH WISDOM
HRAZUL — *Disciple*
YUNI — *Disciple*
ZOIA — *Mapmaker*

ZERUHAWI
Atheistic / Militant

METHODICISTS
Agnostic / Defensive

AZHAKH-NA
Philosophical / Pacifist

ZOARAN POLITICAL ALLEGIANCES

I, ENOK

Enok's attempt to prove his equality with Zmee yields completely unintended results ... Meanwhile, a chance event gives the Zeruhawi cabal a way to further their cause and rid Zoar of Enok in a stroke.

FOR TWO SIX-DAYS, ENOK HAD planned and planned again every nuance of this action. Jin-jin and Snei were now wound fast to the bench and unable to follow. By staying put, a dozen dreary futures sought to smother him, but now his downhill momentum quashed all indecision and committed everything to wild and crazy faith.

On the dais, the exasperated Convener of Ceremonies kept waving the gong mallet emphatically, repeatedly pleading for the last candidate, that 'Firstling of Self,' to finally make herself known.

"The parchments were in such tiny writing and void of any imprimatur. Who is the supervising Oracle? Of which school? This is highly improper! Will none come forward?"

Rising chants of "Stargazer! Stargazer!" and "Make her an Oracle! Not just some Venerable!" from rowdy Northerners turned to peals of outrage as they sighted Enok. Nervous glances sideways told him few routes were free of their red-and-black.

"Odious beast!" growled one.

"Stone the obscenity!" raged another.

"Great Zhmee! It's the Prime Mapmaker's slave!"

As an angry throng spilled onto the central aisle hissing and jostling, younglings from the north, who had never met his kind before and confused by the commotion, beat their stubby little wings and scattered to the winds. On the gravelly common, the crowd parted to leave him standing alone and face-to-belly with the criers. He slipped past them onto the dais to present himself to the Convener and to Old Black Feathers herself, Ukhaz, the Chief Oracle of Law.

THIS IS IT.

From amidst the assembled Oracles came the unmistakable hiss of mistress Zoia. "You Zeruhawi go too far!"

NOW, ENOK!

He recited the disciple's formula and finished with a flourish of his own. "I am Enok, no one's firstling, and egg of none. I have long forgotten my egg-bearer's name, and lack all memory of my people. And it would seem I passed the trials, else you would not have issued summons. So, despite whatever colors your opinion, I submit to you that I am no mere beast but a being."

Where he had expected protest, he was met instead with silence. The Convener was stunned, and even the chief crier went quiet when others hadn't followed her lead.

Ukhaz, however, had been grumbling all along, and now erupted. "Pestilent gnat! Irreverent slave!" With wings outstretched, and tendrils abandoned to rage, she reared high, poised to strike.

KEEP GOING, Enok steeled himself, and continued.

"If I truly am a being, you cannot deny me my privileges; though, if I'm just a beast, then your scholarship is hardly better." He surveyed the elders on the dais, seeking first acknowledgment from every eye, and finally from any. "I petition the Oracles assembled here to reconsider my status. I am not an animal. I want to be Zmee."

The chief crier spun, seeking guidance and silently asking, «Do we broadcast this?»

Wrenching the mallet from the Convener's hand, Ukhaz struck the gong angrily. "Behold, the firstling of fools!" she thundered, swaying side-to-side with eyes gauging her victim. "Oh such wonderful powers of mimicry! In its own cleverness, though, it proves itself a dolt. For as a beast, *it* makes a useful slave. As a being, though, is *he* then not our enemy?"

As the criers began their echo, she struck with serpent speed. Instinctively, lids defended eyes as a shielding arm shot up; however, instead of being felled by the impact, a strange calm enveloped him. Then all to be heard was a frustrated hiss, and when Enok dared peek, Ukhaz was swinging the mallet again with the full force of her coil. But she missed again, and her jowls collided loudly with the platform.

The rising buzz from the crowd subsided quickly when the old matriarch herself took center stage. The blue-feathered miter and vest of pure white down studded with blue gems engendered the silence the High Wisdom's office deserved. She had long commanded great respect for her knowledge and intellect, and was supposedly of great age, yet amazingly youthful, or so they said. Because of the great frill-necked mask she wore in public, no one alive had ever seen her face.

Now the throb of his own pulse gave the pregnant silence meter. Ukhaz, who was still fuming and massaging her jaw, slid aside to admit her.

Snout-to-nose and eyes creased in that well-remembered glare that seemed to sight his very bones, the High Wisdom whispered so softly behind her mask that it almost seemed imagined. "Thou art as thou thinkest."

"Yes, but in my eyes only," he replied. "I want to *be* what I know I am."

She rolled her great head disapprovingly. "And for all to see?" And she added, sighing, "'Good opinions forge no destiny.' Hast thou learned nothing from me?" «Truly? Nothing?» "'Unseasonal blooms die fruitless.' Hast thou never read?"

The quotations were among her favorites from the Aphorisms. However, before he could respond, a great finger stoppered his lips. «Much danger. Trust me!» "We have been betrayed. I pray thee, Enokhi, say thou not one word more!"

Her usual High Zmeezh was abnormally grim, but she had never addressed him so intimately before. Just how grave did she think things were set to become? Then she quickly assured the assembly that he had intention neither to offend nor to graduate. His actions were simply a plea amok. After all, these were indeed the intercalary hours. Harmless fun. And it was surely was no crime to aspire to be more. Would that every slave were as such! However, just when he thought she was defending him, there came instead a diatribe against the barbarity of his people and their attacks upon helpless Zmee settlements.

"And it mattered not," she continued, "whether they imagined themselves as beasts or beings, for any creature so despicably rapacious is, by definition, just a beast. But I gave this animal sanctuary that we might better understand our foes. It's in the public record. Though after fifty years of careful observation, I have yet to sight even a hint of belligerence, and we are thus left none the wiser.

"Maybe the Ish become more hostile with age, or perhaps the madness that overwhelms them transmits itself through contact. The trouble is," she confessed, "after nearly an entire Zmee lifetime, the creature only now matures, and so further study is required. For the moment, I say, let it be."

Enok felt his chances plummet. The High Wisdom had just made his stance irrelevant. He had rehearsed this scenario a dozen times, and it had never resulted in this!

There were no jeers or accusations now, and the crowd was strangely attentive — as if the struggle over his future was merely another chapter in the evening's entertainment.

As elders shepherded the younglings back and settled reassuringly among them, the High Wisdom boomed slowly and deliberately, "If ye aspire to the Azhakh-Na calling, mark ye well what that entails." She struck out with the mallet — *gong, gang-gang, gong* — and held the other arm skyward until the echoes were a memory. "Where is thy home, thy true home?"

"*The dominion of Zoriyan,*" the younglings chanted in unison.

"And where is that dominion?"

"*It is lost but we will find it.*"

"How will ye find it?"

"*With hope, with diligence, we will search. We will not stop. We will succeed.*"

"How should ye prepare?"

"*Disciples we will be, learn all that can be learned.*"

"What shall ye do with what ye learn?"
"The living stones must live again, to scale the Ascending Way."
"And when the Way is open?"
"Zoriyan will be our home again, without Ish, or beasts, or terror."
"And what awaits us there?"

"The midday heat is cool,
And Ssla hurts not the eye.
A place of countless, green canals,
Where water turns to stone.
The earth is red, its valleys deep,
The mountains reach a rich green sky.
The air is thick, and clouds weep rain,
Where Zmee can fly and breathe with ease,
Where life is lived ten thousand years,
Zoriyan is our journey's end."

The High Wisdom allowed the ensuing hush to linger, inviting the wayward to recommit to the common cause. Though their bodies were still, tendril after tendril twitched an affirmation that rippled like a radial wave through the assembly. A grander vision was hard to imagine. He must have been thinking audibly, for her next words were particularly apt.

"This is what we have all long striven towards," she delivered privately in Low Zmiysh with an aura fraught of ... of ... Was it disappointment? Betrayal? "Whether you knew it or not, as a beast and a servant you were part of that dream. In the fullness of years, you would have gloriously become what you were meant to be. But now, you risk everything!"

"I want —"

"Though I have been faithful, how could I not wish upon yours that curse that has overwhelmed mine!"

"— to understand."

«Understand?» "Grasp instead what it's like to watch helplessly as generations of eggs grow ignorant of the splendid culture that birthed them, of their true home and how to find their way back! We Zmee had a grand home — *have* a glorious home, little one, somewhere — and this is not it. What need would there be for cowering in the isles of the sea except for the savagery of your kind? The artifacts left by our ancestors, here on Zoar and scattered abroad, they are the living stones, Enokhi. Living stones! Can you imagine such a thing? You barbarians robbed them of their spirit, the very stones that would have led us home. In a manner of speaking, when they died, we died."

"I am no such barbarian."

"Did I rescue you as an eggling for your own sake? My prayer now is you apprehend a little as to why."

The flicking tendrils, the quiver of her neck wings: every language of her body painted her distraught. It was unnerving to see this normally stolid Zmee struggling for composure.

Ukhaz snarled, "You? What's with this 'you'? Do you really think it's your equal?" She rounded in rage upon Enok. "Between *me* and *thee, thine* and *thou* art one!" She was towering above him again, upper wings outstretched, poised for a killing blow.

Luckily, the High Wisdom intervened as a shield. "Ukhaz!" she growled in lowered tones. "Have the breeding fires clouded your mind? Be mindful of your station, Lawmaker or — by the stones of the Temple! — I will have you replaced!"

The rebuke stung Ukhaz into submission, and now with her scepter aimed at the pyramid, the matriarch boomed, "For the benefit of the younglings, that is a replica of the almanac. According to legend, it was a timepiece of the heavens."

The Oracles moved aside so all could see the face of the relic that was, ironically, in the shadow of the great over-towering ceremonial torch. It was smooth and three-sided, hewn from a single stone that was about twice Enok's height, and etched with runes. The concentric circles of its face almost invited target practice. Whenever he had inquired about it, the reply had always been the same: it was a reminder of the greatness of the past, and they would leave it at that.

Was it one of the living stones?

The old dame continued. "That almanac bears witness of by-gone glories, a reminder to all of a greatness lost. Until the stones lives again, I could never consider the Ish as anything more than barbarians, much less this servant as a Zmee."

"Till they live again," came the chant from the common.

Of all people, he thought, the High Wisdom would surely have taken his side. She had rescued him from some kind of struggle on the mainland. It was all too dim to remember now. He had been her servant for twenty-four years before she passed him off to Oracle Zoia. And now the turn was his to feel betrayal's sting.

With a sudden jerk of her two great hands, she lifted and held him high.

"How fear you one so scrawny? Who among you owns the scars of its maws? See for yourself, it has barely the strength of a youngling. Be assured, when the Shav'yat next convenes, we will settle its future."

Enok fell to the floor as she released him. Despite her age, she was ever vital and stout as a bull. But if Zmee were so strong, then why so afraid?

"Are you all so thin-tendriled?" Ukhaz seemed intent on making a scene. "Where you Azhakh-Na see the insect, the Zeruhawi see the swarm. Isn't a hill like the mountains that surround it, or a branch ever like the tree itself? The myopic philosophy of your Southern cult keeps you from perceiving the obvious."

"Which is?" the High Wisdom inquired.

"Have you forgotten the barbarian that escaped? Ukhaz roared for all to hear, and waited for the criers' echo. "Most of you were still in the shell, but I remember! See? This Ish is *nothing at all* like its warlike sire, or even its mainland kin. And why is that? Because these Azhakh-Na deceive us all. I say the slave's a spy!"

"*Pshaw*," came the response. Even the Convener, herself a Zeruhawi, struggled to believe it.

"Consider: what if it escaped the island? It's tried before, you know. It's in the public record. And if its mainland kin discovered whence it came, then the only defense we have, the fragile secrecy that shrouds us, will evaporate like dew on the dunes and this sanctuary will be doomed. The Zeruhawi believe —"

"Far too many *ifs* in your argument," dismissed the High Wisdom. "And those brutish Ish have never plied the seas, let alone built anything akin to our Dragon Boat," she laughed to approval from her peers.

Ukhaz's great tail was flailing about, and her feathered headdress was wriggling from the animated tendrils it concealed. Hysteria had overcome her, but how could that be? The irrational behavior of which the Zmee had long accused his kind was here, right now, apparent in no less a person than the preeminent Zmee Lawmaker. Enok had always presumed his petition would evoke a response that was cerebral, orderly — and nothing like *this!*

Murmurs began to multiply as Ukhaz's antipathy resonated among the very same crowd that had but moments earlier embraced the High Wisdom's noble vision.

"It's a menace!" barked one.

"If it should die that we might live," raged another, "what loss is that to us?"

The Convener pled for silence, though with little effect. The debate on what to do with him had gone public. The Oracles on the dais huddled in a private meeting. Behind the younglings on the common, an agitator with a bandaged snout was rousing the crowd, but to their credit, they remained largely peaceful.

Oh for the comfort of but a single friendly face! Emotionally numb and strangely detached, Enok awaited their decision. When the pronouncement came, it seemed dreamy, distant, as if heard through another's ears. His status as merely a beast was unchanged, and he would continue to serve but under a new mistress. The council of the Shav'yat would make the appointment before the annual pilgrimage began.

Cries of disappointment ringing the amphitheater, "Next year? Next year!" quickly morphed to ones of "No! Now! Now!" while others took up chanting "Oracle! Oracle! Make Stargazer an Oracle!" so loudly that they drowned out everything else.

His mind was still floating, numb to the pandemonium, when a familiar voice whispered nervously, "Oh, Enokhi, you should have trusted me! Don't you remember me saying I would approach the Shav'yat on your behalf?" Hrazul was beside him, eyes wide and frantic. "We had such hopes for you! But now, you must flee! So many Northerners have come today — Zeruhawi agitators! — who would sooner see you dead." With a worried sideways glance, she added, "And we would be powerless to prevent it. Please hurry, or everything is lost."

She nudged him, and nudged him again with her snout until he woke from his stupor. With a forced dignity, he stepped from the dais and made slowly for the avenue exiting the plaza. Rising jubilant behind him, a thousand wings drummed Zmee huzzahs. The scoffers were having their day. He so wanted to silence the ridicule then fill the void with reciprocal malice, yet a more noble part of him knew that cursing would only fuel the fire. He continued stoically as humiliation burned his cheeks, and when the shadows claimed him, ran quickly from the town.

A watch had passed, maybe two. Having climbed the lower flanks of Mount Oush, Enok had found haven high in the weeping aerial roots of a parasitic fig he hadn't visited in years.

Nestled now in a great hollow between a knotty web of the strangler and the trunk of its host, he pondered what forgotten creature had once roosted here. For there, high above his reach even now, was an ancient scar in the bark of some great three-peaked knobble. It was clearly artificial.

That scar had once inspired a mark of his own. With such an inner storm of hopelessness and self-loathing after tonight's ordeal, it was comforting to find his childhood inscription.

I speak, it read.

Below it, and barely discernible now was an earlier scar. It used to read:

I question.

And now with a blade pulled from his wrist-wrap, an older and much taller Enok carved another above them all. First, the symbol for *I*, and then, not his butterfly glyph, but his name in Mapmakers' ciphers.

I, Enok.

All was calm in the rain forest. The Lesser Light was always full on New Year's Eve, and by its rising glow he could now discern the dim outline of the lush hills of the island's far interior. Below, a thick carpet of mist obscured the city. Soon the zephyrs of Night's Kiss would smother all but the loftiest height of this mountain. The hazy glow from the festive torches was the only reminder that somewhere below were Zoia, Hrazul, Snei, and that desolate, ill-omened hill where he and Jin-jin had sat only twice before.

So much for the 'third time lucky' theory! Perhaps, instead, bad luck ran in threes! Maybe everything did.

All at once, a cloud of something like red and green fireflies began to rise through the mist and drift towards the sea. It was the sky-lantern ceremony where the new disciples released their paper lanterns. On each would have been written a wish for peace, for success, or for wisdom — all rising by the heat of their inner candles like prayers upon Night's Kiss to the Great Zhmee himself.

It was unusually quiet in the treetops of the rain forest, a silence broken only by the occasional stridulating insect and the night cries of a solitary zhrat rooster. These were orange-horned leaping tree lizards that signaled a feed to wake the very forest but then fought like fury to defend it. They were such insatiable, comical creatures.

Plop!

A young zhaga had fallen onto a nearby branch from a higher limb, and was clinging with a salamander's tenacity as its new membranes began to unfurl. By morning's light, the yellow-and-green sky-frog would be gliding with the adults. Mere months were the span of its life, all of them spent here, feeding on blossoms, or the tiny figs sprouting from the trunk of the strangler. Soon its world would no longer be a single tree but a forest wide beyond imagining.

The zhaga's new wings gave him cause to wonder, about himself, about tonight. What once satisfied the younger Enok failed the older now. He knew almost every tree and track of the southern tip of this island and he too wanted to fly.

New trees. New forests. New worlds.

He pondered what his future might be after tonight. Things had certainly drifted from plan! FIFTY YEARS, came the unhappy thought. More than twice twelve as the High Wisdom's, and as many again as Zoia's: fifty years was far too long a servitude. Why, even the very worst of slaves redeemed their status in six — unless, of course, they'd met with execution. So what great change had his efforts wrought this night? None, except that a new mistress would rule him instead of Zoia.

What would he do for the next fifty? Would he even live that long, or might he outlive everyone?

"Just be glad that Ukhaz and Xira live elsewhere," he found his own mouth saying. Zu'u-Shoran had long been free of Zeruhawi influence, and he was thankful for that. But tonight's debacle — well, there was no explaining it, except in the light of Xira's untimely confirmation.

Rotten eggs those Zeruhawi! Their intervention had scuttled his struggle for acceptance. And now it was clear that his own desperate need to belong somewhere, anywhere, had blinded him to the reality that he would never find acceptance here.

I CAN NEVER BE A ZMEE, he realized sadly, *EVER*.

Mulling over a dozen uncertain futures was exhausting, and his thoughts shifted with an ungovernable yawn to dwell instead on the past.

'*SOMETIMES WORDS FAIL MY THOUGHTS*,' Hrazul had once mused, '*AND I FEEL LIKE I NEED ANOTHER LANGUAGE!*'

ANOTHER LANGUAGE, ANOTHER LANGUAGE, he kept thinking in imagined sounds, and every hissing syllable a serpent's. But when had he begun thinking in Zmiysh? When had his native tongue turned foreign?

As he began to doze, his mind drifted pleasantly to the face now appearing in dream. Its smooth, tawny skin and wide yearning eyes were charged with an emotional latency beyond explaining. It was calling to him and awakening a reciprocal longing. And in the last two moons especially, these dreams had evoked a hard tumescence and a clammy ending.

Was that phantom a female of his kind — the memory of the word took a long time coming — an *Isha*? Snei had broached the subject of parents. Was that, perhaps, his egg-bearer? Ah, his *mother*?

For long, long years, her name had eluded him, always hovering in dream and vanishing in the waking moment. Wide and moist, looking down from above, her round brown eyes with their elegant lashes were beyond forgetting, and too the warmth of her touch.

'*MAY THE ... PROTECT AND DEFEND ... MAY ... WATCH OVER ...*'

He recalled the tune more so than the words. She would cantor like a zhrat, then for some unfathomable reason, as her ebony tresses fell about his face, tickling him, she would rub noses, tickle him with her blinking lashes, then end with moistened lips upon his forehead. Oh how every treetop orchid brought to mind her musty, floral fragrance.

'*GOODNIGHT LITTLE ... WATCH OVER YOU.*'

That emptied all memories of mother.

Perhaps her song had affected him more than deeply than he knew, for there were moments when he imagined that someone really was watching over him. The day he nearly drowned far out past the barrier reefs in his first attempt to escape the island would haunt him forever. He had clung unconscious to the precious wreckage of his outrigger only to find himself on the beach once again. A part of him had always assumed that tide and current had been his saviors; but another knew he had drifted too far towards the dawn and there was simply wasn't any way they could have brought him back.

And he remembered the great handprints in the sand about him when he woke. But what kind of creature walks on its hands?

Another was his first encounter with jellyfish swarms on the outer reefs. Puzzled by the annual disappearance of the tree crabs, and drawn by the distant spectral glow of the Shine Water, which occurred but one night in the year, he had found himself corralled by thousands of luminous creatures, mindless as vegetables, yet collectively as fearsome as any predator of the deep. An unavoidable curtain of their long trailing organs, sparkling with deadly and deceptive beauty, had stung him to excruciation.

His legs had seized and weighed like anchors. Every breath had become a labor. His outrigger had been nearby yet beyond all reach. Then suddenly, a pair of yash'kh had appeared in the dead of night in that turbid summer sea and given him a means of escape. Never again would he consider fat old Puzo and his sibling Zoub as merely simple-minded brutes.

Still vivid too were the memories of the burning acid pain and finding himself back on the beach surrounded by a pod of the great reef dragons and half-destroyed trails of those curious handprints.

And through it all, he had felt a peculiar sensation of stillness, the presence of his invisible Watcher.

Just recently, on Breakfast Island, Hrazul had returned him to the surface, but what — or who — had dragged him under to a pocket of air? It had probably saved him from a deathblow by one of Zakon's guards. And tonight, for example, that incident on the platform when Oracle Ukhaz had been unable to strike him: twice she had tried and twice she had failed.

As Ukhaz had struck out, something invisible had shielded him. And he had felt again that stilling presence. Of course, he knew this was impossible. Nothing solid could be so invisible. Nevertheless, Ukhaz, only an arm's length distant, had missed twice, and, surely, that too was impossible.

A wild yawn overpowered him. Only the mating call of a zhrat kept him from sleep. Somewhere above him was another lonely rooster with an uncertain future.

MALES.

He held different memories of his father: tall as bamboo and as stout; a prickly, hairy face; russet hair, straight as a stick and tied in tails at the rear; rough-skinned hands that would fling him into the sky and sit him on his shoulders; a strong and lively person. However, little of it jelled with what the Lawmaker Ukhaz had said a moon ago about a 'furry monster.' And again, tonight, Ukhaz had decried his sire as though he too had once been captive here, yet not a shard of memory supported it.

Enok fingered his sprouting whiskers for the umpteenth time that day. Perhaps this facial fluff would thicken and become like his father's. Or would he too become a 'furry monster'? As he held that thought, the single word that would shape his fate escaped his lips.

"Father!"

'I LOVE YOU, BOY,' his father had said in parting long ago.

He closed his eyes to dream the dreams that made the night less dark, and while part of him slept, another began to remember, and in that hour, in those least understood depths of himself, that which had no name was infused with a renewed sense of belonging.

"My father's name is Yared.

"I am the son of Yared.

"I am not a Zmee."

ZAKON HAD BEEN CELEBRATING WITH Zeruhawi dignitaries in the uppermost level of the library. It was almost dawn, he guessed, and many had already retired for an early homeward start. It came as a surprise when they declined Xira's banquet and denounced this quaint little town as simply too drab to linger. That had left him alone with Ukhaz, the host herself, the old Chronicler Skazaar, and the one-eyed Healer Thaazh. And, of course, a mountain of delicacies: barnacles (his favorite), betel nuts, succulent grapes, and veritably wicked piles of gorgeous, luscious chechi. For the indulgent, though, it not only bared the soul but every secret with it. Slow growing and highly prized, it was the toast of pilgrim's banquets. That Xira had managed to procure so grand a cache surely stamped her as a miscreant.

The water-fire lanterns were dying, and likewise all reflection off the burnished reliefs of the celling. The balcony louvers had been left ajar and the mists of Night's Kiss had wet the rugs. He was free now of all official duties, so that crimson arc of plumage that ran lengthwise along his headdress, Zakon had detached from its mounting rosette. Stripped now of all regalia but the helm, he was relaxing at last after long and interesting celebrations.

The leading six-day after New Year was a blessed reprieve from duty. It was a time — if not *the* time — to renew acquaintances and generally relax. The cleanup after the Amok of the younglings was not his concern. The Prefects would see to that. He toyed with the idea of holidaying in this unhurried, becalming locale. But next to the High Wisdom, he was arguably the busiest Zmee in Zoar. Ironically, the price of power was the loss of freedom. Title held him prisoner, and even with Prefects at the helm, he was certain that duty would draw him northwards sooner than his nerves would allow.

Across the room, a drunken Thaazh had discarded all her regalia. Her one good eye hadn't blinked in ages. It was said she slept with it open. Nestled against her, hoary old Skazaar was out cold, likewise bare, and wheezing in her sleep. The contrast between these sleepers and old Black Feathers (such was Ukhaz's epithet), though, was telling. Despite her belly bulging from betel nuts, she was coiled as stiff as a sarcophagus to preserve her headgear's plumage. The nuts were intoxicating. Yet being chechi-giddy and nut-drunk, decorum reigned supreme.

She was Ukhaz, Chief Oracle of Law, even now, even here.

Xira, that utter sensualist, glorying in her new title of Venerable Stargazer, had gorged herself on chechi. Her lips and tendrils were red with it. And the bandage on her snout as well. Now belly-up, with her trademark brass helmet discarded amidst a jumble of lacquer-ware, she was soused as a pickle and even more naked than she had been on Breakfast Island.

Unlike the others, though, she had no crown sprouts at all — as if she'd never grown up, which was completely odd — so that at least was forgivable. But the great burnished tendrils of her helm were a very sculpture of nudity and provocative, if not downright obscene. And that peculiar redolence that seemed to follow her everywhere: it was becoming annoying. No decent Zmee would ever tolerate any kind of body odor except perhaps a festive spray. But thankfully, her attendants had decked the chamber with great bouquets, and that too exposed her contempt for tradition. Such flowers were for the pilgrimage and she was certainly no pilgrim.

The sky-lantern ceremony had been a triumph for Xira personally. The floating paper-and-candle lanterns had been the invention of a younger self. She had long wanted to gloat in her hometown before the very Oracles she had spurned so long ago. And now, as the intoxicated Venerable of Sky, the press to parade her sky-boats here had rendered her even more ebullient.

At every mention of the upcoming event, Ukhaz returned her grins. Chechi had made a pair of younglings of them.

As wagging tongues were wont to do, the talk had fallen to politics. And after the tonight's spectacle, there was no avoiding the question of the Enokhi creature. That was, after all, what had drawn him here. Though the masses had taken the mischief for an intercalary prank, his colleagues here knew better. The South abhorred such tradition.

Indeed, a naïve Southern spy had brought to light what the Azhakh-Na had long been concealing: the little Ish was unusually clever, and most unlike its forebears. There was risk here, and veritably screaming at the listening ear.

As his head swam against the chechi, Zakon wondered whether to mention Xira's Breakfast Island challenge, and how she had been duped. She was particularly vengeful, and such was her loathing of the Enokhi creature, she was sure to do something rash.

«No!» he decided. Uphold the law, that's what he'd do, and let events naturally unfold.

«No? What?» Ukhaz wondered.

«Forget it,» Zakon signed, realizing he'd been thinking aloud.

"I hear it plays zhakh, too," Xira moaned, nursing her swollen belly. "Apparently, the disciple's been teaching it."

«What?» Ukhaz uncoiled with a start.

"The Upholder's informant is very reliable," Xira bubbled. "Naïve as my sky is high, but reliable. 'It won in several moves,' she droned, and 'from a losing position.' A classic horns-against-fist maneuver, I managed deduce."

Ukhaz hissed, "I recently spoke with Mapmaker about the slave's higher abilities. After much dissembling she replied, 'It does indeed climb trees.'"

«Funny,» Zakon signed.

«Great Zhmee!» Ukhaz scowled. She had never been one for humor. "Have you seen the mess the younglings make when they plaster each other with dyes? At least they keep to their ranks. Even the Amok has its etiquette. However, last night's prank crossed all borders. It was no such Amok as the High Wisdom claimed. These conniving Azhakh-Na have such a talent for obscuring the truth!"

Zakon could only wonder why the Zeruhawi, Northerners all, had such antipathy for the South. So itching for an enemy to fight, were they now turning upon their own kind?

"The Ish are the enemy, Oracle of Law," said Zakon emphatically. "Do you *really* need reminding?"

«Definitely not!» "The intimate of my enemy is no darling of mine, even if they *are* Zmee. Anyhow, enough of that. I would love to hear how you swindled-out the key to the Reliquary. You have rendered the Zeruhawi the greatest of service."

"Bribery and bluff," he cooed at length. "Never underestimate their usefulness. That snotty little biped is too wily by half. Once my spy had the proof I needed, I forced a deal: my silent tendrils in exchange for the key."

Xira laughed so hard, her snout bandages slipped.

And Ukhaz could barely contain her rejoicing. "Sly old snake! You bargained for the key when you knew all along the creature was about to expose itself!" «Capital! Capital!»

Xira laughed again. "How her tendrils must be burning!"

"Hotter than steam when she finds out about the balloon!"

«Finds out what?» Zakon was puzzled. "To show your sky-boat? It was she who invited you."

Ukhaz's tendrils spread in a grin. "Ah, but she doesn't know that Xira's daubed it. The red-and-black! Here in Zu'u-Shoran!"

Zakon baulked. Oh, what chechi revealed. "A touch puerile, don't you think?"

With a hiss of announcement, a Scout in the simple rubberized kit of coastal militia slid hurriedly through the wide oval arches and made obeisance as her partner remained by the threshold.

"Venerable Upholder, a boat has been sighted among the south-western reefs."

All talk of balloons and politics collapsed.

Sobering, "What kind of boat? Ours?" Ukhaz demanded.

«The Ish!» "A primitive thing."

Zakon snorted dismissively. "It's junk then. More debris."

The Scout bowed again. "No, Venerable, but a shipwreck of barbarians!" «Fearful.»

«Ooh!» Xira seemed thrilled. "Ish? Here? How many?"

Zakon was incredulous, even though he had long dreaded this very event. "They just can't be Ish, surely. Are you certain?"

The Scout shared worried looks with her partner before facing Zakon squarely. "We were patrolling along the outer Razor and were hardly a dozen tails distant. There was no mistaking them."

Zakon stroked his tendrils lazily as if pondering some grave decision, but actually was wondering if he wasn't too inebriated to properly respond.

"How many again?" he inquired as his genius sparked. If the Zeruhawi needed an opponent, perhaps here was one worthy of their hatred — and it could help defuse brewing political tensions.

"Not more than six, we believe. They are floundering badly."

«Obviously!» chuckled Xira mirthlessly. "Water is our element, not theirs."

"These beasts seem to swim just fine," the Scout interjected. "But their craft is in tatters, and so are they."

The Scout in the doorway piped hurriedly, "These aren't like any mainlanders we've ever seen, Upholder! These are hairless!"

«Hairless?» Zakon wondered. "Like Mapmaker's slave?"

Where the guard shrugged, Xira and Ukhaz exchanged knowing looks. What his colleagues were up to was unclear. Maybe they had guessed his thoughts.

"Have you informed anyone else?" Xira demanded.

«Me?» the Reef Scout responded.

«Fool.» "Yes, you!"

"No, Oracle. It's the New Year: full bellies and empty heads: everyone sleeps."

«Excellent!» Xira's tendrils curled happily.

"Keep this private," Ukhaz charged, "until the Upholder says so."

The Scout was puzzled. "Upholder?"

Xira scowled, "You wouldn't want to alarm our people just over a few half-dead Ish, would you?" and then she grinned again like some youngling.

«No,» the Scout replied cautiously.

Ukhaz was wide-eyed and signing excitedly. «Send away! Far! Now!»

Even Xira sat up, signing, «Yes! Away!»

Zakon thought to play along for the moment. What were these two Zeruhawi scheming? "Proceed to the armory at Ur-Hozhai and report to the Prefect. On the triple!"

«Confusion.» The Scout blinked vapidly. "Forgive me for saying, Upholder, but that's completely in the opposite direction."

"Then why are you still here?" Xira jibed.

"Yes, Oracles. Yes, Upholder." «At once.» The Scout bowed again and spun to exit with her grumbling partner who had wagged her head at the wasted food.

Ukhaz yawned, "These southerly Scouts are so dreary," while Xira's tendrils twitched delightedly by contrast.

«Kill,» Zakon signed. His companions here would surely enjoy the spectacle of his j'Na-Zeru dismembering the barbarians.

Ukhaz disagreed. «No, not kill!»

Zakon was bemused. «Not kill?»

"How can you be so thin-tendriled?" Ukhaz taunted. "This isn't about them, it's about bringing the High Wisdom to account. 'The Ish have never plied the seas,' she said so very publicly. Remember? Yet here they are." «Ooh!» "What a gift!"

"As the Upholder, the safety of Zoar is my highest priority. Invading Ish must be dealt with severely. The vermin are like ants: to ignore one is to invite others. Exterminate them like zhrat, I say, before the cry of one summons all."

"You need to lift your vision," Ukhaz urged. "Do you really think our people are prepared for that event you described where one indeed summons all? You've long been hovering in secret to see what risk that Enokhi beast presents." «Yes, I know!» "Great blasphemy!" she continued. "It was on the brink of reciting from the Aphorisms at the very Pillar of Zmee! Is that what you've armed yourself for, Upholder? An invasion by philosophers?"

«Indeed!» Xira chimed. "If you truly wish to prepare our people against what you yourself have fought, then, admit it, we desperately need a change in policy, and a rallying cry. These shipwrecked barbarians —"

He caught on. "Ah, so you're hoping these are *violent* Elim, are you?" [xxxiii]

«Just so!» Ukhaz was positively beaming. "In a day or so, they will make landfall, recover their strength, and then — barbarism!" «Ooh!» "Exquisitely ... detestable ... barbarism."

"And the veil that blinds these Ish-loving Azhakh-Na will be lifted. When it does ... it will expose the old High Wisdom as both a liar and a fool ... with her softly-softly policies," bubbled Xira as she emptied a goblet. "Imagine the outcry to dispatch these beasts ... and that Enokhi creature with them."

Ukhaz snickered, "And we enlighten them to the better way." She peered out onto the balcony, hoping to take in the view of the Zu'u-Shoran common by moonlight, but Night's Kiss was smothering everything. "Trust me, not long now and the red-and-black standard will be firmly planted in this nest of dissenters. And you, Upholder, when you slay those shipwrecked brutes," Ukhaz shared wide-eyed looks with Xira, "you will be hailed the people's champion."

Others made laws, others made ships, others raised younglings, but Zakon was the Upholder, the one responsible for keeping the peace and defending all that they as a society had built. He hated the Ish as much as anyone did, and although he could appreciate the zeal of these two Zeruhawi, having their level of confidence was a different matter entirely. Even the simplest of schemes had risk.

---

xxxiii For Zmee, the terms *Elim* and *Ish* are interchangeable, since an Ish is merely a male Elim, the more combative and hated of the sexes.

However, there were only six Ish — *real* Ish — perhaps only five, but if they were anywhere near as crafty as that Enokhi —

"The reefs are already cutting them badly," voiced Ukhaz slyly as indecision played on his tendrils.

"And once the jellyfish are through with them," Xira chuckled, "it's unlikely more than one or two would survive."

"Believe me," old Ukhaz chimed, "two barbarians will be just the tonic!"

One thing still worried him. "Unless, of course, that Breakfast Island shelters —"

Xira jumped in. "It's moved on. There's little respite for these invaders now."

Zakon found himself warming to the idea. "And then we dispose of them *and* Mapmaker's slave." WITH ALL RISK ERADICATED, came the pleasing afterthought.

Ukhaz was insistent. «Yes. Yes.» "No fuss. No casualties. Simple."

«Simple?» Zakon wondered.

«Yes. Yes. Yes,» signed Ukhaz eagerly.

«Yes! Yes!» "And be rid of that fire-bird too!" Xira tore the bandage from her snout. "Look how that turkey mauled me!"

Quiet for a moment, Zakon finally let slip a grin.

«Yes.»

THE NEVER-KISS

While leaving some cryptic clues as to his imminent future, Hrazul bids Enok farewell before departing on her pilgrimage. However, events beyond their control ensure they will never enjoy each other's company again.

ENOK WOKE LAMINATED WITH SWEAT, and perplexed by his body's strange independence. The haunting eyes of dream had teased him yet again in the dark, and with the usual messy effects. The sweet exudation of flowers, the soft brown lips, the wild tangled hair and the erogenous touch had set afire the lower reaches and stirred something visceral and nameless, urging him to climb the very treetop and shout his name to the night.

Instead, he descended the roost and ran, ran along the beach until even the most stubborn stars had winked farewell; until sea and sky glowed coral with the dawn; ran panting until exhaustion before quenching himself in the surf.

These dream-bidden emissions, were they harmful? Was he ill? Were Zoia's daily tonics a poison? Whom could he ask? And what or whose were those almond shaped eyes that continued to remain so elusive? Conjuring them over Hrazul's beatific snout proved fruitless, for they had not the soul of serpent's nor of anything from memory.

Naked, he braced himself as wave after wave kept urging him forward, luring him to futures across the sea and with he the ancestor of them. But the thought was fantasy indeed, and he merely sunk deeper into the sand. Contact with his kind had been utterly severed. For all its vastness, the island with its myriad reefs and sandbars was a cage, and after fifty years, he was left with neither hope nor the means of escape. He was surely destined to die here.

The brown velvety skin, the soft lips, and the wistful gaze belonged to a face, the face of a girl. She was calling to him, needing him — needing him as much as he did her. He had run far and fast, and his heart felt like bursting, but the cramp in his breast was of another order entirely. It was anguish. He could never reply to those eyes.

Days of relaxation followed the New Year's festivities. While slaves cleaned-up after the Amok, Oracles, Venerables, Prominents, students, and ordinary folk too, took pleasure in criss-crossing the island, renewing old acquaintances with egg-sisters, old mentors, or dissipating their days among Zoar's many reefs. And in various flying carnivals, the athletic would spring from cliffside towers and compete to glide longer than their peers.

Doubtless Hrazul would be cheering Alazar Gray-face worst all southern opponents. The High Wisdom's disciple reigned supreme in both distance and zigzag gliding. She was the pride of Zu'u-Shoran. Kite-maker Hozny could almost match her for speed, but she was a city darling for other reasons entirely. Zu'u-Shoran was fast becoming renown for its New Year's kites soaring in the isthmus breeze: box kites, tube kites and wing kites in confident colors yet with dark streamers betokening personal worries one hoped the wind might spirit away. These were principally Hozny's creations, a sight Enok chose to admire from a distance, for Hozny had learned her craft from a younger Xira, and any reminder of Stargazer simply biled the gorge.

No wind-prayer could ever cleanse *her* misdeeds.

Though Oracle Zoia had made no demands, he had little time for leisure and even less cause for rejoicing. To begin with, nothing of circumstance seemed to have changed.

NOTHING!

The New Year's Eve that should have meant his liberation had been, instead, the greatest anticlimax of his life. Would he still be confined to the promontory of Sha-Noa? Would the world beyond Zu'u-Shoran remain as great a mystery as ever? Would he never get to see what lay beyond the majestic Isthmus Gates? He was living under a cloud of uncertainty, and there was nothing he hated more.

Four days had passed and he still had no idea of whom he would be serving and whether he would be forced to leave his possessions behind. And right now, even his almond-eyed phantasm was of little consolation.

In the foul mood that had possessed him after the New Year's graduations, he had smashed Hrazul's game squares and thrown most of his instruments over the cliff: the wind flutes, the wind-powered xylophone, his favorite gong and all but the largest drum. They had met a better end than he, and certainly a swifter one.

He had been denied self-determination, and his rampage had been a final act of defiance. He could not be robbed of that which he'd already robbed himself. Though darkly poetic, it was doubly pleasing. No more music here, he decided: nothing harmonic, nothing melodious, only percussion, for music expressed the song in his soul, and that which once had sung in him was truly, surely dead.

Work was now his only meter.

Repetition. Repetition.

That was why this early morning found him on his knees at the mouth of a wide cinnamon creek, preparing a rawhide for tanning. He was immersed in his work, struggling with equal measure to dwell on neither past nor future or whether the song in him could ever live again.

But who could prevail when nature conspired, and mocked all self-deception? The zhaga were singing. The deep, reverberant grunts of the yash'kh came no less faint with the distance. Even waves, those incessant drums of the sea, were breaking to an even rhythm.

Boom, boom, boom went the breakers.

While scraping fell and flesh from hide, the sound of happy munching soon revealed a scaly vermilion head with its golden beak and lusty cobalt dewlap. It was Jin-jin enjoying one of deir many breakfasts. The bird extended a wing claw to share a half-chewed insect.

Enok winced at the offer. "Thank-you, but no. Tanning kills my appetite."

The bird began bobbing excitedly, pecking at his waist pouch.

"Just quit it! I have no for you treats today."

The pecking ceased, and the pile of fleshings by his side were examined bird-like, an eye at a time, until Jin-jin gave a high-pitched sneeze.

"Disgusted? Believe me, this is no great fun for me either. Like you, I do what I must."

Amidst the beach almonds growing along the sandy banks of the creek, a number of young zhaga had congregated. A late bloom of tadpoles had been maturing from frog to triphibian, and were now sprouting membranous wings. Red damselflies had swarmed from the mangroves, and these adolescent zhaga were gamboling between trees in a feast while dodging an enraptured Jin-jin.

"Zhaga. Zhaga," the bird chirped happily at his feet.

Enok cringed at the sight of yet another of Jin-jin's offerings. "Ugh! Barbaric! *Grapes to Enok,*" he growled in his native tongue. "*Understand? Grapes.*"

Jin-jin squawked a negative and Enok understood: there were none to be had. Something had systematically scoured the beachside groves of his favorite fruit, taking not just individual grapes but whole stems. In his fore pouch lay the shriveled gleanings of the luckless morning harvest. It was hardly enough for a meal.

"You're probably right," he sighed in serpent-speak. "We'll go foraging for figs later, alright?"

Drawn again by the cloud of damselflies, Jin-jin abandoned deir mangled catch, and Enok flung the grisly remains over his shoulder. It brought instant regret, for a rustle in the bushes and irritating shrieks meant a happy zhrat had begun to gloat and summon more of its kindred.

I SHOULD HAVE THROWN IT TO THE SANDWORMS!

And now inflaming Enok's petulance, a horde of its noisy little brethren scurried past in pursuit of the braggart who had fled with corpse in tow. Any moment now, experience told him, the vulgar squabbling over the zhaga's carcass would begin. There would be squawking and posturing, counter-squawking and counter-posturing as zhrat employed an arsenal of trickery using their hands, feet, and horns to claim their prize. Though it rarely came to maiming blows, they spent more time in dispute than in feasting.

To their credit, though, zhrat were not entirely ill tempered. These odd little creatures would mass in the forest's emergent layer to make melody at sunset. With all eyes fixed on the dying of the day, the cantors would raise their bulky orange-horned beaks to the heavens and tell a story in song — sagas that Enok had increasingly come to understand. Others would join in and the tale would grow, embellished with each telling, and wend its way through the forest. A good yarn could last for days.

Why he could understand Jin-jin, the songs of the zhrat, and progressively more creatures over the years, remained a mystery. Who knew? Maybe all the Elim could.

Two nights ago, for example, they sang of a Great-Sea-Beast slain by Giant-Two-Legs. They had sung of his exploits before, so the epithet was familiar: it was him they were singing about, and, of course, a dead yash'kh. Sure enough, the following day he had chanced upon the creature's carcass with dozens of the comical scavengers dancing gleefully upon it. But the sea beast's demise had been no fault of his, and how mortifying if it were! How could the cantors have been so mistaken?

Nonetheless, such a quantity of hide was a prize indeed! Enok had cut away the translucent skin between the tall dorsal spines for his own use, and much of the soft underbelly as well. It made good leather, both supple and robust in a way that other hides were not. And today he was determined to tan the last of it before the day warmed and the hide began to *really* stink. This grim industry had more than one good result, though: it kept him from sulking. Perhaps smashing his instruments had been a tad foolish.

What had Ukhaz called him, the 'Firstling of Fools'?

Satisfied with his handiwork now stretched taut beneath the tawny water, he wondered about the items to be made in the days ahead: new sandals, breechcloth, wrist-wraps, and who knew what else. The sailfin of a yash'kh was special, and a wonder to behold as it progressed from pinks to blues in the cooling stream.

Just then, from across the creek, rang the sound of Hrazul's disgust. "By the very stones of the Temple!" she gagged. "What a stink!" And instead of the usual Alazar, accompanying her was a youngling as verdant as the newborn leaf.

Enok judged she was Yuni, the High Wisdom's youngest disciple that everyone called Little Greeny. Both wore lei's and garlands, and held great festive floral sprays.

"It's not polite to sneak up on people, you know."

«Sneak?» We were calling from the cliff top," Hrazul explained. "Didn't you hear us banging your drum?"

"Sorry. I thought I was imagining. I'm really busy right now. Am happy to see you, of course. You too, young disciple."

"I'd normally be pleased to see you too," replied Hrazul, "but not when there's such a reeking busyness!" «Ooh! The odor!» Beyond the words and signing, Hrazul was making eyes and nodding subtly towards the youngling, who hovered shyly behind a bouquet.

Of course! Now in her second year, Yuni would have been strutting with new armband phylacteries. So despite appearances, this was a fresher. She was so young, in fact, she hadn't even sprouted tendrils.

Hrazul beamed at his spreading grin and widening eyes that grasped the truth before him. "Clumsy me! Your first disciple!"

Fanning the air with a spray of plumeria, the disciple only managed "Sickly" and "Sweet" between coughs.

"Oh, this is nothing," Enok quipped. "Wait till the stench of bloated gizzards hits you. When the zhrat sang of a dead yash'kh, I was worried it might be old Puzo or Zoub. They've not come for their treats in well over a six-day, and — Hey! Careful of the skins," he cautioned as the pair forded the creek.

«You misunderstand,» signed Hrazul. "You really need to wash, for you smell like a banquet compared to what's around you. She is struggling to keep herself from licking you."

"Oh? Ah."

"Notice, youngling, how he ascribes personality to unreasoning creatures. Because he understands beast talk —"

"Beast *song*," Enok corrected. "Besides, they saved my life, that pair of dragons, and more than once for sure. To me, yash'kh are people too, no less so than any Zmee or Jin-jin."

He began to bow and greet them formally as every slave must do, but Hrazul forbade him with a toss of her head, and the youngling ducked suddenly behind her.

"Eh?" Enok wondered. "I'm confused."

"You no longer serve me, remember?"

"But you're an Oracle —"

With a hand raised in protest, she whispered, "Let's not discuss that now. I hope formalities will never come between us, at least in private."

"I did not mean to offend," the youngling squeaked.

Enok was baffled. "Offend?"

Hrazul queried the youngster with a look. "Ah, your biters," she explained, stabbing a fang with a finger. "Your expressions take some getting used to. They're on permanent display, those teeth of yours, and it sends an unfortunate signal." To the youngling, "Despite what you may have been taught," she soothed, "Enokhi is quite amiable."

"Ssla! Truly? Why so many fangs then?"

Ignoring the query, her new mentor let a hibiscus fall amidst the tawny eddies and followed its meandering course. "After twelve years of toil and joy together," Hrazul managed, "goodbyes simply won't come out."

"Oh. The j'Athra-Ya?"[xxxiv] It was a rhetorical question. The pilgrim's flowers as good as said a farewell.

«Leaving. Tomorrow.»

"Me too," the youngster chimed.

"So soon?" The knife slipped from Enok's hand, and it seemed ages before anyone broke the silence.

No more forthcoming than a stone wall at a time when he so wanted details, Hrazul slid quietly ahead towards the spreading mouth of the creek. And the youngling began to drag him after her, which served as a cue for those half-hidden zhrat who had already been eyeing the fleshings.

"No, wait! Those little bandits will rip —" The youngling was insistent and strong, forcing an awkward gait of him as she sped

---

xxxiv *j'Athra-Ya.* A Zmee's reproductive pilgrimage. A sacred obligation, but only for those who are broody as part of their six-year cycle.

towards her teacher. "Hey, slow down!" cried Enok. "Besides, you're supposed to be afraid of me."

"Not any more, though you're not what I expected. Certainly smellier, though in a delicious sort of way." Eye-to-eye, she fingered his whiskers with a youngling's curiosity. "This fur really is quite ugly, did you know?" Having caught up with Hrazul, she added randomly, "So, do you believe in the First Cause too?"

"Say again?" Puzzled, he sought explanation from Hrazul, who merely shrugged and slid further away, tossing her entire bouquet into the creek and whistling for her pupil.

Perhaps a three-way conversation annoyed her, for she had never been much of a talker. Or maybe it was just the grisly sights of the tannery. Anyhow, all work was postponed now, and justifiably so, since this happy moment could well be their last.

The tree ferns of the creek gave way to succulents and ropy creepers as the youngling continued dragging Enok to the beach. He groaned inwardly as the piercing calls of squabbling zhrat overtook him, drowning every natural sound. Anything shiny and the roosters would steal it for their courting bower. By now, his knife would surely be gone.

Instead of keeping to the banks, the youngling dragged him into the shallows, laughing at his efforts to keep up. "You're *so* awkward!"

"No, go *that* way," Enok cautioned. "Follow your Oracle. The hides have flavored the water here. There are sandworms —"

"Zoiks!" The youngling leapt and pulled him into deeper water. "They bite hard!"

"T-told you so!" he spluttered, and directed her gaze to the eyeless head burrowing upwards through the sand and with mandibles as wide as his wrist. "And that's only a little one!"

Perhaps, old Tshipai herself, the enormous mother-of-all-sandworms, had given the disciple a hearty nip, for she sprang now like a cricket and come crashing hard upon him.

"Great Ssla! You almost drowned, me!" Enok chided. "*And* you've lost your coronet and bouquet, *and* your lei is in tatters." But it was wonderful, came the thought, that he had found a new friend, and too that Hrazul had been wise to bring her, for few things were as diverting as a youngling's clumsy antics.

*

On the broad sweep of the beach, far from the tannery and its sandworms, purple midge-crabs scattered or burrowed at the trio's approach. Ahead, quarreling yash'kh flashed their towering dorsal fins in intimidating displays of color. The resplendent dorsal membranes of the reef dragons, iridescent with blues and greens, melded with equally captivating hues of pink in the sunshine.

"Not too close," Hrazul cautioned.

Enok agreed. "They're easily unnerved. Besides, there's a half-eaten carcass ahead. It's no sight for tender stomachs."

On a knoll above the tidemark, sheltered by overhanging casuarinas and palmettos, they settled to admire the spectacle. Orienting a dorsal fin to catch the unbroken morning light seemed insufficient, Enok explained, it was about pride of place as well.

The endless jockeying for the best waterside positions left ambitious youngsters scarred and bleeding. Closest to the water lay the leader of the pod, thundering — *Ga-runt! Ga-runt!* — at all the humbled challengers. At the risk of further provocation, none dared swim before it.

He hadn't noticed it beneath her lei before, but Hrazul had been wearing her graduation necklace, which she now fondled wistfully as they shared significant looks. After a dozen years of intimacy, simple gestures transcended words, and together they shared the warmth of the sun on their cheeks, replaying a scene of countless dawns. But the Greater Light, or Ssla as Zmee poetically termed it, was climbing high into the sky, and the ritual seemed a little hollow.

With candid sighs of boredom, the youngling appropriated the silence with loud inbreathing as a prelude to something unsaid, until: "What happened to your toys on the bluff?"

"Eh?"

"Your things, up there. All but one are gone, my Oracle said."

"An accident," Enok replied. Zmee had words for anger and rage but strangely none for despair. It wasn't worth explaining. True, his old totem, the dreaming pole, had survived his rampage, though mostly because it was half-enveloped by jungle.

Hrazul snorted. «Lie-of-misinformation!»

"Ssla! There would have to have been at least five accidents," the younger stated logically.

"No," Enok sighed. "Just a very big one."

"As big as a balloon, I'd say!" gushed the youngling.

"Balloon?"

"There's a sky-boat on show in town. It can outreach the New Year's kites! Don't you know anything?"

Enok shrugged. "Apparently not."

«X – I – R – A,» signed Hrazul in Mapmakers' code.

"There's a reason why I'm here today," the youngling chirped.

"Oh?"

"I've come to challenge you. Ho-Za!" Her enthusiasm was obvious in the way she extracted a fold-up board for zhakh from her chest-sack and positioned the game pieces for a novice's one-board challenge. "I know the rules, but this will be my first real contest," she piped as Enok and Hrazul talked with their eyes.

There were Adji, Oracles and Prefects, Commanders of Sixty and Captains of Six, then the Scouts, Deceivers, Pike Bearers and finally the Civil Guards — all set up with their identities concealed, and aligned in three ranks on opposite sides of the board: red at one end, and black at the other.

Red and black: how ominous they suddenly appeared. So Zeruhawi! It soured his taste for the game and drew thoughts once again to endings.

I don't want you to go, his said with his eyes of the pilgrimage.

His only friend would be gone for nearly a year. How could she even think of games at such a time as this? Thrice before she had abandoned him for lengthy map-making voyages. He couldn't stand a fourth — not alone and with so much uncertainty. But Hrazul seemed strangely absorbed as her eyes kept roving from his cliff-top camp, to the estuary, to the posturing yash'kh, then back again to the bluff.

"Ssla, that's exciting!" the youngling chirped. "Six moons for a round-trip. And we camp an additional six at the Temple!"

"Oh." The announcement came as a shock. First Xira's balloons in Zu'u-Shoran, now this. Hrazul would be gone for almost a year. Was there no *good news* today?

Then, meeting his gaze, Hrazul tipped her snout and blinked reassuringly. *Fear not.*

Enok wagged back. *I'm not afraid.*

Not? Her eyes widened quizzically.

Should I be? he inquired with a look, then shuddered when Hrazul arched her neck to draw a circle in the sky with her eyes. She meant a Na-Zeru standard, of course. That meant his new keeper was surely a demon — a Zeruhawi for sure.

The youngling was mesmerized by the interplay. "Are you both somehow ... *talking?*"

Enok arched his fingers suggestively. *Feathers? Old Black-feathered Ukhaz?*

Hrazul nodded a negative so deliberately that he knew it was worse than he'd feared. But who could be more terrible than Ukhaz?

"Any weapon can rebound on an attacker, if you can but learn to wield it," Hrazul explained at last.

Enok was mystified. "That's not one of the Aphorisms," he said, half-asking with his eyes.

"Listen, my time here is short. You caused us —" She checked herself and began afresh. "I know you meant well, but you roused your most powerful adversaries. The exams —"

"You read what I wrote?"

«Stop interjecting.» I know the chief examiner," she confessed. "Anyhow, you were meant to answer the questions, not criticize —"

"Well, most of them were ambiguous, or poorly —"

«Let me speak!» "All the pieces of the game are in your mind, how they relate, and all the possible outcomes. And I should know that better than anyone, for I have been studying you my whole life, yet only to discover a reflection of myself."

"You're speaking now of zhakh?"

"No, of life. In all the ways that matter, we are not so very different, you and I. You've all the makings of a great Mapmaker, little one. The urge to explore wells deep in you. But a somewhat different exploration beckons now: a chance to learn the law."

Her signing was forced, her voice faltered. The serene features of the face he treasured were turning blanched and nervous. It conjured memories of that awful day at Breakfast Island with Xira when Zakon's goons had tried to drown him.

"You're no mere beast, and now the Zeruhawi know it. But not every weapon is wielded with the hand, Enokhi. Each realm has it customs and weapons. In zhakh, just as rules invert across the boards, so 'Trident and shield can be one and the same.' See?" Hrazul sighed deeply, furtively scanning the horizon again. "So in any war of ideas, 'There are times when nothing can be something.'" [xxxv]

Enok was perplexed. Hrazul was almost trembling, making every effort at composure, suggesting that something far worse than the Zeruhawi was troubling her. And half-quoting from the Aphorisms in a manner that was both cryptic and candid, whatever she was hoping to convey, it seemed important to have voiced it.

But — honestly! — what exactly had she said?

At the youngling's insistence, the game began, and after several turns with her mentor's assistance, Enok appeared to be losing. He found it hard to focus on the game knowing his only friend was about to leave, perhaps forever, and that fate had cruelly shunted him into Zeruhawi claws.

A low-ranking warrior vanquished one of his Prefects. The youngling gloated at the little victory. "Can you *really* play zhakh? My Oracle warned you were good."

"Careful, now," her Oracle cautioned. "Whether it's z'hadai or zhakh, Enokhi is far more devious than he seems. His Commanders of Sixty and the Deceivers are the ones to watch out for. Yes, especially the Deceivers."

Mischief twinkled in his eyes. Hrazul obviously had some lesson in mind. Well, he would offer some schooling of his own. "Deception, eh?" He pointed to the bluff a-rear with a cry, "Ho! j'Na-Zeru there!"

«No! Already?» "What?" Hrazul was aghast.

As both sought the figment, Enok deftly rearranged the board in his favor. He was counting on their poor side vision; however in the midst of the deed, Hrazul's long blue tongue lashed out suddenly, grabbing his wrist. Enok shrieked beneath the subsequent lunge that pinned him winded to the sand.

She was five times his length, and no lightweight!

"You know me," Enok wheezed, "oh too well!"

"I have long observed Little Animal lacks any kind of scruple in a challenge."

"Me? Animal? Really! You sound just like Sneak-tail!"

---

xxxv   From the Aphorisms. The quotes form part of a stanza on a pacifistic response to conflict.

Hrazul continued with complete composure. "Base subterfuge, deceit — he can be frightfully unpredictable."

"Nonsense!" Enok groaned. "Crushing ... me!"

"Ah, much like a Zmee bull," noted the youngling equally dryly.

"You're ... squeezing ... yesterday's dinner! *Help!*"

"Oh, he can be sour too, a source of the most pitiful squeals. From 'Nobody wants me,' to 'I'm all alone on this rock,' 'What's the purpose of my life,' or even 'I want to crawl back into my egg.'"

"Ha-ha! Not true! Get off, you ... you scrawny yash'kh! *Help!*"

"When my Oracle forbade him something, he'd do it secretly anyway, just for the pleasure of being contrary. It's a perversity of behavior, I suppose —"

"Perverse? That's hardly funny. *Enokhi dying here!*"

"— that must surely be a character flaw. Whether it's moral deviance, or bouts of self-pity, you can either work him to exhaustion, or, even better, roll him until he's unconscious. Either way, he's as good as cured — that is, until the next episode."

The youngling was keeping clear of the tussle yet constantly hovering and committing every word to memory. She was so much like the young Hrazul. "So, even though he isn't red, I should treat him like a bull, Ssla?"

"He's not exactly like our males — nor quite female either. He is —" For a moment, Hrazul's eyes flashed with gold.

"Don't believe a word of it!" Enok squealed. "*Somebody, help!*"

"Witness the reversion to his native tongue. He uses it on the bald-headed bird and other favorite animals."

"Are we his favorites, then? Where is the Jin-jin fire-bird? I thought they were inseparable."

"*Help! Heeeelp!*" Enok squealed mock pleas in his childhood tongue as they crushed the game board.

"You squawk like a zhrat," whispered Hrazul. "Is *that* what you'd call an apology? What a sorry exemplar you are of your race! And before my very first disciple!"

Her eyes had turned wide and golden again, her tendrils were moist and trembling, caressing his face. She entwined herself about him, then began rolling them both about like a log with dizzying speed, first this way then another, while the youngling pried between coils at the interludes, checking on his welfare.

Forgive me, said Hrazul with her eyes as she released him.

Enok stretched with a groan and shrugged in response. *What's to forgive?*

Hrazul couldn't cry, but the sorrow in her eyes said plenty: *For all the things we never did.*

Suddenly there was a muffled squeal and the handsome emerald youngling flopped face-forward beside him, her eyes dulled and narrowed from pain. Enok was stunned and bewildered. Then with a strange bark, Hrazul too shuddered. The smooth lines of her face creased in agony.

Horror struck him as blue-green blood trickled from her lips and onto his chest. Her eyes, those golden pools that beheld him as no others ever had, glazed over.

In the thousand ways of the sorrowed recollections in the friendless years ahead, Enok would relive in measured, tortured, pantomime the image of her tongue hang lazily, her head tip sideways, and her torso hit the sand with a thud.

"Wise-eye!" he cried. "Hrazul!"

But Hrazul would never answer him again.

KINDRED OF THE DARK

On an elevated bluff, Zakon takes stock of the murder scene below ... Oblivious to the onlookers, Enok tracks the slayer to its lair and discovers survivors of a shipwreck, both Zmee and Elim alike.

THE SHA-NOA PENINSULA ABOUNDED with all manner of exotic beasts, sweet-fruiting vines, and flowering or aromatic plants imported by local Mapmakers and Biotists from their many expeditions. Four successive generations had rendered it a comparatively alien landscape. Though exotic flowers were now widely cultivated, much of what lived or grew here was found nowhere else on the island.

Since access here was so strictly controlled, Zakon couldn't help but wonder what secret treasures these plants possessed that the Azhakh-Na wanted for themselves. Hypnotics? Tranquilizers? Toxins? Any new poison would come in handy.

And this southernmost extremity was buffeted by winds of all sorts by night as well as by day: Land's Breath, Sea Broom, Night's Kiss, Star Wash. This bluff was a flyer's delight! But even with the Broom now in full blow, his tendrils caught whiff of a bittersweet scent, and one unmistakably Ish. Evidently, Hrazul and her beast spent much time here together.

"Did it sleep here too?" he inquired of his spy. Her interest in espionage had flared naïvely, but now he sensed a qualm.

«Sometimes,» signed Sneak-tail Snei. "Or somewhere nearby."

It was approaching midday and already unbearably bright. Zakon removed his goggles and raised naked, squinting eyes upon Mount Oush's lofty balds and its crags of squabbling khrii.

So HIGH. So UNASSAILABLE. AND SO BEYOND MY REACH, he thought, for nesting khrii were merciless defenders, and, for all their weaponry, even his accompanying j'Na-Zeru would scarce prevail beneath a thousand stabbing beaks.

"I heard whispers of a network of caves that run through the mountain. Up there, above the rookeries, is probably its lair."

«Doubtful,» Zakon reasoned. "The slave spent most of its time in the city, so nearer the outskirts is likelier."

Snei drummed her fingers on a contraption of hide and bamboo. "There used to be a number of such noise-makers: windmills, and various tubes that whistled in the wind. And there were lanterns of pumice-stone that often lit the night."

"Stolen New Year's thuribles, most likely."

«No.» "Animal-shaped."

«Animal?» "Why? And whose?"

"Self-made, I am sure of it."

"I find that hard to believe." Zakon struck the drum, wondering why anyone, in this case any-thing, would pursue pointless sounds. Only beasts and younglings so salved their disquiet. The truest beauty was silence; indeed, the splendors of contemplation were hardly expected of a barbarian mind.

He still held that thought when, across the clearing, Snei parted young plantains to reveal another artifact and was fingering it almost reverently. It was an ebony pole, square-sided, thick as a tree trunk, and intricately carved with the blocky, stylized heads of various creatures. Crowning it, the semblance of a toothy bird perched with gripping claws, great nacreous eyes, and outstretched wings was so lifelike, it seemed as if the bird was poised to transport the entire edifice across the sea.

In many ways, this resembled a sort of blocky Pillar of Zmee, and was an extraordinary piece of craft. When asked, Snei thought it the product of some local artisan, but he quickly came to realize that this was not Zmee art at all; nothing serpentine graced it. However, neither was this some primitive barbarian work.

He had invisibly observed that Enokhi creature working in town on several occasions and had never once sighted the least cause for concern. It was employed for only the most menial tasks, and rather tedious ones at that. And rightly so for a slave! Notwithstanding, in light of recent events, the evidence was mounting that the Azhakh-Na Oracles had all conspired to deceive the very Lord Upholder. Why, even the ground here confirmed his suspicions. Two great impressions remained where slabs of pumice once reposed, with shards the only evidence of deliberate destruction.

"There must have been game squares here. Is this where you played zhakh?"

«Yes,» replied Snei hesitantly.

"These must have been champion work. And *two* game squares? Even *I* would have trouble with that! I wonder where the pieces went. And about that khwatl creature? You're certain you overheard the slave giving it commands?"

"Yes, Upholder, but in some barbarous tongue. He often rode it into the city then let it graze on the outskirts."

«Without a tether?»

Snei paused, remembering. «Unsure.» "Little Animal merely called its name, and it would come."

"A name? Beasts naming beasts!" «Go on.»

"Chik-chik or Chira-chuk, I think."

"Stones of the Temple! A strange creature indeed."

"It's his habit," she explained. "All his creatures have an intimate name. He's not like us, but I don't believe he's inherently bad."

«His? He!» Zakon was incensed. "We, all of us, can only work together if we continue to believe together. Could you kill an *it?* Or likewise a *she?*" «Answer me!»

«A she? No! No!» "I could never be a murderer!"

«Exactly!» "There's a world of difference between the *it* and the *she*, so what you *believe* concerns us all. Don't tell me those insipid Azhakh-Na have infected you."

«N-no,» she faltered. The reply lacked conviction.

"Why not complete your studies in a Zeruhawi canton? I owe you that, young disciple. And should you share your Oracle's hobby, the butterfly house in Ur-Hozhai is grander than you can imagine. I have," tendrils curled in a grin, "some influence there. And the flowers! Spreading tulip trees, ixoras, winding groves of plumeria. And orris, a perfumers delight! Six different kinds of plantains abound there, some with truly spectacular blooms."

Snei bowed. «Thank-you.» "Abandoning one Oracle for another is unheard of, but ... the City of Flowers" «I shall consider.»

"I must admit," Zakon mused, "the notion of harnessing beasts for labor intrigues me, though the concept's a mite redolent. Why exhaust ourselves in a world teeming with such living tools, eh? Think how we could have dredged the Susyaan canal with their labor!"

"Don't you think it a little strange, Upholder, that the idea was birthed in an animal's mind?"

Zakon's tendrils fell limp. The symmetry of the idea was faintly amusing, but studying her face, he could swear he caught a whiff of insolence — that, or religion. "My guards will commandeer this bluff-land khwatl and any others they find. I'll teach them to respond to Zmee command."

«Yes, Upholder.» "Maybe we should ask Enokhi. Perhaps he —"

Zakon's tendrils darkened. «What!»

"I mean the slave of my Lord Upholder. He's achieved ... It's accomplished something you ... we had never considered before." Snei cringed in the open-palmed bow of a slave, knowing she was giving offense. "It's at your disposal now. If we were to observe —"

«Enough!» "So where is that pestilent creature? You and Kite-maker both long jawed that you knew its every movement."

"There is another place we could look," she suggested, never daring to raise her eyes. "On the southeastern headlands, towards the city."

Zakon summoned his guards. «Lead on,» he signed to Snei. "And do not fail me again."

The taste of the Ish was thick on his tendrils, though there was still no sign of it. From a grassy clearing at the edge of a beach-side bluff beneath an overlook swarming with chattering khrii, Zakon surveyed the great sandy coastline as it curved back towards Zu'u-Shoran beyond the foot of the great mountain. Viewed from this angle, the rocky escarpments of Mount Oush formed a daunting sight. The sheer drops of this aspect were as crisp as a plumb line. There was nothing else like it anywhere.

Nearby, forming some great sentinel at the bluff's edge was a drum made of hide over a hollowed log carved in intricate geometries. First sight suggested theft, however, the discovery of a miniature toolkit bundled in oilcloth told otherwise. The bestial servant had carved it.

Behind it, and half-covered in wild growth, a new pillar of pumice had been taking shape. Even unfinished, the outline of two chiseled palm prints positioned like menacing eyes was shocking to contemplate. The larger was the Grand Oracle's personal motif, a six-fingered hand centered on a spiral, the ultimate symbol of power; and beside it, a smaller five fingered one of similar style. It was clearly the servant's own hand. The implications enraged him, and with a vicious *hiss* Zakon frightened a khrii off the cliff.

Beyond, specks in the sky told of the great festive prayer kites for which the Zu'u-Shoranians were famous — Stargazer's inventions all, if you believed all that Xira brayed of herself. Though wholly unknown in the north, locals championed Hozny Kitemaker as the perfecter of the art. Like Snei, she had long been Xira's snoop, and he could leverage that, Zakon mused, if Snei lost heart in her duty.

Further afield, a pod of yash'kh postured on the beach. Closer to the bluff, an unusual trio lay in spindlewood shade. Two were Zmee, he could easily see. The third brought to mind the image of zhrat on a carcass.

Zakon peeled off a goggle. "Have you a spyglass?" «Hurry!»

«Yes.» Snei fumbled through her pouch, then gasped as she focused on the scene below. "So much blood!"

«Blood?» "Give me that," he hissed, snatching the instrument. A creature resembling the slave was hovering over a youngling who seemed unnaturally sprawled and far too still for a youngster. "What could leaky-eye mean for the Ish?"

«Uncertain.» "First Disciple would know."

"Your Wise-eye was an Oracle. Now she's dead," Zakon hissed, staring numbly through the spyglass. "Tell me of the Ish: is it the breeding fires, perhaps? Or rage?"

«Rage?» "How should I know? Am I Wise-eye? But maybe!"

Zakon's tendrils then rippled with rage of their own. "Guards! To the beach immediately. Seize the murderer!"

The pair sped towards him, and bowed. «Yes?»

"Down there!" An angry finger stabbed at the three dots on the beach-scape. "It's that wretched Ish! Don't let it escape!"

The guards bowed again and made to retrace their path through the scrub.

"Fools! Glide, you legless lizards!" «Fly! Fly!»

As the j'Na-Zeru took a flying leap, he returned the spyglass to Snei, whose tendrils then wept at the sight.

The slave had been standing over a youngling, lancing her with a massive pike, and smeared with her blood. A dead Oracle lay beside her. At first he thought the murderer might have been one of Ukhaz's invaders, but Snei readily identified the Enokhi creature — the twin locks of russet fur, the flimsy leather garment about its loins, and of course, the copper manacle of a slave. And now it was making a run for it, half-dragging the heavy weapon. As if it could escape his airborne guards!

So here it was: barbarism, undiluted, mad, and pointless. It had been only four days since the invaders crossed the reefs. How quickly the slave had succumbed to their influence! The 'infection' had spread even faster than Xira and Ukhaz dared hope. No doubt, they would be giddy with glee at the news. However, he was the Upholder, the custodian of civilization, and he abhorred this darker side of duty, for only in the likes of modest Hrazul had he ever found a reflection of all he truly cherished.

That she died was simply awful.

And regrettable.

But necessary.

ENOK ROSE ON HIS ELBOWS in shock. Where a Zmee would instinctively flee, he found himself frozen to the spot, stunned by the horror assaulting his eyes. Without warning, a tremendous force jerked him upright, bringing him face-to-chest with the largest ... the tallest ...

Just what exactly was it?

The creature stooped to look him in the eye.

Its face was round, flat and with a nub for snout, a thin crack for a mouth, and the merest of dots for eyes.

No scales. No tendrils. Hairless.

Then came words that sounded like gibberish at first, guttural, incoherent, and so unexpected that anxious moments passed before recognition dawned. It was Enok's own childhood language, and the creature was an Elim youth but of such impossible size!

"Your cry for help ... healing ... sea serpents. Come now," urged the beast-boy motioning him to follow. Was it really a boy?

HOW STRANGE IT SOUNDS WITHOUT THE HISSING, Enok thought, AND AFTER SO MANY YEARS, HOW ALIEN.

Tree crabs strung over the stranger's shoulder struggled hopelessly for freedom. And it became clear as the boy rounded that he was not completely hairless: a single fettered lock grew behind a mangled lobeless ear.

With clenched fists, a part of Enok wanted to kill this Ish-beast-boy, or whatever the creature was. The better part demanded he stay and tend to his only friend. His heart was racing. Hands trembled with rage. Eyes were wide from shock and confusion. An inchoate wail cramped his mouth. Realizing the youngling was still twitching, he knelt over her tenderly, and the words of a half-forgotten language, propelled by the overwhelming outpouring of emotion, burst from stammering lips.

"What ... you ... done!?" he howled at the stranger.

Drawn by the youngling's whimpering, the beast-boy returned with his long black pike, and made to skewer the little disciple through the heart. Enok's hands grappled to resist the stranger's, but were ineffectual against that hideous strength, and through that unholy contact, he sensed not hatred, but a dark moral force aloft of any guilt, that accepted the rightness of the slaying as the pike plunged effortlessly down, sickeningly down, down through flesh, sinew and bone and deep into sand.

With his vision blurred and tasting salty tears, Enok collapsed to his knees with hands still on the weapon — while the barbarian fled jabbering as if no more affected by death than a zhrat.

Enok strove to wrench the pike free, but it was stuck fast. There was naught now but one thing to do. Leaning with all his might, tears coursing down his cheeks, he kept wobbling the great shaft till it loosened. When it finally came free, he brandished the heavy thing with overburdened hands. This wickedness of wood would wreak justice, he swore, for one more creature would be slain this day.

Kneeling over Hrazul, anxious for signs of life but finding none, he whispered lovingly, drying his cheeks with a bloodstained hand, "Goodbye my egg-sister, and my only *friend*." Then in barbarian tongue he growled for every ear to hear:

"*I ... Enok ... beast ... kill!*"

He turned to pursue the beast-boy, but all that remained was a trail of huge footprints that led through rather than around the pod of yash'kh. He hurriedly followed the trail, dragging the heavy weapon, taking two for every step of the stranger's while steering clear of the sea beasts. Beyond the pod, he caught sight of the trail again as it curved sharply landward and continued along the foot of a sandy escarpment.

"First he asks for help, and then he runs away!" Maybe he's afraid, Enok thought, but surely not of me. What kind of help would a giant want anyway?

The beach narrowed then broadened again at the mouth of the pebbly cove where his outrigger lay careened under spindlewoods by a freshet. How tiny his craft now seemed beside the wreckage of an alien pontoon. And there, in an arrangement too orderly to have been left by the tide, lay piled his discarded instruments. The beast-boy was here, somewhere.

He searched wildly for any telltale signs of traffic, but the pebbles precluded that. Had the giant scaled the cliff? On the far side of the cove, a sandy overhang had collapsed into a great jumble of sandstone boulders and ruined vegetation. And there amidst sprays of sand were the imprints he sought: a heel here, toes there.

There had to be a cave!

Behind boulders and a loose drapery of pea-vines, his suspicions were confirmed. A narrow-mouthed cave had been tunneled into the cliff-face. But where was the excavated sand? This made no sense — unless the cave had been covertly dug!

Enok hesitated, fearful of imagined dangers and possibly even of victory. Killing was for barbarians, he knew, but after witnessing the stranger's unflinching brutality, what other options were there? Surely justice and revenge here were one and the same? With practiced ease, it had murdered two beautiful, gentle, and intelligent creatures — not for food, not in defense, but for some other unfathomable reason. Was there any predicting how this madness would end?

Enok was still burning with fury, the tragedy and the agony of Hrazul's final expression indelibly etched in his mind. He decided against caution and embraced the darkest certainty. A life for a life, the price would be paid, even at the forfeit of his own.

With both hands firmly on the weapon, Enok dragged it into the cave, and there he was immediately astonished by its size. No effort, this, of some hurried digging. The hollowed-out inverted sculpture, with high-domed ceiling and vents, and a raised circular bed to one side bore all the hallmarks of Zmee design.

Necks, charred rib cages, and broiled zhrat legs curled from agony littered the blackened hearth at its center. Fleshy strips dangled from a makeshift bamboo tripod, curing in the smoke. The globular fats of an eviscerated yash'kh had made a bucket of one of his drums. The horned and wrinkled head of a tusked tortoise hung limply from the hollow of its upturned shell. Two wings of a large bull khrii hung proudly, the trophy given false animation by the flickering flames as they cast long leaping shadows upon the walls of cave. And dancing round the flames was his fire-bird pet.

"Jin-jin!"

In all, the sights and the smells were a horror surpassing any tannery or scenes of bloated carcasses as scavengers' buffets. Enok let slip the heavy weapon by the hearth, and smoldering ash hissed wickedly as he doubled over and retched.

From amidst the darkness came another kind of hiss, the unmistakable breath of a serpent.

On hands and knees, from the corner of an eye, the visage of a cowering Zmee sobered him. With its hands bound, neck and tail shackled and fettered to a thick peg in the ground, there was little chance of escape. A twisted fingerless hand suggested torture. The cripple eyed him briefly with all the apathy of the condemned, no trace of recognition in her eyes. This was not someone he knew.

Enok whispered, "Are you alright?"

The prisoner gave no response.

"Who are you? Where have you come from?"

Again, no reply.

This was hardly the time for etiquette, he decided, and made a poor attempt at soliciting her name in his native tongue.

"Zaraza," she replied in his language. "Sons of gods ... coming. They take ... life ... stones."

"Stones? Gods?" She was using words he had never heard before, and everything was baffling.

A moan caught his attention.

Almost spanning the circle of the bed lay a feverish barbarian. Poultices of ash, sea lettuce, and some alien fabric made a veritable corpse of the body. Though superior in size to himself, this new stranger was clearly outmatched by the giant boy, and like the boy, was attired in skimpy hides, though more elaborately embroidered. Their tight and narrow leather tunic seemed an outright useless garment. Yet, with so much to assimilate, it was the limbs that drew the eye. The castaway had remarkably delicate feet, and the legs seemed rather lovely despite the bloodied drapery.

A shuffling at the doorway and a passing shadow shattered the inspection. The giant had returned with a leaky pail improvised of one of Enok's own drums. And it was with surprising tenderness that he knelt to prop his patient's head with a pillow of sponges and began to water their lips from a conch. Despite their more elegant dimensions, the bed-bound barbarian seemed the elder, and was hairless too but for a single lock of hair.

Ruddy-brown was Enok's own, or so Hrazul defined it, but the strangers' hair glistened like the midday sand. Could they really be his kindred? Their enormous size was puzzling, and he felt like a runt beside them. Judging by the cuts and weals on their arms and legs, they had both survived a terrible ordeal. Not surprising, really, for he too had once been nearly pummeled to death on the razor reefs and tormented by jellyfish swarms.

"Sea serpents," spoke the giant boy. More gibberish, then: "Sink boat ... eat ... much heal ... help."

Interpreting was difficult. Had they been ravaged by sea serpents? Is that how he lost half an ear? Did the smaller one need medicine? Then why hadn't he just asked Hrazul instead of murdering her? Angry and confused, enraged but curious, Enok examined the sleeper more closely. The poultices against jellyfish burns were a Zmee trick. How had the stranger learned of it?

"Why ... Ish ... k-kill ... Zmee?" Enok stammered.

"Save you," the giant replied.

Save him? Did they think he was being attacked? This was 'kill first and think later,' the very atrociousness of which the Zmee had long arraigned of his kind.

The sleeper's forehead was hot to the touch; a foul humor reigned. Poultices were insufficient on their own. Healing herbs were needed, and soon.

Their greater size notwithstanding, the proportions of the sleeper's chest and shoulders seemed more elegant the boy's. The neck was slender, and beneath the soot and grime the skin was as velvety as lilies. Indeed, beyond the fetor, there lingered something floral, sweet, and musky; something from childhood and once familiar but now hopelessly forgotten. How unexpected then was the rush of memories: a caring face with soft brown eyes, moist lips to the forehead, the rubbing of noses.

'GOODNIGHT, LITTLE RASCAL,' his mother had sung, and Enok shuddered at the revelation: this was not another *he* but a *she*.

An inner voice now sounded caution. Zmee died of old age, or rare accidents in the mines and forges. 'Noble deaths' the Zmee called them. However, what Enok had witnessed today was monstrous. Murder, the most heinous of crimes, was unheard of in Zoar since Zakon ruled as Upholder. How could he break this unhappy news to Zoia and the others? What was he to do about these Ish? Could he just exit quietly, or would this giant snuff him like he slew Hrazul?

PERHAPS NOT, Enok thought, HE NEEDS MY HELP, BUT WHAT IF I JUST BOLTED AND HID BETWEEN THE YASH'KH?

Jin-jin was tugging at scraps from the hearth. Enok shuffled the bird angrily towards the doorway. "Not now, glutton! Outside!"

The entrance was free. And the giant youth was gone again! If there was ever a chance to run for help, this was surely it. He hurried to free the captive, remembering too late that his knife was back at the tannery. The zhrat had almost certainly stolen it by now. And the tethering stake refused to budge. The cripple would have to remain where she was.

I REALLY SHOULD FLEE WHILE I CAN!

The Zmee gave a small hiccup. Jin-jin squawked in alarm, and hissing at a shadow in the entrance.

"Not past me," snarled the shadow, and Enok realized he had been thinking aloud.

The shape entered the cave, leading with a three-pronged spear. Another Zmee followed, their paler features contrasting against the dark now threatening with a weapon at Enok's throat. It was the dreaded Upholder himself!

"Watch out!" Enok cautioned. "There's a giant Ish —"

"Silence!" Zakon roared. "I have seen more than enough."

"Sneak-tail, is that you?"

«O Servant! O Servant!» The disciple's neck was arched, her tendrils in spasms, and her mouth open wide and wheezing in the Zmee equivalent of crying.

Zakon addressed the tethered Zmee without success.

"She does not understand you," Enok explained.

«Nonsense!» "Abducting a Zmee! Outrageous!"

"No, I found her this way!"

"What?" Zakon spat. "In the slave's own hideaway?" «Liar!»

Snei struggled to free the cripple, but the rope held fast.

Zakon proffered a hand. "Take the dagger from my wrist-wrap."

Snei cut the cords, and motioned the cripple outside. The newcomer met and held Enok's trailing gaze with a sardonic grin as she left.

«Out! Out!» Zakon gestured gruffly. "Everybody, go!"

Outside, the point of Zakon's weapon forced Enok against the boulders. The Zmee trident was a deadly harpoon. Trigger released, its three darts would be propelled at tremendous speed, any one of which would rip a hole in his body wider than a serpent's thumb. There were many uses for the vulcanized latex of the thaakh tree, and this was its deadliest.

Under the spindlewoods, Snei struggled to communicate with the newcomer, while two angry j'Na-Zeru rummaged through the giant's debris.

"Her name is Zaraza," Enok managed, wiping his brow of tension's sweat and chillingly aware of the conclusions now being drawn from the sight of his blue bloodied hands.

Snei refused to face him, but he guessed her thoughts.

"She ... she told me so," he stammered, "in Ish-glot."

"Ish-glot? In barbarian tongue?" Zakon was incredulous. "And she divulged her private name to a beast?" «Preposterous!»

"You don't —"

The trident pressed hard against his throat. The wounds coiled within it were tangible. No need for any trigger to invoke death now, just one sharp thrust would end him. Hrazul had never feared anything except j'Na-Zeru guards, the Upholder, and Zeruhawi in a bad mood. In Zakon, all three met.

"You don't have all the facts," croaked Enok.

"The evidence speaks for itself." Behind his insectoid goggles, Zakon's eyes were fixed on Enok's blood-rubbed brow. "Hidden in a cove, guarded by yash'kh evening and morning, our most active times of day." He leaned forward, baring yellowed fangs. "It has learned our ways too well. And now I do what I must."

"Her own tongue is foreign to her," observed Snei mournfully. "She must have been reared in captivity. See the docked hand?" «Barbaric!»

Even hands burnt at the forges still had some digits. So, to Enok's eyes, the deformity seemed more likely a defect of birth. Pink stubs in place of fingers, the objects of Snei's gall, evoked all the more sympathy as it was her left hand, the primary hand of a Zmee.

Beyond the crippled Zmee lay his beloved outrigger, ruined. It was all just wreckage now, strewn across the escarpment as Zakon's over-zealous goons delighted in tearing it apart.

Enok shuddered. The sense of foreboding was palpable. "Look, these are tragic circumstances, but, by Ssla above, I've done nothing wrong! The Isha in the cave —"

"An Isha? A female? You there! Guards!" Zakon cried, halting the destruction. "Fetch the sow from the hollow!"

"'Breeding fires render all Ish savage,'" wailed Snei. "So say all the lore.[xxxvi] You — it! — almost had me convinced. On New Year's Eve, oh such an eloquent story of mistaken intention, of ill-chanced location and time. Is the same excuse to be pleaded again?"

---

xxxvi   A misquote of the Aphorisms: *If breeding fires render all beasts savage, then in our time Zmee too are beasts.*

Her hands and tendrils were trembling from shock and from rage and from everything else.

"And now we discover the brood! An Isha guarded by the Jin-jin fire-bird! Murderer! Murderer! Murderer!" she wailed.

"What? No! And Jin-jin's harmless. Please, let me explain —"

Jin-jin had been perched atop a boulder hissing angrily, but at the mention of deir name, dey fell biting and clawing upon Zakon's tail. The response was immediate. With a resounding *whip!* he dashed Jin-jin against the rocks with such a force that it left the bird unconscious.

Zakon growled lowly, tendrils bristling. «Barbarian! Deceiver!» "I saw the murder from the cliff top, the Oracle lying still, and the slave — the beast! — gloating over the youngling with its hands upon the weapon. We both saw it!"

"You didn't see everything! Look at the evidence logically. Won't you at least let me defend myself?"

With astonishing speed, too quick for evasive action, the blur that was Zakon's trident swung about and — *crack!* — clubbed him with such force that Enok felt sure he'd been decapitated.

In that last heartbeat, that timeless moment separating life and whatever came after it, darkness fell swiftly as he heard the dragon's reply.

"No!"

EPISODE 9

WEB OF IRON

A drugged and imprisoned Enok receives a visit from Hrazul's egg-bearer, who informs him of the coming inquest ... Meanwhile, the Zeruhawi conspire to create an incident with the barbarous giant as its centerpiece.

PAIN: IT WAS THE FIRST of signs and worst of signs that life yet beat within. Each fresh stroke of pounding head and throbbing eyes reinforced the thought:

I'M NOT DEAD. I'M NOT DEAD.

One eyed opened thinly, more intrepid than its equal. By first impressions, he was hard against a smooth sandstone wall. It yawned like a dark and windswept beach, smooth and boundless. Everything else was a blur, gyrating, pulsating, a confusion of shadow and light. Only the wall seemed real. It was cool, solid, eternal.

KEEP STILL, FOOL. PERHAPS THE PAIN WILL SUBSIDE.

Light. Shadow. Light again.

How long had he been standing like this? Was he even really standing?

He remembered Zakon's felling blow. And if all that remained was a severed head, for how long could it see or think? Maybe this is how it felt to die, not all at once, but like waves ebbing with the tide. As surroundings came slowly into focus, the pressing world was seen for the floor it was. He was in a chamber. Smooth-walled. Round. Three great luminous pearl-snails inched towards the ceiling.

"I really am alive," Enok mumbled as feeling returned to his hands, and too the sense of a body. "More alive than dead, anyhow." Well, at least his neck still had its head.

The room brightened with time, its contours sharpened, and the teetering twilight world became a little less confusing. Propped now against a wall, Enok began massaging the knot in his neck, and its rival, the great tender swelling at the base of the skull. Ooh, they hurt. So much for appealing to Zakon's logic. Now, where exactly was he? Was he back inside the giant's cave?

Across the room, opposite the luminous snails, a broad arch framed a massive black grille. Metal straps crisscrossed diagonally in broad curves like overlapping waves. It was thick and heavy, and solid enough to keep even a horde of giants at bay.

Keep out? Maybe it was designed to keep something in. Rattling it was a dumb idea, he discovered too late, for it was solid, immovable, and only doubled the hammering behind the eyes.

The defining smell of the place was musty, with fresh mortar most likely the cause. And it seemed hasty work too, for it lacked all mythic adornment. To the inquisitive hand, the stucco hadn't quite cured. It was only three days old, he judged, or a six-day at most.

A light in the corridor.

A distinctive shuffle and the scutter of wheels heralded visitors. A gnarly old Oracle with a gaudy bandolier appeared sooner than he would have liked, and with a crown made lopsided by its asymmetrical headdress. He was in no shape for company, and assumed a sleeping posture.

A plain-looking assistant in simple livery and helm, trundling a two-wheeled barrow, coughed, and coughed again until he reluctantly sat to attention. By its yellow-green light, the barrow's water-fire lantern highlighted a triple stack of food, and the sight of it being shoved under the grille mellowed the chagrin of having his sleepy pretense laid bare.

Enok rose to bow respectfully — "Ooh!" — and winced from the throbbing. "I thank thee, Oracle." Manners forbade giving mere underlings credit. These were strangers, and address in High Zmiysh was mandatory for slaves.

The gnarled hands of the Oracle tightened around a thick cylinder of knobs and harlequin segments. "Has the prisoner just awoken?" she asked her assistant though with a lour aimed squarely at him.

At first he thought she had come to poison him, that is until the cylinder's motif swung clearly into view. It was the Twain Serpent, the symbol of renewing life. The tube was a medicine stick, a portable kit of various herbs and lotions. In the compartments of her bandolier, he recognized spatulas, weights, and other tools of trade. Though he had never met her like, she was clearly an apothecary, if not a Healer proper.[xxxvii]

"Yes. Just," he slowly confirmed, massaging his neck.

The Oracle proffered the cylinder to her attendant, who then passed it through. "This is for the health of the other."

Enok was genuinely puzzled. "But I'm alone."

The serpents studied him carefully before sharing a gesture where tendrils darkened and quivered briefly in unison. He had seen this before, between Zoia and the High Wisdom, between Hrazul and Zoia: a subtlety of tendril talk he had yet to understand.

«It reads?» the old Oracle asked her attendant.

«And writes,» was the reply.

Relics of some alchemical mishap, a gouged cheek, and a patched-over eye were rendered all the more severe by lantern's light as the old Oracle slid forward, eyeing him grimly before inquiring of her attendant, "The slave is familiar with these markings?"

Enok wagged a Zmee-style *yes*. The crowning sigils read *Healer,* of course, but the personal glyph was unfamiliar, though it could possibly translate as *Thaazh.*

"Twist and pull the top knob," was the instruction to her underling, who then relayed the message though with eyes that kept dissecting him.

"All the sections can then easily swing out," the attendant added, with further directions that led him to an orange tonic.

---

xxxvii Healer Oracles may have multiple specialties: apothecary, alchemist, physician, mortician; while lower class Venerables can have but one.

The vial was there as Thaazh had said, but his thanks fell short of her ears, muttering as she was about diminishing supplies.

"Serve the cordial twice a day," she told the attendant as though he wasn't even present. "Three drops to the goblet."

«Hastens recovery,» the attendant explained, then continued with her own tips for cleaning and dressing wounds "There should be a goblet in the wash room."

«Waste of effort,» signed Thaazh, with her rancor clear by lantern's light.

Enok bowed gratefully. "But surely, Healer, the healing arts are for *thee* to perform."

The response was rich in contempt. "Kindred to kindred, but beast to beast! The High Wisdom has convened an inquest, and she wants all the prisoners fit and sober, whether I like it or not. Tell the creature *that*, Steam-maker."

The Oracle shook the grille, appraising its strength, as the attendant added, "Keep the other's head cool until the fever subsides."

Satisfied the grille would confine him, Thaazh uncoiled and departed with mutters of anathemas upon his bones. "May the medicine turn poison, or a pox rot them both."

However, the assistant remained. Thaazh had called her Steam-maker. While Enok was certain they had never met before, there was something familiar about her piercing mantid stare. If not for the obvious signs of age, she and Hrazul might well have been eggs from the one brood. But was the awkward silence and staring a kind of ritual, or was she was simply working up to something? More than twice she had been on the verge of speaking, but instead sighed loudly with a peculiar twitch of the tendrils that indeed was so like Hrazul.

"Thy Oracle has left," he remarked, lubricating the moment. "Dost thou require something of me?"

"The former First Disciple, the new Oracle, she was my ..." There was pain in the restraint.

"As I mourn for her, I grieve with thee."

First a pause, then: "I'm told you're the murderer, though Mapmaker's disciple dares that maybe —"

"Sneak-tale, Snei: is she safe? The giant —" Enok's legs suddenly gave out and he clutched at the grille. "I feel giddy."

"So, are you innocent?" «Spare the deception!»

"Huh? Aye. *Aye*. I enjoyed Hrazul's company more than thou canst know. 'Violence is the tool of the barbarous,' so the Aphorisms say, 'and thus the righteous decry it.'"

"Quoting scripture?" «How dare you!» "You are no Believer!"

"As thou sayest. But neither am I some infidel." Still weak, he sank against the bars. "And my head hurts mightily."

"That would be the effect of the draft. It will pass soon enough."

Did she mean a sleeping draft? Left unconscious from Zakon's blow, why would he have needed it? Just how long had he been asleep anyway?

"Whether thou believest me or not, there truly was another Ish. Well, I think it was. Take care for thyself, he has greater strength than a Zmee's."

"We found only the Isha and the cripple," maintained the Zmee. "The facts speak for themselves!"

"No, they do not!" Enok shot back. "Facts *cannot* speak for themselves: *people* speak, and tint whatever logic the facts uphold with the hue of their own intention."

How could truth be self-evident when shrouded by prejudice? Where Hrazul might employ the facts to exonerate him, the Zeruhawi would indict him with very same. Was she Zeruhawi?

"I am no murderer!" he protested.

Unaware, perhaps, of the fury within, the Zmee made no response, and her tendrils hung idly in a look of spreading acceptance that again was all too familiar. Her speech was accented strangely, he noticed finally, almost melodic, and for her he was no mere beast. She lacked the red-and-black armbands of the Zeruhawi, or pendants or phylacteries, or, well, anything that signaled her rank. Like Hrazul, there was the touch of the ascetic about her.

"Believe what thou wilt, but I *know* what happened despite the accusations. And suddenly," he continued, brandishing a russet banana to indicate the entirety of the cell, "I find myself here, nauseous, and with my head banging like a New Year's gong. My apologies if thou findest me uncivil." Given the lowness of his station, there was no safer way of showing anger.

A pause ruled, longer than before. She wavered more than once between staying and leaving.

"Wise-eye and I enjoyed a special confidence. Nevertheless, we disagreed on the matter of yourself. She gave up much for you," the serpent noted of Hrazul. "Did you know? I wonder if perhaps she esteemed you far more highly than you did her."

"No egg-sister could ever suffer the death that *I* died when the giant robbed her of life. It happened so quickly, so very quickly, and I reproach myself for being so ..." He could feel his throat thickening, and he faltered with lowered head, "For being so powerless. Whatever she was to thee, she was mountains more to me. I miss her greatly."

"As do I. However, she was not my egg-sister. Both she and the murdered youngling were my eggs. And I defy all local custom to profess it." The reverence was tangible as she whispered their names for invisible ears. "Let it honor the dead."

"Hrazul and Aysha," Enok repeated, quietly reliving the events of that awful, awful day. The magnitude of her loss compounded with his own was now just too much to bear. "I am so very, very sorry," he wept. "Young Aysha was beautiful indeed."

"They were both exceptional. Why do your eyes water?" «Pain?» "Is it the draft?"

A lubricant for the worst of grief, of ten thousand lonely nights, of abandoned hopes for an acceptance that now would never be forthcoming, purgers of remorse and impotence and self-loathing, tears were a thing he could barely explain to himself let alone to a being whose eyes would never shed a single one.

He bowed clumsily. "Best I take my leave of thee now."

Another pause.

"First Disciple always believed in you, but for the longest time I refused to support her. She was my best egg. She saw what many could not, or perhaps, would not. I may doubt you, but not her. Yet if I don't doubt her, then I wonder why it is that I'm doubting you."

Finally, she jerked away from the grille to leave.

"Wait!" Enok implored. "If Zakon plans to have me killed, thou couldst, at least, say so."

She bent her gaze towards him, arching her neck in a facial negative like Hrazul would have done. "Why the rudeness? Please refer to him by title. But you're right. To withhold such a thing would be, perhaps, unkind. Besides, that's not for the Upholder alone to decide. A special sitting of the Shav'yat will decide your fate. And not just yours but all the Ish. The decision will be final."

"Well, I hope it excludes the Upholder. I know what I saw in his eyes that day. None of it was good."

A snort diverted the topic. "My egg once jested, 'If our bulls were like my servant, we wouldn't need a pilgrimage.'"

"Oh." A compliment? Why hadn't Hrazul ever told him herself?

"Be prepared," she warned. "If your testimony is true, then you may find the Isha equally unpredictable, possibly treacherous."

Then it finally struck him. He was truly not alone in the cell.

"You're not a Healer, so may I inquire of the reason that brought thee hither?"

"'Eyes are the soul's window,' or so the Writ says. I needed to ascertain for myself whether you're the villain everyone claims."

"I am no murderer," he denied in appeal. "Better for all if *I* had died that day instead of Hrazul. If I could, I would, but I cannot change the past. But should the truth be slain as well? That in no way honors her memory."

The Zmee seemed to hesitate, the two ends of her great body swaying arrhythmically as if head and tail would part company, much like Hrazul at some personal watershed.

"'Judge not the contents by their vessel.' Did you know? That was the one scripture among all her phylacteries that she never changed with the years." At length the visitor appeared to have made up her mind, and returning to the grille, laid a palm against the metal, inviting him to the same.

"I do this for Wise-eye, not for you. I am Zelen the Ever Curious, the Steam-maker."

Her hand was twice the size of his. Enok reciprocated, and Zelen maintained contact for uncomfortably longer than custom. Her piercing gaze relaxed now to one of acceptance, and for a long and pregnant moment, neither made a sound — till challenge rose in her voice.

"As the Writ itself says, 'In the Crucible of Now one's truth is revealed.'"

"I was not aware the Zeruhawi studied the Aphorisms."

Zelen's eyes him drilled him. "I once discipled in Zu'u-Shoran too, you know. Anyhow, unexpected stresses expose both the flaws of character and the doors of destiny. That's what the proverb means. So I believe the next three days will be your crucible, your actions spelling what manner of creature you truly are, with the Isha as the catalyst."

She paused, breaking contact. "You have one great decision remaining, little Ish. You spoke of honor, but, hereafter, how will *your* deeds honor the memory of my eggs — and of all those who died that you might live?"

Now introduced, formal speech was unnecessary. "'To believe what you see, stop seeing what you believe.'" voiced Enok in Low Zmiysh. "Hrazul taught me that. I thought you'd like to know."

A delicate smile crept up from her tendrils and into her eyes. "She had a wise egg-bearer. And one more thing: you should refrain from using people's intimate names, especially in public. It can only lead to trouble." «It's important. Understand?» "Maintain decorum and all may turn out well."

Decorum? Into trouble? Was that a Zmee joke? However, he knew well the reprimanding glare of an Oracle when it came.

As Zelen slid away, Enok slumped to the floor with his knees to his chest. He realized only later that the tickle in his belly that had percolated to fill the cell was a gift unique to his race.

It was laughter.

 IN THE UPPER STORY EXPANSE of the local lyceum where the historian Skazaar held office, a number of senior Zeruhawi had gathered to hear firsthand the capture of the giant Ish. Notable among them were Ukhaz the Chief Oracle of Law, one-eyed Thaazh the Healer, her face malefic with scars, and Xira the Stargazer, she who thrived on applause yet rarely appeared publicly.

It was midday now, the shutters were drawn, and the thick walls rendered it pleasantly cool.

A number of Southerners had died apprehending the invader — not militia, the Civils, but untrained citizens from the High Wisdom's hometown. And when the giant had fled northwards into the local precinct, his martial j'Na-Zeru had fared little better. This was hardly the first time that Zakon had shared the story of how he had stalked and captured the Ish-beast single-handedly where a dozen of his best had failed. He was a male. He was the Upholder. Now he was a legend. And he found himself liking it.

True, the failures of others had only boosted his chances; however, Zoar needed a champion, whatever the truth. And ought not worthy ears meet such praises graciously?

His figs-on-the-tree camouflage had been perfect, or so he had thought, yet the giant had anticipated just such a ruse. It had whirled and lunged, catching Zakon unprepared. He had barely managed to spring to where tensioned nets had lain waiting. And all too vivid was the memory of lying in a shallow brook and mimicking a tongue of river wash while removing the massive barbarian dagger that had pierced through his wrist. His squirting blue life-blood had given him away, but he had slipped aside at the very moment the trap was beginning to spring.

Rubberized rope enwebbed the giant. It was unbreakable. Yet it had fought unrelentingly, writhing and spitting with the brute force of some hate-crazed yashurakh. And surely the image of that massive barbarian spear that had, by the grace of his ancestors, punctured nothing more than a wing membrane, would surely haunt him for years! He winced at the memory of his own impuissance, where the dagger kept stabbing him all over again.

The giant was a monster! How could an Ish grow so large? Or so unbelievably strong? Would that slave Enokhi attain such a measure? It was a worrying thought, but not for much longer if the Zmee gathered here had their way. Their talk was abuzz with Thaazh's new poison — a drug of death like no other.

The story of the first Ish-beast the Mapmakers of Zu'u-Shoran had captured (assuming it really was an Ish) and brought to the island had been hushed up. The adult had proven violent and untrainable, and had escaped the Sha-Noan sanctuary, leaving its hatchling Enokhi behind. Ssla alone knew what became of it. But these new giants, the Isha in the cell and especially the barbarian male, challenged everything everyone knew of Ish-kind.

Simply put, Zmee cows were green, bulls red; Ish were furry, Isha not. But the slave in the cell was almost furless like the new barbarian female, and indeed the other male. And why so great a discrepancy in size between the Enokhi creature and the new barbarian male? After so many years, how could the slave still be such a youngling? After all, it was already nearly twice his age! Something was seriously amiss with all the lore; even a one-eyed Zmee could see that.

The evidence against the Southern Oracles was mounting by the day. They had clearly been deceitful about everything and anything regarding that slave. But why? What were they protecting?

«So?» "What do you think?" Xira the Stargazer asked.

Zakon broke from reminiscence with a shake of the head. "About the venom? Would that all our fangs had such!" «Yes, yes.» "Quite useful on a prong, I daresay. How much is there?"

«No!» "About the inquest, you sleepy-tendriled bull."

«Oh? Sorry.»

"Why would the High Wisdom insist on *not* keeping the slave in Zu'u-Shoran? Why her insistence on having the inquest here?"

Preoccupied as he had been with tracking the giant, recent newsworthy events had escaped him. "Perhaps," he began, voicing a whimsical thought, "by saying the converse of what she really wants, she makes us suspicious, thereby prompting us to offer the opposite of what she doesn't really want."

«Clever!» Xira signed.

«What?» Ukhaz, the aging Chief Oracle of Law was a little slow comprehending. «Ah!» "The Logic of Not. Good, because I accepted her proposal at face value. We are holding the inquest here, just as she requested. Imagine, what a statement we could make!"

«Statement?» It was Zakon's turn to be lost.

"For the Cause," explained Xira. She meant the Zeruhawi one.

«Apprehensive,» Zakon's tendrils twitched. Whatever these two were proposing this time, he was already uneasy about it. That he was privately mourning Hrazul was something best kept to himself. She needn't have died, and the fault was surely his. "No more lives must be lost. This has gone far enough."

"A Zmee's word is unbreakable." Ukhaz shared a look with Xira, then faced him squarely. «Isn't it?»

Skazaar's ornate desk was littered high with parchments, which she parted abruptly, jumping forward with misgivings blushing her tendrils. "I agree with the Upholder." «Enough!»

«Statement? Statement!» "Just how much barbarism do we need? Hasn't this 'statement' already been made?" added Thaazh. "As an apothecary, physician and *mortician*, shouldn't I know that better than most? The plan has already seen far too many die."

"Indeed!" Zakon signed «Thank you, Healer!» to Thaazh. When exactly had *she* become privy to Xira and Ukhaz's nefarious plan? Hadn't she been unconscious when he, Ukhaz and Xira had agreed to all this mayhem? Obviously, someone in this room had loose tendrils, and it piqued him. "The assembly at the inquest," he fumed, "will hear how dangerous these Ish can be."

"Hearing may not be enough. It's best they see for themselves," Xira recommended. "It has to be public."

"And unforgettable," Ukhaz chimed. "With representatives here from every province, this will be quite an event. A little scuffle —"

«Cease! All of you!» "It's no! No! And no!" Zakon growled at each of the conspirators in turn. "Just to be safe, I'll have a beast drag that reeking barbarian to the assembly. I want none defiled from its touch. And I'm having it roped so tightly it will have to breathe through its ears!" Zakon uncoiled himself, wings trembling furiously. "Great Zhmee forfend! That giant was nigh the ruin of me! And I have a dozen guards minus a limb or a tendril whimpering half-dead in Healer's chambers!

"Think about what you're proposing. Is it the dagger that ends a life, or the one who wields it? To kill, to allow being killed — how small the divide! How you all fretted over a beast becoming Zmee," Zakon chided. "Mine is with Zmee becoming beasts."

«Oh, witty!» Xira and her sarcasm.

"You must understand, Upholder," Ukhaz began, "that our people are at a great crossroad. The Stargazer, the Chronicler here, and many others — myself included — have labored our whole lives to change the very way our people think, to free them from fear and imbue them with a sense of hope.

"The Zeruhawi dream is so close now," she sighed wistfully, "so close. Perhaps just moons away. Our people — after such a long and fearful sleep — now clamor for change, and all that holds them back is a stubborn coterie of die-hards clinging to their precious myths."

"Luddites!" Xira hissed. «Antiquated!»

"Zu'u-Shoran especially," Zakon shared. "I know, perhaps too well, how little you esteem them."

"They dominate all the councils, they manipulate every agenda, they control the Great Pilgrimage," Xira hissed. "They slink about with impunity, because they enjoy the favor of the Grand Oracle, that old masked High Wisdom herself. And unjustly so!

"Now, I understand some from Zu'u-Shoran died at the hands of the giant. They were but Prominents and common folk, thank Zulyi. Now, imagine how the delegates from Zu'u-Shoran — including Oracles and Venerables from all the provinces, people of real influence — would react if there were, ah, a *public* incident with the giant? Then we could parade the slain around the city for a few days. That should raise people's ire. Then we could mobilize —"

"Stargazer! That's unspeakable!" Even the old historian was outraged.

«Absolutely not!» "The people won't tolerate any desecration of our egg-sisters, and I won't either!" Zakon was adamant. "Your 'antiquated' is but the normalcy of the peaceful, and I would sooner have that than —"

"Upholder. *Zakon,*" cooed Xira in conciliatory tones, "you are like an egg-brother to us all, and we won't argue. As the Upholder, the final say is yours." She bowed deferentially. "Come, Newcomer," she beckoned to silent Zaraza, who had been so unobtrusive he hadn't even noticed her. "The Oracle of Law has shown you the catacombs, now let me show you my manufactory and my sky-boats."

"Sky ... boats?" Zaraza wondered aloud.

"With your permission, Upholder?" Xira inquired. "There is much I can teach her."

Zakon wondered briefly whether Xira and Ukhaz hadn't taught her too much already, for she had adopted Zeruhawi armbands, one of which holstered an honorary j'Na-Zeru dagger. He was loath to part with her, for he was desperate to learn more about her overlords. But part they would if she were sucked too deeply into Xira's orb. If only her mastery of the true language were better.

IN TIME, he thought. ALL IN GOOD TIME. The Upholder was patient, if nothing else.

He threw a glance at Zaraza, euphemistically called Newcomer, with his tendrils bidding farewell. The two were on the cusp of leaving when Xira whirled with a knowing grin.

"Upholder, won't you join us? There's something I believe you really ought to see."

«Explain.»

"Why, your very own sky-boat, of course."

«My own?» "Balloon?"

The tendrils of every Zmee in the room were positively beaming. This was clearly a public secret.

She bowed unctuously. "It's ready when you are."

EATING THE FRUIT THAT ZELEN had brought, Enok sat with his back against the grille, ruminating on the events of the last few days, and thankful that the nausea and dizziness were at last subsiding. The more he pondered Zelen's conversation, the more like Hrazul she became in his mind. He was glad to have met her, and glad that in those precious moments he had been granted forgiveness from the least likely source of all, Hrazul's own egg-bearer.

Like her offspring, she too was a little cryptic. Her comment 'Died that he might live' made no sense at all. *Like egg-bearer, like egg,* went the old Southern proverb, and now how true it seemed to be.

Beside him lay a physician's medicine stick, a nest of compartments in the shape of a tube as thick as his trunk and almost as long as he was tall. It had ointment for the Isha, and he knew what was expected of him. However, his present predicament was all the fault of that giant, and that Isha included! Why should she be allowed to live when Hrazul and little Aysha had died? The very idea that he and she might be kindred was repugnant.

Now, about that female: where was she?

The cell around him was small by Zmee standards, stretching about thirty serpent cubits wide and half that in height. And now it seemed anything but round. In fact, it was rectangular, which was strangely un-serpentine. Any sort of sharp-edged design was anathema to modern masons.

Again, he massaged the knot in his neck, and quietly marveled at the alchemy under whose influence he had made circles of rectangles, and slugs of windows. "That was some drug," he mused. Well, at least he had counted correctly: there were three square windows at different heights above the floor.

Exploring the prison revealed two smaller rooms at opposite ends, separated from the main chamber by thick masonry partitions. Drawn by the sound of lively water, he discovered the first was for ablutions and toiletry, and there a tall barred window framed a vista of a languid pine-studded bay edged with pale ruby sands.

Ruby: the golden beaches of the world he had known were far, far away.

The other contained the unconscious stranger of the beachside cave, the Isha. She lay half-swaddled in old sailcloth upon a grand straw-filled mattress within a circular camphor-wood frame. It was standard Zmee bedding. And she remained as bloodied, bruised and filthy as when he had first clapped eyes on her. Removing the makeshift blanket revealed a strange creature indeed. With neither snout nor tail, she was tendril-less and gangly, with a puny undersized head and pebbles for eyes. And here the songs of the zhrat came to mind.

They had dubbed him *Two-leg-food-giver,* or just *Two-legs* in their sagas, as though his body so lacked definition. It seemed a mite insulting; however, as he now beheld an image of himself in flesh, he had to admit they were right. This Isha was mostly legs.

But what should he do with her? Too heavy to drag to the water, he would have to bathe her where she lay, presenting him problems of an altogether different kind. Should he do as directed and apply the medicine? Was a murderer's life worth redeeming? All the Aphorisms said *No!* — a bizarre twist, he thought, for in saving her life he was breaking the law.

On the other hand, might not she be innocent?

But the mere sight of her was alien. Instinct painted her as something bestial and primitive. After all, here was the object of a lifetime of warnings: a soulless barbarian, crooked of speech, a bloodthirsty slayer who lived for the hunt. Her recovery could well spell his doom. He might fall asleep and never awaken; and if he cried for help, who would hear? Or even care?

And yet, this Isha and the giant boy were the first real people to fill his eyes for almost fifty years.

Fifty years!

Thus, Enok had questions — so many the questions! — and with only one route to the answers. The Healer was right. To uncover the truth, he would have to see her well. Like it as not, he was caged with her, and there was nothing he could do about it right now.

Except ... sleep lightly.

NAAMA

Enok becomes fascinated by the female shipwreck survivor, and realizes his people are not the brutish savages Zmee have long proclaimed them to be ... Hrazul's egg-bearer suggests a possible means of escape, but for Enok alone.

THE CELL, ENOK OBSERVED IN a lonely moment gone, had been carved high into a precipice of sandstone, the roost of a myriad of cliff-dwelling twitterlings.

It seemed about early morning now. On the floor by a window with his hands about his knees, he stared absently upon the narrow vista of a dark jade sea and ruby sands of a sheltered cove. Its lazy waters were redolent of seaweed and the rut musk of reef dragons, so he found himself grateful for the bed's camphor odors.

Darksome beaches dotted most of Zoar's coastline except near his southern hometown of Zu'u-Shoran and especially its promontory. There, fine golden sand squeaking between his toes was far more inviting than the rubies and charcoals of elsewhere. He was thus north of the isthmus in any one of the four coastal cities.

Even the worst of Mapmakers should have some sense of where they were. Normally, he could orient himself from some familiar landmark or the passage of the Greater Light across the sky, but the view from the cell afforded little of these, and that made deducing his location all the more difficult, if not impossible. The sense of impotence was dispiriting.

Ga-runt. Ga-runt. Ga-runt.

Though hidden from view, their reverberant grunts confirmed the presence of yash'kh, which meant he was unlikely to be in the uttermost north. There, barren, steaming dunes and bubbling mud were matched only by boiling lagoons and a scalding sea where nothing sizable grew. But their familiar sound spoke of sea and wind and wave, of long yawning beaches where he alone was master, and of home, and of the innocence of bygone days.

More so than the forests or the mountains, he had always loved the sea, and the taste of salty air rekindled half-buried memories of escape. He had canoed around the island twice before, and now it seemed like a lifetime ago. The circumnavigations had almost cost him his life, for in the pastures of the sea roamed boat-crushing leviathans beside which even bull yash'kh were hatchlings. Indeed, the pelagic deep bore terrors to rend one's very soul. Would now that he had died at the mercy of the sea, for the Zmee had no concept of mercy, and death — yes, he could sense it drawing near — like birth, was the only other verity of being.

No longer was he the young boy on a barnacled log, desperate for a means of escape. The lad had discovered the stretching majesty of Zoar, a mountainous island ringed by reefs and sandbars of turquoise, emerald, and gold, and surrounded by a pitiless ocean that mocked the very sky for blueness. An older and wiser Enok relived these memories like episodes from another life. Escape was futile, this knew the man; however, to feel the wind in the hair, sea-spray on the cheeks, to hold a halyard with one hand and a tiller with the other, to sail and sail the course of his choosing, humbled and elated between the two skies, these were the dreams of the boy.

Stop it! he chided himself.

After three days in the cell, with far too much of dwelling on the past, the outside world flirted with him, taunting him with his own memories.

Not much had transpired since Hrazul's egg-bearer Zelen had come calling, except for visits by a strange featherless bird, midway between a twitterling and Jin-jin for size, and with eyes as black as zhuk beetles. It was perched now on the bedroom partition as though checking on his welfare. The leathery avian had hazarded sunset and sunrise when the twitterlings themselves were madly aflight, and it was now cooing contentedly, anticipating a breakfast treat.

His thoughts fell naturally to the ever-hungry Jin-jin, when a groan from the bedchamber arrested his musing.

The face he had once thought featureless had grown increasingly less alien in sleep as he had studied its every movement. And now, after long hours of staring and wondering, the long eyelashes, the high cheekbones and slender chin, the ruby lips and skin as smooth as a newborn petal, all comprised features that were anything but ugly. Indeed, they had given fresh form to the face of his midnight dreams. Those wide brown eyes and delicate lips that so filled him with longing were much clearer now in his mind, but sadly these here were not them.

Lately, the shipwrecked Isha had been tossing and turning, punctuating the silence of the night with moans and whimpers. 'Keep its head cool until the fever subsides,' was the Healer's parting instruction. It had kept him busy and deprived of sleep, and it was a great relief to see her improving at last.

Just after dawn, lying on her side with an eye half open and the other encrusted with sleep, she had groggily reached for some water, then slumbered again. He was certain she had seen him, and now as he beheld her sleeping form, two open eyes met and held his gaze.

"Wh— where am I?' she moaned in the guttural language of the giant. It was the idiom of primitives and cutthroat barbarians, the vernacular of his kin. What followed made little sense, then: "Or one of the hells?"

"Zoar," Enok offered.

Groan. Yawn. "What's a Zoar?"

"Place in much Zmee," he replied clumsily.

What more could be said? Zoar just meant Zoar, nothing else that he knew of. Maybe it was a diminutive of 'Zoriyan,' the fabled Zmee homeland, but how did one translate that into Ish-glot? The long years of isolation, he was embarrassed to admit, had left his vocabulary wanting.

"Zmee? It's Traitor's Hell, then," she spat. "Though I don't *feel* dead." There came a squeal as she disappeared under the sailcloth blanket. *That*, he understood. After "Where are my ...?" the rest was gibberish, though it seemed likely about her clothes.

"There." A pointing hand nominated the grille beyond the partition where her garments hung drying. "I do to water."

"You washed my stuff, did you?"

Impolite as it was among the Zmee, "What ... name ... you?" he queried slowly. For someone to yield their name rather than title held special significance. However, as everyone kept pointing out, he was no Zmee — and neither was this Isha.

"You mean, what is my name?"

"Yes," he confirmed. "What is my name."

The Isha sat up, clutching the blanket high, looking dazed and perhaps a little angry when she commanded with terse and deliberate slowness, "Bring. Clothes. Here. Now."

Enok understood and brought her buckskins. SHE DIDN'T GIVE ME HER NAME, he thought. Perhaps his people had similar taboos.

Then came a withering stare and a paddling motion with a hand. "Scat, scat."

The words themselves meant little, but her strange flat face was creased with language aplenty. She wanted him to leave.

"I scat-scat," he replied, rounding the partition to sit against the wall, yet with a curious ear at its lip.

Judging by the sounds from her chamber, she was talking to herself, posing questions, answering them, and arguing over the response. He found that rather comforting, for Zmee never did. And how many times had Hrazul jibed him about it?

"Where's Refa? And the others?" she called. "Are they here too?"

He understood the 'they here' part. She was inquiring after her companions, maybe even the giant boy. That she should speak their intimate names to a stranger was an appalling lack of manners, yet it seemed so accepting of his company as an equal.

A grunt followed a spell of quiet, broken when she peered mumbling over the masonry wall. Was she ever tall! (Whereas his crown barely reached the partition, her chin easily cleared it. And her boy-giant companion would dwarf even that.) With a crinkled nose and eyes drawn thin to blindness, her mumbling found its focus in the sniff of an armpit.

"Phew! I reek of bahalazh!"

Bahalazh. Another new word, and he hungrily absorbed it.

"Oil, I put you," he explained, still wondering what kind of thing a bahalazh might be. [xxxviii]

"You rubbed an ointment on me, did you? What a ..." More gibberish followed.

Rubbed. Ointment. More new words. "You eat?"

"Food? I'm famished." Her eyes followed his pointing finger to fresh provisions, upon which she paddle-signaled again.

Enok spun about. "I scat-scat."

"No, bring! Bring. Food. *Here.*"

Did she want to eat where she slept? What an appalling lack of decorum.

"Where are Refa and the others?" she inquired again.

"Not. Thinking. You." Is that how you said it? Conversing in his own language now seemed more difficult than he remembered. Throwing a few words to his pets now and again was an entirely different matter.

With hands raised high then wide, the Isha sketched something of great size. "Refa."

"No Refa," he answered. Who knew where the giant boy was?

"Did anyone else survive?"

Blank looks were all he could offer.

"Where's my ... Zaraza?"

Now, Zaraza, he knew. That was the cripple from the beachside cave, but what did she mean by 'my'? Was it her servant? It smacked of wrongness, didn't it, a Zmee serving an Ish?

"Zaraza breathe, Refa breathe," he replied. "Not see place."

"So, they're alive but you don't know where they are. Is that it?"

"Yes," he affirmed with growing confidence. "Not ... know where ... they are."

"Who are you, young Ish? What ... is ... your ... name?"

She commanded like an Oracle. Maybe she was one.

"Enok. Enok, I name is."

"A rather common name, Enok. *Ee-no-k. Hee-no-kh.* Named after the old city, I suppose: Qr-Ai-Henokhi. Just about every other

---

xxxviii *Bahalazh* can describe any fetid dragon dung, though specifically from a trr-bahal, which is particularly smelly.

pathetic refugee calls their firstborn man-child Henokh, Eenok, or some such thing these days. And no doubt inspired by some ancient Ab-Sethi prophecy about a … a crying butterfly? A serpent's butterfly? Pah! So, what's your father's name? Or your clan's? I wonder if you even know who you are."

So many unfamiliar words. "Refugee? Prophecy?"

"Never mind," she growled dismissively. "The Ab-Sethi prophets are loopy. And I need to wash this stink off me."

"Wash? Wash!" Enok indicated the other room. "Water muchly there."

Then with a furrowed bow and an exaggerated version of her scat-scat sign, she commanded him from her sight.

The sloshing in the washroom came mingled with unmistakable moans of pleasure. Enok listened intently to its every gurgle. Here at last was a being more like himself than any Zmee he had ever known.

After a while — a very long while! — the Isha emerged wearing her buckskins, standing tall, clean, and proud. How very different she was now to that whimpering bloodied form he had been nursing through the nights.

Completely transformed, she looked magnificent: skin the color of leather, hair the color of straw flowing in a single lock from behind an ear, and with eyes bluer than the midday sea. What was once flaccid now rippled with energy and Enok could naught but help admire the obvious strength of her.

"My skirt's too tight. I don't think you should've washed it." She made that bring-bring sign again. "Attend me." The words bore all the assurance of one used to giving instructions to those who obeyed, and right now, how very frail he seemed beside her!

Finally, she introduced herself. Had she been an Oracle, it would have been proper to divulge her specialty, like 'The Mariner' or even by some private moniker, such as 'Blue Eyes,' but instead it was just plain 'Naama,' and nothing more. Being untitled was the ultimate shame. Only the condemned or the lowest of the low had such a paucity of names. For a lesser being, she sure acted imperiously.

When she had asked him to serve her, and he proffered a cluster of grapes, she recoiled, proclaiming him 'Zmee-handed' (whatever that meant) and thereafter greedily partook of the fruit and vegetables herself, discarding anything touched by him, yet all the while casting eyes for something else.

In addition to the melons, bean pods, sweet drupes of the red-stalked palm, and boiled turtle eggs, the Zmee had provided a salty broth of sea lettuce, and a veritable mountain of grapes. Almost everything, though, was either half-plucked or squashed. They were clearly someone's leftovers.

The odd little zhuk-eyed visitor cooed loudly and Enok threw fleshy pips to the floor. "Here, bird."

"What's a gholuj doing here?"

Enok was puzzled. "Gholuj?"

"*That* is a gholuj, a snake-pigeon, or something very like it. I've never seen one outside a city before. Are we in a city?"

"Not see," was all he could say.

"You don't know where you are? Blood of the gods! You're not very useful. Well, wherever there's food and fools to feed them — and cities breed fools more than anywhere else. Believe me, we're in a city." She wiped her mouth with the back of a hand and asked, "Where's the meat?"

"What 'meat'?"

"What is meat? You know, broiled animals. Over a fire?"

Gholuj. Fire. Meat. "Naama eat animals on fire?"

"Why, don't you? Everything has to eat something, and some animals eat others. Things have always been that way, the weak falling prey to the strong."

Enok bristled. "Zmee not eat animals."

"*Huh.* Is that what they tell you?" Her face contorted strangely. Perhaps it was contempt. "I'm no Zmee, and neither are you."

Springing to mind were the sights and smells of the beachside cave where he had first clapped eyes on her. The mental picture of blackened, hollowed crab shells, charred bones and the strips of flesh curing over a smoky fire made him queasy. Beasts ate beasts, but that was scavenging. However, the notion of people killing beasts deliberately was unconscionable. How could one stomach the flesh of a creature after hearing the song of its soul?

What would come next? Harvesting people for food? Shudders sprang from the thought.

He lounged against the wall, studying her every movement as she ate, and privately mimicking the way her fingers made strange rituals over their selections. Every relished item she named in Ishglot while he reciprocated in Zmiysh. Progressing to objects and then to themselves, it was both surprising and thrilling to learn that many words were similar.

"Where's my belt?" she inquired with a motion.

Enok understood. The Zmee word was similar. From the grille beyond the room, he retrieved her holster of fangs. Each was intricately carved, and both capped and pointed with electrum. He watched attentively as she gave one a twist, and with a dip of a finger, began to daub herself behind the ears and nape of her neck. Oh the fragrance! The very soul of every orchid released in an instant!

"That flower water?"

"Flower oil, actually. From the desert rose. Do you like it?"

"Many times, yes."

"Here." She daubed a little on his wrist. "It's called perfume."

Enok partook shut-eyed of its fragrance, imagining himself roaming through the rain forest canopy. He had never smelled anything so wonderful.

Having opened another fang, Enok watched spellbound as the Isha smeared blue paste on her upper eyelids and, as if that were insufficient, proceed to draw a curved black line above the eyelash with a tiny bristle then down along the crease of the eye to end in a flourish.

Examining the fangs as she slept, he had assumed they were daggers. It was clear now that they were merely vessels. The embarrassing truth was that he been afraid of being murdered in his sleep, and so had placed them out of reach. One should never take chances with barbarians.

Now with her face arched forward, she was blinking slowly. "How's the kohl? Nice and neat?"

The meaning of this bewildering ritual escaped him. How was he to know what its outcome should have been? He shook his head and hoped that would suffice.

She scowled. At least he thought she did. The language of her face was somewhat different to a Zmee's.

From the same utility belt, the Isha produced what resembled two black shells and began rubbing them against her head. Falling bristles taught a lesson: barbarians denuded themselves in adornment. In the armpits too, he realized. He had often trimmed his own hair when it grew past the shoulders, though never to the scalp.

"You could use a cut as well, you know. Maybe shave your chin?"

"No." Enok nodded vigorously. "Enok do hair-face." Why destroy what nature intended?

"So it's a beard you're wanting to grow," she judged, half asking, half stating the obvious.

"Beard, yes, much." Finally, someone understood!

"Well for starters, this is a 'yes,'" she nodded slowly. "And this is a 'no,'" she demonstrated with shakes of the head. "You've been too long among the snakes," she noted with a curious gaze at his shackle. "Hmmm, too long indeed. That defines you, doesn't it? And you've lost your Y'lan."

"Not know Y-Y'lan."

"Y'lan: your native language: Ish-glot. Zmee hiss and blither, but we possess the true tongue. Anyhow, it will be a few years before the beard thickens. Trust me, it's just a nuisance till then." Then large but gentle fingers inspected his hair so softly he shivered. "So, have you never trimmed your hair?"

"Yes, I cut," he nodded mechanically, affirming. It felt so back-to-front.

"Well then, it's the same thing really, except on the face. Here, try one."

Enok eagerly accepted a shell, only to drop it yelping at the sight of his own blood.

"Careful, lost-boy! They're sharp. You've never *really* done this before, have you?"

Instinctively Enok nodded, then corrected with a shake of the head.

The Isha examined his finger before pressing her lips to it and sucking it clean. "Now I have some of you in me." She retrieved the razor, wiping it against her skirt with spittle. "Hold very still," she intoned, and holding his jaw with one hand, she proceeded to shave with the other. "It's been quite a while since I've done this myself. Don't want to mar those handsome jowls, eh?"

"Handsome?"

"Stop talking."

How warm were the hands and how gentle her touch came as a real surprise. The Isha's eyes were closer now than any in memory, and the most minute features were absorbing: the curve of her neck, the throb of her temple, the shape of an ear with its tiny, velvety fur. Her skin was smooth and unblemished. As she worked intently, something deep within him stirred.

Face completed, she began cropping his hair, pulling tufts taut with her left hand, and with a skilled scissor action, the right, to give him his first ever haircut at the hands of another. Her every movement was poetic under the narcotic rhythm of the grab-stretch-cut, grab-stretch-cut, as his hair was pulled first in one direction then another. Her naked midriff brushing him was pleasantly warm, yet strangely gave him shivers. The scent of perfume, mellowed by her chemistry, exceeded all the zephyrs of Land's Breath for sweetness, and he prayed this exquisite tension would last forever. This was bliss, and no dreamed girl of the night could top it.

The holiday of the mind ended abruptly when she pinned him with powerful hands. "Answer me truly, yes or no. Did you sight me naked?"

Enok trembled at this sudden souring. The caressing hands were now weapons at his neck. "Not understanding you."

"Naked. Without my clothes. The skin I was born with."

"Y-yes."

"I have every right to poison you for the offense, or by Havilan law you must best me in combat or die. And I have no intention of losing."

"Enok not live?"

"You saved my life, but you've dishonored me too, so my Goddess demands that you fight me. For the present, I repay my debt by reprieving you until we stand free again beneath her sky. We will not speak of this again. Say if you agree."

Her hands loosed their grip. Enok gulped and settled. What had begun as a wonderful encounter now filled him instead with dread. Would this barbarian murder him after all? He ought never have yielded her kit!

A shuffling by the portcullis.

The gholuj racketed out the window.

The barbarian dimensions of Naama were frightening and it had little to do with her size. Grateful for any excuse, Enok leapt from the chamber. Zelen had returned, and her pronouncement through the grille was the second jolt of the morning.

«Prepare!» "They come for you shortly."

Enok bowed. "It pleases me to see thee again."

«Not like that.» "You may address me informally. They found the Ish-beast you spoke of. As you warned, it's tremendously strong."

"I am glad thou believest — I mean, that you believe me now."

Naama peered over the partition. She and Zelen eyed each other silently, with stares clashing like weapons. Naama muttered something profane, *humphed*, and resumed her preening.

«Fearful,» twitched Zelen nervously. "This will almost certainly be my last chance to speak with you privately."

"Is the outlook that bad?"

"Before we managed to subdue it, the giant murdered six in your hometown of Zu'u-Shoran, and a number of j'Na-Zeru were badly wounded — three mortally. It's likely even the wounded won't survive. Moreover, the Upholder himself was very nearly killed."

"Zakon?" Enok wondered aloud. "That wasn't very helpful."

«Indeed not.» Zelen's expression was grim. "There will almost certainly be a mob at the inquest."

Enok blanched. "A mob?" Another new word, and with such portentous imagery.

"We Zmee pride ourselves on logic, but logic is a sensitive guest, and the larger the crowd, the less welcome it is. 'The solitary ember dies,' my Oracle once taught, 'but many such together make a smelting forge.'" A pause, then, "And so it is with bigotry. In this respect at least, I'm shamed to admit, our peoples could be very much alike."

Enok slumped to the floor. "I was hoping for *good* news."

"On behalf of my eggs, there is something I must tell you."

Another shuffle in the corridor distracted them. A stranger had appeared behind Zelen to slouch against a wall. It was Zaraza, the Zmee castaway that all were calling Newcomer.

"What ... you ... want?" Enok asked slowly in barbarian glot.

"Nothing, really," Zaraza replied. "Just observing." Her tendrils, however, were clearly laughing.

Naama emerged from the bedchamber, brushing trimmings off her shoulders. "I don't follow this snake-speak. Is there trouble?"

"Refa kill much Zmee."

"How many?"

Enok held up nine fingers.

"Only nine? Too bad."

Zelen asked about the Isha and what had just transpired.

Enok replied, "I think she says that was a bad thing to do."

"A barbarian with a soul? That's new. However, as you say, she seems saddened by the death of our people. Perhaps like the captive, Newcomer, she too is a victim. Or might she be one of the giants?"

"I don't know. But I am beginning to wonder why *I'm* so small."

It was then that Naama noticed Zaraza lying prostrate in the corridor. She kicked the grille with half-mumbled curses, summoning murrains upon the cripple before returning to her cubicle. Zaraza, however, kept laughing with her tendrils.

No harm could come of letting Zaraza remain. Since the Zmee tongue was alien to her, the pair continued as before.

"Servant, on New Year's Eve, at the graduation, what you attempted was evidence of either genius or madness, and I'm undecided as to which."

TRY DESPAIR, he wanted to say, but there was no Zmee word for it. "Settle for madness then."

"You see, I was the chief examiner."

"Oh," Enok blushed. "Forgive me, mistress. I didn't realize you were an Oracle."

"I like to build rather than teach. How an unschooled barbarian could perceive things that I myself had overlooked —"

"Please, I do not understand."

"'A barrow's wheel is a rotating lever,' you wrote. Rather insightful, I thought. I'm beginning to understand what my egg had been trying to tell me. But then, I had long given up on the plan and the old creed."

PLAN? CREED? Familiar words but empty of meaning.

«Fool.» "Anyway, it hardly matters anymore. What you did was extremely ill-considered, and now, whether you realize it or not, you have become the concern of the Chief Oracle of Law rather than the High Wisdom."

He shuddered at the memory of his last encounter with Ukhaz, that wizened, splenetic Lawmaker, though to what Zelen was alluding escaped him, and he said so. In return, she privately signed with her tendrils, pointing out that Zaraza might not be here by coincidence, and that the Ukhaz had explained his predicament to his very face on New Year's Eve.

«Remember?»

"Hrazul had been trying to explain something before she ... she died, though I never quite grasped it. For a cartographer she seemed to know a lot about ... well, everything. She would have made an ever greater Oracle of Maps than —"

«Not so.» "My egg was no maker of maps."

"But she became an Oracle. I saw it myself."

"You saw Wise-eye graduate, but her appointment came later, just before freeing the sky-lanterns. She become Hrazul Wise-eye, the Oracle of Ish. I'm surprised she never told you."

"We were ... cut short."

«So impatient!» "She lobbied hard to take you to the mainland with her, and she succeeded too, but then because of your —"

Enok groaned. How things could have been different! *"Please* don't say it."

"She had a curious notion that, with your help, our two peoples might learn to stop fearing each other." «Silly?»

"Not as crazy as some might think." While his future was poised now to smother him, there was sympathy here in the Zmee's great eyes. "We have to escape," he submitted. No other option remained.

«You and only you,» signed Zelen emphatically.

"The Isha has done no harm. Let her go."

"It's not in my power, Servant, you know that. At first light tomorrow, the boat ferrying pilgrims begins its circuit to the mainland. Do your utmost to be on it. It's your only —" She checked herself, realizing that Zaraza was still lying in the corridor. «Boat. Only hope. Zeruhawi. M-murder!»

The Zeruhawi were scheming to have him killed, she privately signed, and there would be no stopping them. But how could she be privy to all this, and yet with blameless tendrils?

"Where is the ... You know." Truly, there were times he wished for tendrils of his own.

«Much danger. Cavern beneath you.» As though in answer to an unframed question, she pressed her snout to the grill and beckoned him closer. "I'm Steam-maker. *The* boilermaker," she explained in a whisper.

"Listen," she continued. "A pair of upturned landing ferries at the rear of the vessel will shelter you. I will ensure they're provisioned and that no one ventures that way. How you get there — well, it's better I not know. On the morning of the third day after crossing the razor reefs, you will have raised a great river delta. The shoals at its head are your best chance for escape. It's littered with a thousand little islands, all perfect places to hide. If all goes to plan, none will ever suspect we had a stowaway."

"Thank you."

"Do you know what a boiler room is?"

Enok ventured, "It has steam-making vessels, I suppose."

«Yes.» "The steam is under great pressure and it spins the wheels of the … Never mind. Just watch out for the underwater paddles. They can chop you to pieces." At his quizzical gaze, she added, "There are four: two fore and two central." «Much danger.»

LIKE THE LEGS ON A YASH'KH, he mused, and while bowing gratefully, he noticed Zaraza was gone.

"Hmmm. Strange how the cripple slipped away so silently. However, if I may be so bold, the 'old creed' you mentioned earlier, I have never seen any parchments —"

"Oh, nothing's written. It's all chants and oral histories." Zelen became visibly uncomfortable. "And not exactly a topic for polite conversation, particularly among the younger Zmee, particularly around here."

Probing wasn't a servant's privilege, and generally earned a sterner rebuke than expressing a dozen misguided opinions. Enok bowed again. The habit was hard to break. "My apologies, Mistress."

After a moment's silence, blood rushed to the fine network of veins in her upper membranes, and she added, "The First Cause."

"First? Eh?"

"The belief that life, every nuance of life, has meaning: that there must be someone greater than ourselves, reveling in our achievements as it were, delighting not just in our delight but the very struggle itself, else all is dust and vanity. Your Southerners call that some-one-thing the First Cause — that force before whom all other causes must bow, from which all other causes derive. Six vespers for the blasphemy of even whispering its name — the sound of howling wind. My life needs no such complications now, though if I were truthful, I'd say rather obligations. A Methodic should be intellectually honest, especially to themselves."

Zelen sighed deeply, and her eyes took on a troubled look. "The Infinite Eternal? Without empirical evidence, how can you believe in that *and* some living corporeal locus? By any definition, there cannot be a finitude to infinity."

"Empirical? I don't follow."

«Oh? Ah. Sorry.» "Strange how I'm still arguing with a memory. Anyhow, I'm not expecting you to understand theology. I don't either." Her tendrils stiffened. "By Methodics, 'there are only atoms and the void.'" The statement lacked conviction, and her expression told more of resignation than belief. "Our lives grow shorter every morning. And I simply cannot wait —"

"Your egg believed in it," Enok ventured, "in the Cause."

«Yes.»

"And Sneak-tail too, I suppose."

«Does it matter?» "They're harmless, those Azhakh-Na, though secretive beyond belief! They built Zu'u-Shoran with a purpose. All your life they were working to a plan. Did you know? If you had not been so impatient —"

"Alright. Alright! Please, don't remind me."

Yet another shuffle in the passageway; the sight made him jump from the grille. Two guards with short-plumed verdigrised helmets had come escorting Ukhaz and Zakon, their animus instantly palpable. They were the Upholder's elite, warrior j'Na-Zeru.

«Oh?» "Steam-maker, what brings you here so soon?" Ukhaz inquired. «Oh yes!» "I should have known! You really do live up to your name, *Ever-curious.*"

"Do I really need permission to sign the death curse upon the slayer of my eggs?"

«Apologies.» "You were of the Azhakh-Na once, so, indeed, you have every right." Ukhaz slid aside, clearing the way.

Naama emerged to view the commotion, looking tense, eyes assaying the guards and with muscles rippling as if ready to pounce.

"Get back!" Zakon hissed as the guards leveled their tridents.

Enok tapped Naama on the arm — it was as tough as the walls of the cell — and gave her the scat-scat sign that she was so fond of dispensing.

"What's the red Zmee saying? I want to know," she growled, evading all his attempts to pull her from the entrance.

"You ... I ... back."

At the tip of a trident, Naama relented. As they retreated, the portcullis rose, squealing in protest until it completely disappeared into the ceiling.

Zakon half-entered the cell, brandishing a small bladed weapon in his one good hand. The other was heavily bandaged.

"Out! Out!" he growled. «Curious.» "Are there others here?"

Enok bowed a little. "Only the Isha and myself."

"There's a peculiar odor here," noted Zakon, tasting the air with both tongue and tendrils. "Something from memory, and it's not the camphor. Anyway, time to go." «Out! Out!»

Suddenly, Naama let shriek a savage cry and bolted past them all. A yelp from further up the corridor was proof, however, that more guards were posted and that escape was futile.

"I will lead," Zelen offered, motioning Enok to walk beside her.

With Zakon and his guards in the rear, he and Zelen followed Ukhaz to a phosphor-washed junction. The light from dying water-fire lanterns made it seem all the grander as its vaulted ceiling of intersecting arches yawned high into the darkness. So many tunnels met here! Six, maybe seven. Some went up, others down. But for some glyphs etched into arch-pillars, one could easily get lost in this warren.

And in a side tunnel, Naama's squeals echoed madly from beneath a mound of Zmee that must have been tasked with fettering her.

After that, it was all downhill for what seemed an age, and all in utter silence. The whitewashed walls with their stuccoes of flowers and mythical scenes gave way at last to a typical Zmee entrance with its pale blue render and overarching benediction.

The party emerged into morning's light, onto a broad red-graveled expanse reminiscent of his hometown common. Everything here, though, was colossally grander. Magnificent buildings ringed the plaza, some with towering spires that jabbed the very sky.

However, where he expected the slender and open form of the Rotunda, there stood instead a massive structure rendered alien by its sharp geometry and size. It was as big as a mountain, dwarfing anything he had ever seen, and free of any hint as to content or purpose. Like the almanac back in Zu'u-Shoran, it was a smooth pyramid of gleaming white stone. Its apex glimmered like gold in the ruddy light of early day. At its base, two doubly serpentine obelisks of contrasting granite, the Twain Serpents, stood guard before a rectangular opening at the head of a long and elegant ramp.

Also like home, the focus of the city common was the dais. That four broad ramps cut through its three encircling steps was familiar, but the edifice as a whole was so monumentally larger.

Its pyramidal almanac, instead of being central, was at the far perimeter, and it seemed comparatively ancient. In a flash, Enok understood. This was the original upon which the one in his home-town was patterned. Just shy of the perimeter, on the nearer side of the dais, a squat cluster of four inward leaning pillars framed a sort of pyramid in outline.

"This certainly isn't Zu'u-Shoran," Enok grabbled.

«Obviously not,» returned Zelen.

Enok sighed. That was hardly informative. He must have been transported over some great distance here while unconscious. That would explain his drugged condition. But transported to where? Recognizing Hrazul in Zelen, that general desire to explain every-thing, he ventured,

"That building, the pyramid topped with gold, it's clearly not a library."

"It's a smaller version of the Zul-Al-Kahhri temple, though with origins lost to history."

Awesome, he wanted to say, but the sheer scale of the structure left him speechless. Naama too was taken with it. The sacred temple on Mount Ur-Atu was said to be grand indeed, so if this was the child, imagine the parent!

Zelen bent her gaze on him, with public words but private tendrils. "It keeps the most sacred relics." «Fifty years past.» "Sealed by the High Wisdom." «No explanation.»

When Zakon growled, "And I've reopened it," it ignited Enok's interest even more.

Reopened?

In this first experience of a foreign city, Enok had a thousand questions that a servant could never ask. He had learned, however, to pose them in roundabout ways.

He only managed to say, "I suppose it has a name," before a trident forced him up a ramp and onto the dais.

Zelen responded, though with a peculiar look, as if surprised he didn't know.

"Indeed," she confirmed. "It's the Reliquary."

EPISODE 11

THE CRUCIBLE OF NOW

Enok finds himself paralyzed with indecision at the most crucial moment of his life ... The giant youth frees himself, and with catastrophic consequences ... An elevated Zakon sentences Naama and Enok to death.

ZU'U-SHORAN HAD SEEMED SO GRAND as a boy, but now by comparison, the world of the isthmus seemed barely a village. This new city was so much larger on every scale, crowded, and teeming with life. For the small-town visitor, the smolder of distant alchemy rendered it all the more unsettling.

For visitors to the south, Enok was more a novelty than the Prime Mapmaker's servant, and he was kept so busy as to be rarely sighted at all. Among the locals of Zu'u-Shoran, however, whether he was skittering along with parchments, trimming among the espaliers, or stomping in the ink vats, his presence only merited the fleeting glance one might spare upon some transient bird. There, he was as much a fixture as its tidal blowhole, its coppered rotunda, or its great festive kites. He was a slave whose diligent labors had earned him at least some tolerance as benign. And there was some comfort in knowing that even indolents forced to remedial slavery ranked lower than he. Wherever this new city was, though, he was none of those here.

Enok paused briefly at the edge of the dais, absorbing the measures of this strange new place, and wondering where he might be among all of Zoar's cities. The earthiness of the air and the moss-grown pediments of the colonnades leading into the plaza brought to mind the swamplands of the island's deep interior. Indeed, beyond the great reliquary and the flat-leaved pines of the neighboring hills loomed an even grander forest. This was a place of lingering mists and towering tree ferns, great spreading cycads, and despite the redolence of industry, blossoms of the fabled thaakh trees heavily scented the air.

Measure for measure, the northern port of Zu'u-Susyaan would be neither so lush nor so humid. Like the mines and forges of Yashau-Zaar, it was mostly subterranean, though Zu'u-Susyaan's network of tunnels and caverns were supposedly blessed with sweeping views over the grand canal made famous for its tidal bore. That left only Ra'a-Zohari and Ur-Hozhai as contenders. The latter was renown for its vanilla-scented orchids, exotic blooms, and nectar-loving hover moths. It was a garden city. Both were coastal metropolises edged by grand forests and equally mazed with aqueducts, or so he had read. For now, it was impossible to decide between them.

However, politics now subsumed all geography, for the sights were veritably spine tingling. Zeruhawi pennants hung from balconies and rooftops everywhere, and in the distance, nervous eyes descried the spiral cupolas of elevated lookouts daubed likewise in the infamous red-and-black. This was surely the mother nest of the Zeruhawi, the haters of all Ish-kind.

The display was clearly recent, for even Zelen, who lived locally, baulked at the flags. Then, in a manner all too familiar, neither signing nor speaking, she partook of his image as though etching its very memory. She and Hrazul were so much alike.

Zakon's j'Na-Zeru were a touchy pair. Their red-and-black armbands should have been warning enough. Do nothing to provoke them, he ought to have cautioned, for one especially enjoyed needling Naama.

TOO LATE!

The sight of her own bleeding elbow frenzied her, and she lunged at the culprit's tendrils, dragging them down to where her angry heel met their serpent eye. However, before a second heel found its mark, the rear guard butted her and sent her sprawling. Naama was unconscious, even as they dragged and bound her to the pillars.

Ropes of copper filament hemp and secured with a screw-lock made almost a web through her fetters. While she may have had a hand free, without a key or a saw-toothed blade, Naama had little hope of escape.

A third guard, and strangely, a Civil, likewise tethered him to a pillar but on a surprisingly long and rather ordinary lead. Also surprising was the extensive matting underfoot and how it nearly carpeted the entire platform. Such was reserved for dignitaries, and they were hardly that!

The sore-eyed guard tested all the restraints, signing «Vermin!» before jabbing Naama in the rump and joining her partner on a lower step. They smacked the stone in unison with the butt of their tridents before coiling to a formal pose.

Along the spiral ramps that circled their towers, Zmee in countless hundreds began descending single file in bursts like condensing green fog, trickling ever downward towards the throng in the common. As the multitude swelled, gliders from nearby lookouts joined their egg-sisters on porches and roofs overlooking the plaza. The solemn hush of the morning gave way to a muted buzz of excitement that grew steadily louder until it became a cacophony. The cacophony settled to a drone resembling a musical chord, waxing and waning like the waves on a beach. Zmee everywhere swayed to its rhythm.

Never had Enok seen so many serpents crammed together, or behaving so peculiarly. Tendril followed tendril until countless hundreds bristled equally:

«One in tendril,
One in hand,
We'll purge the Ish from every land.»

Swollen as it had been with Zeruhawi agitators, the crowd at New Year's Eve had been intimidating; however, this was positively frightening, for here was the suspension of the very rationality that Zmee claimed to laud. They had surrendered to a baser self exactly as Zelen had foreseen. This was a mob.

When Naama woke muttering, it was reassuring at first, but her next words proved chilling. "I don't know if you perceive what I do, serpent-boy," she began, massaging her neck, "but they certainly mean to have us by sundown. And I'd sooner torch my mother than die without a fight." Salivaed fingers wiped her elbow of blood. "And what are all these green-skins doing here, anyway?"

They were all females. What was she expecting? Fear could often muddy one's thinking. Was she afraid? "Mothers," Enok explained, searching for the right words. "Mother Zmee be that."

"Oh, so females are always green? And that the red bull there — are there no other males?"

"No," he replied, a little puzzled, and indicating a height with a hand. "Only little Zmee."

Criers began to space themselves on the lowest step of the dais. A backwards-facing hearing-horn and a funnel-shaped mouthpiece melded into a single contortion of brass that transformed their heads into something weirdly alien, clumsy, indeed comical.

At the clangor of far-flung gongs, a startled gholuj of a nearby portico led a cloud of her fellows to flight. Secondary criers now slid through the crowd, taking positions on conical pedestals, and gongs resounded again to herald what the criers termed The Beast. A commotion from behind the almanac was next to be seen as a trio of j'Na-Zeru goaded a shrieking khwatl onto the platform. It struggled, lathered, against the sheer mass of its burden, a heavy three-wheeled wagon with a long central beam. Refa's lifeless body hung from it like a trophy.

Khwatl weren't native to Zoar, and the few that roamed the reserves of Sha-Noa all looked much alike, but even muzzled and blinkered, this terror bird bore an uncanny resemblance to Chiruk, his bluff-land pet.

However, it was Refa that drew Naama's sympathy. "Take heart, brave one!" she cried. "Today we enter the Halls of the Fallen!" But the boy-giant made no reply.

"He is killed?"

"Don't be daft," Naama spat. "He's not dead."

The absence of blood on the cart boded well. Refa might yet be alive. "He's not dead," Enok mimicked lamely. Though how could she tell?

Chirr-awk! Chirr-awk!

The khwatl squawked miserably under goading from tridents. Despite their fearsome appearance, khwatl were gentle, solitary creatures that preferred the refuge of forest. It trembled violently, and as a blinder came free it caught sight of Enok with a pain-filled eye. It was indeed Chiruk.

"Chiruk!" cried Enok, "Chiruk! Hush now! Be steady!"

And the prodding guards parked Refa's cart directly across the dais, chocking its wheels as best as Chiruk's tottering allowed.

Then loud and long rang the gongs again as the criers introduced the Shav'yat, the Council of Oracles, who then settled at the foot of the almanac. The ceremonial vestments of their respective offices took form in feathered miters and decorative vests or collars. Most were from Zu'u-Shoran, but to his amazement, Zelen had reappeared in downy white armbands and a matching cap rimmed with black pearls and sporting plumage salvaged from, of all things, Hrazul's graduation necklace. He would never have guessed that she too was a councilor.

LIKE EGG-BEARER, LIKE EGG, went the old Southern saying.

An ancient Zmee propped by the speaker's scepter slid forward. It was the same Convener from the New Year's Eve ceremony. The scepter itself was more like a staff, and crowned with a four-legged serpent in shape of a wheel. She spread her wings and raised her free hand skyward until all chatter subsided.

"In the name of the Great Zhmee, our prime forebear; in the name of Zulyi, our ancient savior; in the name of orthodox civilization and all Zmee: I adjure silence upon all until the witnesses and the Council have spoken." A gong rang solemnly. "Be assured, all you present, that justice will be seen to prevail this day. We are gathered here and now to consider both the guilt and the fate of all these Ish."

Enok was clearly the object of her ire, for she added chillingly while meeting his gaze, "To the guilty, the law is a trident, but to the innocent, a shield."

Trident? Shield? Hadn't Hrazul voiced similar thoughts?

As the criers broadcast the address, much of the crowd wagged agreement. Thereafter, a thick silence descended on the plaza. All tendrils fell limp, and all eyes were on the dais. Ukhaz, the Chief Oracle of Law, outlined the order of the proceedings, then summoned Sneak-tail to testify. Sliding past, young Snei ignored him. Not that he'd ever valued her opinion, but he found himself crushed by the snub. He was incapable of murder, especially of Hrazul. Surely she ought to have known that by now.

Ukhaz began the interview. The crowd hung on every word from the criers. "So, from your position on the bluff, you saw nothing of the giant at all, did you? Yes, or no."

Snei had barely replied, "No," before struck with:

"But it was the Ish slave that you saw lancing the youngling as she struggled for her last breath, her innocence rent by such a heinous betrayal."

Snei looked pained. «Uncertain.» "I had come as the Upholder's guide. I saw only Servant standing over ... its hands on the weapon."

"Yes, or no."

"Yes," barely came out before:

"But the slave never had such a weapon previously, did it?"

«Uncertain.» "I do not recall —"

"Yes, or no."

"No."

"So it appears that the giant stranger must have given the slave the weapon, that they were in collusion. Yes, or no."

"It would seem —"

"Yes, or no!" prompted Ukhaz while signing «Yes! Yes! Yes!»

Every question was an insinuating thread, and with each success-ive strand, Ukhaz was twining a slanderous noose. Whatever an inquest was meant to be, there was nothing of fairness here.

Enok's vexation erupted. "You're promoting your own opinions above the actual facts!"

Ukhaz returned a withering stare as dark as her ebony feathers. "Am I not the Prime Lawmaker here? Guards! Silence the animal!"

The Upholder, too, gave his version of events.

Ukhaz probed, "Was the giant Ish nowhere to be seen?"

"I saw no others, except the Isha with the cripple." Before Ukhaz could insist on a 'yes or no' answer, Zakon added, "Yes."

"And speaking of caves and castaways, that must have been the slave's lair. Yes, or no."

Enok's roar needed no criers. "That was not my lair!"

"Hush now, or die, beast!" hissed a j'Na-Zeru, forcing him to his knees with a trident at his neck. "Its turn to speak will come." «If it's still alive!»

This was looking increasingly like the preamble to an execution rather than a simple inquest. He dearly hoped that Oracle Zoia and Zelen would speak up for him, and he sought reassurance from Naama. She seemed curiously detached, though, and had removed her sandals to sit cross-legged on the matting, yawning strangely in some mute barbarian rite. But following her gaze, he came to realize she was pulling faces, and that Refa was awake and reciprocating.

They were mouthing words.

An unfamiliar Oracle displayed remnants of the shipwreck found near the giant's cave. The Convener introduced her merely as Shipwright, but such was Y'shur's renown, everyone knew of the Oracle of Ships.

"This was once part of a vessel," Shipwright pronounced while holding high a bundle of reeds. "A reconstruction of the wreckage found strewn along the peninsula shows that it was little more than pontoons and netting: a flimsy, clumsy construction. I once saw at a distance river-dwelling Ish use reed in this way, but the original size of this wreck would have dwarfed anything built heretofore. This was not some river-craft gone astray but a first attempt at an ocean-going vessel — not unlike our own first barges, if memory serves me rightly."

As the criers kept repeating 'ocean-going' for dramatic effect, a scarred Zmee took the speaker's scepter. Her perforated eyewear shielded sensitive eyes from sunlight, giving her an almost insectoid appearance. Here was First Metalsmith from the forges of the Yashau-Zaar deeps. Much of what she went on to say was in long-winded jargon, but for the captive raised on contrary truths, her summary was liberating: his people could hardly be the savages that folktales so loved to malign.

Enok thought on his companion. She was neither fool nor primitive, and grasped new concepts as quickly as any Zmee.

The smith: "... and so the Ish have learned to smelt ores, and brass is the product of no small metallurgy. Even more interesting was the metal sliver housed in amber — and Ssla forgive me! — that always settles on south. "But what disturbs me most are its markings: they're indisputably Zmiysh."

She paused as the criers conveyed her words, allowing their gravity to have its effect.

As a buzz spread through the crowd, she held a jeweled and enameled dagger high for all to see. Its gems sparkled in the light. "If you doubt my words," her voice faltered, "this alone should convince any skeptic. The craft-work is intricate beyond anything I've ever seen, surpassing even what our own two-thumbed hands could achieve. Their culture is a curious amalgam of the most primitive and the most sophisticated. The only way any of this can possibly make sense is if … if …"

ZAKON HAD ALREADY TESTIFIED AND was now merely a spectator amidst the Shav'yat, albeit one anxiously tugging his tendrils. Every fresh revelation unnerved him. What had begun as simply a risk, was now an imminent barbarian threat.

Great Zhmee! What was he to do?

The din from the plaza was rising as the crowds were reaching their own conclusions. The Convener flagged the criers to desist, beckoning the Oracles to the almanac for a private discussion.

«Confess!» the Convener demanded. "You are being disruptive, you mine-worm! What exactly are your intentions?"

"A third force has arisen," Zhaal the Metalsmith asserted. "It's the only explanation. I merely voice the truth."

Ukhaz glowered at her. «By my oath! I swear retribution!» "Since when is truth for the public? We agreed to keep this private!"

«Defiance!» "This is too important!" Zhaal hissed. "This is way beyond me, and certainly you! Am I supposed to keep this from my egg-sisters? Not on my life!"

«Life ends,» Ukhaz signed with a stare that could kill.

"I must say, Smithy," a Northerner sneered, "your 'third force' hypothesis is absurd. The barbarians are thieves. That's all I see."

"The smith speaks true," the shipwright averred, "as any with sense will agree. The Ish reek of primitivity, except their metals and that Ssla-insulting direction finder. They are permeated with Zmee influence, for on so many artifacts we find either the image of a Zmee or markings in our ancient script."

«Thievery! Simple thievery!» signed the Northerner.

Zakon met Ukhaz's angry stare just as she erupted, "Great genius is hardly required to identify this mysterious 'third force.'"

«Who?»

«The Males!» replied Ukhaz. «Yes! YES!»

«Impossible!» Even the Convener could scarce believe it. "Zmee and Ish cooperating?" «Never!»

«Absurd!» Zakon signed. "My egg-brothers on the mainland would never willingly —"

A hoary voice interjected. "Why only males, and what makes you think they were willing?"

All eyes were on the High Wisdom as she emerged from a huddle with intimates. She signed privately to Mapmaker Zoia, who then melted away. "What is clear to me," she continued, "is that some tribe of the Ish have forced our people to labor. These artifacts and the captive cripple, a stranger to her own tongue, are proof enough of slavery. Have we not all wondered why fewer each year answer the great call to Ur-Atu? Colony after colony has fallen silent, and with not even a whisper as to why. In these barbarians we may yet find the answer."

Shipwright's hands and tendrils gestured emphatically. "This is all very academic," she complained, forestalling any objection, "but you, High Wisdom, and all the councilors have missed the central point."

«WHICH IS?» signed Ukhaz impatiently.

"Though having built a means to do so, they were unprepared for what they found. Don't you see? They *chose* to come here."

Ukhaz was livid. Her black-feathered miter nearly fell from her crown. "But that barbarian script was just Mapmakers' code! Who now dares deny a conspiracy? And where has that Mapmaker gone?"

Snei leapt to the defense of her Oracle. "You suspect the Ish know the secret of Zoar, and there's little more we could add to it, except to say that it's a supposition, nothing more. More likely, the currents took them where they least expected." Embarrassed by her outburst, she bowed.

«Is that so?» Zakon eyed her suspiciously, then reconsidered. She was merely showing devotion to her Oracle. He could hardly reproach her for that. Only Xira had ever been as faithless as Xira. "But, one is left to wonder," he mulled, pausing for thoughts to crystallize, "how *did* they learn of Zoar if not from a map? Or some cartographer's tendril?"

"By the Great Hallowed Zhmee, I can guess whose!" Ukhaz was now eyeing the High Wisdom. «The Azhakh-Na!»

"Perhaps these were just a scouting party," someone piped. "We urgently need to assay if more barbarians are coming!"

«Indeed!» «Exactly!» The question was on everyone's tendrils — all except the High Wisdom's. She was strangely serene, pondering, oblivious to the doom-saying. But given the great mask that covered everything except her tendrils, who could really say?

And now the old Lawmaker was boring her gaze into Zoia's slave, fuming under her breath. Everyone, it seemed, was the object of her suspicion today. She had once held the office of Upholder — enforcer, judge and executioner — and reviled the Ish even more than himself. She really was skilled at hating, and her tendrils were now so agitated he could almost read her thoughts:

THE SLAVE! WHO BUT MAPMAKERS HAVE ACCESS TO MAPS? AND WHO BUT AN ISH WOULD BETRAY THEM?

But the question of an invasion was moot. As the Upholder, his concerns were more immediate. He considered Zoia's slave and wondered what had ever happened to its sire. After years of searching, no one really knew. Maybe it escaped back to the mainland, as unlikely as that was. Or perhaps there really were spies here, right now, on Zoar.

NO, NOT SPIES, he decided, but something irredeemably worse. TRAITORS!

A COMMOTION BY THE GRAND LYCEUM at the plaza's edge caught Enok's attention. One of the criers had reversed her great mouth-horn into a hearing aid, and with help from the ear-flute, had eavesdropped on the huddle of Oracles, distilling their conversation. As chaos spread like a wave, Zakon kept striking the gong with the butt of a trident to arrest the burgeoning uproar. The huddle of Oracles dissolved. The criers coiled to attention.

"Noble brood of Zmiya! How easily you forget your own superiority! Let these Ish die, then let's bolster our defenses. Should more barbarians come, then it's a war at sea, and there we reign supreme."

He made a deliberate show of laughing. "Ha! An invasion on such flimsy reed pontoons? Most won't even make landfall — and as for the rest, well, fine dining for the crabs!"

ZAKON WAS RIGHT, thought Enok. A seaborne invasion could never succeed, and not just because of the reefs. Zmee were more adroit in the water than out, and nigh impossible to drown. But why would anyone want to invade Zoar anyway? And what had the private meeting been about? The Shav'yat seemed severely troubled, and Ukhaz, that malevolent Chief Oracle of Law, was eyeing him as if he, a mere servant, were the very cause of it all.

Silence fell across the common as the High Wisdom, the Grand Oracle of Oracles herself, slid forward and motioned for the criers to resume. For a brief moment, their eyes met, and in them he saw Zelen's great sympathetic ovals.

"We must remember," she bayed in a sonorous tone, "that this gathering is an inquest, not a public debate or a council of war. From the outset, the accused maintained that another stranger had also come ashore, as subsequent events proved."

The scepter drew all eyes to the slung form of the giant, and Enok thought it curious that first the time in history, she was speaking plainly, and not in her usual High Zmiysh.

"Who is accountable for dismissing the warning?" she continued, lancing Zakon with a look. "And how did the barbarians slip past the patrols? And in such a shoddy craft? Isn't that exactly what reef reconnaissance is supposed to prevent? That was sloppy work indeed, unless, of course, someone foiled the preventing."

Another rash of murmurs broke out on the common. Ukhaz and Zakon exchanged furtive glances.

"Thus far we've heard only the Lawmaker's assertions. However, we have assembled here today to consider all perspectives — from aye-sayer and nay-sayer alike," the matriarch boomed. "Moreover, I believe the results of the Healer's truth-saying potion will interest you all, as Steam-maker will testify. You see, the issues before us are not as one-sided as some would have us believe. We are all Zmee, are we not? Do we not all value reason above instinct? Upon the slayers and those found to be complicit ..."

Enok could swear he saw the High Wisdom exchange a mean look with Ukhaz. What politics were in play here?

"… justice will surely fall."

Rowdy disagreements exploded across the common. Patrolling j'Na-Zeru hectored the crowd till they settled.

"Servant," a guard addressed him. "It's time to speak."

After a reverent bow to the council, Enok relived the events of that fateful morning, sparing neither his emotions, his privacy, nor his dignity. He gave them the unembellished truth without wilting under Ukhaz's harangue.

"I've never willingly hurt anybody, as all Zu'u-Shoran knows. Besides, see for yourselves the size of the barbarian! If it's true that a dozen Zmee perished and the Upholder himself was very nearly slain, what aid could I, at half its size, possibly have rendered?"

Ukhaz pressed her interrogation. "So, the servant denies it was protecting the Isha in its lair?" The tip of her tail quivered anxiously. "Yes, or no."

"I had never seen the so-called lair until that day."

«Yes, or no!» the black-feathered Lawmaker kept prompting with her tendrils.

"It was so cleverly concealed. I only discovered it by following the giant's trail."

"Answer, yes, or no!"

"I had assumed that he dug it out of the cliff face, but the layout was typically Zmee."

Ukhaz's tendrils curled in a smirk. «He? Who?»

Enok pointed to the hanging giant.

"Yes — or no!" the Lawmaker insisted.

"That's not a 'yes or no' answer! *He* is Refa."

«Aha!» "The accused knows it by name? By its *personal name?*" Ukhaz was delighted. She bypassed the criers, shouting directly at the crowd. "See the intimacy? Judge for yourselves!"

With a nod from the Convener, the criers paused and the crowd slipped to murmuring again. A menacing trident urged him back to the pillar, and a spiteful tug on the cord tripped him up, forcing him to crawl.

"I haven't finished!" he growled at the guards.

Jeers of "Spy!" and "Liar!" and widespread hooting, however, drowned his every protest. "These animals must die!" a crier trumpeted. "To harbor the Ish imperils us all!"

The thousand angry insults struck Enok like a wall. The crowd was fast becoming a mob again. A hurled stone narrowly missed him, and Ukhaz, that black-feathered dragon, was wearing the wickedest of grins.

The Steam-maker Zelen then took up his defense and gave her reading of recent events. That might explain her visits, Enok thought, to satisfy herself that defending him was no betrayal of her egg Hrazul.

As she was speaking, he noticed Refa had chewed through his bindings, and was now flexing his fingers, his face contorted and ugly. For the second time in a six-day, Enok found himself frozen with indecision. Unless he alerted the Zmee, Refa would be free any moment, and mayhem was certain.

Naama's eyes met his. Her furrowed brows and a slight shake of the head were a kind of covert gesture.

SHE KNOWS, he realized, BUT COMMANDS TO RAISE NO ALARM!

But how could he not? His mind churned with the weight of his dilemma. Whose side was he on anyway?

They crowd had relish for neither truth nor Zelen's eloquence. Their hiss and the beat of their wings were now deafening, even drowning out the criers. With very little prompting, this mob would choke him with their bare hands, law or no law. Were these to be his egg-sisters, or the barbarians who shared his fate? Here was that crucible moment, the irrevocable choice between loyalties. But why this pick between race and race, instead of friend and foe?

A call from the High Wisdom galvanized a Civil behind her. "Summon the Reef Scouts!"

Lawmaker Ukhaz, more vexed than ever, wrenched the speaker's scepter from Zelen and signaled a break to the criers.

"Game of the snakes! What plot now stews by your hand, Grand First Causer! Ish religion is rooted in Hra-Adin, there at the Great Rejection! The First Cause drove them out like the vermin they are! I know your secret beliefs!" Ukhaz now leveled the scepter at Enok. "And the insolent beasts blame us! Deny that, barbarian!"

The Lawmaker was clearly enraged, but her words were empty of meaning. Where was this Hra-Adin and why were Zmee and Ish together there anyway? Had they once been friends? Was Hra-Adin the original wellspring of hatreds?

"So, even by their own accounts," continued Ukhaz with spasming tendrils, "their own deity hates them. In return, these flesh-eaters hate both themselves and us!" «Ha!» "They even rage against the very One you Azhakh-Na revere! But we are of sky and they are of earth. Peace between the races —"

Her last words, however, were never relayed.

Crashing to the platform, the giant boy had broken loose of his bindings, and with surprising speed, slipped his feet free of the beam.

A nearby guard had realized too late what had happened. She had aimed the trident, preparing to shoot, but the giant had crouched and pulled the handle of the weapon from below, and flipping it over, engaged all its triggers.

Three darts: three victims. One had caught the guard in the throat, its partner toppled Zelen, leaving a viscous blue streak be-tween her eyes.

With a shrieking battle cry, Refa had hurdled over the fallen guard's body, impaling Ukhaz amid-speech upon the blunt of the trident through the soft underside of her jaw.

All this in a heartbeat.

Now completely berserk, he roared again, filling the air with curses.

Two more Civils rushed low at him with the Zmee cry of victory. "Khozaa!"

He sidestepped one, deftly hurling her into the solid forward wheel of the cart with a sickening crunch, and impaling her skull upon the spike of her own crushed helmet.

Her lagging partner fired all her darts in a stroke, and a barb caught the giant in the shoulder. He stumbled, howling, then yanked it free and flung it back, striking the Zmee in the eye. She shrieked, letting slip the empty weapon. The boy-giant seized it, snapped it in half, and plunged a jagged stake into her neck, and its brother into an onrushing Oracle. Blue serpent blood shot him in the face.

Two of Zakon's j'Na-Zeru that had sped for the dais from arear were intercepted by an agitated Chiruk who had panicked in the melee and slipped free of the muzzle. In a vicious snap, the lizard-bird dismembered a guard, sending limb and buckler flying.

The injured j'Na-Zeru shrieked, tumbling into the barbarian boy, while her squealing partner fought off Chiruk's pitiless beak.

Refa pithed the handless serpent with a broken haft, and in moments had acquired two more tridents. Bedlam erupted on the common as he discharged one bolt after another into the Oracles: six darts, and then as many dead.

Naama was on her feet, shrilling barbarian curses with mock kicks and one-handed swipes through the air. A crier, shot in the back, fell to the gravel. Darts of return fire whizzed across the platform. A wild projectile struck the khwatl. With an agonized screech and a mighty back-kick, the harness tore and the bird leapt free of the wagon and into the crowd, severing limb and tendril from any hapless serpent in its path.

Meanwhile, Enok forced the amazon to crouch between the stubby columns as more darts fired of onrushing guards streaked overhead, heedless of whom they might strike. A buckler from a severed arm he held high as their only protection. Sparks flew off the sheltering posts as wild darts ricocheted.

Valiant commoners intent on caging the barbarian took flight as j'Na-Zeru and militia rushed the platform. A lone Reef Scout with a serrated spontoon joined the Civil corralling Enok and Naama, blocking their view. Before the carnage was completely occluded, Refa toppled from a great bleeding gouge in his back and a dart lodged in his skull. Beyond his prostrate form, a discharged trident showed briefly from behind the large forward wheel of the cart, and held by a sanguine hand.

A spear point scraped Enok's nose. "Stay put," the Civil warned, "or share the dead barbarian's fate." «Only faster!»

"Dead? I don't think —" Enok choked at the press of weapon.

Tossing the buckler aside, Naama leapt up to encourage the boy. "Go on, Refa! Go on! One more for the gods!"

Enok was shocked and confused. "Why ... Refa ... kill Zmee!?"

"Six hells for the coward!" Kohl streaked her cheeks. "But to die with your blood afire is to free your soul for the afterworld!"

Whatever the meaning of 'coward,' she seemed to admire this wanton ruin. She was beautiful — and like him, she could cry! — but sadly, with all this talk of blood and gods, she remained every jot the barbarian.

"Gol! Gol!" cried the giant, coughing up blood, and marshaling his energies to rise. However, the doughtiest of Zakon's j'Na-Zeru blindsided the giant with the stub of a weapon, sending the half-staved face earthward with a spray of broken teeth. "Finally ... I am ... free," he wheezed, then whatever else the youth attempted faded with the spreading crimson of his soul as it mingled with the spilth of his victims.

Naama stiffened, and uttered softly, "You gave your blood in honor, boy, and conquered your tormentor. Be at peace now, and rest forgiven."

"Refa changing now to be gods?"

"What? No, Enok. Refa *is* a god, or rather a godling. As a Son of the Gods, he always was."

"Help me!" Zakon squealed from beneath a knot of corpses, summoning reluctant Civils to untangle him. His blue blood sprayed in squirts between fingers as he clutched at a wicked barb in his arm. "Imbeciles! Forget defilement! Grab a dead crier's horn and call for One-eye! Now! Before I bleed out completely!" [xxxix]

Still pressing his wound, Zakon nudged Refa's crumpled form sideways with his tail, satisfying himself that his enemy was truly dead. On his orders, guards rolled the corpse off the platform in some urgent act of cleansing.

"We need neither witnesses nor testimony," Zakon hissed. "The inquest is over."

Enok steeled himself at Zakon's approach.

Blood still dripped through the fingers of a wrist-clutching hand. Rage smoldered in his eyes, and his tendrils, betraying his thoughts, were signing the same words repeatedly. They were anguished and difficult to make out, and tense moments passed before they registered.

«Final ... verdict ... death!»

---

xxxix *Defilement:* To touch the dead, their blood, or things attached, renders a Zmee and all ensuing contacts ritually unclean, and generally forbidden from food and civic duty until after three days of ablutions.

WAKE, YE LIVING STONES

A relic of a lost age comes dazzlingly and unexpectedly to life ... The boy-giant is not of his own race after all, Enok realizes ... Zakon experiences firsthand the ancient forces of the Ascending Way, and is shocked by what he finds.

MOST ZMEE HAD FLED FOR dear skin and few now remained on the common. Refugees from Chiruk's rampage crowded nearby rooftops and the distant shrieks of frantic serpents were a telling reminder that its massive aquiline beak was still wreaking havoc somewhere in the city.

The High Wisdom lay crumpled at the base of the almanac, blood-spattered but clearly alive. Her headpiece was intact, but her great gilt frill-necked mask had been ripped from her face and broken. The features long hidden from public view twitched feebly in her vain attempt to rise.

«Help ... me.»

Enok was amazed. If not for the heavier tendrils, he would have mistaken her for a youngster! Sure, her length and membranes were elder-dark, but her complexion was smooth and verdant bright, possessing an ageless beauty. Why, then, the eternal mask? What could there possibly be to hide?

He explained Zakon's pronouncement to Naama. She struggled vainly against the shackles, muttering all manner of things, few of which made any sense.

"Latrine worms! Bahalazh eaters! When Gol learns of this outrage," she was livid, swiping her palms through the air like a blade, "he'll raze this snake-infested cesspit! Oh, Goddess! Enok, mind the blood!"

The carpet was sponging in patches from the blue-green blood of the slain. Enok instinctively leapt and leapt again in revulsion to land upon a clear plot of stone, and amazed, despite all the stray darts, that his own crimson had kept to its skin.

Nearby, Zakon was crouching over the lifeless body of Ukhaz, his tendrils twitching like anguished snakes, and with a sharp intake of breath was swelling in volume and rage at the pronouncement:

"*I* am the Prime Lawmaker now, as well as its Upholder; indeed, and all that remains of the Shav'yat. The decree of this inquest: these prisoners must die!"

Snei, bruised but alright, assisted the High Wisdom to rise. "Upholder, we all want justice," she faltered under the weight of the old matriarch, "but do you alone ... have the right —"

Rearing high, Zakon cut her short. «No more argument!» "Look around you, young Mapmaker. All the other councilors are dead, and I have made my decision! No more lives will be risked on account of these perfidious barbarians!"

"What about assembling a new council? Surely the law —"

«Naïve youngling!» "Will the outcome will be any different?" He waved a spent trident, showing its empty breeches. "My egg-brothers on the mainland are at war. Between the two races there is no peace, and whether we like it or not, the war has come to us." In a fit of rage, he struck the fallen gong once, twice, and a third time and calling in High Zmiysh to the rooftops, "How cry ye, egg-sisters? How cry ye? Spare Zoar, or spare the Ish?"

"But if Servant is a sapient ... and innocent ... then we have no right to just take its life ... *his* life ... without good cause," Snei stammered, then meeting Zakon's challenging eyes, her reply rang equally loud. "It's over! The barbarian slayer is dead! Don't you see? If we act like it, we become like it! Upholder — my lord! — surely you must know that."

"Better than you," returned Zakon, looking more tormented than ever. "This is hardly some game of zhakh, youngling, but a profoundly simple equation. All Ish are barbarians. These are Ish: these are barbarians. I fight for our very existence! Remember, war now shrouds you too. So, what are *you* fighting for? However," he continued, smugly routing her come-back, "I won't be soiling myself with their deaths. As you say, that would be," a wry smile crept into his tendrils, "uncivilized. Let the sea dispense its justice by its own eternal laws."

The comment was cryptic, his expression chilling. The guards chuckled. They seemed to know exactly what Zakon had in mind. For a moment, though, Enok had been proud of Snei. Defiant and unyielding, she had spoken with conviction instead of agreeing blindly, and had risen against not just some Oracle, but the very Upholder himself. He was thinking that maybe, just maybe, she was ready to take up Hrazul's mantle when the words of her own mouth confirmed it.

«Justice, Upholder?» "'True justice isn't vengeful but healing.'[xl] Perhaps my war, your war and *his* war ... are not the same at all."

Meanwhile, Enok anxiously searched for Zoia. She at least would plead on his behalf, but his mistress was nowhere to be seen. Hrazul had fallen, Zelen too, and now it seemed Zoia as well. Of all Enok's trusted Oracles, only the High Wisdom remained. With her great neck arched low, toothy mouth agape and drooling, and with eyes narrowed and wrinkled with pain, she looked little better than the slain around her — then suddenly animated, she leapt away from the almanac with a shaky cry.

"Wait! Wait!" Snei echoed.

"Guilt by association," began the old matriarch hoarsely, "it's a sinister legality."

Zakon tossed his trident to Zaraza. "I'm not convinced she isn't behind all this. Any attempt to escape," he delivered slowly in Zmiysh, "shoot only the tail. Do ... you ... understand?"

---

xl   From the Aphorisms. Southern justice attempts to be restorative; however, the punitive ones of the North apply universally.

The newcomer gestured acknowledgment.

A brief sparkle of rubies caught his eye. The High Wisdom had acquired the giant's dagger, and seemed to want it hidden.

"You won't be needing this," he spat, snatching it with his tail — and with a yelp! The dagger was as sharp as a razor!

"Please, there is much you have yet to understand," the High Wisdom wailed. "For fifty years, we —"

"Blind fools, you Azhakh-Na! Your leniency towards the Ish is the ruin of us all! You so love your butterflies, but these are wasps, and no sweet treatment morphs one to the other! To their kind," Zakon sputtered, with eyes and snout accusing Enok, "each one of us alive, and every Zmee that will ever be born, seems subject to some sort of collective guilt. This 'sinister legality,' as you jowl it, is *their* invention, not mine."

"The young disciple spoke well," the High Wisdom managed weakly, coughing. "Do you not yet see? Hostility solves nothing. 'Hatred makes two enemies alike.'[xli] In its own culture, the giant was a Zeruhawi too. So, here's the result of both your philosophies."

The rebuke earned her a jab in the flanks from Zaraza. "Silence!" the cripple hissed in Y'lan.

"Don't you dare criticize me," chided Zakon, "till memory torments you with the sights I've seen: massacres of peaceful tribes, expeditions ambushed and butchered, their carcasses left for the zhrat. Of all my clan, I alone remained —"

"And of all the betrayals this passing moon, yours now cuts the deepest. Who was it that rescued you, and gave you another life? I was there that day. Remember? This is no way to repay —"

"Oh, I'm grateful: grateful enough to let you live," Zakon growled, clutching his bleeding wound. "If nothing but our death can purge our guilt, then so be it. Nothing but death will expunge theirs. I spit on the Ish and your creation myths! And my excrement upon Hra-Adin!"

"Myth? Your Zeruhawi made it so," the High Wisdom returned, now rising feebly by herself. A raw cut at the base of the neck bled freely where a dart had scraped her, and she winced a little under

---

xli   The Azhakh-Na call to pacifism. A quote from the Aphorisms, and a
       tenet the Zeruhawi especially abhor.

Snei's care. "Follow me." The invitation was personal, and her eyes seemed to search for a reciprocal something in his. "Let me show you what you dare not —"

With the danger now passed, folk were trickling back to the common as Thaazh's disciples and fellow physicians ministered.

"Stones of the Temple!" a gravelly voice rumbled across the dais. "All this from a single barbarian!" One-eyed Thaazh herself had arrived with two of her tubular medicine sticks. "By Zulyi, we should have drowned the lot on sight!"

«Healer! Finally!» Zakon signed. "I have lost much blood. My old wound has reopened. And the slain need —"

"No need to fret, the morticians are coming."

As the Healer attended to the gash in Zakon's arm, the plaza echoed with cries of amazement. Enok instinctively looked for Refa, thinking perhaps he was still alive. The audience, however, were looking skywards.

The air above the almanac had begun to shimmer and flicker like blue fire, yet without heat or flame. A faint metallic squeal rang in his ears, it was almost melodic, and his palate tasted uncannily of metal. His nape bristled. His companion's face creased puzzlingly. She was feeling it too.

With a flash, a sunrise assaulted their eyes. Their wide eyes sensitive to light, Zmee everywhere winced. Through a crack between fingers, Enok beheld what most could not. The golden apex of the massive Reliquary now pulsed with purples, greens, and reds, synchronized to beautiful but almost inaudible harmonies emanating from everywhere and nowhere.

"Oh my!" Naama gasped. "What is it?"

"The runes are glowing!" a guard exclaimed. "The almanac! It's coming to life!"

The face of that great long-dead stone now shone like a paper lantern. Three nested circles ringed its alabaster face in colors of the purest turquoise, glimmering with columns of symbols. The sight set all thoughts ablaze. Each of the rings had its cartouche, and there was one in particular that even a youngling should recognize:

Zoriyan.

Tendrils everywhere were signing amazement. Zaraza had abandoned her trident in favor of the slain Metalsmith's goggles, and was now too transfixed by the sight. Zoriyan was their fabled homeland, and it seemed fable no more.

While the cartouches and larger symbols were in pictographic Zmiysh, the smaller symbols were in the phonemic alphabet that only a maker of maps would know.

Without hint of friction, the three cartouches began to orbit their rings, spinning faster and faster until they had blurred into streaks. Then just as quickly, each individually slowed to a stop. Enok puzzled over the Zoriyan cartouche of the middle ring, for it throbbed steadily with Mapmakers' ciphers beneath it, reading something odd:

No Advocate.

The very name almanac suggested the stone was a kind of season-keeper, so what kind of season was it indicating now?

An urgent tap on the shoulder from Naama: "The snakes are distracted, so don't you be! You're on a longer lead, so — quickly! — rummage for a weapon while you still can!"

However, Enok was mesmerized by the glyphs now aglow on the faces of the stubby posts. And instantly their glassy tops began to make sense. They were a kind of instrumental tableau, and the slope and skew of the pillars were all products of design. And however fleeting the thought, it was ineradicable: they had been made for a creature with manifold faces or eyes. Naama's column was especially pocked with strange geometric depressions, and one in particular matched the High Wisdom's hexagonal pendant.

Hadn't she been fidgeting before the exams with just such an emerald, muttering something to invisible ears about 'popping the chrysalis'?

"Hopeless dreamer!" Naama muttered, inching towards a dead j'Na-Zeru. She had almost managed to ply a blade from the corpse before confronted by a Civil.

"Back to the pillar, barbarian!" hissed the Civil, edging her back with a trident.

Naama retreated warily with eyes leveled on the guard. "This is our best chance for a blade, serpent-boy," she whispered sideways. "I'll make a distraction —"

As she fell back against her post, pale blue arrows of light shot upwards from glowing lines on floor, striking an invisible point high in the air, which responded in kind, returning two for every one. In heartbeats, the irruption of arrows had geometrically multiplied to incalculable dozens of thousands, forming four walls of living, writhing light in the shape of a pyramid, and trapping all but the prisoners, the guard, and Chiruk's cart.

The guard whirled, dumbstruck by the pyrotechnics.

Naama indicated corpses by the ramp. "Enok! There! Fetch a knife!" she whispered as loudly as she dared.

While navigating his way around the pools of blood, the stone of the flooring grew unbelievably cold. Suddenly, there was a loud *whoop*, and Enok spun about.

The shimmering pyramid had vanished.

And everything within it was gone.

IN AN INSTANT, THE WORLD became stranger as myths were enlivened and cherished convictions upturned. Zakon was still grappling with the impossible hope of a Zoriyan reborn, when suddenly — a tingle of the flesh, and a flash of blue light — he found himself surrounded by ... by walls of something that beggared all language. Pearlescent flashes? Woven lightning?

IMPOSSIBLE. AND YET ...

These walls were rapidly misting, diluting the outside world to a memory. Otherwise, everything was as it had been, except — yet another berserk invader! Towering over the slave was a splendid biped with a tapered head and in complex garb, and brandishing some great war staff.

Zakon's sustained thought was: GOOD! KILL THE ISH!

However, the giant merely assumed a defensive posture and ... and the slave's tether was severed! The giant must have freed it and was now protecting it! The stranger's green eyes widened as they met his. Each could see the other.

That instant filled Zakon with dread. Was the slave in league with giants? Indeed! It made consummate sense! But from where could this invader have suddenly sprung?

The walls of light solidified. At the sensation of floating, Zakon grinned like a youngling. The crushing weight that reigned from birth to death had fled. And now came the unmistakable awareness of ascension in jumps. Then again, and again, and again. Oh, wonderful feeling! He was born for this, every instinct told him. He was to the first to spread his wings and fly.

Like the Great Zhmee himself!

There was a loud sudden *whoop* as the plaza, the surrounding hillsides and the distant forest vanished. The cowering Ish and the defending giant were also nowhere to be seen. Instead, before him was the vista of a wan cerulean sky, rusty windswept barrens, and a cluster of crumbling towers on a twilight horizon. Yet, beneath them all seemed the very same dais.

"Where did Ra'a-Zohari go?" a bewildered guard asked.

Approaching the wall of light, Snei wondered, "Is this some kind of window into Zoriyan?"

"You must not touch it," the High Wisdom cautioned. "And keep to the floor!"

Made carefree by the novelty of being weightless, the scar-faced Healer gingerly extended a finger. "Ai-ai!" she winced as a sudden discharge zapped her. «Sorry!»

"It's as though we've traveled without moving," noted Zakon, hovering midair, "but this barren reddish land cannot be Zoriyan. It just *can't* be."

However, the sight of twin moons told otherwise. By legends only Azhakh-Na still believed, there were two night-time Zoriyan luminaries, the larger green and the smaller red. And here before his very eyes, sight and myth were one. But this desolation was nothing at all like the Zoriyan of fame.

A pair of agitated j'Na-Zeru kept attempting a breakout, but the walls of light would not permit them, coruscating furiously at every attempt.

Again the scenery changed. It was early dawn. Lone Zeruha and a familiar moon graced the remnants of a night sky. The reddish alien landscape had been replaced with a vast sandy expanse, like endless beach without ocean, and dotted with prickly low-growing plants and copses of thick-boled palms.

Zakon prepared to throw a lance. "It resembles the Dunes of Sookh. Let's find out."

The warning from the High Wisdom, "No, don't!" came too late. He struck hard at a wall of light with a wooden shaft. The weapon ricocheted and clattered to the floor. Hovering high, he hissed, "A final test." With his one good hand, he practiced a swing with the confiscated dagger.

«No! No!» "Nothing metallic!" Wisdom pleaded, coiling tightly to cones with Snei.

In no mood for advice, Zakon cast it violently. Immediately, there was a flash of light and a loud crash like breaking glass, flooring everyone. The desert panorama vanished. The shimmering blue walls of the lighting ark instantly collapsed. Zakon fell onto corpses, crushing his injured hand. But pain of the flesh was nothing compared to the loss of his aerial joy. He swore silently, for he was humbled again by heaviness, and slimed now with the blood of the dead.

«Great Zhmee!» "What happened to us?"

The guards, physician — all were stunned from the fall, and now they too had become defiled by contact with the blood of their fallen sisters. The blast had caught everyone by surprise. Everyone, that is, except the High Wisdom and young disciple Snei.

And now, wherever it was they'd been, they were back again in Ra'a-Zohari.

WHILE ZAKON, THE HIGH WISDOM, and the others had been trapped inside the pyramid of light, Enok, Naama, the Civil, and the come-lately Scout had been abandoned on the dais.

In fact, Enok had trouble believing his eyes. What was, was not. An outline of a great square was all that remained of the tangle of flesh, and of even the bloodied matting beneath them. The stone floor had been scoured clean, as if some preternatural force had sliced the carpets by razor and dissolved absolutely everything upon it.

IMPOSSIBLE. AND YET ...

A squeal from Naama bid him return. The Civil had become emboldened by the Scout and was growling with a trident at Naama's neck, screaming, "What did you do! Where is the Upholder!"

The amazon took it for a death threat and deftly spun the trident about before kicking it free of the guard's hands and off the platform, sending the Zmee scooting after it. The Scout, however, proved a curious contrast. She seemed strangely serene, lacking any kind of weapon, and merely slid around to examine the glyphs on the posts.

"Is that Zmee writing?" voiced Naama, looking sideways at the Scout whose great snout was much too close for comfort.

Flashing at the top of a column beside him:

Ur-Atu.

Mount Ur-Atu was the site for the j'Athra-Ya, the annual fertility pilgrimage. The great temple of Zul-Al-Kahhri stood there. While some cartouches were unfamiliar, ciphers below made them clear: *Hra-Adin, Hlukzor, Sha'ai, Havilaa* — exotic locales, and more besides, to excite even the dullest of Mapmakers.

"Hra-Adin," escaped on a breath. Wasn't that the place Ukhaz had mentioned in her mad diatribe? Something about his people's prehistory?

"Hra-Adin? The snakes' name for A'din," muttered Naama drawing close, though wary of the Scout beside her. "Zmee lies and Ab-Sethi folktales both. Remember our objective. Don't get distracted."

"A'din? Look, see," he whispered, sharing a glance with the very same Scout, who smiled a little at the antics of the Civil guard who was now becoming increasingly distressed. An invisible force was preventing her from violating the space once commanded by the pyramid of light.

A quarrel of twitterlings, soaring and ducking in chase, struck the invisible wall. *Poof!* A cloud of wattle and feathers. Some bounced off dazed. Others vanished completely.

Running a finger over *Hra-Adin* evoked a weak flash of light from the stone, and a new warning.

"Conflict," Enok echoed.

The Scout made a facial negative, and spun as if to catch a distant sound, then made a show of corralling the prisoners.

"What, by all the gods, was that?" a wide-eyed Naama inquired. "Can you make sense of all this?"

Enok nodded. Yes, he could read it, though with scant idea what it really meant. "Here is ... Ha-vi-laa."

"Did you say *Havilaa?*"

Enok nodded.

"Now *I'm* distracted. That's home! Try it now!"

"Flee and you die!" The original Civil had returned, frantically menacing with a trident. If not for the presence of the tranquil Scout, she would doubtless have caused them harm.

Upon the press of a finger, another flash escaped the almanac with a piercing metallic shriek. The Civil's trident fell to earth as she clutched at her ears in pain.

In a column of names on the tableau, the cartouche for *Zoar* blinked. Enok took a breath, and again ran a finger across it. The pyramid of light reappeared briefly then — *BANG!* — exploded, leveling everyone.

Zakon, the High Wisdom, and the others had returned with Zaraza, bloodied matting, slain, and all.

"Great dung of a ..." Naama was the first to recover, cursing as usual.

Beside her, Enok asked groggily, "What means this?"

However, it wasn't Naama who answered but Zaraza, with tendrils curling gleefully. "It means," she cheered in Y'lan, "the reign of your kind will finally be ended."

"Conniving fool," Naama sneered in return. "It means the gods won't need *you* anymore."

EVERYTHING IRRITATED THE UPHOLDER now. He was beyond the limits of patience. The gathering crowd in the plaza was now pouring onto the dais, reaching for the now dormant almanac as though it held some curative power. Disciples too were scrambling up to find their slain Oracle, and defiling themselves with the contact.

"Peace to Thee! Noble One! Peace to Thee!" they all ritually wailed. "Thy disciples honor thy going!"

"How shall we deal with so much death?" cried a pupil, caressing the lifeless body of Shipwright. "Upholder?"

"It's like the legends!" whooped another. "The old stones came to life! Forgive me, High Wisdom, I did not believe in the Ascending Way! But Zoriyan is no myth, and we're all going home!"

So many Zeruhawi too were excited by the pyramid of light — its disappearance and spectacular reappearance — and now with all this talk of folktale Zoriyan, it dishonored the dead. A single marvel, and all sense of propriety evaporates! Though vexed, Zakon's tendrils couldn't help but curl in sorrow at the sight of so many slain. He, they, and the bloodied mats had shared a journey to astonish the very hopes of the Azhakh-Na.

"Healer! Clear the dais!" he cried "Let's put our dead to rest!"

But the physician too was still recovering from the blast, and responded reluctantly. "My lord?"

"Can I leave you to organize the funerals?"

"Certainly, Upholder, but who's organizing mine?"

"Stop the foolery, One-eye. Ho! You there!" he summoned the prisoners' guard. "Where's the other giant? You, Civil: speak up!"

"The giant is dead, my lord. We flung its unholy carcass off the dais earlier." The Civil bowed. "Just as you ordered."

«Fool!» "The *other* giant! I witnessed another two-legged colossus flourishing a war staff. How could you have missed it?"

The Civil made a show of guarding the Ish, stabbing her trident towards them. "Upholder, I have been here the whole time: myself and the Scout here who came to my aid. There *was* no other giant. There *is* no other giant. You shed much blood in the melee. Perhaps —" The guard bowed again, almost to the ground.

"Not that much!" Zakon spat, as he inadvertently locked sight with the slave. Was that fear in its eyes, or defiance? Hailing fresh guards from the common, he leveled a quavering finger. "Get them out of here! Now!"

Then he rounded on Snei, eye-to-eye. "Disciple Mapmaker! You and I will have words!"

THE SERENE SCOUT GAVE ENOK a small, almost rueful acknowledgment in obedience to Zakon's orders to remove him from the dais. While others were babbling agog, or in shock, she had always been amazingly composed, much like Zelen or Hrazul might have been.

An Ish-like grin spread across her face as if it were the most natural thing in the world for a Zmee, when in truth it really wasn't. Enok thought that especially strange. Then she returned his sandals as if *she* was the servant, all while beaming disarmingly with those mesmerizing eyes of black-within-black. She was zhuk-eyed, like the gholuj in the cell. These were not Zmee eyes at all, and neither was her grin. A dainty cord with a little golden dagger hung about her neck. It was oddly frail jewelry for such as size as hers.

And the Scout's presence was in no way provocative. Even Naama had taken a shine to her — insofar as was possible for the amazon. The Scout made a sign of haste before freeing Naama with a quick swipe of a spontoon, all the while grinning to herself as her partner, the Civil, seemed tetchier than ever. The black-eyed Scout's own bleeding fingers stained the ropes as she pared the remaining knots away. She must have been injured during the melee, so her composure seemed all the more surreal amidst the surrounding bedlam.

Her serenity was infectious, and for a moment Enok forgot himself, and began to reason with her like with a confidant.

"I might have saved us, you know, if Refa hadn't acted so rashly. You need to choose a weapon appropriate to the battle. I understand that now. Not the law, but the lack of law regarding my particulars: that would have been the key."

A black eye winked.

Enok continued: "Absent law, there can be no offense. Right?"

Yes, that must have been the shield Hrazul had spoken about: a legal shield. In the epiphany of the moment he became oblivious to the living myths, the slain, and everything except a dim new hope.

"If it's not too late, I can use Zmee law to my advantage."

Naama scowled. "Stop hissing! Speak Y'lan, will you!"

"I save us. Not die," he summarized in barbarous tongue. Just as the thought formed of persuading Snei to petition the Upholder, the very prospect was trounced by the image of the young disciple cowering under Zakon's rebuke.

Naama *humphed*. "Did you even get a blade when you had the chance? Pshaw, you can't even save —"

Suddenly, Zakon's burgundy snout came bursting between the guards, his anguished tendrils dashing any hope.

«Save? Save?» "You are already dead!"

As the zhuk-eyed Scout escorted the prisoners down the ramp and through the common, Enok was struck by the harsh treatment of

Refa's remains as wounded guards had been reliving the battle, feigning attack, crying "Khozaa!" and rudely with "Khozaa rakh-zhaar!" then beating the corpse until every bone was in fragments. And when they slung it over the great beam of the wagon, quarantining it from their hallowed dead, it hung formless and mangled like the broken meats of Refa's own hearth.

Naama refused to look. With clenched jaws, her eyes wide and nostrils flared, her face had taken on a frightening aspect. She was seeing not what was, but what soon would be, and the curse under her breath through grinding teeth told a reckoning was sure, and that her very hands would wield it.

As the wagon rolled past, and a great hairless arm hung limply just shy of the gravel, something about it caught his attention. Lacerated and spattered with Zmee blood, with burns on the wrist from the bindings, it was a powerful hand, as big as a Zmee's, but the remarkable feature owed nothing to size.

Rubbing deceit from his eyes, Enok re-counted. There was no mistaking the sight.

It had six fingers, just like a Zmee.

THE ZEPHYRS OF STAR WASH had not yet swept Night's Kiss aside. All slept, but Zakon lay coiled on the dais alone, too perturbed to retire. He'd been pondering why the Grand Oracle, that Southern High Wisdom, had hidden behind a mask for so many years like some perpetual actor.

By Zulyi! She was the very epitome of beauty! The manifold tendrils of her crown bespoke a greater age than anyone could guess, but that lime-green face with its piercing black-in-gold orbs was surely the image of eternal youth. Even if she wore that thespian mask for the rest of her life, it was something he'd never forget.

There were other things, much darker things, that he would also never forget.

So many the bodies. So hideous their deaths.

Not designed for such skinny profiles, or even for use at short range, his weapons had been clumsy against the giant. The tactics of the militia had also proven largely ineffective. They had all given such a poor account of themselves in the melee. He needed new weapons, new strategies, and a group of fighters more effective than Forest Spotters, Reef Scouts, Civils and other such militia. More j'Na-Zeru is what he needed, trained in hand-to-hand combat, spike-armored, and bristling with weaponry.

How timely, then, was Thaazh's discovery of a coral fish poison. Northern apothecaries were abuzz at the news — more potent than jellyfish venom, they all assured. If the tiniest prick numbed a Zmee, it should fell an Ish in a heartbeat.

On the day he had announced the giant's capture, someone had whooped 'Death prong! Death prong!' at news of the toxin — but whether Ukhaz or Xira, he could no longer recall. Indeed, the last six-day had been so tumultuous, all his memories were jumbling. All the whens, whats, and hows seemed now like memories lifted from the dead. His one clear and abiding recollection was of his complicity in what had led to this ill-fated day.

By his orders, the dais had been washed.

And again.

And again.

Even the mats and timber ramps made at the old matriarch's command, he had ordered burned, and still he felt plagued by guilt and remorse.

He continued to gaze transfixed by the turquoise markings of the almanac that glowed all the brighter by night. But even as they blurred in the mist, in the solitary quiet he discerned more concretely an ineffable tugging on his tendrils — and, too, a faint ethereal squeal, waxing and waning in cycles, synchronized to the spectral radiance still crowning the Reliquary's apex. It had made something shine in him that had never shone before.

He had earlier removed his helm, closed his eyes, and mapped an invisible landscape of forces. His crown and facial tendrils had come alive with an awareness that defied all reason. Hot spots, cold spots, pathways, and archways: the dais was so much more than eyes could discern or fingers apprehend.

Clearly, those ancient stones, the lesser and greater pyramids were all one vast mechanism, but how had they come alive again after so many generations of silence. And why especially now?

As he continued randomly pondering, his thoughts fell to the image of the beast's carcass being carted off to the limekilns.

Nothing survived lime-fire, not even a soul, some sage had once propounded in a superstitious age. Well, there would be no afterlife for this barbarian, he was making certain of that! The morticians had laughed at his reasoning, and he had laughed along with them. A soul? 'Nothing but atoms and the void' was one of the pillars of Methodics and foundational to every civic system.

But his tendrils were now partaking of something invisible, intangible, yet nonetheless real. Things *did* exist that Methodics could not explain. Regardless, whatever it was that he sensed, it was intoxicating, and he wanted more.

Anyhow, all frivolity aside, something else had caught his eye, though, and it was no laughing matter. The towering terror bird's harness had been fatally weakened with several strategic cuts.

And the giant's hand, large as it had been, was hardly remarkable, though its lacerations were odd. Some were wounds, others were rope burns, and then there was an odd, almost insignificant incision, perpendicular to all the others — one that could only have been made by a razor, and the very same that had nearly severed the terror bird's harness.

The conclusion was inescapable: someone had cut the giant free. Perhaps beforehand, or possibly while 'hidden in plain sight' disguised as a guard. A j'Na-Zeru zealot, or perhaps a Zeruhawi extremist could easily be blamed. However, ordinary hemp had been substituted for the copper filament cord that he had personally delivered. And together the actions spoke as much of treason as conspiracy.

Zakon juddered with laughter. He had placed moles in Zu'u-Shoran, and connived with Xira and Ukhaz in the worst possible way, and now it seemed that Azhakh-Na spies had infiltrated not just the Zeruhawi but his most trusted j'Na-Zeru as well. That had to be it. How else could the High Wisdom have learned of the sea patrol he had ordered to the uttermost north? It was *she* who had demanded to have the inquest here. It was *she* who then insisted on mats for the ramps and dais, and brooked no opposition to a score of minutia.

But why would she have deliberately jeopardized herself by freeing the giant? Most of those who died were from her own hometown. They were Azhakh-Na and she was their chief patron.

True, the Azhakh-Na were loopy pacifists clinging to ancient beliefs, but mightn't those who live solely for religion just as easily die for it?

Or maybe First Metalsmith had been right. Perhaps there really was a 'third force,' and it was here, under his very tendrils, every bit as devious as himself, disguised as a Zmee.

Or maybe they could become invisible.

Yes, like that second giant, the one he had briefly spied standing guard over the bestial slave. When the dais had returned from the other realm, that giant was nowhere to be seen, and none who had been left behind had seen anything suspicious. Perhaps the prisoners' guard was right. Still dazed and losing blood, he had merely imagined it.

Every dimension of Zakon sighed. Just as the High Wisdom had solemnly warned, he had indeed 'opened the door to the whirlwind'. So many now were the funerals, so many now the regrets, but the most stinging of these was the self-accusation:

You're a failure as the Upholder; this is all your fault.

WATERSHED

E nok formulates a plan of escape while becoming stirred by
the realization that Naama isn't just some fresh companion
but a female ... The news that Enok's mistress is the traitor who
freed the giant Ish leaves Zakon confused and more suspicious
than ever.

A RENOWNED TWILIGHT FEATURE OF many coastal cantons
was the mass congregation of twitterlings. Like twirling
smoke-cloud, thousands of the gray little avians swooped
in endlessly shifting formation until finally roosting, all chirping
maddeningly at their cliffside burrows.

Unfortunately, the Zmee holding cell had been hewn in the midst
of their colony. Tonight especially, several had flown in through
the windows, disoriented, darting about with piercing shrieks and
pooping almost everywhere.

Enok had exhausted himself in swatting them out, and now
was pacing and muttering angrily, tormented even further by
revelations and regret. What a fool he had been, unwittingly playing
into Zeruhawi hands! The Zmee had always needed a legal basis
for dealing with him, and ironically, it was only because of their
own law that Ukhaz, that maleficent Chief Oracle of Law, had been
unable to touch him.

No doubt, this was Hrazul's 'nothing that was something' and his only protection. Her 'nothing' was his loss of freedom; her 'something' was life itself. Even Hrazul's own egg-bearer, Zelen the Steam-maker, had given him a clue, reminding him of what Lawmaker Ukhaz had bayed on graduation eve: 'As beast, *it* makes a useful slave. As being, is *he* not then our enemy?'

To live content as a thrall was his safety. That was Hrazul's 'shield.' And in the fullness of time he could have become — no, *would* have become hopefully so much more.

And now he chided himself on how utterly flawed his judgment had been. For all the years the High Wisdom and mistress Zoia had been confining him to servitude, they had actually been protecting him, nurturing him, educating him — at least, in a passive sort of way.

Moreover, Zelen must have overheard the Zeruhawi plans to bait him, but her discreet if not cryptic forewarning had been given in vain, and he doubted he could ever forgive himself.

"You tendril-less idiot!" he muttered aloud.

But why had no one confided in him, especially Hrazul and Oracle Zoia? It might have meant treason to say anything openly, and they certainly were no traitors. Even so, fifty years was far too long to keep someone in the proverbial dark!

'Unseasonal blooms die fruitless,' the High Wisdom had chided on New Year's Eve, and the image of her beaten posture was haunting. It was about patience and timing, she'd been trying to say. But now he was desperate. He had run out of time.

In the sum of his life, these past few days would surely stand memorial: death upon death upon future denied. Short of the extraordinary, tomorrow's dawn would be his twilight. No doubt Zakon was deriving some dark satisfaction from its wicked symmetry, and this one thought kept all others hostage. There was no promise of peace, not even in sleep.

THINK, ENOK, THINK. ALL BURROWS HAVE EXITS. ALL ROOMS HAVE WINDOWS AND DOORS.

The echo of waves told of incoming tide, and he gazed yearningly at the beach below. From this height, a fall would be fatal. There was no hope of escape through the window, he realized. There had to be another way.

Naama, however, was napping on the great bed despite the din of the birds. She seemed rather relaxed about the whole affair, or was perhaps just exhausted from her many ordeals. In the last few days she had narrowly survived an attack of sea serpents, drowning on the barrier reefs, poisonous jellyfish, fever, hunger and who knew what else. Frankly, her speed of recovery amazed him.

And noting hunger, where *was* the food? Right now, any moldy morsel would be welcome. The absence only intensified his anguish. A twilight at dawn, the image of Zakon triumphant, the racket of twitterlings, hollow belly and crowded head — Enok's mind raced through a dozen escape plans but all of them futile.

IF NOT DOWN THROUGH THE WINDOW, THEN WHAT ABOUT UP?

However, as he hung precariously from the washroom window, the image of an oversailing cliff thwarted any hope.

Oh, how he wished for Hrazul or Zoia. They were great problem solvers and thought in strange, lateral ways. He missed Hrazul's intimate yet laconic manner, and Zoia's abrupt but challenging counsel: 'Think in opposites!' And she was always quoting from the Aphorisms. 'Better to round the mountain than climb it,' she was often apt to say.

Had she ever suspected that one of her most diligent students had not, in fact, been Zmee? What had she thought of his graduation efforts? There were so many questions he would like to have asked ask her, and now so much he would never know. In a way, she would always be with him, as long as her legacy survived. And in this his most desperate hour, the lessons given unwittingly nagged him like a conscience:

'TO ASCERTAIN WHAT *CAN* BE DONE, FIRST ELIMINATE WHAT *CANNOT* BE DONE.'

With no way down and no way up, he had to either open the grille or get around it somehow. The room had been freshly plastered. Perhaps it was still soft in places. Maybe there was a weakness somewhere.

"Stop it, will you! You're worse than the birds!" complained Naama from her quarters. "I can't sleep with that all shuffling. At least take your sandals off."

Offending footwear removed, Enok sat again by the windows in the sleeping chamber. "I angry be much. I thinking out getting."

"So *now* he wants to escape," she muttered. "Did you grab a blade when you had the chance? *Huh.* Clearly not." Then eyeing him squarely, "The opposite of life isn't death," she added, "but resignation and atrophy."

"I want to *grow* life … be good … by Zmee *rules*," he lisped, mixing Zmiysh with Y'lan, but she seemed to get the drift of it.

"Be good? You mean, obey their laws?"

The Isha gasped for air and spat — or was it a cough? — as if gagging on wormwood. Was she mocking him? He stiffened, feeling his cheeks burn.

She seemed to have sensed his discomfort, for her expression changed suddenly — to one of concern? — and reaching out, patted the edge of the bed.

"You're so naïve, it's almost cute." Parting lips revealed rows of pearly white teeth. "Come, sit here."

Enok hesitated. Those teeth — was that a threat? And her clothes, all of them, lay at the end of the enormous bed, and the scent of a fresh anointing of perfume lingered heavily.

"It's alright," she reassured him, still patting the bed. "I don't bite."

He sat cautiously beside her, his temperature rising, wondering if the flashing teeth and dimpled corners of her mouth betrayed a little lie. Maybe she *did* bite. He had so become accustomed to her as a patient — unconscious, defenseless, unmoving — that seeing her so self-assured, in command, almost predatory, made him uneasy.

He reciprocated the gesture, feeling his face, now understanding what had frightened Hrazul's new disciple on that awful, awful day.

AH, A SIGNAL OF HAPPINESS. IS THAT WHAT I LOOK LIKE?

Naama rolled her eyes in some alien gesture. "It's only a smile. Listen," she resumed, looking serious again, "I think I understand what you're trying to say, but let me tell you this: any warrior that goes into battle using the enemy's rules" — a click of the tongue, a slash of her throat with a thumb — "is dead before they even draw their sword."

A new word. "Sword?"

"A weapon," she explained. "You *never* let the enemy make the rules. Got that?"

"Enemy?" Another meaningless word.

Again came the eye-roll, though with a sound half-sigh half-moan. "Bad people."

Zakon's decree came to mind. "Zmee speaking sea kill I."

"*Me*. Kill *me*," Naama corrected with a curious touch to the breast. "You really *have* been here too long. You needn't keep apologizing for them, you know. To kill, or to allow to be killed, the intent and the result seem the same to me. The Zmee are your enemy now. You no longer have any choice in the matter."

Enok smarted at this lesson in ethics. And from a barbarian at that! Could she possibly be right? Though didn't the Aphorisms say that 'Hatred makes two enemies alike'?

He had lived like a Zmee and thought like a Zmee for longer than he cared to remember. He was used to the signposts at every crossroad. Forward, backwards, left or right: there was always a choice. He had no desire to hate or be hated, and granted the power he would choose friendship over enmity. So why was this choice denied him now?

Zoia had often lectured about life's endless possibilities. Surely its corollary would be endless choice, yet now he was at the greatest juncture of his life and this corollary was nowhere in sight.

He shot up from the bed. "No!" If this were his fate, he would not resign to it willingly.

"Yes!" Naama countered with equal conviction. "Look, sometimes you get to choose your enemies, but mostly they get to pick you first. It's just the way the world is. Get used to it, lost boy."

"But Zmee —"

"Forget the Zmee! You are dead to them, and they must be dead to you. We are getting out of here, somehow, and you have to prepare yourself mentally." A finger tapped her forehead.

"Prepare?"

"Warriors rarely exceed their self-expectations, and I know this all too well. See, one does as one imagines, so you tend to become what you profess you are. Believe me, the foremost challenge is the battle within, and I've seen wars lost before the lance was even drawn. On your tongue is the first of victories, for by your own words you slay the doubting coward and feed the lusting heart."

She paused, searching perhaps for simpler words. The way her eyebrows rose and fell, and her lips and eyes too — these elements of body-speak were alien, and every bit as complex as Zmee signing. So what were her features telling? Was she frustrated too?

"If you're going to survive this, the first person you must be thinking about," she stabbed his breast with a finger, "is yourself. You're an Ish of the Elim. Start thinking like one and — by the Sons of the Gods! — start *acting* like one."

There was a long uncomfortable silence, and Naama had the wisdom to appease it. He was having a final struggle for identity. Wholly Ish or solely Zmee — was there no other choice? In a manner of speaking, he had already chosen his path, high in the rain forest canopy on New Year's Eve. And yet, there was a tinge of regret. Why not be something of both?

His expression must have given something of his inner conflict away, for Naama placed her hand reassuringly over his own in a series of slaps.

"So what are you, a Zmee that drops it bowels at the mere mention of trouble, or an Ish who devours it?" Her eyes brightened when she added, "Muzzled in carcass to the eyeballs! That's the Havilan way."

Why were life's great conjunctions too often *ors* instead of *ands*? Why never some latitude to redefine the big questions!

"I can tell you're a thinker. You must already have a plan."

"A plan?" Enok echoed.

"To escape. All that moaning back there, I know you've been playing around with it, so if you've got something, give it to me."

Enok struggled for words to say "Nothing as yet." Blank looks said it for him.

"You must have *something*."

"Very big ... big ..." Lost for the right words, he gestured grandly in response to her widening eyes. "Big ground."

"A big island? Is that what you mean? I figured that already."

"Yes, big island. Much places to ..." he covered his eyes with his fingers. "I know place to put me."

She sighed and mumbled something in an undertone. "So, you have a few places to hide, is that what you're trying to say?"

"Yes, hide."

"I'm not hiding; I'm getting off this rock. Think again."

Well, Zmee were amphibious and rarely strayed far from water. The northern dunes of Sookh were too arid for them. He couldn't imagine ever crossing paths with Zakon there. Or, there was his secluded retreat (his home, actually) on the elevated flanks of Mount Oush in the island's south. However, that would entail backtracking through Zu'u-Shoran's isthmus. Fortunately, in the middle of the day, Zmee were either indoors, underwater or underground.

If they avoided beaches and the deeper forests, creeping about the main roads at noon, they stood a fair chance of making good their escape.

Yes, Mount Oush: a place of solitude that none would disturb. Zmee ran short of breath in a chase, and perhaps with their peculiar anatomy, a prolonged vertical climb would be impossible. He remembered the happy times: the berries and edible flowers that grew on the several small plateaus this time of year, the uninterrupted views of deepest blue in every direction, that unbroken horizon which saw the birth and death of the Greater Light, and its blazing arc across the sky.

That was the place to go. There they could hold out for moons, perhaps even years.

"I know," he made a peak with his fingers, "good living place."

Naama's forehead wrinkled in yet another strange expression.

"Enough of this worm-ridden island! As I said, I'm getting off; with you preferably, without you if I must. What if I were to have children? That red snake would hound me till the very last drop of his blue stinking blood. He hates me, clear enough, but something even deeper darkens his eye's whenever he takes stock of you, Enok. You cannot stay here either. So, think harder."

CHILDREN? He lingered on the thought, savoring the implications without yielding to its prurience. She moistened her lips. Her eyes were big and wide, much like Hrazul's, and drinking in the very sight of him. He was beginning to see Naama in a whole new light. She was at once warlike and scheming, but these were as nothing compared to her feminine, alien dimensions. Was the matter of their coupling a foregone conclusion?

She had already said he would have to fight her merely for sighting her flesh! Did she plan on losing? Had he no more say in the matter than carrion beneath a school of dancing zhrat? Perhaps, one day, this carrion would enjoy being a feast, but it would be a day of his own choosing, not another's. Nevertheless, what she was saying made sense, albeit in a vulgar sort of way. Surviving and living were poles apart. If they remained on the island, concealed somehow, they would live forever as little more than fugitives scurrying about the margins of his former home.

Naama was right, and Hrazul, Zoia, Zelen; and after seeing firsthand what a giant could do, perhaps he could even spare the Zeruhawi a little mercy. Surely some good could be salvaged from the sum of hopes and fears of so many people, Ish and Zmee alike.

'Children,' 'war,' and 'leaving,' she had said. Flee the island, sure, but to where? Perhaps they could sail to one of the rocky archipelagos. Ssla! He forgot. Zakon's goons had smashed his boat.

Sail! Yes, of course! He thought of Zelen and the pilgrim's boat. "There is ..." Enok signed with cupped hands.

"A cradle?"

He waved afresh.

"A boat?"

"Yes. Zmee have big boat." Odd that she should know the word.

"Excellent. Use the enemy's weapons against them. And where would that be?"

He pointed vaguely downwards.

"Beneath us? How do we get there?"

He nodded, mouth open in a Zmee shrug, though it was clear the meaning escaped her. OF COURSE NOT, YOU DOLT, he said in his mind. IT'S A ZMEE GESTURE. "I not knowing," he responded lamely.

She rolled her eyes again. Perhaps it was disappointment.

Breaking out and getting to the boat were different problems entirely. How to crack both at once? Drawing a blank with the former, he considered the latter. Perhaps in solving a piece, the whole would follow.

The boat was already provisioned for departure and at first light would be leaving for the mainland. Stones of the Temple! The boat was right underneath him, but how to get at it? Once again, it was Zoia's voice that guided him.

THINK IN OPPOSITES! his mistress lectured now in his mind. WHEN IN DOUBT, FIRST ELIMINATE WHAT CANNOT BE DONE.

"Don't know where it is exactly, don't know how to find it," he pondered in Zmee, "but what about where it *will* be?"

Yes, that's it. Interception, Zoia's voice applauded.

He could visualize Zoia's approving tendrils, and Hrazul's.

"I know where the boat is going to be, so all I have to do is to be there when it passes."

I knew you could do it.

"But how do I get there?"

Where does it go?

"Out of the cove, past the headlands and then south, passing Sha-Noa on the way to Pilgrim Channel."

And pausing at the Chechi Archipelago, where the reef dragons feed.

"Yes, to gather supplies of the chechi sea lettuce, a treat no pilgrim can resist."

Ga-runt! Ga-runt! Ga-runt!

Forty cubits below, yash'kh were rutting, engaged in their endless disputes over primacy.

Naama cut short his soliloquy. "Do you have to be so annoying? Speak Y'lan, will you! That Zmee hissy-lisp gets under my skin."

"Yash'kh!" With a pointing finger, the sailfinned dragons below were conscripted. Then Enok gestured with a hand, "Boat." And with fingers of the other, "Yash'kh and I."

"Us," she corrected.

Then with a sweeping motion, merging hands traced the plan.

"You're mad!" she exclaimed, adding, "Brilliant! Simple, really. All we need to do now is get out of here."

Get out, yes of course, though 'simple' was hardly the word for it. He had yet to figure a way of how to slip past the grating. It would be too heavy to lift. He had to break through it somehow.

"So, serpent-boy," Naama asked, yawning and fluffing a straw-filled pillow she had made for herself, "what do you think we'll need?" A shoulder and the smooth flaxen skin of her back were exposed. She was lying on her side, head on hand, with eyes heavy and sensual. "Well?" she prompted with a slow yawn, watching him mime the objects they required. "Rope. Hooks. Nothing more?"

"Nothing more," he confirmed.

"Good. Now come to bed." Naama lifted the blanket, but he shot up, awkward and uncertain.

The mores of his people were baffling. His face and neck burned like fire, and with nowhere to plant the eyes. Were there even words for such feelings as these?

"No hostilities until we're under open sky. You have" — *yawn* — "a Havilan's word, and I ..." The rest was lost in the stretch of her breath, and the blanket withdrew its offer. "Have you ridden these beasts before?"

Enok nodded mechanically.

"I figure we have about three watches until dawn.[xlii] I'll get us out, you get us to the boat. Agreed?" With eyes snuggling behind their lids, her words slurred as a deeper yawn possessed her. "Just three ... *huum* ... watches, then we ... *haaw*... *yide* the *yashuwak*."

He pulled the blanket up over her shoulders and watched her curl into a ball, hugging her pillow tightly. The rhythm of her breathing became slow and regular as sleep wrought its transformation. She had gone from helpless to powerful to helpless again.

NIGHT HAD FALLEN, BUT THE VAULT of Boat Harbor shone like the nacre of some gargantuan clam. What had begun as a purely natural formation hidden deep in a sheltered cove of Yzhau Bay, centuries of Zmee ingenuity had transformed beyond recognition.

A honeycombed expanse over a hundred cubits high is what it was, and more akin to a beehive than a shipyard. Rocky outcrops had been hewn into platform or a causeway. Everything else had been smoothed, then paneled with hexagonal mirrors of burnished tin. Here the keenest Zmee minds had labored for generations to ensure the survival and the supremacy of their race.

"While the Reliquary embodies a forgotten past, here lies Zoar's very future," claimed Zakon, awed afresh by the sight.

And surely, he thought, something so grand deserved a more engaging name. True, Boat Harbor was as apt a description as any, but here to be found wasn't just any old ferry, but the pinnacle of Zoar's maritime experience, the most complicated device the

---

xlii In Zmee and Elim cultures, a *watch* is equivalent to two hours, but only Zmee have water clocks than can graduate time more finely.

Zmee had ever built. It lay moored nearby, a dozen cubits below the sinuous causeway, and Zaraza couldn't help but hang over the guardrail in stiff-tendriled wonder. Even the j'Na-Zeru with him were speechless, for few indeed had ever even heard of it before.

"It's been christened the 'Dragon Boat,'" Zakon noted, smiling a little at Zaraza's reaction. The newcomer had an insatiable curiosity and was a veritable sponge for anything new. "That, at least, is more prepossessing than 'Pilgrim Ferry.'" «Eh?»

In her life as a slave to the barbarians, she had missed much. And the impending Great Pilgrimage was a tremendous opportunity for her, no doubt at all. But the pilgrimage was as much about duty as biology. Every sixth year of their adult life, as the breed-shine moistened their tendrils and clouded the mind, Zoarans trekked bravely to the twin balds of Mount Ur-Atu. And there, nestled safely between its great escarpments, the sacred lake boiled with the eternal dance of the sexes to begin the cycle of life anew.

As Zaraza lacked the breed-shine and the peculiar thickening of tendrils, it was clearly not her time; nevertheless, by means of signs and her few words, she had pleaded to go. After what she had suffered, and in no small measure to Stargazer's lobbying, Zakon had resolved not to deny her. Besides, her knowledge of the Ish and their ways could prove valuable in a crisis.

His smile was short-lived, however, for he was jealous of her, this enigmatic cripple. A vessel's first voyage carried a certain prestige, and now with the dredging of the Susyaan canal, it would shave more than a day off the island circuit. It was a doubly inaugural voyage, but a double honor he would not be sharing.

Indeed, gone were the days when a hundred Zmee struggled against the current towing a great lumbering barge. Gone too were the galley-slaves laboring over the paddle-wheels that once propelled the older craft with their precious cargoes of hatchlings.

This new boat was almost twice the size of its predecessor: that barnacle-infested paddleboat-*cum*-sailship dry-docked across the cavern. It had recently returned from some expedition to the farthest north, from a cluster of islands bathed in perpetual daylight. It was about to be decommissioned.

The new craft with its copper paneled hull was both self-powered and wind-powered. Excepting a small section abaft, there was no external deck. It was completely enclosed. The multi-masted sail was loosely modeled after the dorsal fin of that most terrifying of creatures, a yash'kh, and from a distance, should easily be mistaken for one. In fact, camouflage and disguise had always been key.

BUT IT'S NO MORE A SEA DRAGON, thought Zakon, THAN I'M A TRUE BULL.

Fire in the tunnels! A young Zakon fled for his life as burning oil came pouring into an underground vestibule.

Outside, several dozen grimy Ish were hacking an elderly Zmee into pieces with flint knives and axes, chanting and dancing around a fire, smearing their russet fur with the old sire's blood. They had caught Zakon, still a youngling, and strung him to a horizontal pole. They had tortured him, mutilated him, in the worst way a male could be.

THEY WOULD PAY FOR IT ONE DAY, he remembered promising himself. YES INDEED, THEY WOULD PAY!

It was amazing how recollections could overtake you unbidden, and almost cripple you with intensity. TRULY, he thought, fingering the bandage on his arm, TIME HEALS SOME WOUNDS BUT DEEPENS OTHERS.

Memories like these had shaped his hatred into a weapon, honed it to a willing tool, for what consolation had he against the solemn fact that he would never be a pilgrim? On the dock below, Oracles and other dignitaries were milling about like younglings on their first excursion. One day, the passengers' descendants might hear with pride how their forebears had plied the great seas in the Dragon Boat.

THEIR DESCENDANTS, he lamented, NOT MINE. There would never be any seed of Zakon the Invisible, the Upholder, the Chief Oracle of Law, and now the High Wisdom of Zoar — a secret shame he would hide indefinitely.

ZAKON THE EUNUCH: A MERE SHELL OF WHAT I COULD HAVE BEEN.

Many of the pilgrims preparing to board the craft had festooned themselves with garlands, skullcaps, or armbands of flowers. In the waiting circle, marshals took pride in buffing the breed-moist tendrils of first-timers' with the exclusive Ur-Hozhai saffron. The early onset of jellyfish swarms had hastened the departure, so the largest of blooms, still in the bud, were notably absent. Flowers were a celebration of life, of reproduction and continuity, saffron too, and in more ways than words could express, they embodied the soul of the pilgrimage.

But the sight of pilgrim seniors so florally festooned being harangued by Xira the Stargazer and others flamboyantly adorned in Zeruhawi colors drew him speedily towards the gangway, with Zaraza and his j'Na-Zeru trailing. If Xira was involved, that new Venerable of Sky, then he needed to quash whatever tension was brewing there before politics put someone in jail.

At the base of the gangway, K'huda the Vessel Mistress, Shukhai the Pilgrim Leader, their disciples and some he didn't recognize, had formed a blockade against Xira and her allies: the old one-eyed Healer Thaazh, Zhaal the Metalsmith and other Oracles. They all seemed to relax a little upon Zakon's arrival, and slid aside to admit him with sighs of relief as if each believed him their savior.

"A truly remarkable vessel," Zakon cheered. "Worthy tendrils guide it, I'm sure, Vessel Mistress," he added, though with eyes locked on Xira.

K'huda bowed graciously. «Thank you.»

Her companion, Shukhai the Pilgrim Leader, offered him a bouquet. It was the traditional invitation to Ur-Atu, which Zakon was forced to decline.

"Sorry, but no." «I'm defiled.»

Shukhai nodded in understanding. «Because of the dead?» "Even so, Upholder, we need your intervention."

"The loss of Steam-maker was a great blow to us all," K'huda wept of Zelen, "but we won't be badgered by some upstart midlander to sail with unqualified replacements."

"Or to be ordered about by some zealot who's not even an Oracle," Shukhai chimed.

«Why not?» Xira pressed. "You need specialists. Here they are."

"The pilgrimage is a holy affair," Shukhai spat, "and I won't have it politicized, especially with pretenders who scorn the ablutions. You stink like animals. All of you."

Xira was dismissive, and seconded by Zhaal. "More Azhakh-Na nonsense, Pilgrim Leader."

"And besides, Upholder," K'huda added, "I'm a navigator, not a boat-builder like our departed Shipwright. This behemoth has yet to be fully tested, and if it flounders on the great deep, what salvation then?"

The air was bitter as the parties glowered over the stalemate.

«I grieve with thee,» Zakon signed to K'huda about Shipwright. "For whom, Vessel Mistress, were you hoping as replacement?"

"One of her former students from Yashau-Zaar. She's a truly formidable Oracle and has a detailed knowledge of —"

A messenger shot up the gangway from the stone-walled dock, and bowed briefly to K'huda. "All the listed dignitaries from these provinces have boarded, Vessel Mistress, except the missing Mapmaker."

«Missing?» Zakon echoed in surprise.

"The Prime Mapmaker of Zu'u-Shoran, my lord," the messenger explained.

Zakon was bemused. "I thought she died," he said of Zoia.

«Apparently not,» signed the one-eyed Healer. "During the funerary preparations we realized she wasn't among the slain. She's a deserter, but we have a replacement here, see?"

The messenger bowed again. "Upholder, the Civils have searched for her everywhere: Civils combing the cities, Scouts across the reefs, Spotters along the forest tree-ways. All we know is that she was last seen on the dais with you during the inquest, and sometime during the melee with the giant, she simply disappeared."

"She's not the only thing that's missing," piped a Zeruhawi disciple. "Someone has ransacked the Reliquary."

"Ransacked?" Zakon was as much intrigued by the crime as thankful the subject had shifted.

THE RELIQUARY, TOMB OF MYSTERY, he mused, SEALED FOR THREE GENERATIONS: AND NOW THIS HAPPENS!

"Explain, Historian," he prompted.

He remembered this youngster, Snakhash, the First Disciple of old Skazaar the Chronicler, the local historian who had died today. By law, Snakhash was her substitute until Skazaar's college of peers chose a successor. Meanwhile, an Oracle's privileges were hers.

"Some history totems and ancient parchments that my Oracle had hoped to examine," she gestured helplessly, "had been vandalized

— but not the sacred tablets of the Aphorisms, or, thankfully, the ancient sarcophagi. Other trinkets seem to be missing."

«Great Zhmee!» Zakon groaned. "Why didn't you send for me, or the Prefects?"

"Ssla's holy light! We only just discovered it," she replied defensively. "It's a real mess inside, but we're salvaging what we can."

"Could the Mapmaker have stolen them?" someone hissed about Zoia. "Missing relics; a missing Oracle. That's hardly a coincidence, surely."

"Prime Mapmaker? In front of the whole assembly?" Pilgrim Leader Shukhai was incredulous. "By Zulyi, why would she have wanted them?"

Privately, Zakon considered how jealously the old Grand Oracle, the former High Wisdom herself, had guarded the key to the Reliquary. And for fifty years to whit! Her reasoning was still a mystery. And, indeed, why would Zoia have needed to steal anything at all?

Vessel Mistress wondered aloud, "Is there any proof that it was her? I mean, what's missing that she would not want anyone to see?"

The young Chronicler thought a little before replying. "Well, the chest of the Ish-beast's records lay utterly smashed and empty."

Ah, thought Zakon, THE HIGH WISDOM'S RECORDS OF THE BARBARIAN SLAVE. He was just beginning to see the connection when Xira Stargazer voiced it:

"That wretched barbarian was once the former High Wisdom's pet — she then entrusted it to the current Prime Mapmaker, her former disciple. After all, they named it after the most prized of butterflies, the blue Grand Enokhi. Surely that means the creature is precious to them, and who doesn't protect their treasure?"

Before Zakon could interject, Xira pressed her point. "Wouldn't that paint them all then as *conspirators*? Is *that* who you want on the pilgrimage?"

The Vessel Mistress baulked. "But Mapmaker was at the inquest too. We all saw her. You're not suggesting she had foreknowledge of the barbarian's rampage and fled, are you? That's stretching the facts too far."

"Big Ish," Zaraza attested, miming an incision to her wrist. "My saws it."

«Me too,» signed Zakon, grasping her pidgin. "Someone cut the giant free. That much is certain." He was not alone in observing it, this clever newcomer Zaraza had too.

"And I recall, no doubt as do you, Prime Mapmaker toying with the barbarian's dagger *before* the inquest began," Zhaal recollected.

Zakon wagged agreement. The Metalsmith was right about the dagger. And she seemed so much more real as a person without those incessant smithy's goggles.

"The High Wisdom — ah, *former* High Wisdom — is the ringleader of those loathsome First Causers. And Mapmaker was not only her student once but also her egg, did you know? Believe me," Xira hissed, "whatever the plot, they are in it together. Revere her if you will, but the ultimate cause of today's tragedy was her lax policy Ish-ward. That's why the Upholder had to confine her. I always sensed she was up to no good with her inquest. This business with the knife now surely confirms it."

Vessel Mistress was unconvinced about Zoia. "Prime Mapmaker of Zu'u-Shoran? The Prime Mapmaker of Zoar? Plotting against her own people? This is sounding increasingly paranoid."

Glancing furtively at Xira, while now avoiding a busy stream of porters, Zakon wondered why she was trying so hard to justify *his* actions. Was *she* the culprit? Perhaps she or the Oracle of Law, Ukhaz, had coerced a Civil to free the giant. After all, a public and unforgettable incident had been their clear desire.

Vivid in his mind was the evening the giant was captured, and likewise the hot debate in the historian's office afterwards. They had all so dreamed of using the monster in galvanizing masses to their cause. Had their plotting backfired? But the knife, the cuts on the giant's wrist, it all pointed to either Zoia or the High Wisdom. After all, the knife had always been in her safekeeping. But neither were Zeruhawi sympathizers.

More troubling, though, was his own cloudy head. Why hadn't he considered posting guards outside the reliquary? Or shut it completely? He alone now had the key. All that stalking and fighting the giant had left him exhausted. He was clearly in no shape to continue as Upholder. But how could he not?

Zakon sighed, stroking his tendrils pensively. "All I see is a knot of intrigue, and it tangles my tendrils to resolve all the plots."

Shukhai the Pilgrim Leader was skeptical. «Plot? Plots?» "Your logic escapes me, Upholder."

Like her partner K'huda, Shukhai was a seasoned explorer from the canal town of Zu'u-Susyaan. Both were veterans of the Great Pilgrimage many times over, though both dolts politically speaking. It was possible that they were just regular Methodicists, but he strongly suspected they were Azhakh-Na converts, and like all new converts, whatever the cause, their brains were off with the butterflies. To such, their passion consumed them, and everything else was simple and easily explained. Zakon knew better.

"Call it intuition," he began clarifying. "Something activated the ancient stones. How many generations has it been? Why all this intrigue now? It all started when I took the key and opened the Reliquary. You weren't on the dais, but I saw the old matriarch jump from the almanac *before* it came to life. And when those walls of light enveloped us, she knew things, I tell you; though what her part in all this …" Zakon's voice trailed away as he caught Healer's expression, a worried, faraway look. «Something wrong?»

"I have one more plot for you to consider," said Thaazh.

«Go on,» everyone signed, all eyes on the physician.

"The size of the strangers always puzzled me, particularly the male. Since I was already defiled, I took the opportunity to examine it more closely. Six digits apiece on the hands, I noted. Single thumbed."

«Really?» The new historian piped nervously. She seemed overwhelmed by her station. "Toes too?"

«Indeed,» signed Thaazh. "Though Ish-like, it *is* something new: its size, six digits and toes, double rows of teeth. It resembles the slave in appearance only, much as we might a salamander or snake."

"Ssla forbid! Then what was it?" Shukhai inquired.

Tendrils hung limp in ignorance. None had a ready answer.

Xira was first to grasp the significance. "It's Smithy's 'third force' hypothesis. Remember?"

«Indeed!» signed Zhaal. "The Ish have an ally, and an incredibly powerful one at that. And if you can't accept this simple truth, then we're all doomed." She sneered at Shukhai, "Do you still think, Pilgrim Leader, that religion can save you?"

Silence again, deeper this time.

"Mere speculation," Zakon offered at length. "Right Newcomer?" Deep down, however, he was becoming increasingly certain that most everything ever believed of the Ish was false. Hrazul had been the only one to have openly said it. And now because of these very Zeruhawi, she was rotting in a crypt. Everything had to be reevaluated if he was to truly know his enemy.

But in whom could he trust?

"Big Ish. Bag egg," Zaraza voiced in broken Zmiysh.

"I think Newcomer means that it was some kind of warm-born, a mutant like our own males."[xliii] By way of explanation, Zakon presented his hand to Zaraza, who seemed nowhere near as embarrassed as the others. Zmee had six fingers, including two thumbs. Zakon, however, had only one among the six, and the sole remaining thumb was hopelessly crooked.

"I never noticed," came a whisper.

"There's no point denying what's been happening," he reasoned. "Fewer full males with each passing generation."

The silence turned palpable. Not only were fewer males being born, but some were missing digits, limbs, or wings — tabooed talk among the green-skins, though he couldn't think of a reason as to why. Only males had ever had hind legs, but there hadn't been a four-legged bull in living memory.

"Anyhow, let's not quench our spirits, shall we?" said Zakon merrily with claps of goodbye. "I came to bring Newcomer and to farewell the pilgrims, not get diverted with wild —"

"Evidence is never wild," Zhaal interjected.

"Pilgrim Leader, see to her ablutions. This is no time to overturn tradition. And what am I as Upholder, if not of tradition too?"

"Well, no sense in waiting for Prime Mapmaker," Vessel Mistress muttered. "We might as well open the doors to the pilgrims. With your blessing, Upholder? And along the way I'll pick my own replacements," sneering sideways at Xira, "as is *traditional*."

In the midst of the agreeing, "Old Wisdom. Helping Ish now," Zaraza hissed, and Thaazh the physician agreed:

"The Grand Oracle? Yes, she may yet try to rescue the creature."

---

xliii *Warm-born (byword).* Proper Zmee embryonic development is interrupted if the egg temperature is too warm and can lead to deformities.

Zakon was beginning to realize that the tangle of plots were best unraveled one thread at a time. "The Newcomer may be right. If she's somehow behind all this ..." A swift decision was being forced of him. "Guards, invite the old mistress here. After all that's happened, the pilgrims are in desperate need of her, ah, *wisdom*. Make certain she doesn't refuse the invitation, and I care not whether she is convalescing in the infirmary, or naked as a melon upon some physician's slab."

To K'huda he added, "And, by Zulyi, make sure she's properly sanctified for the journey, Vessel Mistress. Delay a little, but see this done." «That's an order!» he snapped, then sighed before adding, "You know, we can't keep calling the old Grand Oracle, the old High Wisdom, by her titles anymore."

Xira responded, "Call her First Deposed, or Old Dame for all I care. The important thing is, she won't be meddling."

"Anyhow, it appears I have a missing Oracle to locate," thought Zakon aloud of Zoia. "If she's alive, then she certainly has some explaining to do!"

"To abandon one's sisters in a crisis, though, makes her a traitor," submitted Xira. "Doesn't it, Upholder?"

While the pilgrims baulked, he could not ignore the accusation.

"Guards, for your second task, send two criers apiece from the armory, armed and helmed to every town. The Prime Mapmaker," he said of Zoia, "is to be apprehended on suspicion of treason. I want this broadcast even down the mines."

"Merely suspicion?" Thaazh inquired.

"My two eyes can judge her, Healer, better than your one. She's no criminal until I've proven her so." Zakon waited for the gangway to clear, then made to leave.

"What about the funerals?" Thaazh inquired. "If we're waiting for the Old Dame, then we might as well delay another day or two and make them an occasion of state. Our slain deserve no less."

«No,» Zakon insisted. "We've both been defiled, so neither of us can officiate. Do we really have time for the lengthy ablutions? The jellyfish swarms make timing critical now; the boat should depart as soon as it can. Anyhow, pilgrims: go," he commanded. "Mount Ur-Atu beckons. I'll escort Newcomer to the novices on the dock. The marshals can prepare her there."

As the last of the pilgrim elders signed farewell and slid into the Dragon Boat, Xira whooped something about a new Zeruhawi government.

"I have been hearing a lot about that lately," piped the new historian with a youngsters naïveté. "Establishing a government centered here in Ra'a-Zohari rather than dowdy Zu'u-Shoran, I mean. If ever there was a time for radical change, this is surely it, isn't it? The Shav'yat is all but dead."

Xira, Thaazh, Zhaal and their coterie — all the Zeruhawi affirmed the notion, signing approvingly.

"The council itself would have had to make that decree, and apart from the deposed Grand Oracle, I mean the Old Dame, I'm the only surviving member," Zakon noted dryly. In sliding aside to admit porters with trolleys, he caught Zhaal and Xira share a curious, significant look.

"What about the prisoners' execution, Upholder?" a j'Na-Zeru inquired. "A just and glorious spectacle! Is it now planned for the morrow, or the day after that?"

«Neither!» Zakon permitted himself a little chuckle. "Why waste any more effort on them? I plan to delight in watching them rot. In fact, the beasts don't even need to be guarded." Zaraza seemed intrigued by the news. "Believe me," he chuckled wickedly, "they are so well secured, they won't be going anywhere — *ever*."

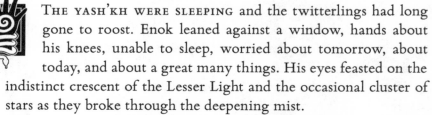 THE YASH'KH WERE SLEEPING and the twitterlings had long gone to roost. Enok leaned against a window, hands about his knees, unable to sleep, worried about tomorrow, about today, and about a great many things. His eyes feasted on the indistinct crescent of the Lesser Light and the occasional cluster of stars as they broke through the deepening mist.

But the clusters weren't just patterns, but symbols somehow, and that one random thought sparked a sudden cascade of long-forgotten words that floated now spectral before him.

HA-AV. KESH-ESH. MANDAL-ARAN.

His father's voice: 'SEE HA-AV UP THERE, AND KESH-ESH BESIDE IT?'

Enok triumphed in the memory. THAT'S IT! CONSTELLATIONS! THEY FORETOLD THE FUTURE! The signs in the sky were a zodiac; the

Mandal-Aran, a great almanac of the ages of grace yet ahead. 'THE WITNESS OF THE STARS IS SURE,' his father had once told a bright-eyed boy straddling his shoulders, 'STRUNG ACROSS THE SKY BY THE MIGHTY HAND OF THE EL.'

Were The El and the First Cause of the Zmee the same?

"Father!" he whispered. "I remember."

A yearning stirred, long suppressed, now inconsolable, triggered by something Naama had said.

CHILDREN.

He had a father and a mother, and perhaps even a whole clan or tribe on the mainland somewhere. For so many years, he had paid them no thought. They were dead to each other. But in the last few moons especially, curious dreams had been dredging his memory, stirring up long-forgotten things, and leaving him more anguished than ever.

And what to make of those almond eyes and ebony features seen in his dreams? He understood them now to frame a girl. The face that gladdened his lonely nights had been beckoning. But to what?

Was she a memory? A spirit?

Perhaps the High Wisdom knew, for she had once rescued him from some kind of mainland battle. Buried so deep under the years, what grief did the forgetting conceal, and why so elusive the memory? She had the answers. He had to get to her, somehow. It was time he knew the truth. All of it.

Sound and emotion took form in a word, AYMA, followed by an image of a different sad-eyed face looking down, long tresses of dark hair tickling him, rubbing his nose with hers.

'GOODNIGHT, LITTLE MOPPET,' whispered the tender-eyed face in a melody. It was his mother. He recalled a little more now.

AYMA! GOODNIGHT, AYMA! he sing-songed in his mind.

With reverence and with sorrow, "My mother's name was Ayma," escaped upon a breath.

There was a soft shuffling in the corridor, the scent of something both spicy and florescent — was that pilgrims' saffron? — and then the unmistakable *clunk* of metal against stone. And again. It seemed to go on for a little while, then — nothing. He sauntered sleepily to the grille and strained his eyes in the dim light, searching. Who was out there, and what had they done?

Silence.

NOBODY THERE NOW, he thought, and frankly, he was too tired to care.

His mind reeling with questions, Enok rested on the massive bed, head-to-toe beside a deep-sleeping Naama. It seemed less intimate this way, and less disturbing. When she was awake, he found her stimulating in ways Hrazul had never been, but that stimulation elicited strange involuntary reactions that only demanded more.

The body should obey the mind, right? Not the other way around?

The scent of camphor from the bed was soothing, as too the echo of waves from below. That swirl of unknowns, and of past and present and future, had all vexed him enough for one day.

"Goodnight, Father. Goodnight, Mother," he mumbled to the phantoms, and surrendered at last to a hope-filled darkness, the son once more of Yared and Ayma.

FUGITIVES

E nok and Naama escape, but an error of judgment ruins their plan. An alternative presents itself, but it means backtracking through the city in broad daylight, pursued by Zakon's infamous j'Na-Zeru troops.

ENOK WOKE TO A JOLT. Oracle Zoia was shaking him, saying, "Drink this, Egg of the Ish. It will strengthen you. Up now, and gird yourself."

Awareness came only slowly. He was on the floor by the windows, head on a makeshift pillow with its corner in his mouth. But Zoia was dead, wasn't she? It had been only a dream, and yet so incredibly vivid. Even the bitter taste of her tonics was still on his tongue.

He rose groggily, yawning as he hung his leaden head from a window. It was not yet light, and bright Zeruha shone like a distant lantern through a hazy remnant of Star Wash. Above the redolence of seaweed, thaakh blossoms laced the pre-dawn air. Neither zephyr nor yash'kh stirred on the beach below. It was deathly calm, unnatural.

The breaking of surf, the chirrup of zhaga, the night cries of zhrat, a plume-wing's warbling salute to the dawn: how he missed the sounds of home. However, now was hardly the time for being melancholy. It was time to outwit that schemer Zakon.

Behind him, the bed was in tatters and with Naama nowhere in sight. He sauntered to the grille in search of her, and there her phantom was straining oddly against it with sweeping movements and alien words.

"What do you?" he yawned.

"Gods! You startled me!"

"*Blech!*" Enok spat the remnants of Zoia's imagined tonics. "Bad dreaming me."

Naama appraised him silently. "Probably just the jitters. You can ill afford to be nervy. You know, self-doubt cripples as effectively as a weapon. Well, since you're up, warm-ups for you too. Watch closely and do as I do."

She pushed herself away from the great portcullis in a slow deliberate manner using only her hands. Then came repeated squats; the straight-legged bending and touching of toes; side stretches, left and right; sit-ups, with knees to the chin, left, right, left, right, again and again; a prolonged straight-legged stretch to the toes; then finally, a strange curl with knees to the forehead. Enok mimicked her as best he could until his abdominals cramped, and likewise rose to finish with a variety of slow, stylized movements, each gracefully executed to a nonsense word. The meaning of these martial rituals was lost on him, but he felt energized and ready for anything.

"Feel more alert, do you?"

"Y-yes," he replied shyly. What 'alert' meant was unclear, but there was no falling back to sleep now.

The flat of her hand reached for his chest and her lips smacked silently in prayer to some ogre god. But with a hand apiece on both their chests, Enok perceived she was counting heartbeats. But why would that be important?

"Good," she decided. "We can outrun them easily."

"What do now?"

Having knelt and replied, "The Gol-Ayat,"[xliv] and produced two fangs from her utility belt, she smeared a waxy paste from ear to ear like a band across her eyes and nose.

---

xliv The *Gol-Ayat* is both an exercise and a war prayer to Ma'nuna coined by Gol, and is accompanied by stylized movements executed to a unique tonal word describing a manner of injury, death, or a stratagem.

"Indigo is for stealth," she intoned. "Goddess, keep me darker than darkness, and fainter than a whisper." Using one of her little razors, a small cut to the arm yielded blood for a mix with another pigment. "Ocher now is for power, the strength of the earth. Goddess, strengthen my hands. May they sever the head of your enemies, and feed the soul of the world with their blood."

In the low light, only sheen differentiated color from color as she smeared this new mixture of blood, imprecations, and pigment over what remained of naked face.

"Kneel with me," Naama commanded. "Honor the Goddess."

Enok's hands waved vigorously, declining. *I'M NO BARBARIAN!*

"Even Gol himself wouldn't dare dishonor the Twain Goddess. You're not a believer yet. I pray she forgives you," she added softly before bowing with her forehead to floor. Then rocking on her knees, with palms extended upwards in a kind of supplication, she droned on for a while in some obscure patois.

Just as Enok thought it would last forever, she sprang upright. "Have you never prayed before?"

"Pray?"

She snorting something derisive, and tossed him an object, growling, "Catch, unbeliever."

He stumbled, surprised, as he caught a heavy metallic rod.

She held another in her hands. "From the toilet window. Soft walls, like you guessed."

To have pried the bars loose was no easy feat. How he had slept through that was a mystery. But why he felt so heavy-headed, or even how he had ended up on the floor with some of Naama's pillow in his mouth and the taste of Zoia's wormwood on his tongue perplexed him ever more.

"How you do —"

"We're headed home, that's all you need to think about. Now, put the bars under the grille. Here, like this." She demonstrated her intention. "Then we slide in these timbers to keep it prized open. Got it?"

Enok nodded. The wood was from the wrecked bed. They slid the bars under the grille, through the feeding gap for purchase, then prepared to lever it up.

"Together — one, two, three — now!"

Enok strained until his back hurt. The familiar screech of metal-on-stone echoed through the tunnels, and after several jerky movements, the grille inched off the floor.

"Quickly!" she groaned. "The timbers with your foot!"

In unison, they slid the props into position, and took a breather.

"Not nearly as hard as I thought!" exclaimed Naama between moans and arching her back.

The ease with which the jail door rose surprised him as well. The overlapping metallic slats were strong yet surprisingly springy and light. Perhaps it had counterweights, or maybe it had never even been bolted. It was hard to believe, though, that any jailer could have made such an oversight. Possibly having them share the cell together had never been the plan. Whatever the reason, they had seriously underestimated this amazon, and so had he.

Naama was kind with his puzzlement. "Like I said, never play by the enemy's rules." The wide shining grin that split her face — well, he presumed it was a grin — looked positively fearsome under all that war paint. "Besides, these dastardly snakes haven't the nous for real war."

She slid her gear through the gap, then squeezed herself after it. "Well, don't wait for an invitation!"

Now they were both outside.

"Good, now let's hide these."

Why the concern for the makeshift tools? They had made enough noise already, and the metallic echoes would surely alert a guard. "Go now," he prompted anxiously.

"No," she growled. "Listen, serpent-boy. She helps those who help themselves, the Goddess of Luck. When you have the advantage, you don't give drums to the heralds. Understand? The longer it takes to discover we've gone, the better our chances."

Again they levered the grille, then scattered the props with a kick. Enok lost his grip. The bar and the grille fell to earth with distinctive peals. Naama pitched the bars through the feeding gap along the floor, yet with such force that they collided loudly under a window.

Enok's heart was racing. In the stillness of the morning, only the dead could be deaf to this clangor. He beckoned furiously, "Go! Go! Go!"

The fugitives crept to the six-way junction, barely daring to breathe. The once spectacular arches were now wreathed in shadow, faintly illuminated by dying water-fire lanterns hanging midway to the ground. There was only one correct tunnel here amid five wrong choices, and all of them certainly deadly.

Naama crouched, groping about in the half-light, whispering "Hey! Zaraza? Zaraza?" Then finally, "To hell with you, then," she spat, rising. "Which way?" she suddenly demanded.

Anxious fingers traced glyphs etched along the arches. SECOND TUNNEL TO THE RIGHT. "Go here," he advised.

"Choose badly, Enok, and we're dead. Are you certain?"

"Y-yes."

"Stretch your left fingers out to the wall, and then run as never before. I'll keep to the right, so hopefully we won't trip over each other. Remember, think of nothing but your goal and your course will be true. Sandals off? Good. Any sound now would certainly betray us. Right! Let's leave these snakes for dust!"

Running: it was both exhilarating and scary, like vinegar and fire wedded in the blood.

Foop-fup, foop-fup went footfall's tempo in the dark, urging him ever forward. Though the flight was downhill, keeping pace was no easy matter. Naama was fearless in her strides, and never once faltered in the darkness.

What if he twisted an ankle? What plans then? So many the possibilities of failure!

JUST DO AS NAAMA SAYS. SELF-DOUBT CAN CRIPPLE. THINK OF NOTHING BUT YOUR GOAL ...

Enok reigned-in his wayward thoughts by conjuring cheery things.

... AND YOUR COURSE WILL BE TRUE.

There was a mainland wide beyond imagining, calling him. He had to keep focusing on the reunion with his family, with his father, with his wondrous midnight girl.

"Homeward bound. Homeward bound," he kept repeating to himself.

OH, FATHER!

*

After what seemed an age of running with his heart in this throat, luck came in the form of a gentler darkness, tall and arched, framing an entrance to Ra'a-Zohari's plaza. Outside, the city was quiet. No patrols. Not even a gholuj stirred.

A thin fog lingered in the plaza, resisting the zephyrs of Star Wash sweeping over the city. In that early twilight, it obscured almost everything except the softly luminescent stones of the dais, the almanac, and the Reliquary.

The Reliquary: palace of records, secrets, and mystery. Who knew what the Oracles had written? Perhaps where they had found him. Possibly details about his family. He had to find out.

"Stop!" Naama stifled a cry. "We're headed the wrong way!"

A yearning finger could only indicate the pyramid across the common, there where a stolen identity lay waiting for Enok in a towering alabaster enigma.

"Inside. Must see."

"Are you crazy?" shot Naama with bated voice. "Our luck could turn any moment. It will be light soon, and those snakes will be stirring." With a toss of the head, she beckoned. "Forget your boyish curiosity. Stick to the plan! I swear —"

But it was too late. Enok had already stepped onto the dew-laden dais. Immediately, it grew cold underfoot. The almanac took on a luminous quality, and once again the crowns of the skewed pillars came aglow with ancient ciphers.

The hand of the man hesitated. The fingers of the boy caressed their glassy surface in wonder and awe. "Oh. Zoar."

"Leave it be!" came Naama's strangled shout.

The dais crackled faintly with sparks as a pale blue pyramid of shimmering light began taking shape.

"Dung of a trr-bahal! You may as well have trumpeted a horn!"

"Trumpet?"

Naama grabbed him forcibly and leapt from the platform. "Get out of the open, fool, or we're both dead!"

As the fugitives sheltered in the portico of a large building at the edge of the common, Enok was astonished at the resourcefulness of his companion. Rope plaited from shredded blanket was coiled about her waist, and the swaddled bundle slung over her shoulder could only be the medicine stick. This barbarian was hot-tempered, sure, yet nothing short of amazing.

"Don't look back," she growled. "Keep moving!"

Down a curved alley, now removed from the plaza, rows of ceremonial incense pots hung from porticoes. At Naama's insistence, they lowered a pot and removed its hooks.

"And this?" Enok proffered the rubbery suspenders.

"Don't know. Need more hooks. Hurry up!"

Within moments, they had what they needed.

"On second thought, wrap one of those cords about your waist," she instructed, miming the motion. Her brow arched meaningfully. "Just in case." With the hooks now tucked into her utility belt, she rose and made that *bring-bring* gesture. "Come on! We have a boat to catch."

A loud *pop* echoed from the plaza. Darkness returned as the blue light fled, and replacing it was the faint and unexpected hiss of conversation.

"Hide!" Enok whispered. "Zmee see us."

Instinctively, Naama flattened against a wall. "At night? Through this fog?"

He pulled her to shelter behind a thick clump of tree ferns, crouching fearfully. "They see hot."

"You mean, body heat? Gods! Who would have known!"

Lying prostrate, Enok peered cautiously towards the plaza. Tall shapes with lances — three, maybe more — were crossing the dais, or so it appeared. It seemed a little odd, though, for guards always traveled in twos.

Enok signaled. *Follow me.*

Creeping down alleys between buildings, running doubled over and listening for the faintest signs of pursuit, finally came to an end. In a sixth of a watch, they had cleared the urban precinct and now found themselves on a track through scrubby woodland. Feet trod sand now instead of pavement, a welcome sign that they were indeed headed beach-ward.

The track was low and narrow, overhung with brush, pendulous tree mosses, and mistletoe, evidently the trail of some smaller creature. Behind him, Naama, had given up on a low-slung gait, and was muttering with every scrape.

Finally, they emerged upon yawning dunes peppered with tussocks of beach grass. Beyond, the somber outline of a sheltered bay greeted them with lapping, rhythmic waves.

Enok sprinted feverishly towards the water.

FREEDOM!

The aura of the Greater Light was just now burnishing the waters, and the great orb itself on the verge of rising. They had escaped the cell, the city, and detection. Thus far, the omens were good.

HOMEWARD BOUND. HOMEWARD BOUND.

Except —

Naama came up panting beside him, echoing his confusion. "This is almost too good to be true. Not a single guard, living or dead. And no boat either." Then, after a short pause, "Are you sure this is the right place?"

Whatever he had been seeing from the jail, this wasn't it. Fine black gravel crunched under heel. Except for a distant bluff, there were no towering cliffs with seams of ruby quartz, no signs of habitation, and no yash'kh. Tall flags hung limp in the distance, awaiting stronger breezes.

Good. They had to find the dragons before the wind picked up.

By the flags, dozens of stout bollards encrusted with mussels framed a chilling site. Half-buried Zmee skeletons in various states of decay were all that remained of at least a dozen lawbreakers. Drowned fare for zhrat and the crabs, they were, and frowning upon their ruin, the four-legged serpent-ring symbol — the very Na-Zeru standard itself, emblem of the Zeruhawi. Very likely, this would have been their own fate too.

Surely no one would search for them here. They were safe for the moment. But —

"No ruby sand, no steep cliffs, no reef dragons — this isn't the cove with the boat, is it, serpent-boy?" Naama spat some foreign expletive, and judging by her painted scowl, no reply would satisfy.

The light was brighter now and the mists were rapidly clearing. A stronger zephyr stirred. The beach was smooth and unbroken. Except their own footprints, no serpent trails or impressions marred its pristine surface. Tall stands of flat-leaved pines continued far into the horizon. A horrible sinking feeling gripped him. Naama was horribly right.

Enok's mind was racing. He repressed a cry of despair.

No-o!

If this was the wrong cove, where then was the right?

Naama led the way, jogging past both skeletons and flags to the remote end of the beach. A steep, near vertical climb up a stony escarpment faced them now, leaving them dangerously exposed and costing precious time. Enok's mind raced for alternatives. Perhaps they should double back.

The amazon, however, gave it no thought at all. She charged the bluff grunting like a yashurakh bull. "Don't overthink this!" she cried, climbing the thick prop roots of pandani clinging to the meager soil. "Just keep moving!"

It was almost daylight. From the crest of the bluff, the vista of a grander bay greeted them. The beach was rubescent and sandy. In the distance, yash'kh were milling about and would soon make a dash for the sea. There was still hope of reaching them in time, though the chances of a dawn patrol either spooking the pod or discovering the fugitives were rapidly rising. And now before them lay a formidable barrier to destiny. Massive crumbling fingers of ruby quartz, remnants of an eroded bluff, stood like a piked trap before them.

Maybe they should detour up the ridge.

Naama was quick. "Stop hesitating! Just do!"

She took a running leap and landed on an outcrop. Then again. And again. And again. And again. These hazards were taking more time to negotiate than the entire escape from the cell!

It seemed an age before they were clear.

Naama hit the sand first. Fearful of being left behind, Enok raced to overhaul her. One final leap left him on a worn gravelly slope, then he ran wildly and carelessly. His heart was racing. Several times he fell, skinning knees, elbows, and swallowing gravel. They should have taken the detour!

Dawn had given way to day. They were running out of time.

Closer now. Redolence of rotting seaweed. No longer mere dots on the beach, the reef dragons were but heartbeats distant.

Ga-runt. Ga-runt. Ga-runt.

Then came another sound, faint yet clear against the dragons' quarreling. Artificial, unmistakable.

Choof-woosh, choof-woosh, choof-woosh.

Emerging from what must have been a concealed cove — their jailing cove — a mechanical behemoth billowing steam and smoke entered the bay. The sight left Enok aghast, and even Naama fell backwards from shock. It was unlike any vessel he had ever imagined. The thing wasn't just shaped like some great yash'kh, it was truly enormous — and was quickly picking up speed!

The pod leader, construing a challenge — something had taken to water before it — took off in pursuit. The pod made to follow.

On the shifting sand, Naama's great strides gave her the advantage. With an ululating trill and hands waving wildly, she ran like fury to catch one of the stragglers. Her battle cry, however, was having a disastrous effect.

In an act of desperation, Enok made for the water's edge, kicking his feet high and wide as he leapt across breaking foam in an effort to beat Naama to the startled remnant.

CLOSE.

SO CLOSE!

NO-O!

Enok fell to his knees in disbelief, and with every breath a labor. Naama came up beside him, gasping and panting with her hands on her knees. The little she managed to say came garbled beyond recognition.

Utter desolation gripped him. Gone! They had missed the yash'kh and the boat along with them. Just like his New Year's Eve acceptance plan, this too had proved a monumental failure.

Pain came. *Pain!* Like the pinch of a tree crab.

Whack! He stumbled from a sharp slap to the head. Naama had struck him!

She was livid. "Just going to" — *pant* — "lie down" — *pant* — "and give up, are you?"

WHAT ELSE CAN I DO? he privately wailed. WE MISSED THE BOAT!

She struck again, now with a force that felled him. Then she kicked him in the behind.

Enok scampered away on all fours from the demon she had become.

SHE'S GONE MAD!

Naama let fall her backpack before slowly undoing her utility belt and tossing it across a limpeted outcrop. She was edging towards him muttering, eyes wide, primal and vicious, nose and lips curled in a sneer like Refa when he slew the Oracles.

Dread filled him. He had failed her, and here they were beneath open sky! Now was the fight she had promised.

Enok kept to the water's edge, still catching his breath, and steeling himself for the assault. A fight in the water bolstered his chances, but his strength was utterly spent!

She struck out with her foot, but he bobbed, catching and lifting it high, causing her to topple. She sprang back to a crouch almost immediately, and with a wide motion, swung a leg out like a cudgel, catching a heel and felling him into the surf.

Fury etched on her painted features, she lunged and would have crushed him but for his sideways leap. She knew she had missed, and crabbed his way as a wave swept over them both. Fingers tore at his copper leg shackle, tripping him, then came the pain of sharpened nails clawing his calves and piecing his skin. Enok rolled desperately, double speed. The instant a leg freed, he planted a heel to her forehead with a dull solid *snap!*

He was sure he had broken her neck. A second heel struck her grasping wrist, liberating his ankle from her wooden fingers. But she was only dazed, and all too briefly. He had barely managed to crawl free when a whip tore through the air. She had somehow used her waist cord as a bolas, and it had snaked above his knee. Now, she pulled hard, dragging him down as another wave broke.

A *splash!* and then another told she was almost upon him and ready to pounce. Clutching a fistful of sand, he rolled, aiming for eyes that had now become airborne, and instinctively, he raised both feet to catch her midriff, and with a spring propelled her beyond her target to drop heavily into shallows.

She had barely a chance to rise and rinse her eyes of sand, when he heaved at the cord to bring her down backwards, then fell upon her chest with a knee to the neck, and roped her hands together. As she gurgled under a wave, Enok pushed back on her thumb with all the force he could muster.

Naama came up gasping, and gurgling obscenities about 'blood and bahalazh' as a wave rolled over and another overturned them. She was done fighting and remained where she lay, crazed between the waves and gesticulating wildly. It was a madness beyond all recollecting: cascades of hiccoughing and bellowing, with teeth biting the air and her eyes still blinded from sand.

But it was laughter — laughter! — wild and carefree!

And it was infectious. He began laughing too at the amazon's comical drowning where each rising was foiled by a wave. It had been so long: the sound of another's laughter had been utterly lost to memory. He proffered a helping hand, but she yanked hard, pulling him into a crashing wave while laughing all the harder.

"Gods! You dart like a viper! Where'd you learn to fight like that, serpent-boy?" Her eyes were still slits. She could barely see.

"Hrazul," he replied. He and Wise-eye had often tussled on the sand, though it was only ever play.

"He was a good teacher," she sputtered on all fours, coughing as a wave receded.

"She," he corrected, kneeling beside her.

"Laughter's a good antidote for misery." A slap to the face, then she leveled a lecturing finger. "But, now, by the Sons of the Gods, take your anger at me," she growled, her finger rounding on the city, "and use it against them! I need you attentive, not whimpering like some dying pup under hostile sky! We can do this. We will find another way."

"'Think of nothing but your goal,'" repeated Enok lamely.

"Exactly! You should study ..." The rest was unintelligible as she washed her eyes of sand. It smeared her war paint. "But you never give up. Never!" Naama trotted to the rocky outcrop and retrieved her kit. "Quickly," she called, "mess up our prints before we quit the beach."

By a tidal creek, and beneath an escarpment overhung with pandani, a sullen Enok considered his next move. Naama was trying to explain the differences between strategy and tactics; however, little made any sense. But this he understood by himself: if this were some game of zhakh, his most valuable piece had been lost in the opening gambit.

"We need another plan." Naama was on her knees, legs tucked underneath, and calmly redoing her face paint in the shadows where a billabong reflected her image. "The unexpected happens.

Even the best of warriors have that challenge. And how you deal with the unexpected is just as important as the objective itself."

Was she being patronizing or encouraging? Though less formal and more temperamental, she resembled an Oracle in many ways — well, a sort of fighting Oracle.

She was sucking her injured thumb after washing her hands when her painted nose crinkled. "Ugh! City water! Small wonder at the brown sand!" She retired to a stiff bench of aerial roots, casually chewing a stalk, and having mentioned something about 'times for thinking, and times for doing,' she yawned and added, "So, have you thought of anything?"

After such an epic failure, it was hard not to despair. Yet, oddly, Naama seemed untroubled by their predicament. With an Oracle, one expected a reprimand and a chastening, but there was none of that here. On the contrary, the imperious undertone was gone, and, despite the war paint, the haughty looks with it. How he knew was beyond explaining, but something had changed in her perception of him.

That she seemed to be pinning all her hopes on him was flattering, if not a little scary, and an accolade beyond any praise from an Oracle. However, there was no redeeming the fact that he had no backup plan. The boat was long gone and with no way to overhaul it.

He cried inwardly as desperate eyes followed the plumes from the tiny speck of a boat as it veered to starboard, exit the great bay, and disappear behind the cape, leaving a trailing pod of yash'kh in its wake.

A large plucked leaf, folded in half, made an instant whistle and he played a simple staccato tune, much to his companion's dismay. She was no lover of music, the pained expression said. In this, and her regimented manner, there was something of Hrazul in her.

He discovered long ago that his best ideas were generated this way, for music helped him relax. As he played, another part of his mind exulted in its triumph of logic as brightened eyes followed the last of the yash'kh exit the bay in the opposite direction.

OPPOSITE!

Yes, the boat had veered to the right! To the north! It ought to have headed south with the yash'kh, to round Sha-Noa, then wend its way through the Chechi Archipelago and the one clear passage through the reefs. So why hadn't it?

He visualized a map of Zoar, and traced an outline of a weedy sea dragon in the pink and brown sand — the shape of Zoar Island — and itemized the few facts to be had. There was a sudden flutter of hope. He now had a better idea now of where they were and what had gone wrong.

The dark, rubescent beaches meant they were certainly north of the isthmus. The thaakh plantations were generally on the western coast, and few bays were as large as this. Very likely, they were at Ra'a-Zohari in the mid-west, or even further north in Ur-Hozhai. The east coast lay only two or three days march through the swamps. That is, assuming there was some kind of road. And though he had only ever seen depictions on a map, those great fingers of stone that had trapped them at the end must have been the Hazards of Yzhau Bay.

I KNOW WHERE WE ARE!

"Boat!" Excitedly he etched its journey northwards for provincial passengers, making enormous circuits in allowance of the island's convolutions before skirting the eastern seaboard on its way to the mainland. "Stop here." He marked the coastal cities. "Three day, four day."

"*¡Mpwa.*" Naama had pursed her lips curiously and sent a little breath towards him, leaving Enok baffled by the gesture. "If I understand you correctly," she ventured, "the boat takes almost four days to circumnavigate the island — perhaps as little as three, depending on Zmee whim. We can't outrun it. But interception is still a possibility this way." Naama drew her own line eastward in the sand, back through the city of Ra'a-Zohari to the Bay of Fires.

Then he shook his head at what that implied. "Much Zmee in city. They catch us!"

"It's the most direct route. Is there an easier one? Or faster?"

He shrugged. "I not knowing."

The amazon suddenly tensed, gripping his arm, and squinting at something afar. A patrol had appeared by the Hazards.

"Great blood and bahalazh! So soon! Dirty snakes, they're tracking us already. We have to keep off the sand." She was instantly energized, and rising, handed him the medicine stick. "Take this.

We have to double back. I guarantee you, that's the last thing they'll expect."

"Back to ... Zmee place?" Enok stammered. "Zmee can" — *sniff-sniff* — "Naama!"

"You mean the snakes will track our scent?"

Enok nodded worriedly.

Her teeth gleamed through her war paint. "Having followed us this far, they're expecting us to flee the city. Since we can't afford to lay another scent trail, we parallel backtrack instead — to slink right through it and intercept the boat on the coast." A large hand weighed on his shoulder. It was surprisingly reassuring.

The ocher-and-indigo face creased queerly. "You're not *afraid*, are you?"

He nodded. "Muchly."

The honesty seemed to surprise her, then she nodded knowingly. "Panic leads to death as sure as any poison, but courage makes its own hope. Remember that." The hand on the shoulder quickly slid to the back of his neck, gripping him eye-to-eye with fingers of wood. "Trust me: if we believe it, we can do it. Just make sure your own mouth keeps saying so." She relaxed her grip when she realized she was hurting him. "So, how long to the other ocean?"

He kneaded the weals where Naama had grabbed him. She was a poor judge of the strength of her grip. Then two fingers shot up. "Two day." With a bent finger he added, "And little."

She nodded, understanding. "Lets err on the side of caution, and say three. That still gives us a day to spare — *if* the terrain is good, and *if*, and *if*, and *if*. ¡Tsk. The greater the ifs, the lesser the luck." She wiped her brow. "Well, let's at least kill one of those ifs right now. The Zmee will lose our tracks in that mess the dragons made, but these need to be covered."

Naama obscured their telltale footprints, and had begun to climb the cliff along ladders of tangled roots while Enok's map-making mind still considered the facts: FERNS. A CREEK THAT SPRUNG FROM NOWHERE. CITY WATER.

'THINK IN OPPOSITES, LITTLE ISH,' Oracle Zoia often said.

Perhaps there was a better route, and safer. "Stop!" he cried.

"We haven't time to waste, Enok!"

"From city come water. With water go city."

That Naama instantly dropped from her height meant she understood. "Hmmm, your Y'lan is improving. And that's actually a really good idea. No tracks, and we wash ourselves of scent. But where does it lead? It seems to flow from yonder thicket."

While she was pointing out how unpleasant it would be to crab all the way back, the pair had crept under thick dense ferns to come before a grand stone arch hewn into the cliff face. The amazon whistled oddly. Sour water lapped his knees.

"You're right. The water from our cell, the city entire, must egress somewhere, and it's here from this artificial cave. It's wide, true, but I'll be stooping all the way."

"Bigger later, Enok think."

"Wading through a Zmee —" Naama spun, crouching. "Voices," she whispered. "Into the toilet. You first."

The sewer tunnel was dark and dank, and Enok thought that amusing. How else should it be at the nadir of his fortunes?

The pair waded with outstretched hands against slimy masonry, and with great uncertainty. Maybe this led so deep under the city there was no way out. Every Zmee settlement had great underground baths, places for meeting and fellowship. Each stratum had their own. Oracles, Venerables and Prominents shared elaborately mosaicked facilities having fountains and waterfalls. The various strata of students and lesser public officials congregated in less stately pools. And then there were the plain public baths for younglings and others. If this tunnel led to any sort of bathhouse — well, they were surely undone.

Naama's original plan had had fewer ifs. Every new doubt tugged at him. *Go back, go back,* they all seemed to say. Enok growled. What was the point of hindsight if it merely crippled the present?

The height forced Naama to go badly astoop, and the hope that this sour-smelling tunnel would open up grew weaker with every step. Nevertheless, the amazon kept her peace — longer than was natural for her. She really *was* relying on his judgment, and that was scarier than the darkness and doubts combined.

Then ahead, a soft haze, and the dribble of unseen flumes.

"Light. And an exit." Naama whispered.

And it was true. They had come to a thick stone grate set into the arch of the ceiling. It was pumice, the same kind of stone Enok had once sculpted as a boy. Water trickled steadily through it.

"I think we're under a building," said Naama, raising her voice.

This was likely connected to a Zmee chamber, and a good sign they had reached the city, but they would need a larger exit.

Naama shared his thoughts. "I think I hear another ahead. Let's try that one."

The next, and the next beyond it were all too much alike. They had to choose one, and soon.

"Hear that?" Naama whispered.

Enok strained to no avail. Naama's hearing was clearly superior.

It seemed louder now, gurgling like an overflow. Its halo beckoned them forward.

At a vaulted junction, pillars with grand capitals made a veritable temple that seemed so out of place in these sewers. Row upon row of columns stretched into endless shadow. And here at the center, a vast lake burbled beneath a waterfall in a dancing shaft of light.

Arms out wide, Naama suddenly cried, "Enok! Enok! Go around and corral it! We mustn't let it escape!"

WHAT? With eyes still adjusting to the brightness and confused, Enok wondered at the sight. It was a Zmee, sort of: an armless mud-colored sprat. First impressions said *serpent*, but its large forward facing ovals, snout tendrils, and bristling neck membranes clearly marked it otherwise, and as an adult Zmee to whit. But it couldn't be a female, could it?

The creature hissed, swaying side-to-side gauging its victims, a typical ploy of Hrazul's before striking.

"Peace to thee! Peace! We mean thee no harm," cried Enok in High Zmeezh, to Naama adding, "Not kill!"

"Either it dies or we do. It's certain to betray us, blast you!"

"No!" Enok growled in return. "Thy life is secure," he promised the creature. "We seek only to escape Zoar without bloodshed. And everyone lives. Agree ye? Agree?"

"Peace?" hissed the serpent in common Low Zmiysh. "What peace can there be for the warm-born dead?"

Before Enok could even respond, it dived at astonishing speed and with barely a ripple. Only the rub of its tail against a leg and the great splash Naama made as she lunged to intercept it marked the event as real and not imagined, and it left them alone now beneath a massive grating and being pummeled by a hearty cascade.

"By the six hells, why would an unarmed Zmee be down here in this cesspool? Part of a posse, perhaps?" While some words were unfamiliar, her sense of confusion was clear.

"That not real Zmee." It sounded untrue even as it rolled off the tongue. It *was* a Zmee, a youngish bull perhaps, and lessened in so many ways, yet a fugitive like themselves. "Here! Up!"

"You're right. No time to waste." With the back of her neck up against the grating, Naama exerted her full force with a mighty grunt. "Blood of th-the g-gods!" she gurgled beneath the cascade. "It's iron!"

The cover flew up with a loud *sloop*, and the amazon finally managed to stand erect with her head free of the tunnel though still struggling to breathe. "Crouch! M-make … a stool!"

With a heel to his bent back, she propelled herself into the outside world, then hoisted him up with her wooden grip to stand in an alleyway beneath an aqueduct's overflow.

She unslung her backpack, arching and burbling, "Oh, Goddess!" as she reveled in the freshwater shower. "I could have drowned in that cavernous toilet! Why build something so low?"

But Enok kept thinking what a young mutant bull was doing in the sewers of an island that permitted only younglings and females.

The respite was short lived. "Where to now, serpent-boy?"

Low buildings surrounded them on all sides, affording a view of tapering spires, grand cupolas, and great forests beyond. This part of the city was nestled in a steep-sided valley that was almost a jail in itself, hemmed as it was by near-vertical revetments. It was wedge-shaped, with the expanse of the common and the Reliquary at its broader end. That was their only way forward, and would leave them more exposed than ever.

The fugitives huddled behind the knobbled foundations of a tower close to the very common where they had once stood captive. Few Zmee seemed to be outdoors today.

So FAR SO GOOD, Enok began thinking before abruptly gesturing *Stop!* As Naama froze, it amazed him how quickly she'd mastered his expressions, a rapport he had once only shared with Hrazul.

Across the dais, on the far side of the common, a typically feathered Oracle emerged from a grand building followed by what seemed like disciples mounted with parchments.

A finger curled a *come-hither* to Naama.

The amazon came crouching beside him, scanning the vacant plaza. "Just one last building to clear," she whispered.

Enok nodded, confirming. The final building was the Reliquary. Beyond lay vast swamps and near-intractable rain forest. Provided they had a good head start and scented themselves with forest litter, they might lose even the best of trackers in that soggy morass. Right now, however, except for the raised crier's pedestals scattered about the common, there was precious little cover.

Enok led the way. "Go!"

From pedestal to pedestal, they dashed slung low; to another, then another; finally to the Reliquary itself, taking a breather behind a great stone corner. Its smooth white surface offered little shelter, and pavement edged it like a final barrier against the jungle.

Naama cocked her painted head. "Can you hear that?"

Voices. And a squawking khwatl. A party of Zmee were approaching along their very route of escape!

A finger of iron poked his ribs: one of her many expressions. Another identified the avenue with the aqueduct from under which they had entered the city. j'Na-Zeru guards were congregating there by the tower and barking instructions to Civils.

"Argh! Enok, we didn't close the grate!" growled Naama as loud as she dared. "And we've left a trail of water!"

They were trapped.

The chatter of Zmee ahead was louder now.

Naama threw her eyes knowingly, indicating the pyramid, and making a snaking gesture. She was suggesting that they pair-up in the shape of a Zmee and slip inside to hide.

Where else could they go?

Enok in the lead, they scurried to a great ebony Pillar of Zmee at the base of the ramp, crouching behind it and barely daring to breathe. An intervening crier's pedestal had been their only cover.

"Blind Zmee could spot us here!" Naama growled. "Either we split up, and one of us plays decoy, or we take shelter inside that mountain."

Enok nodded, accepting the risk as yet another party had begun to casually skirt the plaza. The portal of the great pyramid was open and unguarded. Right now, it was their only place to hide.

At that very moment, there was a diversion in the form of a flash of light high above the almanac on the dais.

Startled disciples dropped their scrolls.

"The blue fire!" exclaimed Naama, peering with bated breath around the column. "Goddess, what a gift!"

This would undoubtedly attract a crowd. Providential or otherwise, it was their one salvation, and they had to act swiftly while everyone's eyes were elsewhere. Enok gave Naama a tug by her backpack, motioning with a nod towards the opening in the massive structure behind them.

"Right. We stick together."

With the hope of the desperate, they snaked with all speed up the smooth stone gangway and into the Reliquary.

PYRAMID OF STARS

While distraught that the reliquary has been ransacked, and all traces of his lost identity gone, Enok stumbles upon a secret chamber that has waited since history's dawn to share secrets beyond imagining.

OUTSIDE, THE RELIQUARY FORMED A stark and glistening mountain. Inside, it was gloomy, cold and eerie. A soft phosphorescent glow seemed to emanate from everywhere but the floor. It was barely enough for the eyes, so Enok marveled by hand at its smooth masonic precision.

Massive stone blocks with almost imperceptible joins formed a broad triangular corridor, as best as he could tell. Shafts had been sculpted into the 'walls' as if designed to showcase something, or perhaps conceal it. These stood brooding like sentinels, semicircular, shadowy, empty.

The amazon had inched warily up the passageway until she disappeared from sight, and had now returned, slumping into one of the alcoves with a groan.

"Thankfully, there's no one here but us," she muttered before angrily elbowing the wall. "But we're still in a race against the boat, and all we can do is play carcass until that outside commotion dies down. I daresay we'll lose a watch, maybe even two, or however long it is until noon. Goddess! Coming in here was a blunder."

It was a grievous delay, an anxious respite, yet this was what Enok had longed for, and he felt a rush of excitement. "Look more. In there," he urged, with eyes zooming up the corridor.

Naama leaned forward into the light. Gone were the wild eyes of a fugitive. They were more like a hunter's now. All was in shadow but for a disembodied face striped in contrasting sheen, and it broke out with gleaming teeth as she studied his expression.

Funny, just a few days ago, he would have instinctively baulked. It was simply unimaginable that some ritual baring of fangs could be anything but hostile — that is, among the Zmee. Yet here it was, an innocent gesture from an alien world, a smile. And it struck him how even the most benign intentions could be misunderstood, how *he* had been misunderstood. Witness the reaction of Hrazul's new disciple on the morning of that awful, awful day. And that segued with a shiver to the haunting image of Hrazul's beautiful, lifeless head falling again to the ground.

The floating head spoke again. "There's something in here you're just itching to see, isn't there?"

He wagged his head. Oops, he was being Zmee again. "Yes," he nodded mechanically.

"Like what? It's just another empty pyramid. The lack of guards is hardly puzzling. Believe me, if there were anything truly precious here, I doubt we'd be alive right now." Something in the way she said 'another' suggested there were others. "But it isn't gritty here at all. Someone opened this pyramid only recently, I'd say, but then why leave it open?"

Enok shrugged. So many questions, so little information. To him, the true mystery of the Reliquary was of another order entirely: what was its purpose, and might it not contain some clues about his past?

"Well, this pile of rock might just have a back door," the painted head mused. "No harm in looking, I suppose. But if we're cornered," her expression turned grave, "prepare to defend yourself."

He recoiled inwardly. To save a life by taking a life was the amazon's proposition. But hadn't there been enough killing already? Every soul was precious. If such a moment ever came, he knew he could never bring himself to murder. But was killing really murder when done in self defense? Nothing he had ever heard or read had ever prepared him for this.

Naama's lips compressed to a disappointed line, and he wondered if all his expressions betrayed him so easily. But it worked both ways, did it not? He briefly imagined, if they survived, what it would be like to live in a community of people like himself: people who understood him, who accepted him, who greeted with a ready smile rather than reprimands and endless lists of chores. To be free among the free, that would really be something.

Naama indicated his feet. "You're not really comfortable in sandals, are you? That'd be a fatal weakness if you were Havilan. Shoes are a warrior's most important armor. I'd slip them back on, if I were you."

Yet another new word. "Armor?"

After a moment's silence, she set his conscience at ease. "Fine. Just guard my rear then. A stab in the back is no way to die. Can you do *that* for me?"

Deeper within the pyramid, at the threshold of a vast low-roofed chamber, astonishment halted the fugitives as they partook of the alien wonder. A water-fire lantern on a three-wheeled trolley bathed the chamber in yellow-green tones, revealing islands of chaos in an otherwise empty room. And Naama barred him entry as she mumbled something about demons and traps.

The most notable feature here, though, was the floor. Alternating dark and light hexagons were as harsh as they were foreign to Zmee organic style. Swirls, flourishes, or anything sinuous found little welcome here. Vacant shelves stood in rows against the far wall. The floor was littered with piles of ancient parchments, statues, and an assortment of artistic artifacts. In a far corner, a number of academic 'genealogy' poles had fallen against a wall. Others had been toppled completely. Elsewhere, piles of shards were all that remained of ornamental scroll cases. The whorled, winged sarcophagi of long-mummified Oracles lay open, desecrated. In all, it was a scene of astonishing devastation.

Enok's heart and mind were racing. It was here, and only here among the rubble, that his past would be uncovered. The smooth feel of the threshold's arch alerted him to another alien influence, the complete lack of traditional rubrics or blessings. Whoever had built the Reliquary, they had clearly been foreign to the Zoar he knew.

He followed as Naama tiptoed into the chamber with some sing-song invocation for blindness on her enemies, and made straight for the grandest sarcophagus

"Deity arks." Her hands delighted over the richness of its textures. "I've only ever heard about these. Strange, though, for Zmee to have such a custom."

The winged and cone-shaped sarcophagus was larger than its peers, and intricately carved in the form of a four-legged dragon. The detail was exquisitely lifelike, down to minute scales and natural imperfections. Ancient runes covered it. Its legs were unnaturally splayed, one for each of the four winds, like the familiar Zeruhawi motif. And it too had been prized rudely open.

"By the Six Hells," whooped Naama, "it must have been a truly glorious fight!"

"Fight?"

"Don't you have eyes? The chamber is a mess, and from a very recent skirmish I'd say." Naama proffered a parchment for examination. It was beautifully gilt and with richly painted cartouches. "No moldering manuscript, this: pristine, not a speck of dust on it. How strange is that?"

The text of High Zmiysh, with its olden serpentine pictographs, was something rarely emulated for beauty. The more familiar Mapmakers' alphabet would certainly have been easier to render. Even so, it told of the early settlement of the island, and the ruins that the settlers had found.

"Zoar Island," he paraphrased simply. "Old, broken place."

First a long plummeting whistle, then, "Are you some sort of Magus that you can read this?" inquired Naama, her painted eyebrows arching. "Take it with you, then, since there's nothing of value here. However, should you find a knife ..." Her eyes widened suggestively.

Even after dozens of parchments, the acceptance was slow and reluctant in coming. Naama was right. There was nothing of interest here. But how could that be? Enok was pondering how generations of Historians had dedicated their lives to preserving this midden of relics when suspicion and anguish converged in a cry.

"Take! Away! Gone!"

All hope evaporated as the truth of it shook him. Nothing of his past was here. The huge mounted lantern was an archivists trolley. The fact that it was still aglow meant he had come too late.

"You mean, stolen? Ransacked?" Naama was skeptical. "You can't know that for certain. What where you expecting, anyhow?" She wandered the chamber, sniffing its vastness like a zhrat on the prowl. "Hey! Now *this* is interesting: fresh blood." She motioned Enok to join her. "Bring that light with you!"

In the far corner where genealogy poles lay fallen, the amazon's superior senses had nosed out a smear on a dark tile. A contrasting sheen had betrayed it. There was a mystery here, and the first clue ended abruptly at the wall as though it had slipped beneath it.

Lantern's light made it clear. It was Zmee blood, and it *did* go under.

"Open!" Naama slapped the impenetrable stone. "I command you to open!"

Silence.

Three pounds of the fist, and still nothing.

She gave way as Enok pushed the cart aside, toppling a relic. His fingers had barely touched the wall when it slid slowly upwards to the sound of scraping stone and revealed a narrow entrance.

"How did you ...? Ah, it was me, after all," she quipped. "It's just a slow door."

Regardless of assertions, what had triggered the door was unclear, though it probably had something to do with the path of one's approach. It had to be serpentine, meandering, and the tiles by the entrance formed a sequence of keys. Zmee loved tricks like that.

Naama forged ahead. "Come on. If there's blood, there's a trail, and perhaps a way out."

As time would reveal, the passage spiraled ever upward and deeper into the pyramid. It led to a spherical room high above the original chamber. Hexagonal patterns were again the motif, barely visible by the light of a large glassy sphere floating head-height above the floor.

The orb shone faintly like crystalline gold as though lit from within, waxing and waning to a slow rhythm. So little of its glory reflected off the walls, and its markings were unlike anything Enok had ever seen: they were moving, appearing and disappearing, changing shape and changing color. It was beautiful beyond words, a product of the same mysterious science as the almanac, and a wonder that beggared the sum of all learning.

Oh how much the Zmee had forgotten! And, indeed, how righteous any sorrow at the loss!

Within the orb, a wheel spun almost imperceptibly, parallel with the floor, and within it another wheel, perpendicular to the first, was revolving slightly faster. At their common hub, an even smaller orb shot rays of light like spokes at its jewel-symboled rims. Eyes drifted occasionally across the surface of the sphere, following some invisible arc. It gave the creepy feeling of being watched.

An eye blinked.

The sphere was alive.

Naama's mouth hung open in rapture. "Great Goddess!" was all she managed, while shrinking dramatically with every step. In no time at all, she appeared much further away than she was. "My, how it's grown!" She swiveled to catch his reaction, her eyes wide and startled. "And so have you!" His approach brought a sigh of relief. "Only the Glorious Ones have magic like this, so why is it here on this worm-ridden island?"

Their relative sizes were normal again, though the object was now twice as large as before. Everything became smaller as it approached the sphere, all distance an illusion.

Her outline distorted as she circled the orb with an inquisitive hand. The golden glass grayed with the contact, spreading like an infection to the rest of the sphere. In mere heartbeats, it was dead, and darkness enveloped the room.

"It feels like metal yet warm." The sphere sprang to life again as her hand withdrew.

Perhaps it was just chance, or the way light played on the room's curved walls. In the transient moment of vision restored, a familiar sheen was revealed. And with the waxing light came understanding: they were smears of a Zmee's bloodied hand. Tiles were keys here too, keys to another hidden door.

Naama rounded at the rumble as another portal appeared. "Well, aren't *you* the favorite son!" she gibed. "What did you do?"

He had pressed the tiles in order of most bloodied to least. Enok's hand was still raised, and she was quick to see it.

"Very clever. You think like a Zmee." With a florid gesture, she bowed in gentle mockery. "Well, lead on, O favored of the gods! Obviously, something or somebody wants to be found." She was still stooping playfully, with her palm towards the doorway, when she gasped, "And I think we just found them."

Amidst a bloody pool, a serpent lay sprawled in the passageway. Her naked crown sprouted tendrils thicker than those of her snout. He'd never seen such exposed before. A festive headdress crumpled half-concealed beneath her was unmistakably mistress Zoia's.

Naama surmised what had happened faster than he. "There's been fighting here. Actually, in the first chamber. Then they chased the Zmee here and she somehow managed to lock herself out." Quick to grasp his smitten looks, she ventured, "Someone you know?"

Enok crouched beside the body, nodding sadly. "Zoia, good Zmee." His eyes closed in a silent promise:

Goodbye, teacher. I will honor your memory. By all you believed in, I swear it.

"The question is, who were the assailants. Not Zmee, that's for sure." Before he could even ask, Naama stiffened as she added, "Zmee remove their dead, or leave an honor token if they can't."

"Always?"

Checking for signs of life, she nudged the corpse with a foot, and nodded. "How can you not know that?"

Following a hasty inspection of the passage ahead, Naama signaled an *all clear*. Then painted eyes drilled him. "Don't you *dare* weep for a Zmee. Don't you dare. Come on. There's nothing you can do for her now."

Suddenly, the orb behind them shone angrily in tones of oranges and reds, shooting brilliant, erratic arcs of light across the room, and the doorway disappeared with a slam.

"Whatever you were after, I think it's ahead," Naama muttered, as she signed some barbarian sigil. "And be prepared. I don't think we're alone."

*

The new triangular passageway twisted smoothly ever higher towards the pyramid's apex. The faint glow from the 'ceiling' lit their way as Naama gingerly ventured ahead, no longer her talkative self. As the gradient leveled, they found themselves at the threshold of another vault. Whereas the first had been a broad, squat rectangle, and the second a sphere, this was a cube.

Naama held him back before throwing herself inside, muttering nonsense about 'death and gold.'

Indeed, gold was everywhere; the room was completely lined with it. Unlike the familiar metal, this was glassy, almost transparent, like the levitating orb. He waited at the threshold, a little apprehensive. Of all the three chambers, this was clearly the smallest, and completely empty, utterly void of grit or mote. No mark blemished its surface. Time was powerless here.

Naama patrolled the chamber, shouting her name, and challenging an unknown god to battle. "Show yourself, coward!"

Odd. There was no echo.

"It's the most valuable stone there is," she informed, scuffing the wall with the tip of her sandal. It was something a youngling might do. "Many have died for just a shard! And here's an entire vault lying useless!" She loosed a plummeting whistle. "What Gol wouldn't do to get ahold of this."

Who was this person Gol, and why he would so value this golden glass? Naama's reply to his badly framed question was, "It's living stone."

Funny, Zmee said the same of the almanac.

"What a Gol?"

"Who is Gol? Honestly? He's third regent of the Glorious Ones! Not a half-cast Anaki like Refa, spawned of some unwilling Isha's loins, but motherless, a true god!"

"Anaki?"

"Who are the Anaki?" The pitch of her voice rose peculiarly. "I can't believe you just asked. Have you *never* heard of the Anaki or the Glorious Ones? Perhaps instead you know them as The Fallen? Though I wouldn't whisper *that* too loudly, unless you're keen on dying. What about the mighty citadel of Bel-Al?" She must have sensed that he still had no idea, for her expression etched one of complete disbelief.

Stiffening and smiting her breast is some gesture of fealty, "The Anaki are my people, and Gol is my lord," she intoned. "The Sons of the Gods shall prevail." It spilt like a youngling's recitation, absent of inflection or passion. Fugitive intimacy died aborning and her eyes took on a distant, troubled look. "We're wasting time here," she grunted in passing. "There is no back door."

Enok, however, wanted to experience this living stone for himself. After all, they had a watch and half until noon and Zmee were under cover again.

Under naked feet, it felt like nothing, neither cold nor warm.

"Your footprints!" Naama cried from behind.

Where he had stood only moments earlier, writing appeared inside the gold of the floor: symbols in different sizes and hues, three dimensional, yet wholly residing within the golden glass. The words darted across the room, up the walls and the ceiling, coalescing, fragmenting, recombining, until only a single symbol remained, a simple triangle yet of infinite complexity — and it seemed to be inverting itself, changing color: first red, then green, then blue, then red again. Or were they just overlapping glyphs?

Whatever it had been, it faded to nothing.

Wa-hwoomp!

The door behind him slammed with an echo, startling him, and the chamber was plunged into darkness.

Even in the deepest of Oush's caves, and even with eyes shut tight, there was always a stray color, the spark of an afterimage, or *something*. This, however, was uttermost darkness, everlasting, not just the absence of light, and Enok sensed beyond all reason that he was no longer *where* he had been or *when* he had been. He could feel neither his hands nor his feet. Was he standing? Falling? He was completely disoriented and began groping wildly, desperate for contact.

Suddenly, a whisper.

"Hello?"

A Presence in the darkness. Need: the need to give, to receive. Need was what he felt. It was too intense to be his own.

Thick darkness boiled.

A light. Such a tiny pinprick. It hovered midair. A pearl, a grain of sun-sand. But it was not the Presence.

Instinctively, he reached for it.

Flash!

In less than a heartbeat, it exploded into countless fragments of color and deafening sound, and with a scorching pain to the hand.

Light! Upon glory! Upon light!

Waves of incandescence began to spread out like the roaring surf of a burning sea, bubbles within bubbles, like orb-shaped ripples, shimmering and blindingly beautiful. In the exhaustion of the primal fire, multiplied thousands of whirlpools of dancing lights flew across their expanding surfaces like so many scattered embers. Enok flinched, instinctively raising a hand to the light. Closed eyes, however, now perceived even more: colors and images beyond any describing, all unutterably wonderful and as bewildering as overlapping mirages, like multiple viewpoints through multiple eyes.

As the outermost bubble spread out, there was an explosion of words on its surface. Were they cartouches of a map? Greetings? Strange winged creatures with multiple faces made a brief appearance, then others with skins of fire darted between the embers.

There was a long pause — and silence.

The High Wisdom had often contemplated other Spheres of Existence with her fellow philosophers. Were these them?

As the second bubble spread out chasing the first, words appeared on its surface too, and he had fleeting glimpses of other strange creatures. Some were serpentine like the Zmee, others furry and winged.

Such an overload of the mind! Images of peoples, cities, worlds, and heavens! How could anything live on the skin of a bubble? Or was it a wave? Enok gave up trying to understand any of it. The images kept bombarding him with the relentless force of a waterfall, and he was powerless against them. His best hope was to keep his real eyes open to limit what he saw.

Again there was a long pause — and utter silence.

The final wave, the innermost bubble of fire, now spread out and grew large and thick. He felt as if he was physically shrinking beyond what anyone could ever hope to measure — and he fell into it.

Sparks! Countless thousands of them!

These too were the children of the primal fire and they flew to greet him. Many burned brightly. Most were now dark. That is, until he closed his eyes to 'see' them whirl past in subtle, delicate hues.

Enok's time among the Zmee philosophers of Zu'u-Shoran served him well. There were realms beyond the visible and he had just seen their birth with preternatural clarity. The flame of understanding roared, and for an instant, it seemed he could comprehend anything. The sparks were stars and clans of stars, and the three bubbles-in-bubbles, a representation of the heavens. Then just as quickly, all comprehension fled like a vanishing dream, leaving only the sadness of having once understood.

The pace of the story was slowing. Wherever the room had taken him, it was nearing its destination.

Darkness again.

Huge orbs flew by. Closer now. Some had children of their own.

Onwards. More slowly. He could feel his journey ending.

Ahead, a swirling disc, a maelstrom with a massive orb at its center. An unborn star? His other 'sight' showed it to be banded with the hues of a fearsome heart. It was not aglow like other stars. Not yet. Perhaps it was Oo-Ssla, the primordial egg from which Zmee believed that Ssla, the great light of day, had emerged.

On the edge of the swirling disc, or cloud, another orb struggled to appear. It was tiny, swaddled in the mists of its mother, bombarded at times with jets beyond steam, at others with cold-hardened water-stone like the ocean bergs of the distant north.

He felt himself falling through the fog, down, down, slowing, slowing down.

Splash!

Water surrounded him everywhere. It was tepid, bittersweet, and syrupy like the sap of a plant. A thick and terrible darkness reigned. Lightning flashed sporadically, indistinct, lacking in both ending and beginning.

Days passed. Or months. Or Years.

Above, a ripple in the darkness. It was that Presence again. No need for eyes to perceive it. He could feel that same burning energy as before. It was alive and pulsing ever more rapidly with agony and ecstasy and —

The feeling he had when his mother used to look down on him and plant her lips on his forehead and sing that tune until he fell asleep. He had long forgotten both the feeling and the words to describe it. Now he remembered both. It was love. Love was here now, breathing life upon the soul of this world. And now, even more urgently than before, this love from above fluttered anxiously overhead.

And there was something else he remembered. The sweet smell of his mother, of Hrazul ... of Naama ... tender and feminine, yet strong and determined. The sense of joyful expectancy was palpable. He could feel the vibrations became feverish, beating madly like the wings of a startled gholuj. The tension peaked in a series of slow intensifying spasms, like a tortoise laying its eggs.

Now — now — *now* — Now — *Now* — NOW — *NOW!*

In the final spasm, a voice boomed. It was high-pitched, low-pitched; it spanned all of yearning, and song, and love, and command. The sound of the voice shook his being. Darkness ebbed as a faint light, the very first sunrise, kissed the world. Then came the blast of a mighty shock, then another, and another, and he felt himself tumbling head over heels. But the agony was gone; only ecstasy remained.

He had little doubt that Oo-Ssla had been enlivened as Ssla, the Greater Light, but what was keeping it so hidden?

A soupy ocean now engulfed him. Enok panicked. He was at once both flying and drowning! Tidal surges ushered him one way, then another. As the light waned, that sensation of fluttering rose.

Darkness. Darkness. Interminable darkness.

Then as light dawned, the tension and agony that had come and gone, returned with increasing urgency.

Now — now — *now* — Now — *Now* — NOW — *NOW!*

The voice boomed, and once again came the sweet release. The waters boiled furiously. The sky — yes sky, he could breathe! — roiled with clouds, and a reassuring solidity came underfoot. Water lapped at his knees. A calm gray horizon stretched to infinity. The ruddy haze beyond it was a sunrise. However weak, it was light, nascent daylight, and he was glad of it.

How had he held his breath for a whole day? The question puzzled him greatly.

It's a waking dream. This cannot be real.

Twilight. Darkness. Dawn. The cycle began anew, more quickly than before.

The voice boomed. And the soul of the world leapt with joy in response to the love above.

From the great deep came a rumbling, as if the deep itself were straining for the light. The ground grew hot underfoot. Rushing waters parted to leave him at their boundary, on the shore of a peaceful lagoon.

Almost instantly, to the receding march of shadow, vegetal life sprouted in forms beyond counting: first in a puddle before him, then radiating outwards to the waters of the lagoon and all the sea and land beyond.

It was hard to explain what he was seeing. Was any of this real, or was it all just some elaborate form of storytelling?

The plants grew with astonishing speed, as if moons had gone by in a heartbeat. And yet, so much of the world was still barren, like a tacit invitation:

Come, and prosper!

Once more the voice rumbled, more softly this time. There was a proclamation, a chorus of triumphant shouts, and of all things, joyous laughter. Someone was pleased, very pleased indeed.

Again, the night; another cycle. Anguish and yearning came rising in waves.

Then a gentle light dispelled the darkness: the fourth dawn. The hazy sky grew crimson and angry. Light like jewels streaked across the sky. Oh the beauty of it!

The blanketing mists boiled furiously, and what had been there since the beginning began to take shape. Ssla, the Greater Light, could now be seen in all her glory. Fierce and bright she shone. Enok considered the dark maelstrom she had once been, and smiled. She was fully grown now, an equal sister in that stellar family, the Backbone of the Night.[xlv]

Darkness came but not as before. Whence this hazy crescent now gracing the horizon? Had this lesser of the lights been seconded

---

xlv *Backbone of the Night.* A common Zmee poetic descriptor for that rarely seen night-time streak of galactic stars.

from obscurity as a witness? A fresh companion to a world born anew?

Stars began to dot the sky. The thick shroud of mist, water and water-stone that had kept them hidden was now a ruin of its former self, dissipated by Ssla's unforgiving blasts. The constellations: he recognized their shapes. The mandal-aran, his father called them. 'The witness of the skies is sure,' the man had once said.

FATHER!

A new dawn completed the cycle, and again the soul below responded in joy to the love above, introducing an overwhelmed and weeping Enok to an even greater level of wonderment as, before his very eyes, from the mud of the very same puddle where he had seen the very first green thing grow, an insect emerged.

At vision's edge, the speed of the imagery was overwhelming. He was desperate to focus on a single thing, to control both what he saw and how quickly, but was powerless.

In mere moments, the verdured world blossomed with animate life. Insects and birds danced overhead. Jellyfish, slugs, and crustaceans frolicked in the seas. Fish rejoiced in pairs by the thousands, then by the thousands of thousands. Even the great deep brought forth minute yet nightmarish creatures of contorted, impossible forms. So many scenes at once, across so many different sites, made understanding anything a challenge.

Yet, when he surveyed the world — the sea, the land, the sky — an emptiness yet beckoned. To all these creatures was the same invitation:

Come, and prosper!

The power he had witnessed was beyond even the maddest hallucination. Immeasurable. Ineffable. Unstoppable.

Yet another cycle began. The agony preceding each dawn grew increasingly intense. Now the same rich voice boomed — and mud began to grow.

Mud! Piles of it oozing upwards in colonies. One spilt open and two lizards crawled out, covered in egg-slime. Another split apart, yielding dragons gasping for their first breath. Then another.

Always in two's, Enok observed. Always with a mate.

Beasts and habitats of every description together formed a theme. From the greatest to the least, each would need the other, and from the least to the greatest, each would complete the other. Somehow he perceived it with perfect clarity. Nothing existed for itself alone. Each was part of an unimaginably intricate, extravagant — indeed, opulent — whole. And if he had witnessed but a fraction of the sum, there had to hundreds of such themes spread across the earth!

Suddenly there was an audience. The deafening beat of a thousand wings startled him. Subdued, excited chatter signaled they were on the cusp of something wonderful.

Before him now spread an island, shrouded in mists and girt by an inland sea. Though dwarfing Zoar in grandeur and size, it was desolate, stillborn, completely untouched by creation. After everything he had witnessed, such barrenness seemed impossible.

And yet, here it was: a womb within a womb.

The veil of mists parted to reveal a mountain in the north, a massif of incomparable height. From its sides, great waterfalls cascaded to merge into rivers that fed the inland sea — the genesis of even greater watercourses. Some wound their way through spreading lands to oceans far beyond.

The meanderings of one particular river found uncanny resemblance in Zoia's maps. The split Gihon river and its delta? Arcing before him were the twin falls of Zhakh. And the vast inland sea — it could only be the Sea of Eloah! The Temple of Zul-Al-Kahhri, site of the Zmee fertility pilgrimage, should be nestled between the twin peaks of Mount Ur-Atu on the nearby mainland. But he searched in vain. The sacred lake of Atu was there yet with no sign of its temple.

Why did Zoia's maps omit the island? And how could he even be enjoying this elevated viewpoint unless he was somehow airborne?

He had missed something! A voice had spoken while he had been busy pondering. FOOL, he thought. THIS IS NO TIME FOR SPECULATION.

A hush descended, all was still, but the aching and the longing were growing intense.

The air thickened like a warm embrace, and it whispered in his mind like a melody. The music rose about him in a joyful crescendo, solidifying with a sparkling rush of color. More wonderful than his windmill xylophones, this; more resonant than all his drums. Song and love took form in the shape of a being — not a Zmee, though he found that perplexing, but instead an Ish like himself.

Enok told himself he was still in the gilt chamber, that none of this was real. It was just an elaborate dream, perhaps a kind of teaching aide built long ago by the Zmee. Right? So who was this new character? A god?

The Ish-god had been speaking, but distracted by his own thoughts Enok had missed something vital again!

Curiously, the stranger was about his own size, shorter and frailer than Naama. Plaits of light brown hair fell about the shoulders. Like his own, the feet were bare, and the short white tunic with its brassy belt were actually rather simple. It was the kind of working garment Enok himself might wear, that is, the habit of a servant. In quiet times Naama had briefly mentioned fabled gods and goddesses of great stature, fearsome in command, sublimely bejeweled and garbed.

There was none of that finery here, though, and it was puzzling. How could a god, rather *this* god, look so ordinary, and take the form of, frankly, a servant?

Whatever the case, Enok grinned. This stranger had a beard, and a good one too! But was this truly one of Naama's gods? He was beginning to suspect not. There was power here, great power, truly immeasurable, yet subtle and shaped instead by humility. That thought drew Enok to pondering again what Steam-maker Zelen had called the Infinite Eternal, and the recurring question of whether The El and the First Cause of the Zmee were the same.

But, who was this person? An emissary? A kind of living thespian mask, that is, what the Oracles might call an avatar? Could the Infinite Eternal truly take a physical form? But then why not a Zmee's or an Isha's? Was there meaning in the choice?

In the blink of an eye, the avatar moved to stand by a river bend. Not a speck of moss or green blade were anywhere to be seen. The island wasn't just barren but utterly, utterly lifeless. Naked feet sank into clay as the avatar wiggled his toes.

The voice of the avatar commanded. He had been hearing it all along, Enok realized, but it was closer now, primal and raw like a chorus of a thousand tongues thundering above the roar of rapids. And it was strange that, if only for an instant, he perceived each word resonating with nuances of meaning across so many dimensions beyond all mortal perception.

The avatar made a show of plunging a single hand into the earth. It was the right hand, and it seemed significant. The hand and clay dissolved into each other, becoming one.

Enok closed his eyes to employ his other 'sight.' The world beneath the visible began to boil, then organize itself around a pattern being absorbed from the hand. Again, the world soul below responded to the love from above. Fingers and earth then separated, leaving a horizontal mass about the avatar's own height. Cracks in the fast-drying clay galvanized the avatar, who urgently broke the surface, peeling away the hardened case to lift a shape to his breast.

Blood and water oozed from the shell. It was another Ish!

Cradling the lifeless form of the mud-man, and grimy from the encounter, the avatar, with a hand over the new being's mouth, and with his lips to the nose ...

He blew.

From the depths of some cavern came a searching call:

"Enok. *Enok.*"

The peak of the great northern mountain now loomed over the avatar and the young-looking mud-man as they conversed by a towering waterfall. But the avatar had somehow changed his attire into something truly splendid. A vest of a thousand gemstones sparked. His skin glistened like brass. And his hair had become bleached beyond even Naama's sea-spray lock.

Could all gods do that?

Mud-man too had appeared in a tunic, wearing what seemed a chest-plate of gold. With a sweeping motion, the avatar indicated the barren hills and lowlands spreading towards the inland sea. Beyond the ringing waters a verdant mainland beckoned, and foremost stood the twin peaks of Ur-Atu backed by a clear cerulean sky.

The avatar laughed with the other. It was like a sunset reunion of twitterlings, noisy and joyous. But why were they laughing? There had been a vital element to the story and Enok had missed it again!

I MUST NOT LET MYSELF BE DISTRACTED, he frowned. "Back. Go back!" he pleaded. The story was becoming familiar somehow, and he wanted to know everything.

Flowering plants were springing up everywhere now and in such a riot colors! Some blooms were as large as a zhrat's bower, and others dwarfed even Ur-Hozhai's fabled beauties. The once barren lowlands instantly greened as fields appeared and trees stretched to the sky!

There was one particular plant, however, that caught Enok's eye. Its copper-colored leaves sparkled invitingly, resplendent as any bloom. It spread lazily by the waterfall almost like a vine, flowerless. His eyes were strangely drawn to it. Though lacking in blossom, perhaps there was fruit.

Suddenly, plume-wings and hover-moths darted playfully. Across lowland fields strolled the most unusual animals: birds entirely feathered and exotically plumed, creatures covered crown-to-tail in fur, grazers with hard shoe-like feet. Where were the yash'kh, the khwatl, the zhrat, the khrii, zhaga, Jin-jin, and all the other creatures he had ever known?

The island seemed peculiar, too ordered, almost cultivated, very different from the rest of the mainland. And mud-man had played his part: first challenged by a question, then mud-man had answered, watching delighted as the avatar had brought plants and creatures to life before mud-man's very eyes, exactly as Enok himself had seen earlier.

And always, always by twos.

With eyes now indicating the summit of the great peak, the avatar looked earnest in explanation, and all smiles were gone as an emphatic hand rested on mud-man's shoulder.

"Enok! *Enok!*"

Closer now. Terror and urgency were calling his name.

Suddenly there were three: an Isha had appeared beside mud-man. From where had *she* suddenly sprung? Enok groaned. Again, he had missed something vital.

Her complexion was striking, like the glory of earth, just a shade or two lighter than her ebony tresses. And the tall forehead and almond-shaped eyes were familiar. Teeth gleaming like pearls behind delicate brown lips brought so many visions to mind. Whereas Naama was a powerhouse, ruggedly pretty, and a hunter, large and tough as a yash'kh, this Isha was compact, graceful and alluring in a way that kept him glued to the very sight of her.

It was surely the girl from his dreams!

But how could that be? And, more importantly, why?

Like carefree younglings, the Ish and Isha were skipping hand-in-hand through a field of flowers, and unaware they lacked even the simplest of clothing. Enok would never have done so with Naama, or even — dare he say it? — Hrazul.

Why were these Elim not birthed as a pair like all the other creatures? And why last of all? And why had that great island at the center of the world been left so deliberately barren? This was typical Zmee storytelling: intentional symbolism, an economy of words yet with hidden layers of meaning. The delight of the wise was to find them.

The avatar, looking more serious now, pointed upwards to the mountain again, and —

The mental whispers died abruptly and a different voice rang in his ears. "Enok. Enok! Get up. Please, wake up!"

A hand covered in something sticky and tasting of metal was slapping his face hard. He blinked slowly several times, orienting himself. He was lying on his back. The air was humid and moldy, the light shadowy and shifting.

And Naama was crouching over him, covered in blood.

EPISODE 16

LORD OF ZOAR

A deputation offers Zakon supreme power in Zoar ... Enok awakes in a forest to discover he has been unconscious for over half a day. Moreover, thanks to Naama, a dear ally he had presumed dead is found to be alive.

ANCIENT ARBOREAL GIANTS RINGED the Lagoon of Souls. It was early evening, low tide, and the ocean was peculiarly calm. Massive ceremonial torches dotted the beach like great tree stumps ablaze, and Zakon lay pensively coiled beneath the flame of one, tormented by the sight of nearly three dozen pyres staining the sea in shimmering pools of coral and gold like a garland of sunsets.

The smoke of crematory spices formed a ghostly veil upon the water. Its perfume was pungent and heady, almost intoxicating. It numbed the tendrils, deadening both bitterness and niggling regret. Mourners could meditate stoically now, in silence, free of bothersome passion.

ALL THINGS COME TO AN END, Zakon brooded. PEOPLE. CULTURES. PERHAPS EVEN WORLDS.

He had never considered himself political like the Zeruhawi, or religious like the Azhakh-Na, but some occasions would remain forever sacred, and the death of a lifelong mentor would surely be among them. True, the deposed High Wisdom had saved him as a youngling from the barbarians, but it was with crusty old Ukhaz that he had found a new home. She had taken him for a disciple when he was a shunned outsider. He had hoped to study Methodics, but she had insisted on martial arts and the law.

Zoar was for green-skins and their younglings, so why had the High Wisdom brought him here against all regulations, and why had Ukhaz so nurtured him, never forcing the adult away?

Most of the mourners had departed, but Zakon had lingered, resolved to watch Ukhaz's glowing embers on her Na-Zeru-shaped pyre until the gentle ripples of the lagoon claimed them forever. His people had sprung from the waters of Zoriyan. Now, in death, the remains of old Ukhaz would return to water.

But this was not their dominion, so the Azhakh-Na kept saying, and these waters could never be home.

He had been the one to recount the many achievements of her life that had earned her a place on the Pillar of Zmee: her treatise *On Reason,* and most famously *The Twelve Pillars of Methodics,* a Zeruhawi classic. Like other pedagogues with great aspirations, she had had her faults, but the public memory of such things never survived. Only the good would remain, and that was as it should be.

Now he silently promised himself to avenge her death, and of all those others — eleven Oracles, eight guards and innocent bystanders from the crowd.

So many. Too many.

AND IT'S ALL MY FAULT, Zakon kept thinking.

Other thoughts troubled him too. The living stones, dead for generations, had come alive and he had experienced the Ascending Way for himself. Though the heavenly road had a will of its own, the city was now ablaze with notions of an imminent return to Zoriyan, their mythical homeland. The Ascending Way would take them all home.

Pah! The blather of fools!

The simple-minded imagined a grand procession in the floating citadel of Azhakh, Zoriyan's capital, with colonnades festooned with flowers, a pilgrim's homecoming. That kind of bosh must surely have sprung from some clerics. Frankly, if such inspirational tales were even remotely true, then why had no one from Zoriyan sought these here out in all the intervening years? Indeed, after so many generations, all hope was naïve. And if what he'd seen of Zoar in the Ascending Way was true and not some visual history, then any explanation was too terrible to contemplate. Could it be that no one knew they were *here* because there was simply no one *there?* If so, then the colony of Zoar was far more precious than any words could express, and his was now a burden heavier than he could ever bear alone.

What was he to do?

Every Zmee alive had ultimately sprung from the six eggs a youngling called Zulyi had secreted from the Ish after they slew the Great Zhmee and the egg-bearer Zmiya. They had been innocent emissaries from Zoriyan, or so Steam-maker had told him. Hra-Adin is where the amity had soured: Hra-Adin, birthplace of the barbarians and too the endless hostilities.

Zelen had been Azhakh-Na once, and steeped in myths that were mocked in equal measure by the Zeruhawi. For them, a new reality existed. *This* was now home, *this* the new Zoriyan, and in desperate need of safeguarding — which is why he had remained so long among the green-skins, however unnatural it seemed. He had resolved long ago to not let this surviving clan fall like all the others. And while it now seemed more critical than ever to support the Zeruhawi cause, could both factions be but pieces of a whole?

They had saved him, the High Wisdom and her First Cause ilk, so many years ago. It was a debt he would certainly repay, though as a subtle and relentless advocate for war. In the face of superior numbers, offense was better than defense. His egg-brothers had found that out too late. Why could the former High Wisdom and her insipid philosophers not see that too?

"Upholder! Upholder!" A young guard's cry disturbed him.

«What!» "I'm meditating. Can it wait?"

"The khwatl: there's been a casualty," she lamented, bowing with her partner.

"'Folly summons the Eternal Night,'" I think the Aphorisms say. «Death?»

«Almost.» "We tried to harness them as you instructed —"

"But did you muzzle them?"

The expression before him was as blank as stone.

«Dimwit!» "So the slave, a lowly Ish, is more able than you!"

"Upholder! Upholder!" Two j'Na-Zeru came speeding anxiously, their wings and tendrils aquiver.

«What now!» Was even a moment's peace to elude him?

"Lord Upholder, the Ish have escaped!"

«Impossible.»

"As you say." The guards bowed meekly, almost fawningly, too aware of the power that the Upholder, Chief Oracle of Law and the new High Wisdom now wielded. "Nevertheless —"

«Explain!»

"We think they leapt from one of the windows, for its bars had been removed. A shore patrol —"

Zakon was disbelieving. "Without wings? Not very likely. They would never have survived the fall."

"— found beachside tracks this morning, but we thought nothing of it until later. And when we checked the cell —"

«Up!» "Stop cringing. You are a Zmee, not some cowering Ish. Where did they lead?"

"Ultimately to Yzhau Bay, where the reef dragons sleep. But we are certain now that they came through here first, probably via the sewers. A grating had —"

Zakon uncoiled himself, now eye-to-eye with the guard, and signing disapproval. «Sloppy work.» "Why didn't you summon me earlier? Or a Prefect?"

"My lord! You were in cleansing with the Healer for the rites. And the attendants said you had ordered not to be disturbed."

"Were there no Prefects in the armory?"

"They had been summoned away by the alchemists, apparently, but none knew to where."

GONE FOR THAAZH'S NEW THE DEATH PRONGS, Zakon remembered.

"My lord, how could the barbarians have escaped? They were so well secured. We and the Newcomer saw to it ourselves."

"It's that overgrown Isha," he deduced with little effort. "It's cunning, to be sure, but die it will and by my hand." He addressed the Civils, "Have the beasts been prepared?"

The two guards shot glances at each other, their fear thick on his tendrils. "They do not respond to us, Upholder, in the same way as the first." «Evil creatures!» "They are just wild beasts."

Zakon tore at his tendrils. "Calamity upon calamity! Perhaps I should make you both apprentice Ish and let that *Enokhi* animal instruct you!"

Using the khwatl was a still a good idea, though. He was so very glad he had thought of it. Whereas Zmee could see wonderfully at dawn and dusk, in broad daylight things became blurry. It hurt the eyes and peripheral vision suffered, and even more so under day-goggles. A trained khwatl would be a priceless treasure. Huge and powerful creatures, they saw perfectly well in full daylight, heard the faintest of whispers, and could even smell another creature almost half a league away. They feared nothing, unfortunately not even their new masters.

"Alright, leave them corralled," he finally said, "but make certain they're properly muzzled. The life of every Zmee is precious."

The Civils lay coiled as if deaf.

"You have your orders. Be gone!"

"Yes, Upholder. Immediately." The patrol bowed so low, their tendrils scraped the sand. It was curious behavior indeed, as though they actually feared him. Or idolized. Either way, he found himself liking it.

IF ONLY THAT NEWCOMER ZARAZA WERE HERE. SHE WOULD CERTAINLY ENJOY STALKING HER CAPTORS, he mused, WITH KHWATL HER BEASTLY AVENGERS. "Now, as for you two —"

"We shall scour the city for those escapees, Upholder!" «Yes!»

«No.» "It's late, and they won't travel in the dark; they don't have night eyes like we do. Instead, have Civils guard every sewer exit and pit — Spotters, Scouts, others: I don't care who you commandeer. Then return to the armory, find the Prefect, and make sure those death prongs are ready. Pikes too. What said the alchemists? Are there sufficient fish for the toxin?"

"I hear more than thirty, my lord."

"More than I hoped. Any Ish is to be killed on sight." «Clear?» "One jab and they die! Oh, and send two of your sisters after those Civils. Otherwise the khwatl will tear those simpletons apart."

«Oh.»"No night posse, Upholder? We're keen for revenge."

«Indeed! As am I.» Zakon closed his eyes and partook off the becalming incense. "I'm not taking any chances with that Isha. Besides, can we be certain she's the only shipwreck survivor? No, too many good souls have already been lost. Better to wait until we have a proper arsenal, with every j'Na-Zeru fully armed."

No more must die. No more.

"And tell the Prefect to convene all your egg-sisters at the armory at first light," Zakon continued, luxuriating in the incense. "I will organize the posses personally."

«Not now?» "My lord, but some of the sisters have already —"

«Relax!» he signed, agitated at all the interruptions. "Where can the barbarians flee to anyway? This is an island, after all."

Complex patterns of light pulsed before him, reminding Enok of the marvelous color-song of jellyfish during the Shine Water. The sights and sensation of wonder seemed very much a re-living of that near fatal boyhood experience, floating innocently among the reefs by night to behold what ultimately became a deadly spectral cascade. And amongst it all, Naama had been looming over him like some bloodied phantom.

And now the phantom had jarred him awake to the gloomy hues of reality. His face was hot and throbbing from a slapping; more than one from the feel of it. And oh his pounding head! It was like waking up drugged in the jail again. Was he back in the cell? Rolling eyes slowly surveyed their surrounds. The great buttressing roots of a truly prodigious tree shaped a mossy shrine around him. The fusty duff and the honeyed scent of blossoms told he was far from the pyramid and deep within the thaakh forest.

"Ooh. My head ... my face."

No, he hadn't been dreaming. Naama was indeed kneeling beside him covered in blood. Zmee blood. Even her war paint couldn't mask the worry beneath it.

"Oh, Enok! Finally! It's been over three watches! We're safe for the moment, but it's a costly safety, this. The day is rapidly fading."

He sat up, slowly, blinking eyes methodically, watching the 'fireflies' evaporate. "How I come here? Not ... remembering."

"I carried you." She felt his forehead, then his cheeks. "I don't sense any fever."

Enok rubbed his jaw. It was tender. His head swam, his ribs ached too, and every joint was afire from the injurious strength of the amazon. It was like being trampled by yash'kh. Naama was anything but delicate.

"Don't give me those looks!" Naama jabbed. "I had to try *something*. After that upper room, you were babbling in a strange language. Just now, you were having convulsions and mumbling more nonsense in yet some other unknown tongue. I had to beat the evil humors out of you somehow. Honestly, would you have preferred a bloodletting?" She nodded skywards. "It will be growing dark soon, and I'm worried a whole day has passed and I haven't made any progress. Time is running out."

"We get out," he groaned. "Is good, yes?"

"Better here than the cell," she conceded, assaying his forehead again. "Will you be alright?"

He set her at ease with a nod, then ran his fingers gently across her waist, feeling the blood. It was still sticky.

"Your friend isn't quite dead, though she's lost a lot of blood."

A look of surprise crossed his face, then confusion. ZOIA ALIVE?

"She's been saying something, but it makes no sense to me. I made a makeshift bandage to stem that blue stuff from bleeding everywhere. She was stabbed very close to the heart." She arched her brows suggestively. "You never know, she might prove useful if she lives."

He bolted upright, fell victim to sudden vertigo, and collapsed against a massive root just as Naama leapt to steady him.

"Whoa, you're still totty. Slowly next time. She's behind you."

Across the arboreal grotto, looking very much like part of the tree itself, Zoia was lying against another wall-like root, chin to earth and eyeing him weakly. Limp and dark, she was a mere shadow of her former verdure, and the fine patina of her aging snout had been made strangely youthful from bruising.

"Mistress!" He fell to his knees beside her. Falling was easier than standing. "We thought thee dead. Naama — the Isha — has a medicine stick!"

"Water," came the feeble response. "Desperate for water. And there's a balm I need. In the orange compartment. A coagulant." «Please. Hurry»

"She keeps repeating the same word," Naama groaned in frustration. "I'm no Zmee-talker. What does she mean?"

"Zmee want water. Help me," Enok begged. "I speak to Zmee."

For a moment, the old Naama was back, a stanchion of disdain and with arms akimbo, before her lips spread in a knowing smile.

"Right, squeeze her for information." With a private wink and a sidelong glance at Zoia, she melded with the shadows of the forest.

"Hold thyself. It cometh," Enok reassured with a stroke.

She recoiled at his touch. «Away!» "Do you wish to glory in my shame? I'm exposed. My headdress ..."

Enok found the crumpled bonnet of feathers half-buried under litter and crowned her with it, though wondering why after so many years of High Zmeezh that she was speaking now so plainly.

"Oracle, new tendrils sprout from thy crown," he observed, and genuinely curious. [xlvi]

"I grew them myself."

Was that humor from Oracle Zoia? He must have misunderstood.

"Did you think our headdress is purely for pomp?" She coiled her great body in slow irregular spasms, arranging her bonnet.

THEY'RE JUST ANOTHER SET OF WORMS TO ME, he kept from saying, unhinging a draw of the medicine stick.

"Take it as a sign of advancing age and ... well, it's a delicate matter," she said in Low Zmiysh. "The older you are, though, the harder they are to control — especially during one's pilgrimage."

While she was on the subject, and being informal, there was surely no harm in probing, right? "I do not understand."

"Emotion. Moods. And other things."

"But the Twelve Pillars proscribe displays of emotion — reason triumphant over the vagaries of flesh, and all that."

"Ironic, isn't it? The Oracle of Law, sad old thing."

Enough had been said to deduce the rest. "But Ukhaz —"

«Enough!» A toss of her head terminated an awkward subject. Maybe Zmee headgear and his loincloth served similar purposes.

"Your presence puzzles me, Oracle. Perhaps you might explain."

«Contrariwise!» "You're the one who should be explaining. Your escape from remand, and without our help, was beyond all hope. Obviously, you managed. It's the tale of tales, I'm sure."

---

xlvi   Zmee sprout additional crown tendrils after puberty every dozen years or so until old age. Ancient Zmee could have eight or more.

He opened the vial with the pungent yellow ointment. "Well, almost. Our plan," it hurt to admit, "has not quite succeeded."

Zoia lifted her breast, and Enok examined the wound. Having been stabbed so close to the heart, she was lucky to be alive. Unlike Naama, the touch of a Zmee was always cool. Zoia, however, was positively cold; not a comforting sign. Well, at least Naama's dressing had stemmed the bleeding.

"I am glad," she hissed softly.

"Hold still. This will sting." Then, "You are?"

Zoia shuddered. "Y-yes. It has given me one last chance to — *Ooh! Ssss!* — save you."

"I'm already saved, I think. But enough about me, mistress. *You* look wretched."

Zoia eyed him circumspectly, tendrils hanging limply in that cool manner he despaired of ever seeing again, and poised to divulge something he might not be prepared to hear.

"So many things we had to keep from you, but believe me when I say it was for your protection."

"I believe you, and I'm sorry if —"

"My First D—" Zoia checked herself, sighing, with questioning eyes to the heavens. "The Zeruhawi murdered Wise-eye," she wept of Hrazul.

"By Northerners? But, I saw the giant —"

«No. No.» "All the result of some intricate plot which, no doubt, has yet to climax."

Enok wagged his head, prompting more. "I'm lost."

"It was no accident that the barbarians beached where they did. Wise-eye was headed for celebrations at Ur-Hozhai —"

"So far north? I do not understand."

"It hardly matters now. Traveling j'Na-Zeru gave it away, gloating in earshot of Northern Civils, one of whom was secretly an Azhakh-Na neophyte, and the other simply appalled at its wickedness. Apparently, the barbarians had been spied floundering on the Razor days before. Hindsight would say that some clique among the Zeruhawi had engineered to have the barbarians shipwrecked near you and to cause havoc at just that moment."

"That's ... that's unspeakable!"

«Agreed!» "When Wise-eye overheard the tale, her first thought was to get to you. See? They lured her away from Zu'u-Shoran until it suited their plans." Zoia hung her great head at the memory of her slain disciple, and Enok began to wonder in the awkward silence whether she blamed him for any of it.

It was quite a while before she spoke again, and when she did, it sent such a frisson of guilt through him that he knew beyond logic the unfurling tale would be a haunt upon him forever.

"She had summoned the Upholder, and hurried to your side in the fervent hope of providing you both an impartial witness and an alibi. However, that her presence on the beach that day had been vital to the Zeruhawi plan was something we never suspected. And the plan had been that she should die."

She moaned so sorrowfully that it brought him to tears. And the image of Hrazul's dying came once again in force.

«Fools. Fools!» "We were all played for fools."

"This is Stargazer's handiwork," Enok growled. "When Wise-eye and I caught her on a breakfast island off Sha-Noa, I just knew there was a deeper reason. She wasn't there for the ghaazli weed, but to personally assess Hrazul."

He had seen firsthand what Xira and her Zeruhawi allies were capable of. The freshly prepared jail, missing grapes ending up as prison food, the concealed Zmee-style lair in the cove, they had all been carefully orchestrated. And his alibi became instead the chief evidence against him.

When they first met, Refa had been saying 'sea serpents.' On reflection, might it not have been 'serpents in the sea'? It explained his attack on Hrazul with so little provocation. It made increasing sense as he gave voice to his theory. He, the giants, Hrazul and her Azhakh-Na, they had all been masterfully manipulated. Perhaps it was Xira and her clique who lured the boat to Zoar. Here was zhakh in its most elevated form. But there were always two games afoot in any challenge. If this was the one, then what was the other?

His analysis left Zoia uncertain. "Anyhow, the High Wisdom asked me to fetch the guards who were witnesses of the plot, and hide them."

"In the Reliquary, I presume."

«Exactly!» She managed a wan smile. "In the sacred sarcophagi. Actually, in Zeruha's own crypt: the sacred original Na-Zeru itself, and the last place a Zeruhawi would look. I found that rather amusing, myself. The guards were to expose what we knew of the plot at the inquest. I went to fetch them. Returning to the dais, I spied a lone Scout sneak into the Reliquary. I felt sure it was another Zeruhawi trick, for Reef Scouts always travel in pairs, and she should not have been patrolling inland anyway."

"It's hard to believe all this happened only yesterday."

She paused as her breathing became labored. "I followed the Scout into the tessellated chamber. I never chanced upon her face, but the flimsy amulet around her neck was distinctive. I would recognize it instantly."

Enok had a sneaking suspicion he knew whom she meant: that zhuk-eyed Scout escorting him from the dais after yesterday's melee. She had been wearing a tiny dagger necklace.

"I remember it becoming light inside the pyramid. I continued to follow her trail. Then she just disappeared." Zoia continued between slow deliberate breaths. "You can imagine my dismay when I found myself trapped inside the hidden chamber with the floating golden orb! How many watches passed, I know not, but the door opened by itself and I wormed my way back to the first chamber, to the Reliquary proper. And was shocked beyond fright when the door opened with a giant standing at the threshold!"

The sights and fears of the dawn just past flashed again through Enok's mind. Was it really only today?

Several tall shapes in the fog had hovered about the dais. They must have been giants like Refa.

"I struggled with one of them," Zoia continued, "while the others ransacked our treasures. I managed to escape back into the hidden chamber. The three of them together could have slain me had they wanted to. They were undoubtedly after for something particular and I was simply a distraction. I cried and cried, but no help —"

She shuddered before resuming. "The Scout had obviously fled, though I cannot fathom how she slipped past." She shrugged quizzically. "Anyhow, I was fighting a losing battle in that spherical chamber with one of the giants, and would have died, but when I saw the smears of blood on the wall — well, it gave me an idea. I struck the sequence of tiles with my tail. The door blinked open, and I sprang through."

«Oh my!» exclaimed Zoia. "It clanged shut so quickly behind me that I thought I'd lost my extremity. The tiles were clearly the key."

Enok was confused. "I thought that was *your* blood on the wall," he said, applying more ointment. "That's what led me to you."

"Ooh," she stifled a cry. "As you can see, it's not my hands that are wounded."

The peculiar amulet, the serene zhuk-eyed smile, and the image of a bloodied palm staining Naama's cords were still sharp in his memory. The dais Scout who freed Naama after the massacre had to be Zoia's mystery Zmee. What other explanation could there be?

Zoia continued. "There's more, though I struggle to believe it. The Upholder is in league with the giants."

Enok made a facial gesture, disbelieving.

«I know what I saw.» "Rummaging through the Reliquary with the barbarians was a red-skin."

OBVIOUSLY A ZMEE BULL, thought Enok. But Zakon colluding with giants? It made little sense. Or did it?

"The rest is hazy. I awoke in the upper corridor and the chamber was sealed." Zoia paused again, clearly overexerting herself. "Little Ish, *Enokhi*, be careful whom you trust. It's unlikely those giants are your people, I can see that now. And I think it no coincidence that your Isha was accompanied by a giant."

"I'm wondering if she might not be one too."

«Oh! Oh!» Zoia braced herself, hissing through clenched teeth as the ointment took effect. "Ooh, that smarts! Better to embrace the Endless Night than to suffer like this! And speaking of dying, when I find that foul egg[xlvii] who abandoned me ..."

Yesterday's tragedies played again in his mind. The zhuk-eyed guard had escaped the Reliquary unseen, to later escort him from the dais. Obviously, the pyramid had more hidden passages than the paltry few they had discovered. But she had used a bloodied hand in the pyramid *before* the fighting began, thus the injury must have been self-inflicted.

"Oracle, that Scout probably saved your life. I know this sounds strange, but I think you were *meant* to be sealed inside that chamber."

---

xlvii   *Foul egg.* A reference to a warm-born egg gone rotten. More profane than being called a *Cracked egg*. The worst of Zmee insults.

«Eh? How?»

"The use of her own blood was deliberate, to mark the secret keys. See? At the inquest, the young giant slew the Shav'yat. If you had remained on the dais, you would almost certainly have —" He choked, suddenly remembering how he had held his tongue. Could he not have prevented the slaughter?

Zoia coughed painfully. «What? No!» "*All* the councilors?"

"All but the Upholder and the High Wisdom. I believe he's had her arrested and he's condemned me to death."

"Second Disciple?" she inquired of Snei, then relaxed as she read the truth in his eyes. "This is dreadful news indeed. Most of them were Azhakh-Na Oracles, my egg-sisters. How the Zeruhawi must be rejoicing now! The Upholder now assumes the role of Chief Oracle of Law as well, and with the Shav'yat gone and ... and the High Wisdom deposed, there's no telling what he might do, or rather be gulled into."

All those years as his mistress must have taught her a little something about the vacant expression behind her former servant's eyes. "He's a bull," she explained. "They can become irrational in the presence of broody females, or thick-witted at best. Even among the Zmee, little Ish, cultured behavior can often be mere gilding over more primal needs."

Enok added, "And sometimes the gilt peels off."

With a touch of sadness, Zoia added, "It has always been that way. When one's season has come, the urge to procreate can be almost debilitating. And the broody odors affect bulls profoundly, whether they themselves are in season or not. That's why the sexes must live apart."

"Then, strange as this sounds, I worry for the Upholder."

«Surely not!»

Enok stroked his chin pensively as he pondered Zakon's behavior. "Well, he has now become the most powerful Zmee in the history of Zoar, at a time when he may be most vulnerable to deception. That cannot be accidental, surely — and now all this tumult with the giants. I can't help but suspect they're connected."

Zoia looked more tired than ever, when she hissed, "I wouldn't be at all surprised. So much for all that Zeruhawi rhetoric about us" — «Us!» — "consorting with barbarians!"

"You said you wanted to save me. But save me from ...?" The habits of a lifetime let silence frame the question.

The eyes of the Oracle narrowed. Contempt was clear on her tendrils. She arched her great neck in the direction Naama had gone, and spat a word like a dagger:

"Her!"

AS THE LAST OF THE GUARDS departed, leaving Zakon alone on the beach to mourn his colleagues, a distant panoply by the water's edge caught his eye. These were neither professional criers, guards nor cinerary attendants. He expected that thurifers with their giant censers would be making one last round of the beach, side-winding formally in the last march of obsequies. However, their bearing was neither unhurried nor solemn. Moreover, the vaunted plumage of the headdresses could only be that of Oracles in formal attire. Whoever they were, with the ceremonies long concluded, there was little doubting their intention.

Was he never allowed any peace?

"Ah, Suraazh," he bowed a little to the Venerable of Law, his Prefect from Yashau-Zaar. That she had missed the funeral of her former mistress was unthinkable.

"Lord Upholder," she saluted bowing low — a little too low, he observed, given the coolness of his greeting. "We come on a matter of utmost importance." She held forth a long ornate cylinder of clay, making sure that everyone knew what it was: an old-style testament marked with Ukhaz's signature glyphs.

Zakon found himself flanked by the Oracles of Law, of Chronicles, Healing, Numerics, Metals, Structures: nearly two dozen of the most senior and respected Oracles, Methodicists and Zeruhawi all. Oracles were the pinnacle of the Zmee social hierarchy and here was the very embodiment of power in Zoar, or what was left of it.

Maybe they were here to protest. He was already the Chief Oracle of Law and its Upholder. Perhaps allowing others to proclaim him the High Wisdom's successor had been a tad hasty.

"I assure you," he disavowed in a conciliatory posture, "it was never my intention to assume the title. It was a popular movement in Ra'a-Zohari, that —"

The Prefect dismissed his confession with a wave of her hand and the way "Something greater bids us here" had rolled off her tongue, it was at once tantalizing and reassuring. They were not here to censure him, and it piqued his interest.

«Oh,» he began, recovering his aplomb. "The inquest and funerals are over. I thought you'd all left for home."

"I believe I speak for all when I say we have no intention of returning just yet. We have another solemn duty to perform."
«Take it.»

Zakon gingerly weighed the cylinder and fingered its intricate design. It was a monumental tome and far too large for anything like a mere testament.

"The rumors are spreading. We must settle this once and for all."

He looked for Xira and her trademark helm. Absent cataclysm, even a recluse like her would hardly have missed such a moment as this. And the reconnaissance Civils he had ordered north never reached the Ur-Hozhai armory. They had been found dead on the dais. Did someone else know of the conspiracy? Was there perhaps a reciprocal one?

"Conspiracy?" he let slip. OOPS. "I mean, rumors?"

"The long-dead heart of the Ascending Way now throbs again, but none alive know why or how."

"And the Ish — more may be coming!" someone cried.

«Exactly.» "With the Shav'yat all but gone, and the Old Dame [xlviii] in custody, too much uncertainty provokes unrest, political trouble. A hole in water cannot remain long."

«So?»

"See? This is the perfect opportunity, and long have we worked towards it. We mean to recreate the Zakkat."

Zakon baulked. Such blunt words surely fomented revolution.

"We are the water to fill the hole. Dusk and dawn stand juxtaposed in Zoar. My lord, though you haven't confessed so publicly, you must surely feel epochal changes tugging on your tendrils, just as we, begging you to choose: to grasp the dawn of the new, and

---

xlviii   *Old Dame*. Titles rule. Zmee etiquette demands addressing adults in public only ever by such. The former Grand Oracle/High Wisdom is now effectively an untitled pariah except for this aweless byname.

let twilight fall on all mossbacked conservatives." Others wagged assent to Prefect Suraazh's counsel.

"The Zakkat? Our ancient form of government? It's just a myth or a poor memory embodied in the game of zhakh, its mechanisms lost to legend. Who now can say how it should be constituted?"

"Break the seal. Kill your doubt."

"Talk is one thing, action another. I have to be sure your intentions are noble," Zakon parried cautiously. What of *his* status in this new regime? "Besides, this needs careful consideration. The details might take some time."

"That time is now, my lord. Why else the proclamation of your succession to the highest cathedrals of Zoar? Recent events force quickness of us," sighed the Prefect.

"It's regrettable, but you were right to unseat the High Wisdom — ah, now the Old Dame," said a Numerist.

"I would depose myself if it meant Zoar's safety."

«Just so!» signed the Prefect. "We recognize in you that same turmoil of the mind that elevates the better of her sisters, that same force of nature dividing sea and land and sky." Suraazh delivered it with complete sincerity and yet ...

"So, are you with us?" the Numerist prompted. She was positively decrepit with age, seventy years old at least. And strangely, she too had missed the ceremonies.

«I suppose,» he signed, still wary of their true motives. "What has this to do with me, exactly? I really should be investigating how the giant was freed, and how the Reliquary —"

«No!» the Prefect interjected. "No," she repeated softly, and somewhat nervously he thought. "Those 'mechanisms lost to legend' as you said, you hold now, written by the Prime Lawmaker's hand. As her former disciple, this was in my keeping in the event of her death. It is addressed to you."

"As Upholder, or succeeding Oracle of Law?"

«Neither.» "To you personally."

«Me?» Zakon ran his fingers over the seal.

The markings were certainly hers. He held the cylinder high and threw it to earth with traditional ceremony. From the shards he retrieved the parchment. It was indeed penned by her hand, and in the blocky calligraphy of judicial pronouncement. It had been recently composed — two years old at most, he judged. Its opening paragraphs told plenty. The rest he would read at leisure.

The Prefect continued: "Five of us will be chosen as governing Adji, one for each of the prefectures, including someone to oversee that nest of meddlesome Ish-lovers in Zu'u-Shoran. And just as every body needs a head, likewise we Adji will need an overruling Aaj."

Suraazh and the others bowed fawningly. "Tomorrow, we want you to accept the role and be the Aaj that Zoar demands."

Zakon's tendrils froze at the suggestion. They were merely mouthing in summary what the testament detailed. Could he refuse his former mistress? According to the legends of their mythical homeland, the Lord Aaj was the absolute ruler of the Zmee — not just the green-skins but of all Zoriyan — and had always been a male. The relationship between the female Adji and the Aaj was unclear. For the present, such minutia could wait. Ukhaz's lengthy scroll would explain it all. It was a truly monumental work, the crowning gift to those she served.

How strange that she had never mentioned it. And stranger still was that a Venerable had been the trustee instead of an Oracle peer.

"Why me?"

The reply was swift. "Because she knew you wouldn't covet it. And there's no one better suited to the task."

Or was it that none of these Zeruhawi could trust each other and needed him to keep the others in check?

Zakon eyed each in turn, searching for a motive; and when none shied away, he mellowed.

Supposedly, Adji had the power of life and death in their fiefdoms, and commanded armies in their own right. So were these here a cabal of extremists so power-hungry, so radical that it was *they* had who had used the giant to hasten a new Zeruhawi polity? Or did they think he already had the evidence to expose them? After all, he was a male. He had the very abilities they feared most of all, and his stealth was legendary.

Zakon the Invisible. That 'invisibility' had captured the giant. The appellative was well earned indeed.

Me as the Lord Aaj, he continued to mull. This was even better than anything the Old Dame had ever enjoyed! Her titles of

Grand Oracle and High Wisdom were based on intellect, learning, and moral leadership. *This*, however, demanded nothing but an unyielding force of character. Supreme and unmerited power was being handed to him willingly, and — by Zulyi! — without a single shard of dissent!

But he had learned, even as a youngling, that when something seemed too good to be true, then it almost certainly was. For now, he would let events unfold and wait to catch the lies.

"The Stargazer has prepared a feast in your honor," the Prefect invited with a sweep of the hand. "We can discuss the parchment's details there."

Zakon returned to staring at Ukhaz's embers still glowing brightly on her Na-Zeru-shaped pontoon. "You all go ahead. I will follow you shortly."

The Prefect understood. "Yes, of course, my lord." She bowed low in unison with her company, then departed.

A breeze whipped through the ancient pines, soughing like voices of the dead. With the Oracles departed, none remained to overhear Zakon's conversation with ghosts.

"You have to admit, old Black Feathers," he said to Ukhaz's smoldering remains, "that one giant did more for your Zeruhawi cause than fifty years of campaigning. Until now, I had no doubt at all that Zoia and the High Wisdom were the traitors who had set that unholy monster free.

"Now I have two dozen more suspects slithering at speed to Stargazer's compound, their tendrils dripping with guilt. Well, old teacher, it seems there have been more conspiracies in play than just our own, though you virtually guaranteed your death when you penned this testament. Or had you planned to die this way? I am the only bull in Zoar and now they need an overruling Aaj. A bull. Tell me, what's the coincidence of that?"

He imbibed of the pungent air with a sigh, and with thoughts drifting like the incense around him. He fingered the green crystal hexagon about his neck uneasily. It was the key to the Reliquary, perhaps to everything. All his troubles began when he had wrested it from the former High Wisdom and opened the pyramid. Some things, he was coming to realize, were better left unopened.

Perhaps he should close it again. If only he could figure out how. More importantly, it behooved him to uncover why the old matriarch had sealed it for so long at all! And why so specific her instructions regarding every little detail of the inquest?

He returned to his monologue, reproving himself for being so easily persuaded by Ukhaz and Xira to allow those barbaric Ish to make landfall. Chechi and betel nuts had proved a heady mix! And now with the sudden appearance of this testament, he'd be a fool to believe in coincidence. And they would be fools to believe he believed.

Zakon's key worries twirled about him like evanescent butter-flies, and he without a net: INVADERS. GIANTS. ZERUHAWI. TRAITORS. AAJ. RELIQUARY. ASCENDING WAY ...

Too much had happened too quickly, he realized, but solving the plots one at a time, that's what a Methodic would do.

"Zmee plotting against Zmee," he whispered absently. "If this is what we've degenerated into, then surely ruin awaits us all. Between the Ish and our own scheming kind, it's becoming increasingly harder to tell who the real savages are."

Zakon uncoiled himself, realizing he was speaking to a memory. IT'S THE EFFECT OF THE INCENSE, he thought. IT'S HARD TO THINK TRUE.

Perhaps it was fitting while remembering the dead that words of lovely Zelen should spring to mind, and with her very voice:

'HRA-ADIN IS WHERE THE AMITY SOURED.' [xlix]

Something cataclysmic had happened there, fomenting the war, and since the hostilities were real, then perhaps Hra-Adin was no myth either.

And suddenly, as though whispered by Hrazul Wise-eye herself, another curious thought formed unbidden behind the eyes:

IF HRA-ADIN TRULY EXISTS, THEN YOU OWE IT TO THE MULTITUDES OF THE FALLEN TO SEE IT FOR YOURSELF. WHO KNOWS? FOR THERE, MAYBE, JUST MAYBE, YOU COULD START TO SET THINGS RIGHT.

Zakon shook the alien voice from his head. Why, the very notion spat on his ancestors! Wounds could be healed but not memories, and if not memories, then how could relations ever be?

---

xlix   See the preface on Thought Bubbles. Telepathically received thoughts are represented in a bold italicized small-cap font.

Alone now and unhelmed, the tendrils of his crown imbibed freely of that numbing perfume. When he had luxuriated long enough with an empty mind and quieted the inner turmoil, Zakon uncoiled himself for a final farewell.

"Sleep well, old teacher. I myself will erect your memorials, one for each of the Twelve Pillars of Methodics. Until the Gha-Ghara crumble, and Ssla refuse to shine, you will never be forgotten. And now I'm compelled to suffer the details of what these schemers are proposing, though, even you will have to admit, this business of an Ascending Way reborn might actually undermine everything you struggled for.

"Besides, even with the best intentions, great change is risky. And social upheaval is the riskiest of all. After all, I'm supposed to the Upholder! My job has always been — and still is, by Zulyi! — to minimize sovereign risk, to quell social disorder, not promote it!"

Zakon sighed. "Better for all if you had died intestate, eh?"

The embers flared briefly as the last of the fuel on Ukhaz's funerary pontoon caught fire, then died with a fizzle and a puff of steam as ash blew into the air and the pyre sunk from sight.

Perhaps that, came the improbable thought, was Ukhaz's reply.

Or worse still, an omen of Zoar itself.

ZOIA'S DEBT

Enok's former mistress suggests a wildly different plan of escape that will recover the lost time. Unfortunately, they have to brave the city yet again and enter Xira's personal domain. The plan succeeds but at a terrible cost.

"Her!"

Such was the venom in Zoia's utterance, and so unexpected, that Enok was left momentarily stunned, and no less so than if she had physically struck him.

"If not for *her* I would still be in the cell, or left rotting for the crabs," Enok shot back. "You are far too harsh in your judgment, Oracle!"

The rejoinder was equally swift. "And you are too hasty with yours."

The silence between them thickened. His old mistress eyed him warily, wanting to speak yet somehow unable. Her great eyelids were droopy and her tendrils leaden, only by shades less haggard than death.

What was the source of her antipathy towards Naama, surely nothing as simple as jealousy? In the end, he felt ashamed. He had never before raised words against Zoia. The tension had grown so palpable that he bowed reflexively in appeasement, but clumsily.

"It's alright," she forgave at length, "You are not my servant anymore. Just remember, this is, practically, your first encounter with your own race. You would be well advised to be cautious."

"I *am* being cautious, Oracle."

"After all, the duplicity of your kind is legend, and a burgeoning intimacy between male and female," she sighed wearily, "warps all rational thought. That is the way of your kind."

"*Humpf.* And not of yours? Storytellers have long had me imagine my people as witless savages. Well, I'm beginning to see things differently now. The Isha is affecting my judgment you say? *Good.* Better the truth than the fable."

«Consider!» "In your lack of experience, you confuse splendor with virtue: that which is beautiful must also be good."

"And the learned Zmee mistake ignorance for stupidity: the Ish who live simply must also be brutish. Both suppositions are false. Civilization, as Zmee would define it, is not the hallmark of intelligence, Oracle. Besides, of itself, ignorance is not a failing. Whereas *willful* ignorance — Oracle, I'm not being funny!"

There was no mistaking the quaint curling and uncurling of Oracle Zoia's tendrils. She was grinning broadly, Zmee style, gleeful as a zhrat at a banquet. "*You* are lecturing *me*." «Yes you are!» In fact, given her weakened state, she was positively beaming. "So, the butterfly emerges at last."

Butterfly? Emerge? Where was the humor in that?

"It's clear that Naama's not fond of Zmee," he admitted weakly, while stowing the ointment away. "Perhaps, given her experiences, like the tragedy on the reefs, she has little reason to. However, I would sooner trust her than a dozen Zakons. And it looks as if she saved your life as well. Or perhaps you would have preferred being entombed alive, slowly bleeding to death, to become another relic for the Reliquary?"

Ignoring the sarcasm, Zoia blinked and narrowed her eyes as indecision played upon the features of her careworn face. After so many years, Enok knew that look only too well. She was considering the possibility that she might be wrong. Of course, she would never actually say so. She was an Oracle, a vaunted authority, and used to dispensing opinions in the guise of wisdom's morsels. And besides, she was as stubborn as granite.

Zoia whispered casually, "The Isha made an excellent bandage."
Though disguised as praise, it was a rare admission.

"She's quite resourceful, Oracle. The Upholder underrated her."

"So it would seem. But, even with your Isha's help, leaving the
safety of Zoar is foolish." «Much danger!»

Disbelief rang in his ears. "Safety? Foolish? Oracle, you cannot
be serious! The Upholder would have posses out scouring all Zoar
by now. We're doomed if we stay here. Surely you must see that."

"Without us, Enok, you are almost certainly doomed if you *do*
go. Where exactly is your destination? The mainland is vast beyond
imagining! And where will this Isha lead you, has she said? And
what do you know about her, really? You may be of the same race,
but you are not of the same kind. Trust is earned, Enok; earned, not
thrown.

"Be warned," Zoia continued, laboring to breathe, "the moment
someone says '*Trust me alone,*' then you know you cannot really
trust them. Stop and think for a moment. Is she truly here through
misadventure? Frankly, why is she here at all? And who are these
giants? I met such brutes once before, so many years ago now. They
were a terror I had hoped to forget."

"The Isha values my judgment. She likes me, and doesn't treat
me like some mere servant." Enok was going to add 'not any more,'
but curbed his tongue. True, Naama's attitude towards him had
originally been imperious. But it had changed suddenly, though he
was loath to admit any of this to Zoia. Not just now, anyway.

"Enok, I have known you nearly all your life, and have been
watching over you closely lo these twice-twelve years.[1] We have
been through much together, and I make no apologies if it has
not always been easy. Your situation required certain precautions.
We were working to a plan — *ooh!*" she winced from some inner
twinge. "I need water."

"Hold on. The Isha won't be long."

«Exasperated!» "I hope one day you'll appreciate the wisdom of
the plan. But how were we to ever know your race matured so very

---

1   Since Zmee are six-fingered, their numbering is based on multiples of
     six and twelve, with the latter seen as the perfect or most compete of
     numbers. All administrative cycles follow this pattern.

slowly? Honestly, there were times when the High Wisdom and I thought you were stunted, or retarded, or something."

PLAN? WHAT PLAN? "You should have confided in me, Oracle. I'm not a youngling anymore."

Zoia grinned weakly. "Nor a servant, it seems. You've changed so much so quickly, I can hardly —"

"I have water." Naama had returned with a huge body-sized leaf of some enormous ginger folded into a temporary bucket. It was flimsy and heavy. A sneeze and it would all fall apart.

Zoia motioned with her snout. "If you could pass me the medicine stick, there's a troche I need."

Enok obliged, and Zoia, coiling her serpentine body and rising from her mossy bed, opened her mouth wide to accept the gift, leaf and all.

With a tilt of the head for gratitude, she hissed slowly in Y'lan, "Thank you," signing «Much. Much,» meaning many of such, but leaving Enok to explain.

Was this a first small step towards reconciliation? He could only wonder. Naama, who had had a Zmee servant, was for once of service to a Zmee, and here was an Oracle, who had had an Ish for a servant (and never once thanked him for anything!) with a debt of gratitude to an Isha.

Symmetry: here it was, woven into the very fabric of life. Was it symbolic of something deeper?

"Ow!" Enok winced from a poke in the ribs. Naama's iron fingers again.

"Don't get too cozy reminiscing. There is still a boat to be caught, and I'm no such darling of any goddess to succeed with time itself my enemy! Has the snake blubbered anything useful?"

Zoia chimed, surprised, "Boat?"

"Boat?" Enok echoed.

"Yes, *boat*," Naama snapped.

"It's the same word in both languages," observed the Oracle. "If I understand your intentions correctly, then you have well and truly missed the boat."

Enok managed to rise and keep standing. The head was clearer now. "We plan to intercept it on the sunrise coast. I beg you, Oracle, do not interfere."

"However slim, your best hope is to aim for the cape between the weedwaters, but it's unlikely you bipeds will make it on foot. Not now, anyway." «Too dangerous!»

Naama was fidgeting impatiently. "Enok, I just can't stay here bantering forever."

"Servant," Zoia began, then realized her mistake. That address was longer appropriate. "Little Ish, I suspect you know the maps as well as any disciple. It's treacherous terrain for something with only legs. Unprepared, we have no chance of surviving the crossing. The Fear! The Fear! There's —"

"Then I shall die trying, Oracle. I meant every word. We cannot stay anymore!"

The three in the grotto faced each other silently. Naama's eyes darted occasionally, probing the gloom, ready to pounce at the slightest movement.

Tok-tok-tok.

The amazon leapt into the open, flashing a makeshift obsidian dagger.

Tok-tok-tok.

A driller-bird pecking a hole in a trunk was the only sound in the forest.

"It's risky, but there *is* an alternative," Zoia suggested, in a slow and tantalizing way.

"I hope it's faster."

"'Better to round the mountain than climb it.'" That was one of her favorite scriptures.

"Oracle, please! No more riddles!"

"You forget this is Stargazer's city. Her compound is just beyond its limits, by the mountain aqueduct."

So, XIRA'S SKY-BOATS ARE NEARBY.

Naama shifted impatiently. "What's the dragon saying? I want to know."

Enok and Zoia, however, continued unbroken.

"Her balloons won't take us to the mainland — not this time of the year. The winds blow in the opposite direction."

«Indeed not,» signed the Oracle, searching for a hint of sky through the thick canopy while tracing an invisible line to the eastern sea.

YES! RIGHT INTO THE PATH OF THE BOAT!

«Quietly!» "We need to retrace our path, then skirt around Ra'a-Zohari to the foothills of the Gha-Ghara."

Enok shuddered as the suggestion struck home. "No, Oracle! Not the city again!"

"We stow aboard one of her sky-boats before the evening mists roll in, and should all go well, we'll have raised the dawn sea long before the pilgrims pass."

"By morning? Then we have a day to spare."

«Wrong!» "No time to lose! The Dragon Boat plies the canal —"

"The Susyaan tidal? It would need a truly grand tide!"

Naama's frustration was rising. "If you're considering options, I need to know —" she began, but faltered under the Oracle's glare.

"The day Wise-eye died," explained Zoia, "the new canal was officially opened. In fact, she had been on her way to celebrations there. Anyhow, tide is no longer a factor. We have less time than you think. Besides, if you truly understood what stalks the eastern swamps you would never have left the cell! All Zmee fear," her tendrils quivered at the thought, "The Fear."

Well, as everyone kept reminding him, he was no Zmee. Why should he fear the — well, whatever they were. Could anything be worse than swarming tree ants? Enok shuddered. One couldn't help but hate green ants. And if The Fear were even worse —

"What's the snake saying?" Naama had broken his pondering with another poke to the ribs. "I have to get going; with you preferably, without you if I must."

"Back to city." He knew of no word in Y'lan for 'balloon.' "Fly," he explained with a fluttering gesture. "We fly."

Naama's mouth hung open, her painted forehead wrinkled and incredulous. "Sailing on yash'kh, and now what? Flying on khrii? By all the hells! Could you even find one my size? And how would you steer them? No, I say go though the forest as planned. What makes you think this will succeed?"

Enok grinned weakly, though with a growing sense of confidence. "Boldness."

"I like it when you smile," she said, returning his. "But — blood of the gods, Enok! — a Zmee is ever a Zmee! Who knows what her true motives might be? And what if it's a trap?"

He took stock of the darkening sky, grin fading as a shadow crossed his brow. "Not certain. Nothing *certain*." And that was the absolute truth. Should he blindly accept the word of the Oracle, his former captor, now, when so much was at stake, or entrust his life to Naama in a blind trek across dangerous terrain? "Zmee not liking forest. Beast at night."

"Well then, if there's something they are afraid of, then they won't be pursuing us, will they? They haven't the gall to their liver. Look, I'm forced to rely on your judgment here. Either she will create a non-existent pressure and force a bad decision, or she may try to lull you with talk of old friendships. *'We have known each other for years,'* blah, blah, blah. *'Can you really trust the Isha?'* is what she's bound to say.

"Trust me," added Naama emphatically, and drawing him close with her hand to the back of his neck, "it's the old divide-and-conquer strategy. These cowards are famous for it. Then they blind-side you. So, no, it's not your ailing friend that worries me, but rather her accomplices."

"Blindside? Accomplices?" Words without meaning.

"A fork in the road is as good as a trap, and when you least expect it," her clawed fingers stabbed him, "the serpents strike." She drew him even closer, whispering emphatically, "I know this from experience, Enok. A Zmee just can't be trusted. Even one you grew up with. This," she flashed her new dagger, "is the only thing I trust. And *'Guard your mouth, and save your skin,'* is the best of rules to live by. So be careful what you tell her, Enok, *and stay alert.*"

It should have been an easy decision. All they had to do was leave Zoia behind and march off into the night, but something niggled him to be cautious. Whose advice should he follow?

On one hand, Zoia kept talking of *we;* on the other, Naama had let slip too many *I*s. And Zoia's reasoning was sound: trust the familiar, not the untried. Both probably meant well, but Zoia had an intimate knowledge of this city, and that could work in their favor. Moreover, if the pilgrim's boat could now ply the Susyaan canal, then they were desperately short of time.

At last, he made up his mind. The risks were incalculable, but the rewards too great to ignore. And with a bit of luck, tonight would turn out better than had today.

"Lead on," he nudged his former mistress. *Follow,* he gestured to Naama as he took up the rear. If he nursed any hope at all now it was that he would never regret this decision.

However, Naama had ideas of her own. Her painted face came within a breath of Zoia's as she ran the flat of the dagger across the serpent's snout. "You might be his *friend,*" she challenged sarcastically, "but if you betray us, I promise by my mother's hearth, I will rip out your blue beating heart and eat it raw." And addressing Enok, she added, "You make certain she understands *that.*"

However, no translation came. Zoia understood the threat well enough on her own. In the blink of an eye, with a whip of her tail from behind, she deftly swept Naama backwards off her feet to disarm her in a stroke. Like a predator poised for the kill, pinning her down with clawed hands, Zoia growled a word in Naama's own tongue:

"Barbarian!" she spat, then added angrily in Zmiysh, "Better for all if *I* keep the dagger."

Enok sighed. Perhaps reconciliation might take a little longer.

So, it was back to the city.

The forest of immense thaakh trees and the labyrinths formed of their buttressing roots were something truly spectacular. Together they were grander and more humbling than anything Enok had imagined from maps.

The trio, led by Zoia, moved erratically through it, pausing frequently for telltale signs of pursuers or workers harvesting latex. Air orchids thrived here. Long strands of glaucous mosses hung like smoke in the air. The forest was wreathed in shadow, and thick with tree ferns, fan palms, and so many kinds of parasitic vines.

No place for Elim eyes, this: here is where Zmee had all the advantage. They were hardly nocturnal yet had the eyes of a night creature, in addition to their other alien senses. Hrazul had often found him in the dark, even in deepest jungle. She could 'see his heat,' she had said, even trace his scent. Now he was relying on Zoia to keep them from straying or being discovered, though her unsteady pace was annoying. It had little to do with age or her weakened condition. Zmee had a habit of dashing in bursts, pausing like a viper to 'taste' the air before dashing forward again.

On the contrary, lagging Naama was skilled in stealth. Creeping sideways with eyes to the rear, she made nary a sound; no rustling branch or snapping twig gave her away. Despite her size, she was graceful in action, enchanting to watch, but her beauty seemed somehow diminished after the Reliquary vision. No time could erase the image of the delicate Isha with the midnight complexion.

As she crept past him, muttering, "Though I feel naked without a blade, if she wasn't your friend, I'd have killed her," he comprehended that her silence had been resentful, for in a single day both an ailing Zmee and an untrained youth had bested her.

He had gloated only for a moment when struck by smears of a distinctive green-blue across where she holstered her fangs. It was Zmee blood. And fresh. But whose?

She met his gaze and winked with a mouth click, "Yes, I would have. Even without a knife."

No longer concerned with guarding the rear, Naama trailed Zoia closely. Then, amidst the primeval landscape, the pair stumbled across a very welcome path. Ornate pumice lanterns bordered it, high to the chin, yet dark and unlit. 'Fire-warders,' Zoia called them.

Gnarled and ancient trees made whispered commentary as Zoia surveyed the road in both directions before speeding across to hide in a labyrinth of roots. On a signal from her tail, Naama followed, then Enok.

«Too risky,» she signed. "A forest worker's road. Civils ought to be lighting the warders soon, to protect —"

"Where to now, then?" asked Naama eagerly.

Zoia addressed Enok. "Two watch-sixth's up the road is the Reliquary.[li] My old disciple's home isn't too far beyond it, but we will have to move bole-to-bole, quarter-circle round the city."

Naama was alert, scanning the treetops. Limb ground against limb as trees groaned a warning. "What's that weird sound?"

"Trees."

"No, Enok. The *other* sound."

---

li   A sixth of a watch, or just *sixth* or *span* in Zmee parlance equals our twenty minutes, though no culture yet reckons time so minutely.

The amazon's ears were exceptional. Moments passed before he heard it too, distant night-howlers hooting wildly.

"Nothing to worry about," Zoia reassured, sensing their growing concern.

THE FEAR! THE FEAR!

Melding with the sough of the wind in the canopy came a lamentation, a song of terror and death that only Enok perceived.

Naama leaned over to whisper, "What did she say?"

Seeing Enok had frozen, listening intently, Zoia inquired, "Ish, what's wrong?"

O SISTER! O SISTER! YOU FELL TO THE FEAR!

Someone had died, someone much beloved.

"We best not go that way. Evil lurks nearby," he answered the Oracle. "Something truly fearful."

«Fearful?» "The Fear! So close to the city? How do you know?" The look of terror on his old teacher's face became one of surprise, then understanding.

SHE KNOWS. Somehow, she had learned of his ever-strengthening gift with beast-song. Odd, he had never told her. Maybe Hrazul or Alazar had.

"Is there a problem?" Naama was feeling left out again.

"Beast here. Danger much. You not hear beast-words?"

Being of the same race, he assumed Naama shared this ability. A wrong assumption, he realized, when she spat, "Don't be silly. No one understands beasts."

"Zmee hear Ish-talk. I hear Zmee-talk."

"That's different," she replied, and gave him the strangest of looks when he asked "How?" in return.

«Danger!» "Come on, bipeds! Both of you!"

Naama wagged her head at Zoia's panicked expression. "¡Tsk. Alright, we stick to the path, and may the Goddess forgive the cowardly." She motioned to Zoia. "Go on, worm-breath. There's no point in lingering."

The trio kept to the open road for longer than Enok thought wise. Though broad, its frequent arcs and lush verges meant little warning of a posse rounding a bend. Zoia was leading in erratic Zmee fashion, noticeably slowing, with Naama distantly shadowing. If danger was present, the amazon clearly believed it to lie behind them again rather than afore.

And now they had come to a fork in the road. The wider path seemed clear and well-used. The divergent trail had become littered and narrowed with encroaching bracken. The Oracle paused for breath by a towering fire-warder that doubled as a roadside marker.

"The forest highway now leads straight to town. I would not consider it safe."

Enok translated, and Naama's kohl-stained eyes widened in reminder. *The fork in the road.*

"This way," Zoia gestured looking frailer than ever, taking the overgrown trail. "If we find water, I need to rest. Ahead should be a ramp into the forest mid-story."

"I'm not sure about this, Oracle. A tree-way leaves little room for maneuvering. I feel safer on the ground."

«Worry not.» "This is an early-season lot. The sap harvesters are further inland; this path is mostly disused. With luck, we might find an abandoned water bladder or two. Besides, this tree-way arcs the city to exit across the aqueduct near Stargazer's compound."

Naama was making eyes and wagging her head.

"There's more you're not telling me, Oracle."

Zoia's great eyes met his and he comprehended the pleading in them. She needed his help as much as he did hers. Zmee were amphibious, and in her present condition, she wouldn't last long without water. The aqueduct would necessarily be high above ground. And the tree-way gained her the elevation she needed while some strength yet remained.

Enok shuddered from the realization: Zoia was even frailer than was she letting on.

"Your eyes are leaking, little Ish."

"Naama calls them *tears*. It's a weeping of the eyes."

«Time for that later.» She gave Naama an up-spiraling gesture, who with lifted eyes to the canopy seemed to grasp the intent.

The scowl confirmed it. "There are gangways in the treetops? We'll have nowhere to flee if confronted. I warned you, Enok. Smells of trap to me."

"Water there. Zmee need water muchly."

"Two scalps with a single swipe, is that what she's saying?"

Another strange new word. "Scalp?"

"Forget it," Naama sighed with a sideways glance at the Oracle. "I'll take up the rear again. Just in case."

The narrow branch of the forest highway ended at the base of a magnificent thaakh tree, then rose again above its great buttressing roots in a wide spiral gangway of roped planks sticky from resinous spilth. Weeping veils of air moss gave it all the looks of some giant spider's lair. In the forest twilight, imagination conjured up arachnid terrors, and Enok, with regular unease, sought comfort in backward glances at Naama. But the haunting sight made even the amazon shudder. When he last checked, she was tottering zigzag across the swaying bridge, growling and pointing upwards at an even higher tree-way that almost paralleled their own.

"Enok!" she cried out as loudly as she dared. "This is insane! A posse could be lying in wait above!" He followed her pointing finger. "Look, over there: more gangways. Up, down, left, right: it's a maze of death for sure."

Enok shared her fears, and even more so as Zoia clearly found the going hard against the grip of the rubbery floor. She was noticeably slowing and dusk was nigh. They had passed dozens of the great trees with still no sign of a water bladder. The many wedge shaped wounds in the trunks had long crusted over, and that fallen leaves carpeted stretches of the tree-way here told of no appreciable traffic for several moons at least. Slim indeed were the chances of finding anything potable here.

At a wide crossroad circling the trunk of a forest giant, they paused. Oracle Zoia's breathing was labored, and she collapsed against the thaakh tree, blue ichor staining the bandage over her heart. "Enok, the sap is a good coagulator. Pull sulfur talc from the medicine stick, then score the tree. Quickly now. Here's the knife."

With Naama's obsidian blade, Enok notched the tree with a down-facing wedge and gummy milk oozed readily.

«Stop!» "Don't toss the bark! Chew it to a paste, then make a salve with the sap and the talc."

While Naama's war-painted eyes kept scanning moss-draped bridges in the higher canopy for the accomplices she was certain lay in ambush, Enok fingered the bitter paste of bark, sap and sulfur into his former Oracle's wounds.

Zoia smarted. "We ... we have to keep moving. Not far now. I hear the aqueduct beckoning. Or am I imagining?"

As Enok strained for water's familiar tinkle, Naama growled and leapt at the Oracle. "I warned you not to trust her! Look!"

From tangential directions, one at their level from the right, the other above and directly towards them, two guards in Civil livery were rapidly converging. The higher called to the lower, who waved in response. The tree-ways quivered from their hastening tempo. Barbarian prophecy had come alive.

"I told you so, Enok!" cried Naama. "Throw me the knife!"

Zoia snatched the blade from Enok's grasp with the tip of her tail. «No! Peace!» "Look, the fire-bird!"

The amazon struggled for the weapon, knocking Enok aside.

The overhead Civil was the nearer of the two. In a deft leap, she plunged with outstretched wings in a swift aerobatic maneuver, arresting her flight with tail to the ropes and a complex somersault to land behind Naama. It was Hozny Kitemaker, masquerading.

"Forwards, Oracle! Hurry!" she cried. "Two Spotters approach from above!" was all she managed to say before Naama had wrested the knife from the aging Oracle, and twisted her arm behind her back and with the blade pressed ready to pith her.

"Stop, or the old dragon dies!"

There was no time for interpreting. The second Civil whizzed down past the trio with wings stretched out like a shield. "Back! Return!" she cried. And swooping after her was Jin-jin! "You're almost at Stargazer's compound. It's madness to continue that way!" The high-pitched cry and gray face were Alazar's, the High Wisdom's senior disciple and Hrazul's deepest confidant.

From an elevated tree-way, a Spotter hissed, firing a trident. A dart zipped past Alazar's loose fitting buckler and into her neck, felling her with a scream. "Oracle! Save Servant — while you still can!"

"Gray-face!" cried Enok in shock. "Why ...? What brings ...?"

"Little Greeny is dead," wailed Alazar of Yuni. The trappings of civil militia ill fit her too and hung loosely. "We were covering your rear, when —"

"Alazar! Enokhi! Above you!" hissed Zoia with all the strength she could muster.

Alazar sprang to shield Enok. The pursuing Spotter fell from a height, felling her in the impact. In the blink of an eye, the disciple wheezed beneath a stranglehold coil.

The Spotter whooped, "Khozaa!"

Recognizing an ally in the two ragtag Civils, Naama released Zoia and at once lunged past Hozny and onto the Spotter, who squealed as much from surprise as from the amazon's obsidian blade. A guttural battle cry masked the instant a fang from Naama's utility belt jabbed its way with barbarian force into the soft underside of the Spotter's jaw.

Young Alazar fell limp as the Spotter released her.

And the Spotter's eyes widened quizzically as her hands lost all strength and the trident tumbled overboard. Defiance and astonishment welded on her features as a brief shudder wracked her before she slumped to the floor, breathing heavily but paralyzed, yet with loathing in her eyes.

This was no time for gloating. "Enok, quickly," urged Naama. "You go on ahead."

"Servant!" cried Hozny. "I need the barbarian's weapon. Look!"

Taking stock of the situation, the second Spotter on the upper tree-way had spread her wings and leapt in a glide to the forest floor and was now slithering away at speed.

In the hope of being understood, Naama growled emphatically with a finger at the escapee. "We have to stop that Spotter!"

Hozny added, "Mistress, the High Wisdom sent us to find and warn you. She's now a prisoner aboard the Dragon Boat, and a host of Zeruhawi now blockade the Isthmus Gates. I'll explain later. Quickly now! I need that poisoned weapon! Ow!" She winced as Jin-jin snapped at her hand.

Enok shooed the bird. "Jin-jin, stop it!"

With a swift swipe of her prehensile tail, Zoia snatched the great fang from Naama; though before she had managed to hiss a thank-you in barbarian tongue, Hozny had stolen it in turn, and taken a flying leap to glide, swerve and ricochet between trees with all the grace for which she was famous. Forest and distance now hid her from sight.

Jin-jin squawked angrily, and fell pecking at the tendrils of the paralyzed Spotter.

"Smart bird," cooed Naama to Jin-jin. "Enok's pet, eh? You've a real talent for discerning enemies."

Meanwhile, eyes met eyes in expectant silence, awaiting a victory whoop from Hozny. However, no 'Khozaa!' echoed through the forest, and eyes and ears were drawn instead to whimpering Alazar. The young disciple and close companion of Hrazul's lay twisted in a spreading stain of blue seeping between the planks, and whimpering as she clutched at the gash in her neck. A dart had also badly grazed her jowls.

"Little Greeny is dead," she whispered weakly of Yuni. "Reeking of the Isha's scent. I am ... defiled. No time for the death chant."

Rage gripped Enok as the truth of her words penetrated. "Naama! You kill little Yuni in woodland!"

Naama stiffened. "What?"

"Little green Zmee. You kill!"

"I was merely hafting my blade when I ambushed a youngling paralleling our trail. That, I admit. But at worst she'll be paralyzed for a watch or so, asleep at best." Naama dug a heel with a curse into the wide-eyed Spotter, causing Jin-jin to leap. "See? Drugged. What do you take me for? A Havilan doesn't kill children, even if they are Zmee."

"Drugged?" he responded, juggling puzzlement and relief while interpreting for Zoia.

"Enok, make another sulfur bandage!" «Hurry!» Zoia ordered. "Don't fret, young disciple. Like the Spotter here, Little Greeny is only tranquilized. She will live, and so must you. Be at peace, you are not defiled."

"Oh, mistress," Alazar whispered, "It begins."

"What begins? Death?" Enok inquired, inadvertently asking in his own language, and was doubly surprised when it was Naama, eyes locked in understanding with Zoia's, who answered.

"No, civil war."

As Zoia rummaged hurriedly through the medicine stick, Naama muzzled herself against the dangling ropes of the tree-way, watching pensively as former slave and mistress battled united to save a life of the race she hated. But Alazar had proven her loyalty in blood. She had saved both Naama and Enok from the darts, and the knowing showed in Naama's expression.

«Dead.» "Yuni … truly dead. Kitemaker … trust not," were Alazar's last words.

Naama seemed genuinely moved as Alazar Gray-face breathed her last. "I can scarce believe what I'm seeing: Ish and Zmee, allied equals. Who could have thought? But for what, I don't understand; however, war I do, and I know what needs to be done."

She dishelmed the Spotter and flung the trophy into the void. Her paralyzed enemy could barely even gurgle when Naama pithed her with the dagger. Enok's horrified expression at her twist of the blade, she dismissed with a curse and a wag of the head, and wiped the blade against her leathers.

"We've sunk to a whole new level now, serpent-boy. It's kill or be killed. You had better get used to it."

MORE SENSELESS BLOODSHED!

"You live for killing! You *did* kill little Yuni!"

"I *survive* by killing. That's *hugely* different." Naama's words were metered as she stiffened, with narrowed lips and eyes. "I am the Havilan of Havilans! My word is better than iron. As I already told you, I did *not* kill the woodland youngling. There wasn't much poison left on my fang, so this enemy Spotter here wouldn't have been paralyzed for long. What? You don't think she would have raised some alarm when she woke?

"Your young Zmee friend here is already dead!" she spat. "And why? Smell her wounds, serpent-brat. Those darts are tipped with some sort of fishy poison. And that means we're being hunted with a kill-on-sight order. I did what I had to do. And your self-righteous mammy here knows it too."

Zoia abandoned dressing Alazar's wounds, and coiled the young disciple into the customary sleeping position. "Rest now, little one. May the First Cause preserve your soul, now and into forever." Then with a sudden whipping motion with her tail, Zoia once again grabbed the dagger, spitting "Barbarian!" before stowing the weapon away.

Meanwhile, Naama had found a dangling oiled rope and, with a hasty loop about the waist, was on the verge of rappelling to the ground. They were high above the forest floor, and a considerable fall awaited her even at rope's end.

The Isha was unfathomable! Enok cried, "Naama! We go now!"

"We've been discovered, and I need to make certain that other Spotter is dead. I'll follow you from the ground."

"But —"

"Great Goddess! Where's your friend's victory cry, eh? Well do I know the smell of war, and even better the stench of Zmee betrayal. Its laughing spittle blinds you both! Jin-jin has better war-sense than both of you combined. Well, don't just gawk. Keep moving!"

Enok translated for Zoia, who chanted something privately over the unconscious disciple, then lifted open hands to the heavens in silent petition while he instead followed Naama's skirling descent with his eyes.

"The Isha could well be right," noted Zoia a little somberly, "that is, from the little I understood. And with the High Wisdom a prisoner, we are in more danger than ever before. If that other Spotter escapes, and with proof of our aid — of *my* aid — it's not just you and the Isha the Zeruhawi would see dead but anyone who stands to protect you, directly or indirectly."

"And by your actions, you represent Zu'u-Shoran and everyone in it. So the Isha's right. Here's the other half of that grand game: war."

Oracle Zoia caressed the crown of the slain youngster. Her gaze was fixed sightless to another realm as she fingered the pupil's phylacteries that embodied everything the Azhakh-Na believed in.

"Winds of change now blow over Zoar, and whither to the North, or the South, it matters not a jot. Such a storm this 'game' will bring will surely ruin us all."

Enok knelt, taking his mistress' hand. "Because of me Hrazul is dead. Because of me, even more died during the giant's rampage. And even now, death traces my every step. I owe my life to all of you, and it's a debt I can never repay. I'm just a lowly servant. If so much is truly at stake then let *me* be the game that you lose."

The Oracle tore her hand away, signing, «Little butterfly! No!» "So much more is at stake here than any Northerner can possibly imagine." In her burst expression, the whole of her life and its bitter terminus were there to be read. "Zoar is undone already, and the only consolation to my lineage is that the Zeruhawi are winning on the wrong board."

*

The journey along the tree-way continued without incident. Even Jin-jin had kept out of trouble. Zoia was now panting hard and had moaned more than once about thirst. The long-anticipated bladders did eventually appear, though someone had deliberately punctured them. They were empty. However, the chime of running water was no illusion now. The mountain aqueduct was close, and so too was Xira's compound.

His former mistress spoke little. Ever the teacher, she was always challenging her students to think, to reason out puzzles randomly pulled from her vast repertoire, but there was none of that today. Striking up any sort of conversation proved fruitless.

Frankly, Enok had never seen her so pensive, or so fragile, and it seemed little to do with it her health. Her eyes and intellect were as sharp as always, but burdened now with a knowledge that was even more disquieting than death. She again the mistress, he again the servant, questions or idle banter were ignored as they ever had been in happier, simpler days.

In concern for her welfare, he kept as close as the tree-way allowed, creeping along like a zhrat with a prize, eyes scanning every tree and creaking branch, imagination conjuring enemies of shadows and familiar friends of every sunbeam. More than once his ears detected the purr of juvenile yash'kh.

Of course, that made little sense since yash'kh were creatures of the sea. Only illusion could place them at such remove or so near to Xira's compound.

The tree-way now began to descend in sagging arcs from lesser trees as the stanchions of the towering thaakh forest with their immense and fantastically contorted limbs gave way to more slender flat-leaved pines, fern-leafed trees, and kauris. Their less majestic canopies afforded less cover; however, it was also less dark in the open and it evened the odds.

And now at a junction circling a kauri, one elevated path spanned the aqueduct, the other spiraled to the forest floor. Tears dewed his lashes again at what this could mean for his mistress when instead of continuing, Zoia cocked her head at the sound of whistling from the base of the ramp and chose the downward spiral.

In a grove of great cycads, Naama was beckoning with her poisoned fang in a blood-stained hand. Hozny Kitemaker lay dead at her feet, half buried in the forest litter. The eyes were wide and her features seemed creased more from hatred than anything else. Zoia and Enok shared tortured looks. What was Hozny doing by Xira's camp?

Jin-jin flew to alight on the corpse, carping and posturing angrily. "Khaa! Khozny!"

Only Naama had the temerity to speak. "Smart bird, that. It really does know its enemies. Don't want to gloat *again*, but I told you so. Your friend and the Spotter met in the underbrush. Your dead companion here did all the talking, but after a little scuffle, the Spotter just zipped back the way we'd come without uttering a syllable, firing her dart-shooting trident into the air before abandoning the useless weapon. Great Goddess, that thing's heavy! Hard to fathom after all that's happened, I know," she mused, tossing him a dagger-like amulet, "but that strange dark-eyed Spotter was no enemy. Recognize that? It belongs to our mystery-snake."

The rest of her story was equally incredible. They had fought viciously, with Hozny darting and ricocheting off trees like a living bolt. However, Naama had managed to turn Hozny Kitemaker's weapons against her. Hozny had long been an intimate of young Snei and had never treated him unkindly. But it was common knowledge too that she been a great admirer of Xira. It rent his soul to relay the amazon's gloating. If Zeruhawi influence had turned friend Hozny traitor, then, frankly, no one was immune.

Naama displayed her fang, then the weapon she had prized off the kite-maker. "Be careful, Enok. It has that same fishy toxin that killed your friend in the tree-ways. This one here," she nudged with her foot, "took only moments to die."

Zoia's face already gravely drawn, weeping in almost human form as she examined the jutting little spikes in Hozny's neck and the weapon's broken remnants. "Wood, poisoned like the barbarian's fang, but it doesn't paralyze, it kills." The Oracle was about to keen a Azhakh-Na death chant over the darling of Zu'u-Shoran, champion flier and celebrated kite-maker, when Enok's discovery of another death prong in Hozny's armband worsted Zoia's already loured mask.

The armband's triskelion marked it as Zakon's. Hozny must have been one of his spies.

"Strange, then," Enok pondered, "to deprive Naama of her fang when Kitemaker had no real need of it."

It seemed like ages before Zoia responded. "Perhaps to use as further evidence against you, claiming you had killed Little Greeny." In a wink, she snatched the prong from Enok's grasp and stabbed it deep into the earth, snapping it with a twist. "Leave it. It's cursed."

Enok's thoughts raced to Yuni. "So, what Gray-face said about Little Greeny in the forest really might true. She isn't just paralyzed, she's dead."

"Murdered, yes, but not, it seems, by your Isha's hand." Her sad eyes met Naama's briefly before bowing her head in gratitude.

"Like I said, serpent-boy, I recognize the stench of betrayal. And this Zoia of yours might just be alright after all. But let's keep moving. I have already scouted ahead, and the best cover is on the far side of the clearing. But — phew! — wherever your old mistress has been leading us, we're here, and I can't say I like the smell if it."

As Naama and Jin-jin led the way through a gully overshadowed with spindly tree ferns, Zoia grabbed Enok with her tail.

«Danger!» "Kitemaker might equally have just been making her way to meet us," she whispered.

Enok baulked. "Unlikely, given all the evidence."

"No witnesses, no proof," came Zoia's rejoinder. "I have never even heard of a death prong like Kitemaker's, much less so fatal a venom. But your Isha seems all too familiar with poisons, and how is it she never discovered that second prong herself? My judgment is she wanted *you* to find it. Or at least to make it seem that way."

"But I thought you said you trusted her now."

"I said nothing of trust, little Ish, only that she may not have killed Little Greeny." When Naama and Jin-jin were out of sight, she added, "This barbarian is no one's ally. Nothing of her report could be true. Don't underestimate her, Enokhi. Keep your tendrils moist, and stay alert."

The vast grassy field of Xira's compound was a stark contrast to the thick, brooding textures of the forest and the Gha-Ghara cordillera beyond it. Whitewashed domes clustering about a grand central rotunda resembled a family of colossal puffballs bursting through the soil. These were nothing like the angular constructions of the city with their twisted columns framing keyhole-style entries, but modern buildings with simple parabolic arches for an entrance. A massive three-lobed tower with parapets amidst the complex didn't just support another aqueduct, it formed part of the watercourse itself. The lobes rose with Zeruhawi defiance to astonishing height, dwarfing nearby trees, and the tallest rivaled the very thaakh for height. Narrow windows punctuated its masonry, following the course of some internal ramp. The lower reaches were fretted with yellow-bracted vines that rambled over the balustrades of the watercourse.

No traditional rubrics hallowed the entrances here. Serpent-ring standards framed every entrance. And great black ensigns with the red dragon-wheel hung roped from the parapets. Enok shuddered. These were kin to those they had seen this morning at execution beach — the Na-Zeru standard. The image of Zeruha's crypt clearly held special meaning for Xira and her cadre.

"Khaa! Hated j'Na-Zeru!" Zoia hissed. "We need to be especially careful." «Instant death!»

Where it narrowed on the eastern side of the clearing, a towering bamboo stockade corralled squawking khwatl. Nearby, as large as a building and swaying gently against the dark curtain of the trees, gigantic gas-filled bladders strained against their netting. As distance dissolved, a hanging basket was easily discerned above the trampled grass. It was big enough for several Zmee together.

The sight transfixed Naama too. "Goddess of Luck, no guards —" she began to say before muffling a sneeze. "Phew-ew! Great blood and bahalazh! What a latrine!"

Enok gagged. "And to think that Wise-eye choked over my insignificant tannery!"

"It's the manufactory. Stargazer makes her flying gas here," Zoia explained, slithering low. "It's hardly floral but not *that* unpleasant, surely? Smells like a fresh batch though."

"Fresh?"Enok hawked. Even Jin-jin sneezed. No wonder Xira stank. The complex reeked of rotting yash'kh, and he said so.

Zoia eyed him queerly. "Few would approve if they knew."

What? Well, at least they were upwind of the manufactory, the source of the fetor. Oh, but the khwatl were downwind! That the stench would mask their scent and the khwatl not raise an alarm was a hope with the odds, but khwatl were unpredictable. Anything could happen.

"Stay low," Naama whispered when they reached the sky-boat. "This great basket should shield us."

Twilight had come. The distinctive glow of a bobbing water-fire lantern lit the archway of the central rotunda.

Xira never stooped to carrying anything, Zoia commented. That meant there had to be at least two Zmee, Xira and a disciple. Nothing to worry about, she signed, before coiling behind the balloon's cradle with tendrils coloring in an expression he'd never seen before. "Tell the Isha to get in and keep her eyes on the buildings for signs of life, then pass me the medicine stick."

Naama hurdled into the gondola, bobbing low, and peering over its lip. "I'll hoot if I see anything."

"Hoot?"

"Wait and see."

Jin-jin perched on the lip of the cradle.

"Get down, crazy bird," Naama barked, drawing Jin-jin to herself. "Stay with me, little fighter, before the snakes spy you out."

"Here, start cutting," Zoia insisted, producing the confiscated blade, while she herself began chewing on a tether.

Naama's makeshift knife worked a treat. The gondola rocked wildly as one by one the restraints fell slack.

"Only one to go, Oracle," he whispered. "This is such a wretched goodbye."

«Move over.» "You need me."

Enok baulked at the idea. Zoia was in desperate need of both water and a physician. The argument did little to dissuade his old mistress. "But your place is here, Oracle, and especially after what Kitemaker said about the blockade." If anything of what that traitor Hozny said was true, then all of Zu'u-Shoran was in danger. "Your people need you more. My life here has brought you nothing but trouble."

«Indeed!» "But a life cut short, I fear, without my guidance. After all, you have no memory of the mainland, and you are still just a youngling."

"Youngling? I'm nearly as old as you!"

"Oh, what a gift you have, Enokhi! Though it took a while to comprehend it. The pyres of the next six generations of Zoar will have long sunk into the sea and you —you! — will still not be as 'old' as I am today. Do you begin to understand now, little Ish, what a withering race we Zmee have become?"

Enok wagged his head in Zmee-style negative. "Please, Oracle, dispense with the riddles. There's no better time for the truth."

"Longevity, Enokhi! We Zmee once lived thousands of years — tens of thousands! And now," she said between mouthfuls of rope, "if we live to six twelves it's an achievement. Until you came," — *spit!* — "we thought such endurance a fanciful myth." *Spit!* "Now, at last, we comprehend: you possess in your blood what we forfeited long ago. You still have so much to learn!"

"Naama will guide me. She will help me find my people."

"A conclusion based on assumptions. My *disciples* ought to know better," she managed to grin. "Now, unswaddle the medicine stick."

Close by, a night creature hooted. INDEED, WAY TOO CLOSE, Enok thought, before realizing it was Naama.

Peering round the gondola, panic rose with recognition. Two copper-helmed guards had appeared by the corral and were barking instructions at Civils.

"Great Zhmee!" exclaimed Enok. "They're the very guards from Breakfast Island!"

They dispatched their orders ruthlessly. 'Dead to every living pleasure save one,' Hrazul had said. And he could easily guess which: killing!

«Wretched guards!» Zoia signed. "The Upholder's j'Na-Zeru elite. They've come with Civils for the khwatl by the looks of it. No cause for alarm." However, her facial tendrils were stiff as twigs, belying her words.

The Zmee had six different words for lying. Pick any, but she was a poor liar. The words had barely escaped her lips when a grand procession began skirting the tower and snake towards the rotunda. Torchbearers, standard-bearers, and gong-bearers slowly beating their gongs, headed a train of Oracles festooned in finest robe.

A youngling shot from the rotunda to protest the presence of torches, but her actions were promptly scolded.

"Looks like Kitemaker didn't tell the half of it," Zoia observed. "If this is what I'm thinking, then night has truly come to Zoar."

She unzipped first one wrist wrap then other, while making sure Naama's eyes were elsewhere. Enok briefly spied three balls of clay marked with runes before she began stuffing them with grass into the medicine stick.

«So little time! So little!» "You wanted the truth? These are what the giants came looking for. Sealing the Reliquary was the only way to protect them."

"Keep safe? I don't —"

"They belonged to your progenitors. Now they are yours."

"My *parents?* I ... I can scarce believe it!"

«Seriously!» "Tell no one, and *never* entrust them to anyone else." His knuckles cracked from the strength of her grip. «Understand?» "Not even the Isha! Better the Zeruhawi win all the boards of that 'elevated Zhakh game' and we all die today, than have these fall into unworthy hands. The lives of all the eggs to come, of our world and yours, depend on this. One day, First Cause be praised, an egg of the Ish will stand again on the Holy Mountain. There, you will speak the name of the Azhakh-Na ..."

Chika-chika. Insects were exceptionally loud tonight.

Naama hooted again. She was quite good at it.

Great Zhmee! The j'Na-Zeru were headed their way!

"I think they have noticed something odd about the sky-boat. Get in and stay down!" Zoia forcibly threw him into the gondola, then hurriedly chewed on the final restraint.

Enok was both shocked and excited by the revelations. "Here, use the knife," he urged through the wicker. "Please, Oracle. You must tell me more of my egg-bearer!"

As Zoia was cutting and remembering a shadowed past, between breaths came fragments of the strangest tale.

"Mapmaker's expedition. Sea of Eloah ... Steam-maker and I, disciples of the High Wisdom then."

"You and Zelen, disciples together? I didn't know."

«Shush!» Your progenitors saved us ... we saved you. Terrible giants!" *Spit!* "We only survived by the aid of your guardian!"

"Guardian? Oracle, I don't understand!"

"A custodian, protector of a tribal leader's egg. A magnificent red-furred beast, forced by the cruelty of Ukhaz and her ilk to flee into the forest, so long ago now my tendrils can scarce recollect it.

But it knew you would be safe with us in the peninsular city we were building." *Spit!*

"Eh? Oh! Zu'u-Shoran!"

"The High Wisdom let everyone believe it was your sire, that it must have perished." *Spit!* «The perfect deception.» "And if its lifespan is anything like yours ..." «No time, now! No time!»

Naama's 'night creature' hooted wildly.

Jin-jin shrilled a warning.

Chika-chika-chika.

The strange rattle from the forest had been steadily growing, distracting Zoia from Naama's warnings.

Then — *thud!* — Naama threw and pinned him to the floor of the cradle, while Zoia rose high like a viper, hissing, and with her upper membranes bristling from shock.

"Ho! Caught the great thief, have I?" The tone was unmistakably Xira's.

"Stargazer, my old disciple! Wh-what a surprise!"

"Surprise indeed, thou wayward pilgrim. We all quit searching, and the Dragon Boat left without you. Did you know? Well, of course you did, because you planned it so. You were off looting the Reliquary. And — lo! — the thief can't help but to steal *again*. It's a childish sort of revenge, though, isn't it?"

«Revenge?» "Your flying gas has pickled your wits."

"Admit it! The kites! The sky-lanterns! My magnificent balloon in the red-and-black! Behold my triumphs in your own hometown! I promised you one day I'd return to hails of acclaim. Now they worship me there! You were always jealous of my genius."

"Arrogant ambition blinds you —"

"Not so blind as to have missed you aiding the prisoners! My informant has solid proof that you freed them. «Traitor!»

«Impossible!» "Three giants attacked me in the Reliquary. I very nearly died! I was lying unconscious —"

«Out cold? Really?» Then why did no one see you?"

"There are secret chambers —"

"An invisible Oracle in an invisible chamber. Another fanciful Azhakh-Na tale? I'm sure my Lord Aaj will be delighted to hear it."

«Excuse me?» "Aaj?"

"He'll be here soon enough. That's his sky-boat you're stealing."

Zoia took stock of the overdressed dignitaries by the rotunda, and snorted. «Bribery?» "Do you really take him for some venal simpleton?"

Xira chuckled. "It's for the greater good, so the means don't matter. You never did understand Methodics."

"I understand all too well your version of it. With reason void of morality, what then keeps lust from consuming us all?"

"Ever the philosopher," Xira sighed. "Action always triumphs over principle, you sad old fool." She hesitated for a moment, studying her former preceptor's bandaged wounds, then cried all the louder, "Guards! Guards! Over here!"

Chika-chika-chika. Louder now.

Khwatl were squawking nervously. Naama slid a hand to her utility belt, gripping her poison-tipped fang.

A lone Forest Spotter exploded from the nearby woodland, signing «The Fear!» and gesturing frantically at the forest.

«Ridiculous!» Xira snorted. "The Fear? How could they be so hard on your tail? I feed them carcass aplenty. They never need to come this far."

At the diversion, Zoia quickly tossed the knife into the gondola, and Jin-jin leapt heckling to the bulwark with wings and claws extended.

Xira spun. "That wretched turkey-vulture again!" she spat with a swipe of her tail. Then her tone softened to a delighted hiss. "So, what else is hiding —"

Jin-jin attacked her before she could finish. Then with one swift and fluid motion, Zoia grabbed Xira's neck in a stranglehold coil.

"Did you think me blind to your despicable scheming? You Zeruhawi murdered my disciple! You killed your own egg-sister! But your 'proof' died with Kitemaker, Stargazer. Your wicked ambition has seen far too many innocents die! But, by all that's sacred, this life I deny you!"

"Ssss ... Kitemaker finally understood ... but Wise-eye was a weakling. I offered her greatness. That Ish ... vermin ... not ... disciple." Xira's words came hoarsely though a crushed throat.

"He's a truer disciple ... than you ever were! Go, youngling. Go!" she squealed to Enok. "Go be our *tears!* Do for us what we could never do for ourselves!"

Grass and divots flew skelter as Zoia and Xira rolled about like serpentine wheels, first one way, then another, with Jin-jin hovering for an opportunity; and the Spotter, instead of helping Xira or calling for aid, made straight for the gondola. Enok blew the dread from his chest, lying frozen, expecting the worst. Naama slipped the poisoned fang from her belt, and was ready to leap when the Spotter peered over the bulwark, met Enok's frightened stare with eyes that seemed colorless in the gray light, and winked. It was the zhuk-eyed Zmee!

Naama recognized her instantly. "You!" To her it was the renegade Spotter from the forest tree-ways; to Enok, the kindly Reef Scout who had led them from the dais after Refa's rampage.

With a gleaming golden blade like none Enok had ever seen, the Spotter sliced through the last strand of rope and the balloon lurched — not up, but sideways — dragging the gondola across the clearing.

He rose in time to witness Zoia, naked head held high, struggling to keep her former disciple subdued. With eyes large and golden like Hrazul's had once been, she was calling out to him, but the voice came faint above the strange forest buzz.

Naama's superior hearing caught the words. "She bids you farewell, I believe."

As she repeated the fragments she'd heard, Enok translated softly to himself. "Zoia the Life-giver. Remember. Butterfly."

The Oracle spun suddenly, barely in time to save herself. A column of something puce yet darkly shiny, following the part in the grass made by the lone zhuk-eyed Spotter, was snaking towards her with surprising speed. It was The Fear: an insect swarm of innumerable thousands, drowning all sound with the drone of their wing.

Alarmed, Jin-jin sped through the air to catch the swiftening gondola, but dey[lii] were a tree-bird and not a great flier. Even so, Jin-jin managed the distance and struck the bulwark clumsily. Naama had been beckoning with outstretched arms and quickly pulled dem to safety.

---

lii   See the preface on Genderless Pronouns: *dey / dem / deir* are the genderless singulars of *they / them / their*.

In the compound, the spooked khwatl broke free of their corral and j'Na-Zeru gave chase. The huddle of Oracles fled for safety. Zoia sped blindly towards the main rotunda, pausing twice to catch her breath and sparing backward glances for her former charge, but Xira was beyond any help. Where teacher and student had struggled mere moments earlier, The Fear now formed a rising mound — a wrenching, bilious sight as the swarm devoured a living being. No blood-curdling shriek split the evening air; no pleas for mercy, or rescue, or death; just a writhing, buzzing mass in the grass, and the spark that was Xira's life was extinguished.

No one deserved to die like that. For all the hubris and vanity, no, not even her.

As the balloon drifted amid-field toward the buildings, the guards abandoned their pursuit of the khwatl, and instead primed their tridents, making haste for the balloon. In a flash, Enok realized they were aiming their weapons high. Too high.

OH! THE BLADDERS!

A single puncture and their flight to freedom would end in disaster!

Zoia must have realized this too. She leapt into the open with waving hands to distract the guards, shouting and pointing to where Xira had fallen. As expected, the guards sped towards her, summoning help.

"Heavy. Too heavy," Enok cried, throwing overboard anything he could find: ropes, hooks, a Mapmaker's spyglass, two huge sacks of provisions.

Both furtively glanced at Jin-jin, deciding the fire-bird would stay. Naama jettisoned a water bladder, then another, and another. The balloon began to rise rapidly higher. They would just clear the trees.

From their height, Enok watched anxiously as more j'Na-Zeru emerged from the central tower holding water-fire lanterns. They paused briefly, then made to intercept Zoia, cutting off all hope of escape. As the guards converged and stilled the cries of his mistress, the helplessness and rage that enveloped him was beyond all describing.

Beyond hatred. Beyond murder. Beyond repenting.

He leapt with impotent fists to the bulwark, determined to shout down the injustice, but a stronger hand forced him down as another clamped his mouth.

"Undisciplined fool! She sacrificed herself — to save *you!* Would you dishonor that by giving yourself away? The guards were only chasing this flying basket; they don't even know we're in here." When the struggling ceased, the hands relaxed. "Who ever dreamed of a day when a snake gives its life for a man? And serpents against serpents? Why, my own mother wouldn't believe me!"

Sensing his grief, she released him slowly, awkwardly, as though uncomfortable with the emotion. He slid away and bowed his head between his knees, for his eyes refused to stay dry. But there was no upbraiding here or some uplifting speech about how warriors should cope with their loss.

Naama too had put some distance between them to sit curled on the far side of the cradle and out of sight of the tower. She kept regarding him with narrowed eyes and with Jin-jin perched on a knee for a head scratch.

"Even more curious were those two younglings in the lower treeway," she finally said "I'm still having trouble accepting what I saw. Sure, one was a traitor, but whatever their motives, they weren't concerned with your ailing Zmee friend at all. Which, being some kind of dignitary — right? — she had every right to expect. But no, they seemed solely concerned with *you*. And then there's Black Eye, neither friend nor enemy, who pops up at the oddest moments, especially when things are at their worst. That silent upper treeway Spotter. The amulet wearer. You know who I mean."

Even with averted eyes, the pierce of her gaze grew palpable. "Who *are* you, Enok, really? And do you even know?"

The gondola skimmed the treetops, drifting into unknown lands. Enok stood propped against the suspension ropes with eyes fixed on Ssla's dying glory. The evening mists were beginning to roll in from sea, hazing Ra'a-Zohari's distant lights.

As branches continued to slap the cradle, Naama lightened the load with anything at hand. Food, water, pillows, anchors: nothing was spared. She had even cut free the trailing moorings and the great ropes coiled on the basket's sides. Her mention of sacrifice continued to echo, echo, and echo; and now he could now think of nothing else but of what Oracle Zoia had done for him, and Steam-maker Zelen, Alazar Gray-face, and Hrazul Wise-eye most of all.

He would miss her greatly. He would miss them all.

The body of law that had given him a life, was the very same that had almost deprived him of it. Hrazul had sensed the winds of change and foreseen the evil ahead. Her years in the archives and immersion in law had all been focused to one end. She had devoted her life to saving him, and how unworthy he felt right now, unworthy — there was no Zmee word for it, and no better way to describe it — of her *love*.

He sacrifice had not been for naught in the end, but was it a price worth paying?

An errant tear worked its way past his nose at the memory of their first encounter. It was in Zu'u-Shoran's butterfly house, a lifetime ago, and yet she'd been ever the same: a mystic, laconic, full of proverbs and half-spoken truths.

'To become what you dream, first know who you are.'

Those were the very first words he remembered her saying and, strangely, had never forgotten.

"But who *am* I?" he whispered into the void. "And where do I belong now?"

His thoughts drifted to his origins, to his parents. Were they dead? It would seem so. Over fifty years ago, they had saved more lives than just his own. Zoia and the High Wisdom had repaid their sacrifice by sheltering him until — until what? What was he to do now? What had been the plan to which had Zoia alluded? And those clay balls now in the medicine stick: what was their purpose, and why were they so valuable?

And her words, 'Stand on the holy mountain,' were equally baffling. Did she mean the one in the Reliquary vision? It had only been a chimera, a dream, and yet with minutia that brooked no forgetting.

An open palm revealed the burn-scar of the primal light. Since, dreams don't sear flesh, he could not have been hallucinating.

And the sacrifice:

Father!

What had driven him this far was the thought of being reunited with his family, and now it seemed he had none.

MOTHER!

They were all beginning to make sense now, those oft-disjointed fragments of memory. His father had been flinging him high in the air, masking worries with a smile; his mother bowed over him, playful yet weeping, her dark tresses caressing his face, singing a song, or a prayer:

'MAY THE EL PROTECT AND DEFEND YOU. MAY THE EL WATCH OVER ALL YOUR DAYS.'

The tune and the words were now a united memory. His parents believed their deaths were certain and had abandoned their child to the Zmee. As decoys, they had saved the lives of Zelen, Zoia, the High Wisdom's — and his own. It was of *their* sacrifice that Zelen had spoken:

'HOW WILL YOUR DEEDS HONOR THE MEMORY OF ALL THOSE WHO DIED THAT YOU MIGHT LIVE?'

And now here was the older Zoia, fifty years later, chief witness to his manumission, reciprocating. What was he seeing? There seemed to be no freedom, no release, no repayment of life-debt without the spilling of blood. And that debt had now been repaid. Mapmaker, Life-giver, Zoia[liii] — that wasn't just her title but all three of her names — the public, the private, and the intimate.[liv] The latter, only her egg-sisters knew. How appropriate they all seemed right now. Her names had been her destiny.

Though he had always secretly known her names, she had never shared them personally. Yet with her last breath, she had accepted him, not just as an equal but something more. And that spoke volumes for what she really thought of him. His mother Ayma had given him life, and Zoia had given him another, and now yet another.

There was deep symbolism here. After what he had seen in the Reliquary, he could never apprehend anything again with merely

---

liii *Zoia.* From *Z'oi*, the Zmee word for *life-force*, or *soul*, that innate metaphysical element that makes consciousness possible, though both Methodic and Zeruhawi modernity denies the existence of such.

liv All Zmee have at least three names: the public titles of formal address, both in long and short forms, the private monikers used by their peers, and the intimate name that few ever know.

earthly eyes. Symmetry and symbolism: they were signatures, for those who sought them, of a higher governing power, a power unwilling to expose itself, and yet strangely reveling in the thrill of being recognized in the coincidences of life.

Was it The El? The First Cause?

"I will never forget you, Oracle. Ever," he whispered into the void. "I promise you all, by the First Cause, by The El, none of you will have died in vain." As a lifetime of despair and loneliness engulfed him, "I *will* be your tears," he promised the slain.

Then he hung his head over the lip of the cradle.

And wept.

ODIUM

Zakon deduces the theft of his sky-boat, and his coronation ends disastrously as judgment falls upon Xira's compound ... Hopelessly adrift in a stolen balloon, Enok and Naama realize that they have no way to land.

ZAKON HAD HASTENED TO XIRA'S compound prepared for anything but this! Rarely had he seen such chaos. The compound blazed with bonfires like another mass funeral. That bravura of Oracles that had beckoned him hither was now disheveled beyond recognition and in complete disarray. Though others had swelled their ranks, it was impossible now to distinguish Oracle from commoner, for nearly every vestige of office had been abandoned or scorched beyond recognition.

Nearby, a copper-helmed j'Na-Zeru argued with an obstinate youngling who seemed intent on dousing the flames with her bucket. Elsewhere, others were setting the grassland perimeter alight, scavenging the khwatl corral for its fuel. White curls of smoke drifted slowly eastwards across the clearing. There was hardly a breathable patch of air anywhere. There was but one remaining haven, Xira's grand rotunda.

He had barely entered the atrium when the j'Na-Zeru and the youngling leapt frantically after him, fleeing a rampaging khwatl.

"I'm no yash'kh carcass! No meat on me!" the youngling cried before colliding with Zakon in a heap. "I'm too young to die!"

"What the deuce?" Zakon rolled instinctively to protect the youngling as the head of the terror bird came crashing through the archway. It was bloodied and frothing, tearing masonry apart with its great wicked beak. The low entrance, thankfully, kept it at bay.

"Be gone, wretched beast!" Zakon commanded with a savage punch to an eye. The khwatl withdrew with an agonized shriek and made for easier prey. He shook his head disparagingly at the guard. "If you had muzzled them like I told you … Once they've frenzied like that … Oh, what's the use! Great Zulyi's eggs! Can someone please explain?"

Venerable Suraazh, a northern Prefect, appeared casually from an antechamber with a funerary attendant bearing a water-fire lantern. Her placid demeanor was a calm in a maelstrom. "The Fear," she explained serenely. "They overtook Stargazer. We are burning the swarm, but it's still deadly out there."

"It's dangerous everywhere!" the youngling bawled. "We must abandon the compound. There's nothing more we can do!"

Zakon snapped, "Youngling, we either work together or die alone." «Hear me?» "Prefect, this is unheard of. What drove The Fear from the swamps? Where are the rest of the Oracles?"

"Out there, fighting remnants of the swarm. Surround and burn, it's the surest way."

"Yes, of course," Zakon agreed. "Unfortunately, I'll lose —" The words 'My new sky-boat' died unborn in his throat.

"Too late. It flew off."

«Eh?» "What do you mean?"

"Your j'Na-Zeru discovered it drifting across the clearing, and would have caught it, but the missing Mapmaker came speeding to warn them of The Fear."

«Disbelieving.» "Prime Mapmaker? Of Zu'u-Shoran?" The news was welcome but perplexing. *Zoia, here, alive?*

"Truly, Upholder!" squealed the youngling.

«She's dead now,» signed the Prefect coldly. "From rather patchy information, it seems that in all the confusion, with khwatl stampeding and the sky-boat loose, the guards thought she carried The Fear on herself, so they —"

"They killed her with a death prong?" «A merciful end,» Zakon shivered. He knew better than most the danger those swamp locusts posed. They weren't just flesh eaters but predators, and could leap from one poor soul to another and burrow into any orifice at hand. Only fools ventured into the thaakh forest unprepared. One never took chances with The Fear.

«No, no!» "You misunderstand, my lord. She had a serious wound to the heart," the guard explained. "She kept saying 'Help me, help me. The Fear.'" The guard bowed with near-incriminating lowness. "We all assumed ... Then she collapsed."

Zakon and the Prefect exchanged skeptical looks.

«Truly,» signed the guard. "Her makeshift bandages fell away at a touch. And her heart bled out. She died from overexertion."

PERHAPS I WAS WRONG ABOUT HER, Zakon considered. SO WHY HAD SHE COME HERE, AND WHY IN SUCH A STATE? "So, she met an honorable death. Eh, Prefect?"

Prefect Suraazh seemed dull or half-dazed and was almost slurring her words. "Upholder, if you please. Light up a torch and grab a pail of incense. At the moment, it's the best weapon we have."

"No flame! Not in here!" the youngling exclaimed, bringing to attention Xira's very first balloon floating high above them. "The manufactory in the tower next door, the sky-boat above —"

"Oh." Suddenly the Prefect understood. "Is that why the roofs are domed?"

"Because they're not roofs!"

"Lord Upholder, the plan is to set the perimeter alight," the j'Na-Zeru explained. "To coral the swarm and destroy them."

"Danger! The gas could ignite!"

The youngling was really getting under his skin. «Alright! Alright!» "I wasn't hatched last night you know," hissed Zakon angrily. "It's a good plan," he affirmed to the guard. EXCEPT THAT IT TRAPS US ALL. "Who are you, youngling?"

"Yelza Sky-watcher, my lord. "First Acolyte of Stargazer. I'm new."

It was painfully obvious, that. She had not yet sprouted facial tendrils, her unhelmed crown was bare, and she still had the flee response of a hatchling. Yelza was barely twelve years old at a guess and surely too immature for an acolyte.

Zakon sighed. "First Acolyte, pair up with a torchbearer and help the Civils. Do *exactly* as they tell you. And by all that's holy, keep your private names to yourself."

Yelza gave no verbal response, but the tightening lips and narrowing eyes of a sideways sneer were loud enough for Zakon's ears. It was that look of reluctant condescension common to initiates, and her newfound self-importance would hardly have tempered under Xira. Right now, however, he had patience for neither children nor arrogance.

On the contrary, Prefect Suraazh showed little trace of anything except serenity. Perhaps the fumes of the incense had numbed her already. "As the Upholder said, 'We either work together, or die alone.' There's an *emergency* here, Acolyte," she urged without emotion. "Here, take this pail of oil. And get moving."

Outside, Zmee of all stations were frantically using anything combustible to either complete the fire ring or burn any insect on sight. Heady ceremonial incense filled the air, masking all scent and sensation but the eye-watering smoke.

A despairing soul in the distance wailed, "Keep together! Work in pairs!"

As he and Suraazh crossed the field, something rubbery burst beneath him, spilling its liquid.

"What's this?" With his tail, Zakon held up what looked like a water bladder just as the Prefect made another discovery.

"And there's a spyglass here," she announced. "Such precious equipment lying in an open field. Really, Upholder! Your j'Na-Zeru can be so brutish. They ought to take more care."

"That's not one of mine. It's celestial."

Glass rattled within the broken device. "Celestial?" «You certain?»

«Absolutely.» "The armory's are collapsible like a Mapmaker's. Stargazer wanted to show me ..." His voice trailed away as his natural suspicion perceived a pattern that was anything but random. And the discovery of yet another water bladder confirmed it.

Smoke curled past him, past Suraazh. He spun with eyes to the mooring posts, following the breeze. Both the spyglass and the bladders could only have come from a gondola.

"My sky-boat was tethered past the tower there, on the far side of the clearing."

«I'm confused.» "The grass there is already alight. Surely, it's imperative to assist with the fire-ring?"

«Not now!» "Leave it to others. There's something I think we ought to check first."

Zakon examined the last known resting place of that ill-fated balloon that had been made especially for him. The nearby fires were fierce and blinding. Tendrils stung from the acrid smoke, and the eyes burned without remedy. A set of Reef Scout's goggles would have been handy.

Through the scorched earth, four squat pillars poked their heads like needles some colossus had buried. They were mooring posts, and threaded through the eyeholes were the charred remains of mooring lines that must have tethered a balloon.

The Prefect invited a closer inspection, holding up a knot of rope. "Look. Definitely cut."

Zakon examined another blackened remnant. "This end is not even singed. It looks more like it was torn apart, or chewed."

The Prefect wondered, "Why would someone cut and chew, when it's easier just to cut?"

"Maybe when you have only one knife between you."

"Someone took the sky-boat deliberately, and they had help. Is that what you're suggesting?"

Zakon stroked his tendrils pensively, following the smoke-drift. The balloon would have taken the same path. And the spyglass and the water bladders had been dumped in the clearing as if —

The Prefect too traced the curling billows, guessing his thoughts. "Azhakh-Na saboteurs! And they must somehow have summoned The Fear — but they're long gone now, whoever they were. Regardless, it's imperative that we complete the fire-ring. Could you carry the incense for a while? Easy does it, it's rather heavy."

"Heavy, heavy," Zakon repeated absently, lifting the pail.

The moment seemed to stretch into days as all thoughts fell to his sky-boat. Why would anyone want to steal it? To escape the monster that they themselves had released? Even so, why would they throw valuables overboard? Where was the balloon headed?

Suddenly, the answer struck him. Heavy! The saboteurs were completely ignorant of sky-boats, otherwise they would have let loose with the ballast instead of jettisoning provisions and rare equipment. The balloon must, therefore, still have had its ballast when it flew. It was clear now: they had only succeeded because they were lighter than a Zmee — indeed, much lighter.

"Upholder, please. Let's forget the saboteurs. We need to focus on the swarm and the fire."

"I decide what's important here! Acolyte! First Acolyte!" Zakon summoned with all his lungs. "Yelza!"

Xira's young acolyte came slithering sideways, low to the ground. Her eyes were narrowed and watery.

She coughed, "Yes, my lord?"

"The flags! Can you get them down?"

"By the Great Zhmee, Upholder!" the Prefect exclaimed. "What has possessed you?"

"Right now?" asked the youngster. "I suppose so, but —"

"Prefect, fetch two guards and follow me. And dismantle the Na-Zeru standards. I need those poles. Now!"

The Prefect flapped her wings impatiently. "I don't understand, Upholder. We *must* complete the fire-ring."

Suddenly, one of the distant towers erupted in flame. The large gas-filled bladders that had been roofing it rose into the air, hissing and blazing with demonic animation. The screams of some unfortunate Zmee being devoured by the monster the flames had become could be heard across the compound before their charred and writhing form struck the earth. And if that wasn't tragedy enough, the tallest tower exploded. Its remainder toppled sideways into what must have been a pit. The death shrieks of Zmee rang across the clearing as escaping yashurakh stampeded.

"Upholder! Upholder! What shall we do? Oh what shall we do?" Yelza was so frantic, only forcible restraint kept her from fleeing. "We are all going to die!"

Zakon was momentarily overwhelmed. "Stones of the Temple! Whence these beastly reef dragons?"

Yelza tugged at Zakon's arm, screaming, "They're the source of Stargazer's gas! I thought she'd killed them already!"

Suraazh dropped her pail of incense, crying matter-of-factly, "Take shelter, or we're all dead." Then, like Yelza, she shot back towards the rotunda where a single sky-boat remained.

It took all of Zakon's strength to maintain his composure at the sight of all the bedlam. Xira's once-beautiful towers were ablaze or in ruins, and her balloons had become floating infernos, rising beacons of catastrophe. When he could endure the sight no longer, his membranes unfurled, all trembling with despair turned to fury and revenge turned to murder. He raised his snout to the heavens and spat a single word like a curse, the most odious word in the world.

"Enok!"

How Xira the Stargazer had ever managed to use a balloon as an observatory was a mystery. High atop the great balds of Mount Oush, above every mist and miasma, Enok once loved watching the constellations of the zodiac slowly arc across the summer evening sky. But now the living shroud that was Night's Kiss admitted but scant views of anything.

If hills hadn't bobbed intermittently through the cloudy blanket, it would have been impossible to tell that there was actually a sprawling forest beneath their very feet. And whatever actually was beneath them, it was absolutely silent, which made it all the eerier. Where the raucous gaiety of Sha-Noa? Where the night-song of the zhrat? The hooting of night-howlers? The chatter of twitterlings returning to roost? Whatever ruled below was cruel, and it had made the jungle a sorrow.

There were few hints of movement in the balloon. Passing hilltops might well be the same merely drifting in and out of the haze. All Enok knew for certain was that they were lucky to have fled Xira's compound unharmed. But who could really say whether this great cloudy tide would sweep them overland towards the sea, or merely come full circle back to that Zeruhawi nest? Whatever happened next, wherever this strange vessel drifted, it was no longer in his power to control.

These were surely now the closing watches of the night, but sleep continued to elude him. There had been too much death, too much loss, too much sorrow, and the strange new amalgam of fire in the blood and conflicting emotions would succumb to naught but something cheery.

The girl in his dreams: would she come again tonight? Would she fill him once more with longing and ecstasy and grant the release that he needed?

Perhaps.

But why had she appeared in the Reliquary vision as the mate of another? Had he been dreaming all along of some spirit?

"You're not sleeping," Naama observed. "You should, you know. The bird certainly is."

Enok toyed with the dagger-shaped talisman that Naama had said was Black Eye's. "I thinking."

"About the little amulet? That's a strange thing for a Zmee to wear. I guess you can keep it. She's probably dead herself now."

Words failed him. "You not ..." A quivering hand to the chest somehow better expressed it.

Naama hazarded, "Hungry? Afraid?"

"You not afraid?" He had been both for a while, and his muscles had trembled like jellyfish. Then desolation had numbed him until Naama brought death to mind again. Hrazul and Zoia were irretrievably gone, and with them every joy of friendship. He was not physically alone, yet he now felt more desolate than ever.

Naama rose, braced herself against the rope webbing and peered down into the foggy abyss.

"Sure I am. Though, it's beautiful here, isn't it?"

Enok shrugged.

She edged her way towards him until their bare flanks met. Zmee generally slithered over each other with little care except for distinctions of class or of ritual defilement. But this was different. The warm press of her flesh triggered so many conflicting emotions — guilt, frustration, desire and rejection — each competing for primacy. Guilt won out and he slid slowly aside.

"Everything has its own kind of splendor. There's beauty in terror. Even in death." Her husky voice faded to a whisper. "Goodbye, Refa."

The knowledge was a selfish comfort that she too was haunted by memories. But what had been their connection? Had Refa been a relative of the giants who plundered the Reliquary? Were they too of the shipwrecked party? Is this what Zoia had been alluding to, that Naama was deliberately withholding information, merely using him to get off the island? If so, how was she expecting her comrades to escape? Had any survived beyond Refa?

So much about the barbarian was cause for suspicion, or uncertainty at best, though it was hard to think ill of her when she stood so close. He decided to wait for the right moment to ask his thousand questions. After all, it would be a long journey — by all accounts, a very long journey — back to his people.

"So," Naama gripped the webbing, testing its strength, "what happened inside the golden room? Did you hear something?"

"You not hear same?"

"No, the door slammed behind me as I left. Remember? I heard absolutely nothing through that thick stone. And when it finally opened, you looked unconscious but were babbling repetitiously in some unearthly glot. It was frightening, and all the more so because I couldn't wake you from it."

Enok fumbled to reply. It would be nigh impossible to distill the vision he'd seen into Zmiysh, let alone his broken Y'lan. Great Zulyi's eggs! How to convey the terror and the majesty of creation's fires, born of a hunger for fellowship that beggared in scale the very night's River of Stars[lv] for desire? Mere language could never describe it. So much would be lost in the telling, each splendid gem of truth tarnished by clumsy vocabulary. He had seen into truths beyond mortal conception, glorious answers to un-askable questions. It left him bereft of any intellectual smugness. He had seen into something so utterly beyond any reckoning, that raw naked power of The El, and he knew now that he knew nothing.

"Then what *did* happen in there? Simply tell me," she implored with a gesture.

This was not something for casual banter. You had to experience the upper room for yourself. Alone. Perhaps that was its purpose, to elevate sensation above argument, personal experience above intellectual satisfaction; a telling that simply said, "I am. This is. Accept it." How he wished it could have satisfied both experience *and* intellect.

Or was feeling a truer kind of knowing?

---

lv   *River of Stars*. Enok's (and the Elim) name for the uncountable stars of the visible galactic arc. Zmee call it the *Backbone of the Night*.

Unequal to the task, "The El," he stated simply, then instantly knew how vague and incomplete that was. The birth of the world had hardly been impersonal. He thought again upon who or what the avatar had been. Zelen herself had mumbled some fragment of her disagreement with Hrazul. Perhaps only philosophers like Zoia could ever truly ponder that 'locus of the infinite.'

So, if the avatar were the Ish of the El, should he simply call them the El-Ish? Or would that cheapen the vision?

"What? Come on, be serious now."

"The El make ..." A pointing finger drew a lazy circle above his head.

"The sky? Everything?"

"Yes! The El make sky. The El make everything. The El make Ish and Isha." In essence, that was it.

"Sons of the Gods!" Naama flounced, slapping her thigh. "Here I am trying to have a serious conversation ... risked my life ... rescued you ..." She punched him playfully in the shoulder. "Is this all you have to say? Great Goddess! You're not Ab-Sethi, are you? Those mendicant fabulists take that nonsense about A'din and the Woebegin far too seriously. Ha! And strut about naked at that!" She moved a little closer. "Come now, you owe me," she urged huskily. "Really! The El? No sight of Ma'nuna? I want the truth."

Strange, he never mentioned A'din, or Hra-Adin as the Zmee called it. He recalled reading its ciphers on the dais when the pyramid of blue light and everything within it had disappeared. Ukhaz, his accuser, had mentioned it too. Was there some big secret everyone knew but him? And where or what was the Woebegin?

"The truth?" he asked innocently.

"You're not telling me the whole truth."

There were half a dozen ways of saying that in Zmiysh, and just as many calling one a liar. Which of twelve might she mean?

The burn to his left palm still made itself felt, a reminder he had not been hallucinating. "Much more," he quietly mused. One day, perhaps, someone with a gift for words might explain it.

A grin broadened on her face, detectable only by gleaming teeth in the moonlight. "I knew you were teasing. The Twain Goddess has truly favored you, Enok. You're wiry and light on your feet, unusually strong for your size, and quick as a ravisher. With the right training, you could be a sung warrior someday, even if you are only a simple Ish. And a Zmee-handed pagan [lvi] at that! I see that in you."

Few of her words made sense. Sung? Zmee-handed? Only Ish? How could he be more?

She made herself comfortable on the crude floor, using an arm for a pillow. "Come." Her tone was more command than request, her palm slapping the rattan. "It's a bit lumpy, but at least we'll manage to keep the cold out."

"Not sleep I," Enok responded. Though he hoped to dream of his midnight girl, in this heightened state he knew that any sleep would elude him.

She had that wide-eyed hungry look again. As he grew aware of her fixed regard, he shied from locking eyes. Strange how dirty his fingernails had become, and he busied himself with their cleaning.

"As you wish," she said rather coolly, "but make sure to wake me if there's any, ah, *excitement*."

EXCITEMENT? HERE? HOW COULD THERE BE?

Naama seemed to have a knack of sleeping anywhere, anytime. Jin-jin too. And when next he checked, her breathing was deep and regular. *She* was the favored one.

Curled against the far side of the cradle, Enok found himself considering afresh the marvelous creature that was his companion. The soft outlines of her golden skin, her long legs, the smooth lines of her shoulder and neck were all rather handsome to the eye, and strangely alluring. He imagined her, as she used to be, clean-faced and free of that hideous war paint. She was intelligent, yes, accepting and highly personable too in so many ways that the Zmee had never been. She was also resourceful, and deadly. Whatever trouble he found himself in, she always managed to pull him out.

IN — OUT. IN — OUT.

He really believed that nothing could harm him as long as he was with her. Down on the ground is where the danger was. Up here, he was safe. Zoia had been right about the balloon. This was

---

lvi All Zmee are left-handed, as is Enok, which would be utterly shameful since for the Elim it's their latrine hand — and never used to handle objects, food or, among some tribes, even touch another person.

so much better than having to inch their way, step upon faltering step, down there in that ancient and deadly forest.

DOWN — UP. DOWN — UP.

It must come down what once when up.

Yes indeed, but how?

Leaning over the edge of the cradle in a precarious search for anything to aid a descent proved vain, and was finally abandoned as the eerie splendor of the night-scape below blanked all but a single thought from his mind, something Naama had stirred.

'YOU'RE NOT AB-SETHI, ARE YOU?'

Ab-Sethi. That word used to mean something. *Father, mother, son,* and *family*: not just words anymore. He strove to imagine their faces, but the only one that would clearly form was the ebony girl's of the vision.

Time stretched to forever. All qualms and strife were forgotten. Stars briefly spangled the sky as the balloon cleared the blanket of Night's Kiss. Then, in the distance, he could swear that in the instant before the mists engulfed him again, a huge and terrifying ball of flame had curled its way into the sky.

EPISODE 19

SERPENT IN THE SKY

While ensnared in the forest canopy, rescue comes by the great paws of a figure from Enok's forgotten past ... Later, nearing their destination, hostile pursuers overtake the fugitives. In a daring aerial counterattack, disaster engulfs them all.

THE ALL-ENCOMPASSING MISTS OF Night's Kiss had long since been swept ahead by Star Wash. The air was crisp, visibility was fast improving, and dawn's ruddy glow made glorious a watery horizon. To the north, the Gha-Ghara cordillera rimmed the graceful arc of the Bay of Fires. There, deep in the island's bowels, molten earth bubbled, and the smoke of Zmee forges rose in columns to strike some invisible ceiling and dissipate in great sprays to the east. To the south lay the broad golden beaches of Zu'u-Shoran, and beyond its isthmus rose towering Oush, that lonely mountain of the Sha-Noa peninsula.

The fugitives and their stolen balloon had left the majestic thaakh forest with its ancient sky-rending giants far behind. Stretching wide beneath them now were the Claw Lakes, long swamps of mint-leaved paper-barks shrouded in an endless miasma of vapors. But last night's sailing had gone anything but smoothly. Skimming the forest with barely a cubit to spare, the cradle had repeatedly collided with treetops. Once, Naama had held her fellow fugitive dangling by the legs in total darkness while he freed them from a snag. Later, when roles were reversed, liberty came only by snapping limbs or savaging the cradle. And when Naama had lost her utility belt, she had let loose with a tide of profanities that darkened the very night and sent even Jin-jin scampering. Later still, after promising to stand vigil while she slept, Enok had been shocked from dream by a startled tree-dweller's screech. They had been snagged again and wasted more valuable time.

No, last night's sailing hadn't gone smoothly at all. The misadventures had climaxed in the most unexpected of tragedies, and Enok had had no fitful sleep as he remembered the Wahoona. The abrupt end to so brief a friendship stabbed like a knife in the soul.

Thud. Crack.

A shout. A cry of agony as the basket lurched. Enok, seated lookout on its lip, felt himself thrown overboard. His fingers clung desperately to the bulwark, and his feet fumbled frantically for purchase. A forest giant had snared the balloon and badly punctured the gondola. The fog seemed to lift a little, and the pallid glow of the Lesser Light shaped a tree of astonishing size. The camphor odors betrayed a swamp turpentine that dwarfed the neighboring thaakh. Its canopy spread so high and wide that an easy escape seemed impossible.

"'Ugh! 'Ugh!"

Naama and her snoring! It sounded like canvas tearing. Nothing seemed to wake her.

The lower branch of a forked limb had gouged its way through the wicker. The upper had missed him by the luckiest of margins, and had tangled itself in the ropes. The basket was stuck fast and with no release short of tearing it apart. This was the fourth time they had struck a tree this night, and Enok was hopping mad until —

"Urrgh. W'a urrgha." Some creature was grunting in pain, and if it wasn't Naama, then who?

Seeing anything clearly in such dim conditions was almost impossible. And hanging onto the basket for fear of becoming stranded whilst also straining to free the balloon was as much as he could bear without also worrying whether he might or might not become food for some nightmarish beast!

"Urrgh. Wa urrgha-gar." Again came these strange groans that sounded almost like a plea.

Louder now. Leaves rustled. A thumping of the trunk, the sound of living flesh against wood, then a visceral grunt sprung from muffled bellows.

What was it? A khrii perhaps? A night-howler? No, the timbre had the richness of a much larger creature, possibly a tree-dwelling frog, but oh a frog of such a size!

Fireflies blinked sporadically, and Jin-jin leapt after them.

"'*Agh!* '*Agh!* Plach-agar wa urrgha-gara." Again came coughs and grunts from a throat that now seemed most unlike any frog's.

They were words! Enok panicked. One of Naama's giants was here!

"Naama here, and Enok!" he cried. "Enok! Enok, I name is!"

Silence followed, punctuated only by the ripping sounds of Naama's sleep.

Instinct bade him retreat to the safety of the basket. Would the giant follow?

Grunt. "Hatan ¡*tke* waha-waha-Wahoona ... ¡*ts* Wahoona-rosh."

Clack. Clack. The sound of stone against stone.

A spark. A flame. A torch roared guttering in the breeze.

A wrinkled face fell into relief: wide-nosed, thick-jawed, and broad-cheeked, buried in tawny fur. Prominent ridges framed the intelligent eyes of a great hairy creature reclining with its head against the trunk. If anything, it seemed more pained than angry, yet eager to communicate.

I WOULD CLEARLY LOSE IN A FIGHT, Enok judged as they sized each other up. It was Ish-like and powerful, but unlike any companion of Naama's.

"'*Ugh!* ¡*tkla* wa'u Enokhi ¡*tke* Ish ¡*tklo*," it uttered.[lvii]

Excepting the coughs, grunts and clicks of the tongue, there seemed real language here.

Yes! It was asking a question: *Are you Enok, an Ish?*

A slight bob of the head and a grunt — "'*Agh!*" — seemed to signify impatience.

---

lvii   See the Linguistics section in Author's Notes for an explanation of grunts and clicks. A full translation may be found at *lostworldtributes.media*

Jin-jin crawled towards the torch as the creature rested it.

"Enok, I name is. Ish am I." The creature's eyes never left his, and seemed to narrow in puzzlement before Enok added: "*¡Tklo* Enokhi *¡tke* Ish."

Did he say it correctly? And then other sounds came unbidden from his own mouth as if they were needed. "*¡Tke* Ish waha-waha *¡ts ¡ts.*"

What seemed a grin of excitement spread across the beast's face. "Khaa! Khaa! W'a Hatan *¡tke* Wahoona. Khaa … khaa … bach-agar Enokhi," and Jin-jin joined in with a cackle.

"You Hatan," Enok ventured, "Hatan of Wahoona?"

The creature, this Wahoona, snorted, flaring its broad leathery nostrils, sniffing, appraising. In all, it seemed peaceable enough, reclining against the trunk. A raised hand extended the torch. Yellow eyes widened as they fell on Enok's leg-shackle.

"Ah! Ah! Enokhi pshew-naga blogass Zmee. Hatan *¡tke* bloga n'ga Zmee. Gujera n'ga gujera *¡tke* bloga Zmee. Ah! Hatan —" A coughing fit cut it short, then it added weakly, "Hatan pshew-agar. Pshew-agar n'ga Hatan."

Talking with a Zmee or an Isha seemed natural enough, and it had just sort of happened with Jin-jin, but then Jin-jin was a very clever bird. The cries of various creatures, their dawn-songs, their night-lamentations, even their prayers to the waxing Lesser Light had made increasingly more sense with the passage of years, so why not now a conversation with a Wahoona? Hatan of the Wahoona: a long-time slave of the Zmee who still vividly recalled the adventures of its escape — of deir escape.[lviii] This Hatan wasn't just some beast, but a person.

Enok's eyes followed the Wahoona's up the tree. And as if to validate the story, should any ever ask, there hung a mangled copper leg-shackle and a prize of Zmee fangs. Hatan the Warrior, the trophies declared; a warrior alone in a forest so deadly, so impenetrable, that even armed Zmee shied to cross it.

This runaway slave was safe in deir sanctuary but condemned to die alone.

---

lviii See the preface on Genderless Pronouns: *dey/dem/deir* are the genderless singulars of *they/them/their.*

The Wahoona wheezed painfully, resting the burden of the torch on the floor. This elevated platform seemed to completely ring the tree — and what a great bastion it was; though at this height, the trunk was narrow and flexing and swayed in the breeze.

Ladders of knotted vines fell to a wider platform below. Maybe this was just a lookout, part of the impressive home dey had built for demself. Much of it seemed frayed, though, and weathered, carpeted in lichens and mosses. Hatan had clearly lived here for decades.

So many the questions requiring an answer! Who were these Ish-like Wahoona? A mainland people, or local forest dwellers? And only slaves were ever shackled like that. They were generally wastrels reprieved from the harshness of old Ukhaz's laws in a final chance to contribute, and treated little better than beasts till reformed. Enok had never heard of other foreign slaves, despite Sha-Noa teeming with exotics. Perhaps this Hatan had once been one of them, though dey had to be old indeed to have escaped before living memory.

Random facts came suddenly together: the Wahoona made their homes in trees, and this one had escaped long enough ago to have lived almost anywhere. It gave him an idea. Kneeling cautiously by the torch, Enok scribed with a twig a squiggle under three mountains on the bark, twin peaks with a tall surmounting third — the symbol he found etched in his New Year's Eve roost.

The response was immediate. "Ah! Ah!" Hatan waved the torch excitedly, causing Jin-jin to leap. "W'a golach. Golach ¡tke Hatan. ¡Tkla Enokhi bach-agar golach ¡tklo."

"Yes, I saws it. You mark tree, and I saws it," Enok replied in his own tongue before attempting it in Hatan's. "And I make Enok mark in same tree."

With deir mouth open wide like a silent roar, a solitary incisor and its yellowed companions bit the air. It seemed like one of Naama's crazed laughs. "Argh! Argh! ¡Ts Elyal ba-bach-agar. Enokhi bach-agar. Enokhi ¡tke ¡ts Elyal."

Jin-jin joined in with a cackle.

Did 'Elyal' mean The El? "You know of The El?"

As the Wahoona's eyes closed wearily, Enok finally understood why Hatan was reclining so stilly. Deir left hand hung limply in shadow, crooked from crushed ribs and shoulder. The collision with the tree had broken Hatan's body. Whether dey understood it to be Enok's fault, or the wind's, or that it was simply an unfortunate accident, Enok had no way of asking, but the Wahoona displayed nothing of fear or anger, though surely every breath was painful.

Hatan yielded the torch, wheezing, eyes rising to something above. Two thick hairy fingers made a sign, "'*Ugh!* Ararat-agat," followed by a single emphatic digit. "'*Ugh!* Elyan-agat ¡*tke* do A'din."

After puffed cheeks came more strange and interrupted sounds: "Enokhi ... wa'u g'khliup-agar khliup-khliupa." After a series of moans, Hatan added, wheezing, "Gosh ... ¡*tklo* ¡*tklo* gosh wa'u ... g'Elyan-agat ... agara ¡*tke* do A'din."

It was there above deir head, carved into the tree, that very symbol of the three mountains. The Wahoona, in that long abandoned roost in the Sha-Noan forest, had sketched a picture of the home that still called dem. What Enok understood from maps and from the vision in the Reliquary suddenly fused together. The twin peaks of Ur-Atu? And the third had to be a mountain beyond both: Elyan-agat the Wahoona called it. Perhaps they meant Elyon, that great mount of the island in the sea at the center of the world, an island the Zmee called Hra-Adin. It was over a dozen Zoars for size yet never shown on any map.

"That be your home, at foot of Ur-Atu — Ararat-agat? — where see you A'din? And khliup-khliupa — is splashing? A river?" Hatan's people lived on a river, most likely the Gihon.

People. A family. A tribe.

Enok made a height with a hand. "Have you little ones? F-family?" The word caught in his throat. Enok, too, had been a lonely captive without any comfort of community.

Moments passed in silence before the Wahoona gave a slow blink of understanding. "¡*Tklo* gujera n'ga gujera Hatan plach-agar ¡*tke* waha gosh ... gosh ¡*tke* wahayawi."

Enok nodded. "You much family. You miss family far away."

With a tap to deir breast, "Mu-ch fam-i-ly," Hatan managed to imitate before the good arm fell heavily and the yellow eyes took on the sight of the basket. "Enokhi pshew! '*Ugh!* '*Ugh!* G'glit-agar khree-gar pshew. Hatan ba-bach-agar."

Then dey laughed like before, but more painfully, while raising a finger at Jin-jin and calling the fire-bird by name. It was clear that Hatan understood exactly what Enok was doing and why, and deir words meant escaping like a khrii, fleeing like a bird, flying. However, short of tearing the basket apart there was no way to free it. To break the impaling limb required enormous strength or some great amount of time. Any more delays would cost them dearly. They would miss the boat and with it any hope of freedom.

Attempting to rise, the Wahoona yowled between clenched jowls, yet with deep-set yellow eyes fixed on the gondola illumined by the flickering torch. Teeth then bared in a snarl at the sound of the amazon's voice.

"Blood of the gods! Stand back, Enok! You are too close." Naama was poised on the lip of the cradle, deciding whether to attack.

Enok waved the torch in her face "No! No! Wahoona friend!"

"Friend? Ugly flea infested brute! It looks more menacing than anything friendly!"

Hatan let loose a deep visceral growl. "Wawa Anaki-blog! *'Ugh! 'Ugh!* W'u ... blogass ... Anaki-blog!" Dey weren't as tall as the giant boy Refa had been, but were easily Naama's size and, with wrists twice as thick as her knees, more than a match for both if dey'd been hale.

Enok rounded on Hatan, waving the torch. "No! Isha! Naama Isha *ɉtke* gosh Enokhi."

"*¡Tkla* poko Naama *ɉtke* Ish-wa-waha *ɉtklo,*" Hatan growled again, brows raised as if to say, *Are you certain she's one of yours?*

Enok was insistent. "Yes! Naama Isha. She with me. Naama *ɉtke* Ish-wa-waha *ɉtke* gosh Enokhi!"

More grunted words through yellow teeth seeming anything but a smile, and Hatan seemed to be asking if he and Naama were really together. Deir reaction had been unexpected and only fueled Enok's suspicions. Were the Wahoona and Naama's people enemies? The Anakiblog: did Hatan mean the Anaki? Naama had mentioned them too.

'The Anaki are my people and Gol is my Lord,' she had once said, but how then had she never met a Wahoona before?

Perhaps it was the war paint that had so startled Hatan. Spittle on a hand wiped some pigment from her cheek.

"See —" he began, but Naama quickly slapped him down.

Hatan took in the scent of things like a zhrat, then rubbed deir abdomen with great eyes suddenly furrowing in concern. "Naama bawoga. Fa-mi-ly." And Enok shook his head quizzically at the words: "¡Tkla bawoga ¡tsk ¡tsk Enokhi ¡tklo."

At the sight of Jin-jin cavorting among fireflies, Naama relaxed a little, though in a tense and awkward silence. The fireflies danced crazily by the trunk as canopy and platform rocked with creaks and groans, and the torch almost guttered to extinction. She and the Wahoona exchanged stares then nodded slowly in unison.

"No, we can't take it. It's dying, and will only slow us down."

What? Her words left him flummoxed, for he had been thinking exactly that. "Hatan get better. Here Zmee healing stick!"

"Idiot do-gooder. There's no medicine for wounds like these. Maybe not today, maybe not tomorrow, but its days are surely ended."

The Wahoona howled as though she had actually lunged with a dagger. This Hatan understood much, if not from Naama's words then from the slow wag of her head.

"Come on, Enok. This friendship ends now."

"Friend," repeated the Wahoona slowly. "¡Tklo Hatan ¡ts ¡ts friend Enokhi."

"Enok, we need to free the sky-boat, tear this great basket apart if we have to. I'll start inside, strip the smaller branches; you on the outside, and jump on board as soon as there's movement. Hurry!"

"Friend Hatan, Enok go now."

A tearing gesture to Hatan, and a mock shove towards the sky-boat and the Wahoona grasped more than the brutish face would suggest.

"Ah! Ah! Glit-agar khree-gar pshew. Hatan ba-bacha glit-glit grrozh gujera-anag-ashag."

The Wahoona's language was becoming increasingly easier to understand.

"Hatan see Zmee fly before? Days before?" Perhaps dey really had seen Xira's balloons come this way. After all, their own sky-boat had.

"Hatan roz-gar glit-glit grrozh." A broad smile quickly crept into those deep-set yellow eyes. "Hatan roz-roz-gar," dey growled softly again. "*'Ugh!* Enokhi g'glit-agar. Enokhi ¡*tkla* ¡*tklo* ba-bach-agar wa-waha ... fa-mi-ly!"

"I find your people too, Hatan. Enokhi gar-ba-bacha wahayawi ¡*ts* Hatana."

At that, the Wahoona let loose an ear-splitting yowl, frightening Jin-jin into Naama's embrace. A wounded zhrat could not have shrieked louder. Awkward moments passed before those piercing eyes reopened, keening moist and stamped with determination. Hatan staggered back to the trunk for that shackle of distant slavery. The copper had been reworked, sharpened into a sort of hand-ax. With it came a fang: one, it seemed, of Hatan's own incisors, awled and strung with large fragments of abalone shell.

A large red-haired hand — five fingered, Enok noted — extended and offered the gift as Enok returned the torch. "¡*Tkla* ¡*tklo* wa'u ¡*tke 'ugh!* daasht wahayawi ¡*ts* Hatana ¡*tke* Ararat-agog ... kliupa-agog."

Strange. 'Daasht' was a Mapmakers' word. "Yes, I give daasht to your family at Ur-Atu — at Ararat-agog."

"Daasht. Zulyi khna-daasht! Waha. Fa-mi-ly. Hatan ¡*ts* Wahoona-rosh!"

Naama had been cursing during the exchange, denuding intruding limbs and tearing away branchlets with gusto. Her sleep had been disrupted and her mood paled the very night that had swallowed her utility belt.

A shove in the back startled Enok.

"Harraga! G'glit-agar!" Again the shove. Hatan had cast the torch aside and was forcing him into the gondola. "*'Ugh!* Hatan grrozh roz-roz-gar!"

With speed and agility barely expected of an able-bodied creature, much less an injured one, Hatan and deir ax tore at the basket with great sweeping slashes.

"G'glit! Pshew, wa'u! Enokhi ¡*tke* Ish-wa-waha. Enokhi ¡*tke* ¡*tke* Elyal-waha."

Groans and yowls mingled with manic grunting lent strength to each fresh swing, and in moments the prodigious strength of the Wahoona had opened a hole big enough to crawl through, but it only allowed for more of the tree to penetrate. Realizing the effect, Hatan crawled to the very edge of the limb, notched a break-line with savage force, then gripping the basket's bulwark, began leaping wildly. The limb wobbled until a great *ca-crack!* split the night.

Behind them all, the torch had ignited the platform. The fire was beginning to spread but Hatan continued bouncing madly, rocking the great limb.

"No, birdy! No!" Naama had to forcibly restrain Jin-jin from leaping back. However, it wasn't the blaze that so beckoned the bird.

"Khata! Khata!" dey cried of Hatan. Jin-jin wanted to stay.

"Wahoona ¡tke ¡tke Elyal. Hatan friend Enokhi-bun-Yared. 'Agh! 'Agh! Hatan grrozh roz-rozgar. Enokhi pshew! Jin-jin pshew! Elyal g'wozh ¡tke w'a wahayawi."

Then the limb snapped completely. Hatan felt it give way underneath, and clung for dear life with a face creased in unimaginable pain. The one-lunged, one-armed giant swung from the cradle, gliding over the tree, continually forcing the sky-boat away. It went on for longer than Enok expected, so long that he was numb to any thought of the catastrophe a detached part of him knew would surely follow. Enok winced to Hatan's every moan. It took no great empathy to guess how much it pained the Wahoona to stand, let alone keep forcing the gondola clear.

"Enokhi-bun-Yared ... Daasht ... Wahayawi ... Hatan ¡ts ¡ts Wahoona-rosh!"

Naama gripped Enok and Jin-jin tightly against her on the far side of the gondola, balancing its lopsided flight. Then the world turned silent in a strange anticlimax. In that peculiar numbness, an awareness of the finality of their encounter, of Hatan's efforts, even of Hatan demself came with syrupy slowness. Not so with the amazon. She leapt to the great gash and prized the beast's fingers from the cradle. In the final instant, Hatan took hold of the intruding limb, extracting it as dey fell.

No sound came. No scream. And no apology.

Jin-jin flew to perch on the bulwark, flapping deir wings and squawking at Naama in a very peculiar way.

"Don't you judge me with those eyes, serpent-boy! It was as good as dead anyway. You couldn't do it, and neither could the creature for itself in the end. Nobody *wants* to die. By the Twain Goddess! I would have done the same to you."

"Kill Enok?"

"A quick death. I expect no less when it's my turn."

Whatever Hatan had used for fuel, dey had wisely kept it high above the lower deck, for now the entire upper platform was ablaze like a pyre, pouring its glory upon the forest of death.

Jin-jin perched on the bulwark, squawking. Enok stared randomly at the burning tree, torn by the sudden revelation of who and what Hatan had been: the red-furred childhood guardian mistress Zoia had spoken of, the beast that Oracle Ukhaz and her Zeruhawi ilk had taken for his sire. 'Enokhi-bun-Yared,' Hatan had said: Enok, son of Yared. And now the one person who knew both his origins and his kin had gone the way of everyone else.

"I'm curious. How did you make sense of beast-talk?" probed Naama, sliding towards him. "Frankly, how is that even possible? Are you a Magus?" Then she sighed, "No, you couldn't be."

"Speaking," he began uncertainly, "sleep in Enok head."

"Language? Something from memory? Honestly, Enok, the longer I know you, the odder you become."

Enok slid away. Right now, he just needed to be alone. "Goodbye, friend Hatan," he choked on the words.

"Friend!" Naama spat. "It would have made a superb enemy. Tell me, what did you give it?"

"Give? Not knowing you."

"Brutes and champions, pansies and deserters, connivers and conquerors: believe me, I've known them all. But no one surrenders their life for nothing in return! You gave it something. You must have." Naama grunted in response to his silence. "How easily you make friends, Enok, and how readily they die for you."

The words smote deeper than she knew. "Hatan —"

"Shut up. Don't look at me! Just shut up, and don't turn around."

The sight of the flaming tree numbed all but the echoes of her private whisper. "Who are you, Enok, really? And, frankly, *what* are you?"

Back in the present, the great tear in the basket screamed of Hatan's legacy, and indeed of Hatan himself. Despite what Oracle Zoia had revealed at the last about his childhood guardian, it made no sense that he and the great man-beast had once been captives together, especially since he had no recollection of anything except fragments of his parents and growing up so terribly alone. And yet, the language of the Wahoona had just come so naturally.

Whoever Hatan had really been, the journey to freedom only continued now because of the Wahoona's sacrifice, and they were now clearing the canopy of this lesser forest by seven cubits, maybe eight. Better than last night anyhow.

LAST NIGHT. HATAN.

Naama greeted the morning with an unbridled yawn, rising slowly, stretching, and smacking her lips. "Did you sleep much?"

She had used her arms for a pillow. Her face paint had smeared badly and it had colored her flesh as well. It was a hideous if not pitiable sight. Honestly, she looked mauled.

Even under all that pigment, her complexion reddened as she caught his appraising gaze. "Well, this is hardly the time for beauty, Enok. And you're hardly one to judge."

Eyes averted, with Jin-jin poised by his side on the bulwark, he engrossed himself with the breathtaking vista of Mount Oush, of home — of anything but the gash.

DAASHT. WAHAYAWI. HOME.

Jin-jin's squawks and pecks broke Enok's concentration. "Zhaga. Zhaga."

The bird was hungry; however, Enok had no food. And his gnawing belly growled a reminder: it had been far too long since he himself had had a proper meal.

"Ooh, this is marvelous! I'm up with the birds! Though there's a strange fat thing flying even higher behind us." There was both wonder and excitement in Naama's voice. The tension was gone, the warrior and the Oracle in her too; only the girl remained, unpretentious and carefree, delighted by nothing more complicated than the pleasure of a lofty view.

"Look! The ocean!"

Though Naama's face was so unlike a Zmee's, the expressions of joy and relief were easily enough read. He too should have felt wonderfully relieved. He was free. He would be going home to his people. After a lifetime of despair, so much had happened so quickly. But Hatan's sacrifice ...

ARARAT-AGAT. A'DIN. KHLIUPA-KHLIUPA.

Thump! The warrior in Naama had suddenly returned.

And it had kicked him!

"Last night never happened. Understand? Excepting a little salve and razors, I've lost my entire utility belt. It's an irredeemable shame for a Havilan, and I suppose I should thank the Goddess for what little she spared me. But do you see me moping over what was and what isn't? Only *now* matters. And tomorrow won't happen unless we survive today. So fix yourself on the present. I'm not used to judging distances from the air. How long to the sea do you reckon? A watch, perhaps? Maybe half?"

Her kick had the desired effect, though forgetting last night wasn't easy. "Smaller than one watch. Half, yes." Naama had figured well.

"That's great, as long as the Zmee haven't been traveling by night. And who knows? They might have dispatched a posse down along the coast from the north. They're as clever as the gods and twice as shifty. Never underestimate them." She bent over the lip of the gondola. "*Whoa-ho-ho,* that's some fall. You expecting me to just — I don't know — drop into a tree?" She gazed back with a lopsided grimace. "Crummy justice if you are. How *am* I going to get down?"

He had been contemplating an ocean leap, striking the water with the narrowest possible profile. Cliff diving with Hrazul had taught him that, and how easily broken were ribs and limbs! More than once he had tried to outdo her and nearly drowned.

"Problems?" she asked. "You're awfully quiet."

She was good at reading faces. Enok averted his gaze lest she read the worry there. A scan of the gondola's exterior revealed nothing of the coils of rope that once hung there. If Naama had not been so zealous last night, something might have remained with which to noose a branch.

"Look, in the sky! Is that really some bird? It doesn't act like one."

Tired and anxious eyes made little of the strange creature trailing distantly. Then all hope of freedom numbed as he realized it was another balloon. Despite large sheets billowing from its sides, it seemed a smaller craft, though soaring loftily higher.

"Talk to me, Enok. I worry when you're too quiet."

In a sudden frisson of terror, he understood: Star Wash! Because of the sails, the breeze was propelling it faster than their own balloon, and it would overtake them long before the sea! Now looming over the fear of plummeting to their doom was the prospect of certain death in the air.

"Zmee!" he shrieked unwittingly. "Zmee death for us!" Could Hatan's inferno have pointed the way?

Naama scowled. "Are you sure? Great blood and bahalazh!"

How many Zmee were pursuing was impossible to say, though likely only two.

"Ah, but they can't reach us," grinned Naama smugly. "Even if they caught up, they would sail right over us. Worm heads!"

That thought had occurred to him as well. But why was a smaller balloon drawn so much higher to the heavens? It was simple really: the more bladders, the more floating-gas you had, and the higher you went. But if this balloon was larger, why were they so heavy?

"Actually, I don't like this at all." She was quick to see the danger and it forged her a fearsome mask. "From this height, they could almost glide forever!" She made a diving gesture. "They killed three of the sisterhood once. Swooped in, took their heads clean off. Remember that glorious clash in the forest tree-ways? For sure they'll have those poisoned forks."

To her the forest battle was a splendid memory; however, all Enok could think of was beautiful Yuni, Little Greeny as they called her, and pray that she had somehow survived, for everyone else he had ever cared about were all destined for a pyre.

Naama swore. "Start thinking! Whatever we do, they'll shadow. They have the advantage. We need to overturn the game."

"Never play by rules of enemy?"

A grimace grew into beaming approval, then, "Look! The sky-boat, it's sinking!"

Though not quite fully daylight, the essentials were readily discerned. The pursuing craft had only a large single bladder, and the ever-clever Zmee had fashioned makeshift sails of flags. And the bladder seemed to sag a little, as if it had a leak.

A leak! Of course! More gas, you go higher; less gas, you sink! Enok berated himself. He should have grasped this principle during the getaway from Xira's compound. Now their pursuers were bleeding gas, preparing to attack. Having made this effort, they would have come prepared. As Naama had intimated, ahead was a fight to the death.

"I know to go down! I knowing now!"

Naama whooped exultantly, then just as quickly disapproved. "No. Bad idea."

"Yes! Make cut, let flying air go. We fall slow." Enok pointed. "Like them."

Naama studied the bladders overhead. "No!" she insisted. "We'll hit the trees. For a moment, we'll be disoriented or injured, very likely both. We'll be at our most vulnerable and, take my word for it, that's when they'll strike. No, Enok, they're counting on exactly that. Have you learned nothing from me at all? Never play by the enemy's rules!"

"Down! We run!"

"Midden-headed serpent-brat! The very blood of victory is surprise!" Her paint-smeared face was etched with fury and the force of it bearing down on him permitted no response save a weak accepting nod. "Up! Up!" she screamed at the top of her lungs. "We have to go up!"

Great Zulyi's eggs! They would have to make themselves lighter, but how? Naama was wondering that too. She leaned over the gondola, searching frantically. Then with sudden intuition, the reason for heaviness seemed simple: payload! They were carrying something heavy. The urgent challenge was to cut it loose. Both sets of eyes met on the rope platform above them.

Enok decided, "Me go see."

Naama took the thongs, the hooks, and groaned angrily as she fumbled instinctively for the missing utility belt. "Still have my knife? Good. Quickly now, turn around. I'll help you re-shoulder the medicine stick. There's little time."

They scrambled madly upwards, and on the higher platform, they found their extra weight: thick rubber sandbags. Hundreds of them! And in surely the strangest of places for ballast!

"Throw!" he cried with a motion.

"Quickly!" Naama seconded.

Then, "Jin-jin!" they called together. "Climb up!"

Entangled precariously in webbing designed for slithering beings, Enok and the amazon hurled ballast frantically overboard. Naama shrieked, wailing about a Zmee with outstretched wings and how it was poised to intercept.

A thought suddenly struck him: THE CRADLE.

The pursuing balloon had a much smaller basket. The single greatest weight they were carrying was likely the gondola itself. Fumbling though the last of the ballast, a finger caught on a copper shackle, the nexus of so many knots.

Of course! The gondolas were interchangeable. Just re-thread and re-hitch! Hence the lofty ballast.

"Naama! Cut this! Cut!" With fear-found strength, Enok severed the bindings. The cradle hung lopsidedly as he pared away first one knot, then another.

"Great Goddess! It's diving!"

Enok imagined a Hozny look-alike with her aerial acrobatics unfurl her wings at the last.

"Cursed snake!" Naama fumed. "It's going to hit!"

The cradle lurched as the Zmee collided. The last knot slipped violently free, knocking the knife from his hand as the rope looped twice through the shackle.

"Dung-worm! You lost our only weapon!"

The balloon surged upwards as the gondola and its open-mouthed passenger plummeted to the forest below. Now the fugitives rose ever higher until the sinking enemy balloon was almost directly underneath.

Enok's heart was pounding. SAFE AT LAST!

And now ahead the broad vista of the morning ocean glowed like polished brass beneath the Greater Light on its diurnal circuit. Whether it was the whip of the wind in his ears or the echo of distant surf was impossible to say. They were rapidly approaching the sea, but at such a dizzying height and with little to prevent him from falling.

Thankfully, Jin-jin was a tree-bird and a good climber. Dey had leapt into the webbing and clawed deir way towards them.

"Brave bird!" Naama cooed before checking her belongings. "Ropes, hooks — everything but the knife! Come on! Come on!" she urged, scrambling ever higher in the webbing, then yelped as the balloon began to list and tumble.

Without the gondola for ballast, the great net of bladders tumbled aimlessly, mocking every attempt to scale it. She changed tactics, and began to savage its fabric. They had risen too high.

"Go, go, go!"

Stones of the Temple! "Go? Go where?" he shouted in return.

"Phew! The stink!" Naama chortled as she tore apart bladder after bladder with her razor shells and her teeth. "There's still a Zmee in the other basket!" she cried with a nod at the sky-boat below. "Jin-jin! Enok! Jump! Now! We have to slay that serpent in the sky!"

Hanging upside-down and watching Naama leap to the other balloon was terrifying. She had sailed like a fisher-bird, opening and collapsing her arms like wings to steer herself right onto the apex of the enemy balloon. Then his efforts to force Jin-jin after her cost valuable time while the balloons drifted apart and his own had pitched again from the shifting weight. Now an endless series of fearful breaths were only delaying the inevitable.

Then courage spoke to him. Or madness.

JUMP!

But he hadn't so much jumped as simply fallen helplessly from an endlessly tumbling balloon, and had landed greatly off-center with nothing but three fingers caught in the bladder's webbing to keep him from plummeting to a certain death.

One of Zoia's quips surfaced as he scolded himself for having hesitated. 'LUCK FAVORS THE QUICK.'

His other hand flailed wildly now, desperate for purchase. His eyes were wide. Everything about him paled. It felt as if reality itself were fading. Each heartbeat grew slower and louder, the pulse resounding in his ears like a slow booming drum.

Louder. Paler. Slipping.

Then something gripped his free hand like the bite of a khwatl. It was Naama. She had reached over backwards, feet entangled in webbing, and grabbed him with an iron grip, pulling him upwards, and cursing.

"Fatherless whelp of a mule!" she scowled. "What were you waiting for? When I say 'jump now,' for Gol's sake just do it!" She reached reflexively for the lost utility belt before letting rip with some obscure oath. "Gods! I'm upside down. I'll spin around." Fearful moments later: "Can you reach my foot?"

"Ye-es!"

"There are two small shells in my ankle-strap," she yelled at the top of her lungs. "Pull one out slowly. They're extremely sharp. Cut the webbing first, then the cloth!"

"We not climb down?"

"Too predictable. We're falling in!" came the shouted reply. "There's another dot on the rear horizon and for sure it's another sky-boat."

"Jin-jin?"

"Faring better than you! Just do it, blast you. Do it now!"

The little black shell of hers easily cut though the net and its underlying rubbery composite. There was a massive *whoosh* as the gas escaped. His hand flew sideways and the razor was blown into the sky. The air was putrid with the stench of rotting yash'kh. The urge to vomit was overpowering.

"Goddess protect us! Go, Enok! *Go, go, go!*"

Fighting nausea, he gulped madly at any remnant of sweet air before following her blood-curdling "Ai-yeeee!" with a leap down into the eerie translucent world of the bladder with fingers clamping his nose.

Whump!

He landed bouncing on his buttocks beside Naama. Her eyes were scarlet and watery, her cheeks swollen like a blowfish.

So desperate for air! Pretend you're underwater. Just like swimming with Hrazul. I'm homeward bound, homeward bound. Ayma! Father! Oh, El!

And now a shadow was creeping down the membrane. It was Jin-jin's silhouette! The bird would give their stratagem away! Naama quickly made a throat-cutting gesture, retrieved another razor from her ankle-strap and slashed madly at the membrane until a small hint of morning sky shone through. Without signal or hesitation, in little more than a heartbeat, she had scrambled through the gash.

Enok struggled to emerge and only managed to poke his head out for air. The medicine stick was caught in the gash. Meanwhile, the amazon must have somersaulted directly into the cradle, for she was now being thrashed about like some great parasite on the Zmee's tail and with Jin-jin darting in-between.

The tail was red at first, then green, then blue, then a rush of shifting colors. What sort of creature was this? Whoever or whatever it was, Naama's strategy had worked. She had caught them unawares, foiling the enemy's attempt to surprise them from behind.

Trembling with tones of deepening red, the tail whipped sharply, flinging Naama headlong into an amphora, smashing it. Seizing the opportunity, the multicolored Zmee sprang back hissing into the gondola, wavering with hue upon hue of rage to smother the semiconscious amazon. It had gripped her in a serpentine coil and was gloating about Zmee superiority.

"I am ... and you are ... Khoza-zhaar!"

That was the imminent victory cry. The killing blow came next.

Jin-jin leapt at the Zmee's snout with open wing-claws and a piercing shriek. The serpent fought with its bare hands as the firebird savaged its tendrils. Then with an anguished cry, Jin-jin was flung by the tail, spiraling into the forest below.

The distraction was fleeting but it offered Enok that precious moment to free himself from the bladder, positioning to strike. His mind was racing. He had to save Naama. He had to.

O EL, GIVE ME WISDOM!

A trident! On the floor within Naama's reach! Had she seen it? Enok fumbled around for a weapon — anything. Beside him lay several of those rubbery ballasting tubes. He threw first one, then another. A direct hit.

Startled, the Zmee looked up, tendrils stiff with surprise.

A little loosening is all Naama needed. Fingers groping for a shard found their weapon, and she stabbed the serpent's hand.

"Khaa!" hissed the Zmee.

With the serpent distracted, Enok leapt from the platform, swinging widely with barely a three-fingered grip on the ropes, hurling himself and using his own momentum as a weapon.

Crack!

Collision. Naama fell with the impact.

"Good aiming! Quickly," she gasped. "Get this weed eater off me! Get it off!"

However, Enok was flat on his back with his legs across her face and struggling to rise. The medicine stick was strapped too tightly. It had left him both rigid and vulnerable.

356 ENOK AND THE WOMB OF GODS

"Roll, for Gol's sake! Roll! And go for the trident!"

But tangled as they were, even rolling was difficult and Naama was pinned by the combined weight of two bodies.

"Push me!" he cried.

With a single free hand, Naama gave a mighty shove. He rolled onto all fours and immediately made for the weapon. Both hands trembled under its weight. He retreated to the gondola's edge, resting its haft on the bulwark, and with shaking hands desperate to aim true.

The colorful hues of the dazed Zmee quickly settled to a terrifying red. And the polished brass helmet lying at his feet filled Enok with dread. The cropped tuft of scarlet feathers uniquely marked it as Zakon's.

Enok had never been in a knockdown fight with a Zmee before, but he remembered all too vividly the blinding speed with which the Upholder had once clubbed him. He was prepared to shoot if he had to, for if things were reversed, he knew that Zakon would be utterly merciless.

The tail twitched.

"Naama. Get you here! Now!"

"It's too heavy and I'm stuck fast. Lend me a hand!"

"Zmee living now. Get you here!" He wanted to help her, but to relinquish the weapon was risky. And his feet just wouldn't budge.

"Blast you, Enok. I can't!"

The plated red hide rippled as muscles came once more to life.

Zakon, bleeding blue where Jin-jin had savaged him, tightened round Naama again, hissing viciously. "Watch the barbarian die as a I crush its skull like an egg."

"I kn-know how to shoot this," Enok stammered, "and I ha-have strength for the triggers. Let her go."

There was a long tense pause as Zakon considered his next move. Enok could hear his companion gurgling. She was desperate for air. He had to act quickly.

"I meant it. Release her now!"

"I turn my head at my peril," Zakon hissed. "I'm as good as dead by a dart anyway."

"No, you're free to go," Enok offered, taking sideways stock of the forest below and the watery horizon. "Just begone!"

Bad luck, though, or sheer blunder had left him in the worst position. The Greater Light had now fully risen, shining right into his eyes. And the fear that shaky hands might accidentally shoot his companion rendered the heavy trident useless as a weapon.

Sensing the weakness, Zakon twisted around to expose Naama as a living shield. «Impertinent animal!» "The word of an Ish is no bond at all," he hissed through gritted teeth. "Savage blood-lapping barbarians —"

"'To believe what you see, stop seeing what you believe.'"

"What?"

"A lesson of the very Southerners you despise! Prejudice, preconception, arrogance: they all blind you to the truth."

"Truth!" spat Zakon. "What is truth?"

"For the last time, let her go —or, by Ssla above, I *will* shoot!"

"The Isha will tell others of Zoar. Its kind will come in force. Many lives will be lost, Zmee and brutes alike. I am the Upholder! I cannot allow —"

"They already know!" It all began to make sense now. Though he would say anything to save Naama, Enok knew this was as true as anything ever could be. Zoia has also figured it out: 'Zoar is already undone,' she had said. "Three giants attacked my Oracle in the Reliquary. Someone somewhere already knows! The Ascending Way: *we* didn't open it, *they* did — and they can come and go as they please!"

"Six kinds of a liar!"

"And you're seven kinds of a fool! [lix] She was trying to expose a plot you Zeruhawi had engineered. You're the Upholder — no, you *were* the Upholder once. Now *you're* the barbarian. You and your kind let the giant murder my only egg-sister before my very eyes! You've been in league with the giants all along!"

"What!?" «Nonsense!» "I have no idea —"

Naama gasped. As Zakon shifted, she managed a gulp of air but was rapidly suffocating. Enok steadied the cumbersome weapon, its great haft on the lip of the gondola.

---

lix   Zmee have six different words for *Liar* as well as for *Fool*. The ultimate lies are those to oneself. The insult is therefore that Enok is utterly delusional. Enok's retort is that Zakon is even worse.

"Don't deny it! It was you — you! — that my Oracle fought in the Reliquary with the giants. Who's the liar now? And I watched her fall at Stargazer's compound at the hands of your murderous j'Na-Zeru."

«Blind egg!» "It's the Isha who's with the giants!"

"Then — as Ssla above is my witness! — I have every reason to pull this trigger and shoot you both together!"

Naama slumped as Zakon finally loosened his grip, but his great orbs were fixed on the weapon, and his quivering tail-tip betrayed some surely budding scheme.

"How can the slave be trusted?"

"The island's secrets are safe with us! By the memory of my egg-sister and my Oracle, I sw—"

Fush. Fush.

Treetops slapped the gondola, shearing off the larboard sail.

The sky-boat spun wildly.

Seizing the opportunity, Zakon lunged to strike, but a great limb smote him from the cradle a mere saving eye-blink before the trident discharged as they careened into a forest giant.

Enok's last memory was one of flying, tumbling headlong through a green sky.

There was a mighty *SMACK!* and then:

Nothing.

NEMESIS‡

Eyda's storytelling is cruelly interrupted by her son Sess's wife, a beautiful titan who is quite the opposite of the monstrous ogres of her stories. Feeling humiliated and unwanted, Eyda renounces storytelling forever.

THE GREATER LIGHT WAS ARDENT in the sky, well beyond the second shadow marker, with midday soon approaching. Admittedly, Eyda's excursion through the 'Pyramid of Stars' was a story unto itself, and perhaps better left as themes for Temple Day singers. At this point in the story, though, it was hard to imagine that scenes of Enok flying headlong into danger could be anything but boring. Nevertheless, a huddle of snickering boys at the rear of the open-air classroom had broken her momentum. The young faces that had earlier been so earnest were now wounding her with simple inattention.

The tattooed boy, Ab, had lassoed one of the colossal marshland dragonflies. It was more than half his size and was circling furiously overhead. Roping them was easy enough, but restraining these winged monsters took near-adult strength. This Ab was far stronger than he looked and it astonished his companions.

SHORT ATTENTION SPANS: THEY'RE ONLY CHILDREN, AFTER ALL, Eyda consoled herself with the thought.

A scowling girl at her feet spun about, searching for the disturbance. "Let it go, and *hush up!*" she growled, then her eyes widened quizzically to the gasps of her peers and her features blanched on return.

Eyda spun about too. "What the …?"

Three women had been standing behind her, Sha-Noa's mother Mehet'abel and two others who were cradling infants. The shorter of the newcomers had that swarthy complexion common in these parts, with lustrous ebony hair coiffed with fragments of shells and colored beads plaited loosely at the temples. The taller seemed the younger of the two, a slender shaven-headed waif and utterly pale, even fairer than the palms of Eyda's hands.

To unfamiliar eyes, it seemed unnatural, even unhealthy. Except for a short skirt of beautifully woven grass, this woman-girl was shockingly exposed, and in this insular world where a lustrous volume was prized, the utterly shorn head doubly disgraced her. These were the strangers from the long-boat, her son Sess's wives.

The youthful prudery of some boys found expression in a false bravado of chuckles. Even some of the older girls, who should have had more sense, were openly giggling at the half naked stranger.

An astonished boy gasped, "She's a slave?"

"She's my mother, sort of, but has to do whatever I say," replied Ab artlessly, releasing his prey. "That's what my tattoos mean, I think."

The dragonfly sped for open water, dragging its tether.

"Hey, but what if *I* get a tattoo?" asked a girl.

"By my father's bones!" whooped a boy. "I wish *my* mother was a slave!"

"She already is, you good-for-nothing loafer," a girl shot back to a chorus of sisterly approvals. "So shut up and let Old Maa get on with the story!"

With her lips pressed thin and nursing the gravid bulge under her gown more tightly than usual, Sha-Noa's mother seemed decidedly troubled, and the sight of all three women so obviously tense was worrying.

"Welcome." Eyda gingerly stretched a hand towards the delicate, half naked stranger. "If you like, you can make yourself comfortable on a bale with the scribe over there."

The young woman's gaze was downcast and sideways, and her complexion reddened as she struggled to cover her exposure with a sleeping infant.

"But please," Eyda offered, sliding the shawl from her shoulders, "take this first."

"She has to learn her place," insisted an approaching stranger. The words were curt; the timbre was resonant and with a distinctly feminine hauteur.

The children's gasps were alarming. Even the scribe blanched.

Feet were the first Eyda saw of this stranger: large feet, elegantly sandaled, with brightly painted toenails — too many toenails, she realized with a shudder.

Not five, but six on each foot.

A GIANT!

Eyda's gaze crept slowly up the impossibly tall flanks of the visitor, admiring the sight and yet loathing the memories, to finally settle on kohl-stained eyes.

It was a woman, yes, but there was nothing delicate about this polished version of an old enemy. Easily head and shoulders above the tallest marshlander, a beautifully proportioned amazon with golden flawless skin, bejeweled, scantily clad in crimson leathers and a silky cape, now towered menacingly over the little storyteller.

Eyda rose to her feet, struggling to suppress the stomach-wrenching memories the very sight of her evoked: the ravishers, the blood, the screams of captives pleading for their lives.

"Y-you are?"

"Throwing my idol into the river was hardly friendly, was it? How do you expect me to beseech the Twain Goddess for offspring without it? You've brought a curse upon yourself."

"Curses! Goddesses!" Eyda spat. "There are no such —"

The titan scowled. "Ignorance of the Glorious Ones is no excuse for rudeness."

"Wh-who are you exactly?" Eyda quavered, studying the giant woman with her semi-shaven head and regal lock of silver-blonde hair behind an ear. She sought consolation in Mehet'abel's eyes but found only terror there.

The giant crouched in overt condescension. *As ONE MIGHT DO,* Eyda shuddered, *WITH A CHILD.*

"I always wanted a mother of my own. Well, then. Hello, *Mother*. You are much smaller than —"

"What are you doing here? We've no place here for the likes of you!"

"Old M-Maa, this is Surai," Mehet'abel began shakily. "She's —"

"I know what she is!"

Eyda nearly toppled from the shock of the words: "Old Maa, Surai is Sess's *wife*."

"Wife? She's an abomination!"

The titan responded with mock outrage. "Oh my! How utterly rude! Your Old Maa sure has a temper."

The youngsters, who had never heard anything good about the giants, responded nervously with *oohs* and *ahs*, for standing before them now was a living representative, and one who was hardly the embodiment of evil they had been led to expect. In fact, she was quite the opposite. Not only was Surai charming, self-assured and imposing, but hypnotically beautiful, and richly bejeweled and attired beyond anything they had ever seen.

"Fight!" a distant boy wagered.

"The Refa you've been hearing about from my *mother*," she paused and squared her shoulders, "died a glorious death. Glorious! Refa Dragon-slayer!"

The words, "I'm no mother to *you*," barely escaped the knot in Eyda's throat.

"Well, he must not have been very good at dragon slaying," some boy mumbled. "The Zmee got him in the end. And what a hideous death!"

"Whose prattle was that?" Large, painted, angry eyes scanned the suddenly hushed assembly and made their way to the cowering fool of a boy who should have fled at their approach.

Surai lifted him by his breeches with a single hand.

"Wow!" boys gasped from a distance. "She's strong!"

"Ugh!" Surai grimaced as the hanging boy wet himself. "You're disgusting, just a bahalazh worm by comparison to Refa. He killed over thirty-six dragons in his time. Thirty-six! So, you show some respect for the memory of a great warrior."

She dropped the whimpering lad onto straw, continuing, "I must say though, I've never heard my brother's greatest victory recounted in such an unflattering way. Bested by the serpents? *Pshaw*. It just doesn't ring true. And any slight on my brother's memory insults me personally."

Eyda was confounded, and struggled for composure. "Wha— what do you mean?" she managed weakly.

Reassurance came by the touch of the scribe from behind. *It's alright. You are not alone.*

"Island?" Surai was disbelieving. "I've never heard *that* before. And it's odd that my lord's consort made no mention of it, especially since she was there at the battle. You live on mud in the middle of a river and, of course, you set your story on an island too. It all seems too contrived, don't you think? Naming that strategy game of zhakh after the Twin Falls of Zhakh? And isn't Zakon's Reach supposed to be downstream of that? Is that where you got the name? Really, these names in your story," Surai gestured dismissively, "seem ridiculously trite."

Surai then faced the anxious children, remarking, "Besides, how could your Old Maa possibly know the thoughts within a dragon's head?" She stooped, rounding on Eyda with the challenge: "You're not a mind reader, are you, Old Maa?"

Eyda instantly perceived a question clear as day in her mind and with her own voice: *WELL, ARE YOU, OLD MAA?*

As she marshaled near forgotten skills and strangled that alien presence, surprise rose in the giant woman's eyes. "You will never know," replied Eyda stiffly.

"And didn't I hear you rave about that noble ancestor keeping mum about that oh-so-secret island? Yet, here you are, doing just the opposite. It seems to me," Surai wagged her head with mock indignation, "Enok must have reneged on his word. ¡Tsk, ¡tsk, ¡tsk. And how telling is that now of you?"

Eyda realized Surai had been listening to her story from behind the schoolhouse. Besides phenomenal strength, giants had exceptionally good hearing.

"Your people know nothing of honor!" spat Eyda.

"And since Naama hailed from the great barrens of Havilaa, if Enok really did sight her mother-born skin and best her in combat — which even a well-armed Fist of a Reaver posse could scarcely have managed! — he would then have had to have fathered her child or she'd have been disgraced as a weakling and an outcast.[lx] See, the Havilans live without menfolk, so by dune law — well, that's just how things are. Such feisty creatures those Havilans!

"Ooh, but that would mean — let me think — that your Baba Sess married his own older sister! Me! Well, half sister. I suppose that means I've been your Old Maa," she indicated Eyda with a sideways sneer, "even longer than her! But you can all just call me Preeminent Mother. Unlike some here, I'm far too vital to ever be called old.

"Anyhow, children, I wouldn't dream of interrupting." Then with calculated charm Surai added, "I just came to see what you were all up to. I'm sure you all want to continue with the story of that musty ancestor you've heard countless times before. But imagine, without the intervention of Refa and his mother, none of you would be here today. Quite a thought, eh?"

A boy stammered timidly, "Are your clothes dipped in b-b-blood?"

"This?" Surai inquired, fingering the leathers of her crimson skirt. "Of course not. It's genuine bull dragon hide. The beast was said to be domesticated, but it attacked me without provocation. Such impudence could not go unpunished. Come," she beckoned. "Don't be afraid."

Two brave boys approached her cautiously and gingerly ran their fingers over the distinctive patterns of the hide as she crouched, looking back with a grin at their peers.

"There really *were* dragons?" a girl behind Sha-Noa asked.

"The Zmee? Well of course there were, though I haven't seen one in the wild for over a hundred years, particularly a male. Bulls have always been scarce, but there are still a few cows in the cities."

"There are?"

"Cities?"

"Oh yes. We free them briefly for the New Year's festival and make them dance. They don plumed garments, some of red, others of green, dazzlingly filigreed with gold, and they form two long chains like snakes. As the pace of the gongs quicken, they weave in

---

lx   The *Fist* is one of two troupe leaders, and is a well-armed battle-hardened para-human Anaki godling.

and out of each other with amazing speed. It's really quite a sight: serpents made of serpents!"

"Chains?" someone wondered.

A mesmerized girl at her feet distracted Surai, asking, "You come from a city? With walls and roofs of stone? It must be really awful to live there."

"The imperial city? Goodness me, no. The finest of fabrics and jewelry!." She flashed the serpentine bands of jewel-studded gold on her upper arms. "And with such exotic delicacies, and your every whim catered to by scores of servants. Oh, it's the most wonderful place imaginable."

Confused and innocent faces looked to Eyda, finding voice in a germ of doubt. "Old Maa, but you said that —"

"The best of you will get a chance to see it for yourselves," Surai pronounced with a knowing smile. "I promise."

"We will?"

Eyda protested, "No, you will not! Even the most beautiful fruit can have a rotten core. Cities are awful, violent places."

"¡*Tsk*," Surai glared in return. "What truth ever came from the mouth of a fabler?" Smiling disarmingly at the youngsters, she added, "There's one old city called Qr-Ai-Henokhi. If cities are so horrible, then how come they named one after your ancestor?"

Teras the scribe could scarce contain himself any longer. "Y-you keep twisting the facts," he puffed, tightening his grip on Eyda's shoulder. "Enok was named after th-the city, n-not the other way round!"

"Irrelevant trivia," went the dismissal as Surai fingered Eyda's coarse garment and a puckish grin lit her face. "I can see these girls would just *hate* city life. I'm sure they would be, um, *thrilled* to spend the rest of their lives barefoot, in these delightfully sanitary marshes, wearing such *exquisite* apparel," remarked Surai, wrinkling her nose. "But who's to say they wouldn't?"

With an exaggerated snuffle, she added, "Oh, there are such perfumes in the city! And the cosmetics! Believe me, a girl can never have enough." She twisted a dragon fang holstered at her waist. "Here, smell this."

After jeering or gesturing at the wet-legged boy now peering from behind the school hut, the youngsters began to resume their positions. The giant newcomer was hardly a threat and was instead preparing to thrill them with exotic tales.

Eyda felt helpless as Surai bumped her sideways to settle on the very bale of reeds that just moments earlier had been her own.

"Ab, dearest," Surai called a little stiffly. "The boat's waiting for you. Take your new friends and let them climb all over it."

"Alright!" came an animated chorus from the boys at the rear.

"I really want to hear about my grandfather. Besides, father said I shouldn't —"

Heavily painted eyes bore down on their son, silencing dissent.

Ab relented. "Yes, Preeminent Mother."

"Your mother's *fantastic*," a boy whispered.

Ab shrugged sheepishly in response.

"W-what about Enok?" the scribe Teras pleaded. "W-wouldn't you like Old Maa t-to finish her story?"

Eyda could tell he was as incensed as she was. Bless him; he had always been a sensitive boy.

"Nah, heard it all before," came the verdict. A few girls and most of the boys leapt after Ab without sparing a thought for their storyteller.

Eyda was lost for words.

"Now, that wondrous imperial city," said Surai, inviting with open palms. "Where shall I begin?"

Their fear all forgotten, girls began questioning with a zest Eyda hadn't seen in a while.

"Is Qr-Ai-Henokhi the imperial city?"

Surai shook her head. "Don't you younglings know anything? It prospered for a while, though it's not as prominent as before. But Bel-Al, now *there's* a magnificent place. Towers taller than the tallest trees, and floating bridges between them, the hanging gardens, the Causeway of the Eternals to the great ziggurat: a city truly fit for the gods. In Bel-Al, everything is bold, bright, and grand."[lxi]

"Why are *you* so big?" wondered a little girl.

"And how come you're not ugly? Old Maa said —"

Surai chuckled. "If you raise your hand politely, then —"

---

lxi   *Bel-Al* is the Anaki capital of towering megaliths perched on a grand meander of the Hidekel river in the distant land of Akad.

Hands shot up like a sea of rushes. "Pick me! Oh, pick me, lady-giant!"

"One at a time, please, children. One at a time. And, remember, it's Preeminent Mother to you."

"Yes, Preeminent Mother! So why *are* you so big?"

A number of younger women with infants had appeared at the edge of the clearing, hovering and uncertain. Young scribes and temple maidens had also abandoned their training. The giant curiosity was quickly drawing a crowd.

Surai gestured a *come-hither* and laughed at the question. "It's just that you're all so very small. What you call 'big' is simply normal. My lord is one of the very Glorious Ones, the gods who rule the Anaki, their earthborn sons and daughters like myself. If you prove yourself worthy, perhaps a god or a godling will take you for a consort among The Blessed in Ur-Namu. And my! What an enclave they have! And what a privilege for you! Think of the honor accorded to your family," she winked at the steadily growing audience, "should you manage to bear. Your children will be godlings like me, an Anaki suzerain, crowned with riches and fearful of nothing."

"She's lovely," Eyda heard one of the younger mothers say.

"Noooo!" Eyda made to strike this insolent titan with both hands, but found herself frozen. She was trembling with rage, wanting to strike, but no matter how she willed her hands to connect, they simply refused. As she held Surai's gaze, alien thoughts formed again in her mind, more strongly than before, and snickering with images of Eyda's face buried in marshland mud:

THEY HAVE **ME** FOR STORIES NOW. YOU'RE JUST A DECREPIT OLD FABULIST WITH NOTHING FRESH TO SAY.

Suddenly, Eyda's immobility vanished and she lunged forward unexpectedly, tripping over a large extended foot, and landing with her face in the dirt.

The children laughed. The young women and dancers laughed.

Everyone was laughing at her.

Surai held out a helping hand, large and six-fingered, one Eyda would never accept.

"Dear me," Surai began with mock sincerity, "you've obviously had an exhausting day. Perhaps you should go and *lie down?*"

More snickering. Young eyes that would never have met Eyda's in a show of recognition now happily beheld her humiliation. The husky, imperious voice speaking over her turned sinister as Eyda rose feebly, spitting mud and straw from her mouth.

"You look positively haggard, *Old Maa.*"

At home by the river, rocking on a flagstone stool and oblivious to lengthening shadow, a furious Eyda had whittled away the remainder of the day.

Why bother with a morning benediction when it reneges on its promise of hope? And in reliving over and over again each humiliating detail of her encounter with Surai, WHY BOTHER WITH PRAYER AT ALL? the bitter thought kept repeating.

How dare that sneering titan call her Old Maa! Love alone granted the right. And how dare she impugn Enok's chasteness! Why, such was his meekness that he hadn't even bedded his own weeping wife until a year after the wedding!

As Eyda's anger had ebbed and given way to self-pity, her thoughts fell to her first confrontation with Surai's loveless kind.

The original giants — the self-styled Glorious Ones — had been taking wives of various races since Eyda was a girl. Like everything else they lusted after, the gods simply took. Offspring from such unions weren't exactly common, but the resultant mules, the Anaki,[lxii] were towering six-fingered tyrants like their fathers; likewise haughty, loveless, and with astonishing capabilities. But rarer still were the Magi, females born with preternatural gifts that surpassed even that of their sires.

And Surai was that rarest and most deadly of mules, a Magus.

Eyda shuddered at the memories, mentally stabbing the image of Surai's fertility idol and thankful that godlings had always been barren.

MERCIFUL EL, MAY IT EVER BE SO!

Though originally few in number, the giants had settled in the land of Akad, amidst that great twist in the Hidekel River. There would always be those who were drawn to power. Some had gone

---

lxii *Anaki.* Often called the *Sons of the Gods*, since the godling mules were overwhelmingly born male. Named for Arag-anak, the first para-human.

groveling with a hope of sharing that power, others to worship it. Such formed the bulk of the mixed-race Akadian society, the Reavers ever hunting for slaves, and especially for the grandest of beauties to serve as courtesans among The Blessed.

Eyda's heart ached as though torn from her chest. She remembered a rebellious younger self, a lovelorn runaway, being caught and taken for a merchant's slave. The nervous smile of the father who never sired her, the reproving tongue of the overanxious mother, the pinioned moment of a secret lover's kiss: last memories all of dear ones never seen again.

O SESS, MY SESS! HOW COULD YOU HAVE MARRIED AN ANAKI? DIDN'T MY STORIES REACH YOU? DIDN'T I LOVE YOU MORE THAN LIFE ITSELF?

It was possible to love too deeply, she now knew, and that left one vulnerable to the greatest wound of all: not of love lost, but of love betrayed, once dear, now trampled underfoot.

She cursed the day she bore Sess. He had always known how she had suffered under the gods, how his father likewise times untold almost lost his life. At great personal risk, Enok never shrank from the truths whispered across the generations from when the world was new, exposing the so-called Glorious Ones as nothing but The Fallen, just another kind of creature from some great beyond.

Some believed at first, but fewer and fewer listened as the spreading fearsome power of the Akadian horde made truth the beliefs of their Anaki masters, to worship what had fallen as divine.

Enok's parting words echoed in her mind.

'*TEACH THE CHILDREN, TEACH THEM FROM YOUR HEART.*'

"I gave up teaching years ago. Don't you know why?"

'*WITHOUT HEART, TRUTH ITSELF WILL BE FORGOTTEN.*'

"My heart's been broken, once, twice, a hundred times. Don't you understand? They just don't care to listen anymore!"

'*IT'S A SACRED STEWARDSHIP, A PRECIOUS GIFT.*'

"Don't you see?" Eyda sobbed. "The world has changed and lies now reap the harvest, Husband. I cannot be your sickle any longer. Oh, Enok. You've been gone so long!"

Even the scribe's plea for her to remain at Temple Island tormented her. "I curse the day I began telling children stories," she had angrily replied. "Never will these little ingrates wheedle another out of me. Death-come-take-me! Never!"

She had been staring vacantly across the marshes for much of the afternoon now. The Greater Light was setting, and her shadow was long and thin, thinner than she remembered, thinner than it should be, stretched long upon the water like a spectral finger pointing to an inevitable end.

"Is that what you expect, for me to cross the Great River[lxiii] and sleep with my mothers? I hate you," she spat with a kick, showering her shadow with dirt and creating a myriad of conflicting ripples. "But you're right. I might as well be dead. I have nothing left worth living for."

NOT EVEN SIMPLE STORYTELLING, rolled the thought in a wave of self-pity. THAT'S ALL I AM AMONG THE SIX FINGERS NOW, JUST A DECREPIT OLD FABULIST WITH NOTHING FRESH TO SAY.

"It's true. I'm *useless*."

She beheld again the age spots and the wrinkles of her timeworn hands. The dark fingers and insipid palms were the very image of her mother's. More than four hundred years had passed since the slavers had spirited a young Eyda away. In just a single night, everything had overturned for the girl who had been Deina.

"Oh, Mother! I should never have forsaken you. Please forgive me."

Debris and eddy-bound foam twirled slowly and endlessly by. It never stood still, this river. What came, only ever lingered briefly, and then never returned.

THEY HAVE SURAI FOR STORIES NOW, she kept weeping.

A single tear worked its way down a cheek to hang wavering on her chin, then it fell and became the river.

---

lxiii   *Great River.* A local euphemism for the separator between life and
         death; based on the notion of certain death beyond the safety of the
         Gihon.

THE VISITATION‡

A b and his sisters visit their chagrined Old Maa by night to coax out the story's conclusion ... A visitation from The El upon the Watchers and the Imperial Emissary surprises them all with new orders. The storytelling must never cease.

DRY, SLOW-BURNING FUEL WAS increasingly harder to come by lately. Now all Eyda had was spent as she yielded her last to the embers of an earlier fire. Lamek's elder sons were the local woodcutters. Rafting upriver for pine cones, pitch, and logs was routine, but they had been gone for an age, and no word had come downriver. Perhaps they'd been caught in a logjam, for it was surely the season for it. Even so, the entire village of Ai-Lamek was worried for other hamlets too had reported missing merchants and were resorting to old burlap or animal dung for fuel.

But there was equal cause for rejoicing. The way her son Mati had been grinning with his chief scribe today, a deal had been struck and there would soon be a wedding. It would be nice to have her favorite family together again for the happy event. Oh, there would be music, dancing, and feasting!

Actually, Lamek was hosting a feast this very night. He had always been such a hoarder, and his longhouses wanted for nothing. He, at least, was sure to have plenty of fuel.

As his grandmother, she had welcomed the perfunctory invitation, but that Preeminent Mother creature had ensconced herself in his compound, and so Eyda had decided simply not to appear. There was no denying the impossibility of keeping a civil tongue while breaking loaves with that smarmy titan.

Despite her somewhat rustic temper, in everything else Naama had had the bearing of a queen. Surai was but a regal brat, and yet surely the most dazzling incarnation of evil that eyes would ever behold. No doubt, the whole village was rapt with her fanciful distortions, charm-spread and disguised with just enough truth to be swallowed whole.

CAN'T THEY SEE? THE PAINTED EYES THAT MESMERIZE ARE A DEATH ADDER'S!

Most locals were Eyda's direct descendants. To them the great stone-walled cities, the giants that reigned over them, and the subtle corrupting power of their lies were simply fables now. Except from the reminiscences of the far-born few, these marshlanders knew little of the wider world. So how could the here-born possibly discern if anything that titan was telling them was true?

ALL THE MORE BITTER, THEN, WILL BE THE LESSON THAT BEAUTY AND GOODNESS FRUIT FROM VERY DIFFERENT TREES.

"Oh, El. Is this now my portion, this cup of sorrow my own Sess makes me drink?"

She knelt by the fire, bowing low.

"I beheld evil today. I pleaded not to. Did You not hear my prayer? Or is there some purpose to this cup spilling on me?

"Oh, that's funny," she chuckled in response to an inner voice. "The spilt drink leaves the vessel empty?

"Fill the empty vessel? *Huh.* You sound like Mati.

"No, I'm not a story teller anymore. I curse the day I ever started. 'Embroider stories like a wedding veil,' do I? See? They take me for some craving fabulist! As if anyone could fabricate such implausible nonsense! The truth, the *real* truth, is even more astounding!

"Honestly, even *I* don't understand all that happened, or what really became of Enok. He said he had Your promise. I wasn't there at the Burning Waters, and it's only hearsay that You took him. So how can I know," she beat her breast bitterly, "ever really *know* that something is absolutely true when my eyes have never seen it?

"You are right. It all depends on faith. Even a simpleton can say 'I believe,' but just how simple must I be?"

"Like a child?" she sniggered at that inner suggestion. "Then pick a younger storyteller. My Mati, my dear Matu-Selah is still too traumatized by the past, and Kush is far too busy. Or what about one of the younger scribes, like Saran? He's a superb orator. Perhaps even Nimur? My, what a memory she has! And they're both great cantors, though Teras, dear boy, is developing a serious stutter, and I really don't think it's from wedding stress.

"My very age makes a spectacle of me now," sighed Eyda, fingering her cheeks and the creases of her brow. "See? No one believes the wrinkled. I'm just a decrepit old fabulist with nothing fresh to say.

"It's all because of the Woebegin, isn't it? You solemnly cautioned First Father: *'In dying, you will die.'* But only now do we begin to understand how long that dying can take! And, surely, a hundred and eighteen years is long enough as a widow. My time," she sighed resignedly, "has long been well and truly over.

"When the sickle blunts, another feasts? Indeed, they have Surai for stories now. I've had my fill of ridicule, and I'm just too tired to keep caring anymore."

The fire crackled and Eyda searched the evening sky.

"I feel You nearby. Have You come for me, to ferry me across the Great River into the bosom of the departed?"

Moist-eyed and kneeling, she stretched her arms out wide in both hope and in welcoming the end of her days. "I'm ready. Take me like You took Enok."

Waves of heat coursed through her body, but coming not from the fire. She felt light, giddy, and the world dissolved beneath her.

IN A REALM UNSEEN BY MORTALS, Elishan stood with Legate Yuriyel beside Eyda's reed hut, watching her stoke the evening fire. Later, as Elishan had observed on countless occasions, she would shift the heat-stones with a sling and place each last benison of warmth beneath her great bed, though he had yet to understand why. It really wasn't cold here.

"That's the last of her fuel," he commented sadly.

The Legate never deigned to chitchat. As stiff as a statue, dey had been listening to Eyda's tale, absorbing every gesture, every word and sigh. [lxiv] Dey had been silent when the titan appeared among the children, and surprisingly stoic when deir accompanying sphere of crystal shot a column of cool fire that solidified into a tall, hoofed, four-faced being. That there had been no locking of gazes or acknowledgment surely told of a prearranged encounter.

Nor had the Legate commented on the anguish of the pale shaven-headed Isha, Sess's youngest wife, or how easily the titan Surai had ingratiated herself with the youngsters — an ease that bespoke a century of practice. And when Sess's other two wives had cried privately to Sha-Noa's mother Mehet'abel and Mati's wife Saz'yana, Yuriyel had kept unnervingly silent.

During a closer inspection of some of the newcomer's children, which evoked subdued commentary from Guardians, even then — even then! — not a sigh escaped the Legate. Dey were typical of deir kind, and now dey were studying Eyda with an intensity matched only by the four-faced creature with its inscrutable eight-eyed perspective.

It stood erect on its hooves by its crystal sphere, as tall as the Legate and equally mute though with each of its faces taking turn at the study. And what curious faces they were, one for each of the four winds and all on a single head: of a feathered bird of prey, of a great-cat, of some buffalo, and an Eloi (like the Ish and Isha, and humanoid like himself).

Helon, who confessed to some experience with Four-faces, believed it was here to witness the Legate's activities. Its kind usually traveled in groups, sometimes as hordes, but never alone. Commonly seen around the throne of The El where life was anything but ordinary, Kheroub seemed out of place almost everywhere else; and whenever they did appear across the heavens, a direct encounter with The El was surely inevitable.

Or so Helon said. Maybe he was right, maybe not. At least he would mutter something occasionally, but the grim dignity of Yuriyel's kind would seem forever baffling.

---

lxiv   As per the preface on Genderless Pronouns: *dey/dem/deir* are the genderless equivalents of the singulars *they/them/their*.

The Kheroub's Eloi-face seemed sad as it looked briefly heavenward, but then harsh as it nodded to the Legate.

"Catastrophe," pronounced Yuriyel solemnly, as his lifted eyes beheld a broadsword tumble to earth from the sky. "We ... here ... are undone."

Elishan was startled. Helon glanced up. Obviously, a skirmish was afoot in the higher realms.

Whump!

Their long-awaited leader Starion materialized abruptly, landing backwards beside the sword and minus an ankle-boot. His classic white-and-tan kilt was tattered, and he held in his hand the severed transverse crest of his war helmet. "Dirty tactics, eh? I'll wipe —" The grimace, a rare one, quickly dissolved beneath the intensity of the Legate's stare. "Oh. I never realized it was *you*."

A silent and subtle exchange of expressions ensued between the bronzed giants, and Elishan followed the interplay with some surprise as their eyes kept returning to the severed crest. A modest smile equated to a guffaw for such stoic beings, so what exactly was transpiring here?

Starion rose to his feet and saluted with an uncustomary flourish. "Legate Yuriyel. Hero of the Six Day War, is it?"

The Kheroub trained its avian face on Starion.

"Hmmm. 'Hero' seems hardly appropriate. In the service of The El," returned the Legate, bowing slightly. "Princeps Starion, defender of the marshlands, I presume."

"You presume wrongly. It's *Adjutant*," Starion corrected, inspecting his broadsword and averting the Legate's gaze. "And it's *failed* marshlands defender now. We routed the scouts, but it won't be long before a more aggressive force arrives."

Elishan realized he must have been wearing the stupidest of looks, for Starion sheathed his weapon, straightened the pleats of his warrior's kilt, and made to explain. "Don't worry, it's just ironic that's all."

"Ironic?"

"The Legate and I have some history between us. And to meet again, like this, here of all the rebel worlds, is surely strange."

"Ah, but 'There's no coincidence under heaven,'" countered Elishan. "Isn't that what you always say?"

Starion yielded a small nod, mumbling as he fingered his severed crest. "I never told you or Helon. I was ashamed, I guess. You would have found out eventually, that —"

"Me," the Legate interrupted. "In attempting to save your world during the Six Day War, your clan and everything you ever knew was blasted to bosons because of *me*."

"Me, actually," confessed Starion. "I was the Legate's military attaché. It was *my* experience that dey relied upon when —"

"Do not punish yourself, Starion," urged the Legate sadly. "None of us were experienced in the arts of war back then." Addressing the Kheroub's avian face, Yuriyel explained, "*I* was that councilor. *I* gave the order to the Princeps here —"

"Adjutant."

"*Princeps.*"

"No, I've demoted myself."

"Put simply," the Legate continued, "on my explicit orders, Starion zigged, when he should have zagged. If not for me, your world might have been saved."

The greenish crystalline sphere beside the Four-face glowed ruby red, flashing with fire-like sparks. Now the feline face was prominent. Was it angry?

Moved by the giant's frankness, Elishan too was on the verge of confessing. Should he tell them of his own mistakes, or of Helon's? The pair had long been confidants. They knew, or they thought they knew, why they had been posted to this dreary terrestrial backwater. What else could it have been but a castigation for their own shortcomings? The cities, that's where the really important assignments were.

On their watery world of Melakh-Anan, his colleague Helon had been an engineer before the war. Floating cities had been his specialty. He had proudly shown off the ... Well, it mattered little now. The rebels vaporized nearly all Melakh-Anan's elders in a single act of terrorism. And Helon's life was forever changed.

His thoughts now drifted to his own failures. So many the clerics who perished that day! And the ancient seers! Gone forever and their prophecies destroyed. The High Councilor, one of the Twelve Exalted, that magnificent angel of light that he had personally escorted into the temple, had been the rebel leader Bel demself.

Shouldn't he have known, or at least suspected that something was amiss?

Anguished by his secrets, Elishan's focus shifted to the dark little Isha stoking her primitive fire. He noticed the Eloi-face of the Kheroub staring at him — at him! — and its haunting eyes, if they really were eyes, seemed unbearably sad. Its sphere shone brilliantly and the small dark depressions, or eye-shaped lenses that would occasionally drift across its surface, began to whiz about excitedly, and the Kheroub itself spread its four wings as all of its eyes began searching the darkening sky.

Helon clutched Elishan by the shoulder. "The El! Brace yourself. They're here."

There appeared a wind, or a whip, or a ribbon — it was all of them and none them. Like a tear in the fabric of reality, it flicked and twisted, glowing and flashing with colors, visible and invisible. It curled around Eyda like smoke-drift. Tendrils of … of … Perhaps there would be tongues to describe it someday. The wisps probed her gingerly, flinching at a touch; restraining itself like a mother with a foundling, hovering and uncertain.

Eyda was kneeling on her mat, eyes closed and with arms out wide as though inviting arrows through the heart. "Please, take me like you took Enok."

Roars and screeches split the air from three faces of the Kheroub, the avian, feline and bovine, while its Eloi-face beheld Eyda, weeping. Electric arcs flashed about her, and she seemed to sense the visitation, falling to her mat in obeisance. The smoke rose whirling and growing into a column taller than a dozen Yuriyels, arcing and flashing in colors that were anything but random. It was the fabled color-speak language, one that only the Kheroub (and formerly the Zmee) truly understood. It bowed, burying the Eloi-face under its membranous wings.

Without warning, the multi-colored smoke became electric fire. Brilliant arcs hit Eyda's life-tapestry. Others curved their way erratically through the marshlands like lighting on a mission.

Wham!

A bolt knocked the invisible beings to their faces. Elishan lost all strength and sensation. Even the Legate lay prostrate, stripped of all rank and pretension, completely helpless before the awesome power of The El, The El in Their effulgent form. Elishan's eyes were clamped tight, yet the radiance was hot and blinding, for it was more than mere light. He could sense the radiation coursing through him from within and from without, separating his very spirit from its body, and bringing up his memories for examination.

No, they were someone else's.

The greatest engineering project of all time sabotaged by bosom friend turned traitor. The cultural achievements of an entire race reduced to dust by war in a single day. City-sized ships wracked with explosions and overturned by monstrous tsunamis. They were the private guilt and terrors of those who lay beside him.

Deception and betrayal on the very steps of the Crystal Temple, the center of worship on Melakh-Anan. MY MEMORY, MY MISTAKE, Elishan lamented, AND MY SHAME.

Between skin and spirit nothing was hidden, all was light. All were naked before The El, before the God they had chosen to serve.

He had been examined and found true. He was no traitor.

The column of raw energy sent an arc across his back, lifting his spirit into the air where he found himself floating with the others, still powerless to control the least part of himself. No head rose higher than any other. Yuriyel had metamorphosed into a magnificent being, luminous and six-winged. Apparently, that was deir true astral form. Indeed, Yuriyel was a Saraf. Like the four-faced Kheroub, dey were a denizen of the highest heaven and old beyond reckoning.

Even the astral form of little Eyda was hovering in the air beside him. With eyes pressed thin, so completely was she pouring out her troubles to The El, so intense was the communion, that both her spirit and her flesh had become oblivious to everything else. Surely, if there was any lesson here, it was that in prayer all were equal and equally important.

The thought had barely formed in his mind when all but Eyda slipped a cubit so that all could see the bitterness poised to strangle her faith like a python. What had begun on her tongue was now in her soul. Then Eyda herself collapsed.

Grace. Sympathy. Worthiness. Feelings of acceptance now came flooding into him. The El were not here to scold him, but to give him hope and a new understanding. Those feelings of inadequacy and guilt that had long plagued him were removed like poison from a wound, and he realized now that these were as much the enemy's weapons as any sword or feint.

Learning from one's mistakes was not limited to mortals, and the truth was, for Elishan and all his colleagues, they had been allowed to serve here not because of their failures, but because of their resolve to ensure such mistakes were never repeated. What they considered their personal weaknesses had become the basis of the very strengths The El would use in what They had foreseen would become one of the most important missions of the war.

From the images impressed upon Elishan, the independent military strategies pursued by the Watcher alliances were failing. The El had always maintained that they would. How many battles, how many failures, how long until not only his own kind but Yuriyel and Starion's people finally learned to forgo all personal quests for justice and trust The El without reservation?

Unfortunately, doubt was one of the consequences of the war. It was the enemy's greatest weapon and one each loyalist had to neutralize for themselves.

The enemy was fighting to win, and so were The El, but on a vastly grander scale and for an infinitely greater glory. And the fate of this world was at the heart of the victory. All four minds could see that now. Like in the Zmee game of zhakh, to win, sometimes the best strategy was, in fact, to lose.

Another image formed in his mind. This mission was now under a new authority — the direct control of The El, and Legate Yuriyel would be the official liaison.

THE INLAND SEA OF ELOAH, came the mental voice, THAT'S WHERE THE MARSHLANDERS NEED TO GO, BUT THEY MUST BE FREE TO CHOOSE.

EYDA, said The El with distinct finality as Elishan marveled at the astral form of his little charge being cradled back into its flesh. THE WORM OF SURAI IS FIXED ON HER TONGUE; HER SELF-CURSING WILL DESTROY HER. UNLESS SHE UNSAYS WHAT BITTERNESS ECHOED, AND TRULY FORGIVES, WE CAN BUT HONOR HER PROFESSING AND THE WORM WILL DEVOUR HER CALLING.

As quickly as The El appeared, They disappeared, and spirits and bodies united again. The four-faced Kheroub had vanished as well, retreating into its crystal sphere which shimmered briefly before vanishing into some higher level of reality. And it left Elishan wondering whether the Four-face really was a being or a projection of some kind, for the spirit of the being was clearly inside its inscrutable crystal sphere.

Yuriyel, returned to inglorious guise, looked up as a scimitar materialized and fell to earth followed by another. Red-and-black: they were enemy swords.

"Looks like we're whipping them good up there," Starion cheered, unsheathing his blade and preparing to join that unseen fray. "With your permission, Legate? My squad needs me. No doubt the enemy will be sending reinforcements — probably on a massive scale, now that they have discovered the villagers and noticed the visitation. They'll be awfully curious, don't you think?"

"Granted. But let them come, Princeps Starion. Let them come." The Legate seemed unperturbed. "You, twins: Elishan, Helon. Tell me more about this zhakh game. When outnumbered and out-maneuvered, what has one left to fight with?"

"Princeps. Princeps," affirmed Starion to himself. His missing kit materialized an arms length distant. "Ah, my boot has found me."

"I know what Enok would have said," Helon offered, dusting his tunic.

"So do I," chimed Elishan, fingers combing his auburn hair.

Yuriyel lifted an eyebrow as if to say, "What?"

They answered both at once: "Guile."

Bo-awk.
Re-ee-bubup. Re-ee-bubup.
Bo-awk.

The evensong of croaking frogs and a host of other creatures rang louder and louder in Eyda's ears. Fang-swans too honked their raucous duets. Night had come and the gentle heat and dying light of her hearth now proved an irresistible attraction. Dragonflies buzzed erratically overhead, and winged geckos preyed noisily on insects drawn to the light. As the embers reflected like sunsets in the eyes of tiny dragons ever-hunting for a cricket, elsewhere across The Moud signal fires dotted island shores like the night-time stars of her childhood.

Eyda rose from her mat, unable to remember how or when she had fallen prostrate, but there was this dim recollection of waiting to cross the Great River and instead finding herself amidst a sky of luminous giants and looking down on herself from above. How was that even possible? Perhaps it was just the distant lights that she now groggily remembered. Indeed, she felt especially woozy now, as if her very blood had been diluted. She had lost track of time too, but that wasn't unusual when pouring out her soul. Yes, bedtime seemed long overdue. She really ought —

"... and this is where Old Maa lives."

"Is she *really* five hundred years old?"

"Almost. She's the oldest person there is, so they say."

Eyda was startled. Sha-Noa had come guiding a party in the dark. The children burst into the clearing, skipping and running with a vigor at odds with the ebb of the day, and Eyda wondered anew why younglings couldn't just *walk* somewhere.

"Hallo again," sang a pretty darkling. It was Sess's daughter, Sha-Noa's look-alike, leading a much younger and paler girl by the hand. Pearly teeth shining by the firelight forged her such a winning smile.

"You're supposed to bow a little," whispered Sha-Noa.

The child tugged Eyda's dress. "Are you also *my* Old Maa?"

"Of course she is, silly," the older girl chided.

Ab had come too. "I'm so sick of living on a boat, Noa. Most times there's nowhere to go, well, except the other boat. This is way better. Besides, I overheard father mumbling to himself that this place is perfect."

"You are?" Sha-Noa was astounded. "This is?"

Ab greeted his grandmother with: "What's wrong with your eyes, Old Maa?" After a moment's silence, he bowed to Sha-Noa's prompt and added, "Shouldn't you, ah, wash or something?"

"Thank you for the beauty tips, young man," returned Eyda curtly, though secretly impressed by his night-sight. She dried the sooty tears with the edge of her sleeve. "Is that better?"

Ab arched his brows and shrugged to the midnight girl beside him, who shook her head slightly.

"No? Well, I appreciate the honesty. Raama, isn't it?"

"Why do you live so far away?" the child asked.

"It's safe here, and I have my independence. Why, what's with the strange look," she asked as Ab made a face.

"It's hardly fun if you're always lonely. You're not dying, are you, Old Maa?"

"Don't say that!" Sha-Noa admonished, then with eyes on Eyda begged, "Are you?"

Eyda grimaced. "What brings you all here?" she asked, trying to regain some sense of composure. They could not have come at a worse time.

Raama looked to her brother Ab, who popped the question.

"Well, why did Ava-Baba Enok not escape the island much sooner, if he knew how to make proper sailboats and *from wood* like Noa says?"

Sha-Noa's name sounded strange when pronounced that way. "Lose your bet, did you?" Eyda chuckled. "Well, since the island was placed where current and sky flew towards the dawn, away from the mainland, it was just too exhausting for one person alone to paddle against them. I think there was a way to use the wind against itself, but perhaps Ava-Baba never knew about such things back then," she offered wistfully. "Remember, he wasn't much older than — ah, how old are you exactly?"

"Thirteen." He bit his lip. "Forty."

Eyda was staggered that this boy did not even know his own age, but let it pass.

"Are there really currents in the great sea, like in a river? Oh. I didn't know that," Ab admitted to Eyda's nod. Taking his place by the fire, he chuckled with Sha-Noa, "My mothers are going to rub me in ashes — all three of them. Do you think I can sleep here tonight, Old Maa, and hear the rest of the story?" The beseeching grin was hard to resist. "I really don't want to go back."

Eyda was about to ask "Why not? What trouble have you caused this time?" when the young girl clinging to Raama squealed happily, "Can I stay too, Old Maa? I don't like Preeminent Mother. She makes my cuddle-mother cry. I want to hear more stories! Cuddle-mother doesn't tell me stories, not like before, not since she lost all her hair."

Eyda considered their requests, eyeing the boys, Ab especially. "I thought you weren't interested in my story."

"Says who?" Ab contested. "It was unlike anything I expected, especially since father hardly ever breathes a word. About Ava-Baba, I mean."

"It's all because of *Preeminent Mother,*" piped Raama, her voice rising like a plea. "She tells all the grown-ups what to do and even what to say. Somehow, they just obey. It's like her voice gets inside their head. I think even daddy's scared of her."

Sha-Noa and the other children, seven in all, sat around the fire. The little girl nestled against Raama produced a squashed loaf of millet and some torn lentil flatbread from pockets in her delicately woven dress. "I saved this for you."

Eyda was touched by this simple act of thoughtfulness, and squeezed her tightly in a kiss to the forehead.

"Old Maa, I'm going to be ... a princess," came her muffled announcement. "... teach me ... sew lilies ... my hair?"

"Don't forget the nuts, Kalmiya," her older sister reminded.

"Story now?"

"Kalmiya. That's a lovely name," cooed Eyda as the child climbed into her lap. "Story now," she confirmed, while briefly wondering how a child could have hands and feet so large.

"So what happened in the sky-boat?" Raama asked. "Did Baba Enok cross the sea to your village? And then you fell in love?"

"¡Tsk." Ab rolled his eyes. "Wrong direction. They were adrift towards the dawn, then crashed! I heard every word of it."

Eyda bored her eyes into the braggart. "While you were showing off with that dragonfly? Doubtful."

"Oh, that," the boy admitted awkwardly. "But hands and mouth don't do the listening, do they?"

Eyda laughed. What a well-practiced line it was!

"Come on! Pine cones!" At Ab's command, two boys emptied a sack into the dying campfire, and it flared crackling from the fresh fuel. "And we've left another two sacks by the hut for later."

"Where did you steal —?"

"It's a fair trade, isn't it? A story for a hearty fire?"

Eyda couldn't help but chuckle at his gumption. "What happened to me 'embroidering stories like a wedding veil'?"

Ab humphed. "'You're 'overly verbose and moralizing,' Preeminent Mother said. And your stories are 'sluggish, and lack emotional resonance,' whatever that's supposed to mean. But we," he shared a nod with his sisters, "we rather like the way you explain things. It's like being inside someone's head."

"And they're 'not really suitable for children,'" Raama chimed, "but we're almost grown-ups too, you know. Besides, daddy says it takes four eyes to see my nose."

"That's not how he says it," Ab corrected with a playful hand to her face. "He means that some things are obvious, but only others can see them."

Raama slapped him back. "Or tell."

"And the way you tell things," said Ab, mockingly goggling his sister, "it *really is* like having four eyes."

Kalmiya nuzzled at Eyda's ear, "I think wedding veils are pretty."

Everyone was silent, attentive, poised for Eyda's response.

"Old Maa?" prompted Ab with raised brows and a florid two-handed gesture. "You're in my debt now. And you *are* a storyteller, aren't you? 'There was a mighty *smack!*' and then?"

Eyda studied this boy with new admiration. Though he played the comic, a head as shrewd as any clearly nested on those shoulders. At length, she nodded.

Another boy nudged Ab gleefully. "Ooh! More fighting!"

Who were all these children? Not all Sess's, surely. Their eager faces beamed at her by the flickering glow of the fire. Perhaps this wasn't such a bad time for stories after all, at night, by the hearth, when fewer things could distract. Why hadn't she thought of that before?

"There was a mighty" — Ugh! Ugh! — "smack," began Eyda, feigning a coughing fit, and it evoked a chorus of complaints.

Now I HAVE THEM.

"There was a mighty *SMACK!*" — Eyda clapped her hands for effect — "and then ..." She paused for dramatic tension, checking that all eyes were upon her. "And then:

"Nothing."

DEADLY GROTTO

Freezing in an underground river, Enok comes perilously close to being eaten alive ... In pursuing scavengers for the stolen emerald, luck grants Zakon a final chance to slay his quarry and save the secrets of Zoar.

ENOK'S LAST MEMORY WAS ONE of flying, tumbling headlong through a green sky. There was a mighty *SMACK!* and then: Nothing.

It was pain that finally woke him. He had been worsted in a conflict with some unyielding tree, as every sinew cried. And a jagged spur had torn his thigh. The gash stung madly at a touch, and he prayed it wasn't as grave as it felt.

It was a confusing world that came next into focus. Everything was gyrating. A riot of orchids and bromeliads in the forks of nearby trees were a mesmerizing anodyne as they swung from side to side. And he shuddered at columns of green ants busily snaking their way up trees. He so hated tree ants.

The muted roar of water formed an enigmatic backdrop. The mist the jungle had sponged overnight cascaded now in either rivulets up tree trunks or came shooting like streams of darts at targets above that just wouldn't keep steady. The Zmee called this 'rain,' the subject of endless elegies to a homeland lost, but it was falling in the wrong direction and in great sweeping arcs.[lxv] And the roar was concerning. Were they near the beach?

"You alright? You alright?" came Naama's distant echoes of concern. When he finally caught sight of her, the image was of an angry insect besieged in some gigantic tangle. "I'll be fine, thanks!" she cried, worming her way out of strangle-vine. "You plan on hanging there forever?"

HANG?

As the strange perspectives righted, the horror of his predicament crystallized. He was upside down, tangled in the ropy filigree of a massive strangler fig, and swaying like a pendulum. Its aerial roots had caught hold of him by the medicine stick, and an entangled leg had kept him from flipping upright.

As Enok struggled to right himself, the ropy material gave way to his weight and he slid once, twice, to stop with a jolt at its terminus.

He shrieked. He could feel the remainder unraveling.

Naama cupped her hands to shout, "Don't make any sudden moves! Catch another vine!"

More instructions followed, though few made any sense. He had to grab ahold of something fast before he fell. If he could just flex himself, extend his reach, but the lifelines kept swinging past too quickly, and the medicine stick made him rigid as a post.

The roots snapped and Enok fell screaming.

Whump!

The web of vines that had netted Naama proved his salvation too. Fingers and toes twitched on command. NOTHING BROKEN, he sighed with relief.

A chill brushed his legs. His wound throbbed.

The sound of rushing water was louder now.

Naama disentangled herself from the last of the vines to rise on solid ground. Her hands were waving urgently.

"Enok! Whatever you do, don't stand up!"

Wiping rain from his eyes and surveying the glade, Enok struggled against the medicine stick while wondering at her concern.

---

lxv   *Rain*. The denser atmosphere of this world sees roving mists more commonly than rain. Few ever see real rain in the lowlands.

A feeble attempt to rise left a foot without purchase, and it hung uselessly. As the net sagged, Naama's tone grew alarming.

"No sudden moves! There's a waterfall right beneath you!"

The web draped a chasm of twenty, maybe thirty cubits brink-to-brink at the narrows, she said, and was rapidly fraying!

The sound of roaring water rose even more ominously now from its depths. And Naama, now crouched at the very precipice, took to savaging a sapling with a sharp-edged rock.

"Wait for my lifeline!"

Dush! Dush!

Its foliage shivered madly. A rocky outcrop made a perfect brace, and with her feet above the ax-breach, she forced the sapling with every savage scrap of strength. Success came after several crisp *cracks!* The ringbarked tree toppled towards him — onto him! Branches whipped his face. The net of vines tore, and instead of rescue, its momentum plunged Enok screaming into the yawning chasm.

Crunch!

The medicine stick crumpled as it struck an elbow of rock.

Feeling and dreading the inexorable descent, he clung desperately to remnants of vine while kicking and probing slime-covered walls for a toehold.

His grip weakened and he plummeted again.

Splash!

The chill and deafening roar numbed all reasoning. Enok leapt about panicking for air in the gloom. His hands swung wildly for buoyancy, and his feet for solid ground. In such a din and such a state, understanding came only in fits between gasps and a panicked search for safety. It took a moment to register that a submerged mound in the underground lake made a shallow, and it was that that had kept him from drowning. Chilling water lapped at his neck. Coarse debris ground between toes. And beyond all reach now was the gray outline of the outside world and the tree that almost killed him.

"Ee-nok! Ee-ee-nok!" came the faint yet urgent echo.

"Living! Living!" he kept hallooing, yet hearing nothing except the waterfall and conjured echoes of reply. How could Naama rescue him now?

Curiously, it wasn't as dark as it should have been here. Shut eyes reopened, appraising. Some kind of luminous slime bathed everything with a greenish glow that gave little of dimension away. It was like being inside a vast water-fire lantern.

It took a while to realize, then, that the height of the water seemed ever the same. But so great a volume exited somewhere, he reasoned, with teeth clenched at the cold. And if they were close to the ocean, that would surely mean a way out!

But should he stay and wait for some great rescue plan, or explore some route of escape? He decided to wait for Naama.

He waited, waited, waited shivering until impatience conjured eternity. Then, a sound, a *slurp* barely audible above the din.

And again.

Something was in the grotto. It seemed nearby.

Louder now.

Frantic eyes, however, could never make the invisible visible. There was simply nothing to see in this spectral-green nether-land.

He shifted nervously on the mound.

Crunch. The sound of breaking bones.

Crack. Snap. Skeletons crumbling.

For a brief and creepy moment, he imagined standing on a skull. Whatever lurked the grotto, it was certainly no herbivore!

Slurp.

What was it?

Slurp.

So close!

SLURP.

It was right beside him and he still couldn't see it! "Oh, El!" he wailed. "Save me!"

ZAKON LAY DAZED AND CONTORTED among colorful treetop orchids, opening first one eye then another, then taking deep and grateful breaths in celebration of survival. So many unusual flowers surrounded him, both great and fragile — an enchantment to all but his j'Na-Zeru guards, and surely every pilgrim's dream. But waking in some floral paradise was poor consolation if the barbarians too still lived.

He quickly fumbled for his wrist-wrap. It still should have two death-forks. Oh, but where was it?

Scratch. Scratch.

The awareness of little claws scampering over him swept everything else from his mind. And his crown was numb and sticky to touch.

"Khaa!" he hissed, tasting his own blood. The blasted zhrat were eating him alive! Their saliva had anesthetic, almost paralyzing qualities. How badly then was he injured?

But whether alive, half-dead or half-eaten, he had to will himself forward. He had made the dead a promise that night as the Lagoon of Souls claimed their embers. Their cries had soughed through the ancient pines, and even now they reverberated, torturing him, accusing him, demanding that justice be served. But in view of what the Ascending Way had shown, what did justice really mean? 'Not revenge,' young Snei would say, but what then sets the brokenness aright? As far as he was concerned, justice wasn't about preserving Zoar anymore but the entire race of the Zmee. The fugitives had to be eliminated. He would not let those barbaric Ish overrun this final remnant, and no effort, no penance, no sacrifice, no murder would ever be too great to preserve its whereabouts a secret.

He was naked. His helmet was missing. Perhaps the zhrat had stolen it. He would find it, he told himself, but later. With an effort of will outshining the most rabid of j'Na-Zeru, he dismembered two of the little scavengers in a snap.

"Vermin!" he spat. Their aftertaste was oily and sickening.

The rest fled higher into canopy, twittering, and spiriting away their treasures: his wrist-wraps! death-forks! and too the green crystal pendant! An orange-horned little devil taunted him with the emerald, sneering with its charcoal eyes.

«Eh?» Since when did zhrat have eyes so black?

The Scout who had failed to puncture the enemy balloon — his balloon! — had had those dark eyes too. Useless mute! She had unfurled her wings too late and collided instead with the gondola. Hadn't she been trained for aerial combat?

And now this insolent rooster was leaping limb-to-vine, ever lower to the forest floor, proudly displaying its prize. That hexagonal emerald was the key the former High Wisdom had yielded, the very same that had somehow awoken the ancient stones and controlled the Ascending Way.

'ZORIYAN WILL BE OUR HOME AGAIN, WITHOUT ISH, OR BEASTS, OR TERROR ... WHERE LIFE IS LIVED TEN THOUSAND YEARS ...'

The memory of the younglings' prayer had compelled a detour of him last night on the way to Xira's compound, and with surprisingly little effort the secrets of the dais became mystery no more. Repositioning the emerald triggered certain events, and one of these had sealed the Reliquary. But if the High Wisdom had long commanded such power, then why hadn't she simply used it to take her cohort home? Was it because she already knew that the fabled Zoriyan was a ruin? If so, then why all the secrecy and pretense? Why not simply embrace the Zeruhawi cause?

Such musings aside, for the present his duty was clear. If the truth of Zoriyan was to be uncovered, he had to retrieve the emerald pendant. But now with two wars at hand, one with the zhrat the other with the runaways, which was the more pressing? The crystal was more important, he decided, for if all had gone to plan another sky-boat of j'Na-Zeru was headed this way. Then he would find his missing Scout, join the other unit, and together they would tear fugitive limbs asunder in a just and bloody requital; for they were guilty, those barbarians, not just for themselves, no, but for all the crimes of their race. *That* would be justice, comprehensive justice: self-preservation, the restoration of order, all flavored with revenge.

He hissed a crooked laugh, for the Ish had nowhere left to flee. He spread his wings and sprang from the orchid bed, but a crippled wing betrayed him and Zakon the Invisible, the Lord of Zoar and conqueror of giants, fell to earth with a sickening *crunch*.

ENOK HAD SWUM FLEEING TO another underwater mound. It was shallower here, but right before the roaring waterfall where even thinking was a labor. Whatever else was present here, his instincts judged it huge.

Slurp.

A stalk. A reed. An orb here, another there, and before his very eyes! A slimy appendage licked a knee underwater.

SLURP.

Hovering eyes without a body.

The creature was virtually indiscernible, and that was surely impossible — unless camouflaged with the same luminescent slime as the grotto!

Heartbeats skipped in terror.

A tentacled snail! And monstrously huge!

Thousands of slippery teeth lightly brushed his thigh.

IT'S TASTING ME!

Two hands gripped an eyestalk with terror-fed strength. The snail reared high, throwing him backwards. A slimy feeler probed again, but recoiled as it scraped against his copper leg-shackle. Seizing the moment, Enok kicked himself away from his assailant, away from the waterfall. Taking in great gulps of air as he surfaced, he leapt panic-stricken through the water, not knowing where to turn. Everything was lit in a pale ethereal green, masking all sense of perspective.

There had to be a way out. There had to be! A thought appeared in Zoia's voice:

WATER FLOWING IN, THEREFORE WATER FLOWING OUT.

"But exiting where?" he cried. "I can't see anything!"

RIGHT BEHIND YOU, came the suggestion, but there was nothing behind him now except the waterfall itself.

Slurp.

He overcame his instincts and willed himself still, hoping to discern a current flowing one way or another. The water was up to his chin and he was simply too numb to sense anything. It was hopeless!

IN — OUT. IN — OUT. FOLLOW THE WATER.

"Where?" he wailed. "Oh, El! To where?!"

High above, the opening to the outside world was the best point of reference, and Naama's murderous sapling the only finger he could follow. He began feeling his way along the edges of the grotto on tiptoe, and now, at the waterfall again, there was nowhere to go, except —

Spla-ash!

Something huge had just tumbled off a hidden cleft. The wave propelled him backwards and into the cascade.

KEEP GOING, urged the inner voice, AND LIVE!

He dove beneath the great cascade, swimming madly through the turbulence and feeling his way through uttermost darkness as the current pulled him long. The passageway seemed endless, and with shifting, jagged dimensions. Frantic hands hit a ceiling everywhere they probed. The current was too strong to double back.

Oh, El! He would surely die!

A light ahead, pale yet beckoning.

JUST A LITTLE FARTHER. YOU CAN MAKE IT!

Enok probed his way to the surface with bursting lungs, to finally tread water and breathe again in palpitating gulps. His breaststroke was frenzied, with every breath metered and laboring against fear.

Were there snails here? Was he safe?

The water here was tranquil, a wide lagoon disturbed by nothing but the swimmer. The only sound here now was the thumping of his own heart, and a droning in the ears from the waterfall past.

The deeper he penetrated into this new cavern, the brighter it became. A different light ruled here. Luminous mushrooms twinkled in great vertical flourishes as though painted with red and orange brushes. In this wonderland of color, the terror of the grotto succumbed to gaping at a vast labyrinth of vaulted precipitate splendor. And here Enok gave obeisance to the invisible idea-giver.

"Thank you. Diving under the waterfall would never have occurred to me."

Then hunger spawned the happy thought that mushrooms make good eating. Though tasteless and a little rubbery, they were food nonetheless. Of course, Jin-jin would eat almost anything. And he wondered if that crazy tree-bird had survived.

Leaning against a stalagmite that melded like a buttress with the cavern wall, he ate, marveling as it crept high towards the ceiling to merge with an even larger stalactite. Unseen cataracts drizzled behind galleries of stone curtains. And from the recesses of that eerie half-illuminated ceiling came soft contented chitters. Creatures hung suspended in the shadows. Harmless little things. Thousands, he estimated. A huge family.

Mighty Hatan had spoken of family too, and even the Azhakh-Na secretly acknowledged blood ties. 'Like egg-bearer, like egg,' went the old saying, and in hindsight, Hrazul had so resembled Zelen, especially about the eyes.

EYES! FAMILY!

Yes! His dream girl with the almond eyes and ebony complexion was not the tawny Isha of the Reliquary vision, but kin to her, family! Though his parents were dead, hope rose in his breast like a brand in the darkness. He would live to see this girl of dream in the flesh. That was his prayer. If her mere phantasm caused him such pleasure, then how much more so the reality!

As he nibbled on the strange orange harvest, pouching some for later, his quieted mind grew concerned again, for there was another girl to consider. Being now so deep underground, how would Naama ever find him?

He struck up a tune and continued his journey. Even a nervous whistle was comforting, and its echo doubled as company. With time, the majestic columns of fungi gave way to featureless rock. The river became shallower and faster flowing as the cavern shrunk to less humbling proportions. Along broad muddy banks, a tribe of popeyed midge-crabs burrowed at his approach. These estuarine creatures rarely strayed far from the sea. And distinctive three-toed tracks meant that zhrat came scavenging here. As he rounded a bend, joy swelled within him at the distant glint of daylight.

YES! SALVATION!

Ahead was the portal to the outside world — and freedom!

How LONG HE HAD LAIN unconscious, Zakon had no way of knowing. Though his jowls throbbed and body ached, his crown was still completely numb from what those hateful zhrat had done to him. He vowed by all his ancestors to never become so vulnerable again.

Holy Ssla! He had escaped death several times today. When the odious slave had fired the trident, he had come as close to dying as he ever had. But all three poisoned barbs had missed him!

I REALLY SHOULD BE DEAD, he thought.

He had no fancy for deities such as the myth the Great Zhmee had become, or that heroic figure of Zeruha for the Zeruhawi, or even the First Cause, the subject of endless Azhakh-Na philosophizing. Pure Methodics would have none of them. It was random chance that had saved him. Pure luck. Or the slave's bad aim.

He slid haphazardly through the thick undergrowth, tasting the air with his tendrils for any sign of those hated little scavengers that had so stripped him bare. And after what seemed an age of snaking through tangles of rattan, above him now the wreckage of his interceptor had made a huge and menacing mushroom of a tree. A tattered flag of the Zeruhawi slid slowly to earth.

The world was strangely blue in that great mushroom's umbrage, instead of pleasing shades of green. Was he hallucinating?

The sound of wave-lap ahead came mingled with the scent of bleaching seaweed and yashurakh musk. Though mildly unpleasant on the tendrils, they were magnificently powerful beasts. The Ish, however, had the sweetest scent yet were truly the most perfidious of creatures. And after all the recent troubles, he was beginning to comprehend the Zeruhawi loathing of those Azhakh-Na and their better-than-thou gravitas, those stoic sensualists (if such a thing could be) who had allowed themselves to be seduced by that Enokhi creature.

But if the Old Dame, at once together the former Grand Oracle, High Wisdom and Azhakh-Na ringleader had commanded the deepest secrets of the Reliquary and the Ascending Way, then what was it about that odious slave she had fought so hard to protect? Hadn't Xira been saying something like that: Enokhi, prized pet of Azhakh-Na? So maybe it wasn't of all Ish, just of Enokhi that she was fond. But why then it alone?

Too many imponderables, he conceded. It was now patently clear he needed a more serious interview with the old deposed matriarch, but she was long gone on the Dragon Boat by now.

The zhrat, he could sense it. It had come this way.

Food. He needed food — anything to cleanse his palate of the greasy aftertaste of the vermin — and oh for a medicine stick!

He succumbed to fatigue in a patch of young tree ferns. The copper of his own blood was rich in his mouth. Without his helmet, his crown tendrils could sense the thoughts and emotions of other Zmee — if any were about and their own crowns were free. It was standard procedure in situations like this. However, there was nothing to perceive. And that almost certainly meant he was alone, and the black-eyed Scout had died in the crash.

Disgraceful mute! How could she have failed a simple aerial

assault? Hadn't she been trained for situations such as this? Had she never flown before?

«Ah!» his snout tendrils twitched at a scent. FOOD AT LAST, he thought happily. They were eggs, probably. Unfamiliar.

A river. A vine-covered wall. The odor of zhrat — of *that* zhrat. The scavenger had fled through the wall!

WHAT'S THE MATTER WITH ME?

Though at the very mouth of a subterranean river, he was only now beginning to see it. Its hues were wrong. There was something amiss with his sight.

He parted the growth to snake the deeps in search of the devilish thief. The river's coolness was refreshing, but he was weaponless, wounded, and alone. And being so vulnerable was no fit state for the nigh-to-be-hailed Aaj, Lord of Zoar.

The zhrat's scent was weaker now. He must have passed its lair without realizing. How easily his flesh now betrayed him.

Luminescent fungi streaked the further reaches of the cave. And what delectable colors too, glowing in bands of reds and purples, and every bit alluring as chechi. Hunger and temptation finally overtook him, and helped purge the distaste of the zhrat from his mouth. Ooh, how hunger makes everything flavorsome. Zakon collapsed underwater with a mouthful of bliss.

Ssss, how that stung! That explained his jaded perceptions! The midair collision had shorn him of his crown tendrils! And the zhrat's saliva had numbed what remained! Or perhaps those scavengers had eaten them! And his eyes too must have filled with blood.

He rose angrily from the water, even more determined to kill every zhrat in sight.

«Eh?» That peculiar sweetness of the Ish came now from both directions. Great Zhmee! It was a classic ambush strategy, and his mind raced to the worst case scenario. Ssla forbid! Had they found the dead Scout and her death prongs?

Weakened and weaponless, he stood little chance of killing them together. Individually, however, he might yet prevail. He should hide until they passed, and wait for his j'Na-Zeru posse.

Echoes now of wading and jabbering sounded through the cavern. The slave was almost upon him! So now more than ever Zakon hoped his fabled powers were intact. Unlike other bulls, he still possessed the ancestral abilities. Like the Great Zhmee himself, he could not only chameleon but see perfectly well in the dark. Better even than the green-skins, and certainly superior to any Ish!

After all, he was Zakon the Invisible, and with rising confidence he knew now that he had the better weapon:

Surprise!

Zakon flattened against a stalagmite and willed a mushroom-studded camouflage.

Splash. Splash.

The slave was but an arm's length distant, and burdened with a battered medicine stick. It was nearly as long as the creature was tall: the top sailed over its head. The beast therefore had scarcely any mobility, and would certainly lose in a fight. And now it was yammering partly in Zmiysh, partly in barbarous tongue, about finding its progenitors and some 'dark eyes of the night.' Was it mazed in the head from the fall?

Let the fool burble. Not a weapon in sight. And the savage was wounded! The odor of its blood was strong.

It paused to sample some fungi while supplicating its god. Then it begged for Zakon's life.

My LIFE!

Not to end it but to spare it! It piped that Zakon was acting in fear and ignorance, beseeching that the Upholder come to see with better eyes. Such impertinence! And a worthless entreaty! As if the Lord of all Zoar could ever be witless or afraid! Then it pressed to know whether the Isha was friend or foe, and that *it* be granted better sight, that *it* not act from ignorance or fear.

Pah! Impudent biped, to want the very same for itself!

Zakon returned with stealth to the river, hardly rippling its surface, to follow the slave as it rounded a bend and stumble over some underwater object. Then it jowled more nonsense as it paused near the very mouth of the cavern to examine a crude arrangement of twigs and pebbles.

The scent of zhrat was stronger there.

No! CALAMITY!

Ahead was the portal to the outside world — and escape!

Zakon summoned every form of malice the image of a pyre-filled lagoon could provoke. By all the blood now gone to ash, he had to halt that creature. Zoar had to be saved! And he urgently needed that medicine stick.

So, kill it, you worster of giants. Kill it now!

THE RIVER NARROWED, AND THE force of its flow bid Enok advance to the pure light that shone through a low, filigreed opening. It was an exit to the world he knew, and it was a great relief to have found one so easily, yet for reasons unknown, he caught himself hesitating instead of rushing madly outside.

Would he emerge simply to find himself in peril again? What lay beyond? Another waterfall?

His own behavior perplexed him, and he was on the cusp of willing himself forwards when struck by the sight of what seemed like moving dirt. With a hand against the light, that dirt turned out to be midge-crabs. Some scattered, some burrowed, but others were fixed on their prize. Above the muddy bank, translucent melons lay fixed in jellied clumps, and hedged by inquisitive crabs.

Snail eggs, Enok shuddered. *Dozens of them!*

He panicked for the exit, only to stumble over a submerged rock, and he rose, sucking air between teeth, fuming over having come so far only to be hobbled by a throbbing toe. He fell upon the opposite bank, on an outcrop forming a natural seat beside a muddy little game trail. The distinctive prints were of zhrat, and Enok followed the trail with his eyes. Here, in the most unlikely of places, a familiar tunnel of twigs made a rooster's courtship bower by the very mouth of the cave.

And it was bursting with all manner of shiny things that were sure to woo a hen: shells, polished river stones, cuttlebone. A rooster would even steal from other bowers, if it could. Why, they had pilfered his own tannery and hideaway often enough! Perhaps he might find something useful here.

All thought of pain vanished at the discovery of a copper shackle. It must have come from a sky-boat. And the bower held an even greater surprise: an emerald sullied by a crust of Zmee blood. Of all the places to find it, the High Wisdom's sacred pendant!

How? Why? What was this emerald doing here?

Zakon must have dropped it. Perhaps he had passed this way!

"Hey! Over here!" called a voice in the light.

With a hand to his eyes, Enok emerged from the cave.

Nearby, with her feet dangling in the river, Naama had taken a giant tortoise for a stool. The sunken-eyed ancient-looking creature struggled under the amazon's weight. She seemed to have made a game of quashing it. At her heels, Jin-jin kept leaping and snapping at a giant buzzing dragonfly she had tethered. Her face, now cleansed of that horrific war paint, was buried in a half-eaten snail egg. Its slimy contents dripped in gooey strands.

Enok pocketed the crystal.

She looked up, grinning. "Ah, you made it! Just knew ... you'd work it out. The echo. I could hear you whistling ... talking to yourself." She wiped her mouth, flicking slime from her fingers. "What *are* you looking at? I'm absolutely ravenous. I can't help you if I have no strength myself, right?"

She continued devouring the egg unabashed while Jin-jin made swift work of a crab claw.

"Try one. Not ... too disgusting. Hardly food of the gods, though. Tortoise eggs ... better," she mumbled thickly between mouthfuls. "And caught a big crab earlier."

There was silence as Enok fought to master yet another shock.

"What?" uttered Naama defensively. "I figured this to be like that sewer beneath the city. Remember? Look behind you. That's masonry under all those vines, not a natural egress. All that water from the waterfall had to come out somewhere, and here I am. Alright, I confess! The bird found the river. And the cave. Way too smart for a bird, this Jin-jin."

Enok was transfixed by the sight.

"What's to gape at? I can't do *everything* for you. Some things you just have to do for yourself. I knew you'd find the exit soon enough. Or are you glaring at me because I've eaten one of your pets?"

Enok kept staring at the broken tree ferns behind her, assessing the stain on the fronds and what that implied. It was the blue blood of a Zmee. Had Naama seen it?

"Where be Zakon?" he trembled, searching for a bloodied trail.

"That red snake? Dead, I hope ... wretched ... weed-eater," she growled, sucking noisily on the last of the egg with all the ill-grace of youngling.

Oracle Zoia's comments, the seeds of doubt she had planted in his mind, chose just this moment to haunt him:

'Can you really trust the Isha?'

When her tree fell, was she trying to save or dispatch him? Now that they had escaped the Zmee, had she abandoned him in the chasm? Perhaps he would never really know.

"Go now," he urged. The brightness of day and the sight of Zmee blood were galvanizing. A breeze had whipped up, rustling the palms. Was it Land's Breath or Sea Broom? If the Broom, then the yash'kh would have already made for the sea. Time was running out. They were vulnerable here. Their pursuers were nearby, and at least one of them was alive and injured but by no means dead.

Naama, however, seemed unhurried. Only slowly did she allow herself to straighten up, moaning and cussing all the way. The dragonfly sped off, dragging its tether.

"By the Havilan-ka! The great desert wind itself! That sky-boat gave us a glorious toss, eh?" Her usual bout of expletives followed as she drunk in the sight of him, eyeing him from foot to face.

"Ooh, that's a nasty gash," she observed, wiping her chin. "Not having the best of days, are we?" Producing a chalky paste from a little fang under her bodice, a remnant from her lost utility belt, she made a salve with her spittle to glue skin and flesh together.

Enok yowled through gritted teeth.

"It stings now, but you will thank me later."

"We living. We down from sky. Go now!"

"Gods, you're positively chilly!" she exclaimed in the midst of a hearty embrace. "That medicine stick probably saved your life. That's funny! Otherwise, you would have broken your neck in the fall. Lucky you, eh?" She twirled him about, examining the tube. "You may as well ditch the tatty thing now. I'd be surprised if anything inside survived."

Did she mean throw it away? Zoia's gift was in there, those clay balls from his parents. Hopefully the swaddling had kept them intact.

"No, I take more."

"Suit yourself." She gave the medicine stick a shake. Broken vials rattled inside. "I'm surprised you can even move with this burden. My fault! My fault," she mumbled. "Here, let me loosen the straps."

Suddenly, Naama froze, tilting her head one way then another in response to a sound that escaped him. Her scowl signaled the end of the interlude.

"Stay alert. While they may be injured, a simple fall wouldn't have killed those snakes, and they'll be coming after us. They have lost their advantage for now," she grinned with a throat-slashing motion, "so we had better deal with them promptly."

Had she spotted the blood after all? Minus the war paint, her expressions were easier to read, and her features were creased in that determined look of hers. Did she mean to hunt the Zmee?

"No! Go now!"

"What do you mean? Don't you see? There are only two of them, which means they've figured out our plan. This is just the vanguard meant to keep us from the boat. What we need to do — what we *must* do — is thwart *their* plan, and we have to do it *here, now,* on *land* while their forces are small, for we'll have no chance at all in the sea! Some kinds of trouble you just can't run from, Enok. Deal with it before it deals with you: surprise it from behind and slit its throat, that's how a Havilan deals with trouble."

"No! I speak life to him!"

"What?"

"I gave him my word!" he growled in Zmiysh, frustrated by his lexical poverty. "Your actions must be as good as your words. I gave him my word and I intend to keep it!" Then in loud, halting Y'lan he added, "Boat ... go ... now!"

"Dung-blooded idiot," Naama hissed. "Keep your voice down!" Then her brows knit together as she surveyed the swaying treetops. "The winds are picking up again, so the boat is our first priority. Is that what you're saying? Normally, I would agree. However, this is combat. This is war. This is what I know best."

Enok shook his head emphatically.

"Hu-uh!" she sighed as loud as the psithuring palms. "There's no point in chasing the boat if we're dead, is there? ¡Tsk. This isn't smart, Enok, is all I have to say." And true to word, though she kept wagging her head, she dared nothing more about it. With a parting kick to the tortoise, she cracked, "Join me for dinner some time."

Behind them, the cave exploded with a thousand little creatures fleeing for their lives: odd little things, flat beaked, khrii-winged and sightless. Some took shelter in nearby trees, swinging upside down, comforting each other in a melody of squawks and chitters.

THE FIGHTING BEASTS, THEY CAUGHT US NOT! NO, NO, THEY CAUGHT US NOT!

"Hurry," Enok urged, trotting over the tortoise-cropped lawn. "You hear that?"

Coming up beside him, Naama threw him strange looks. "Snake-speak, bird-speak, even last night. What is it with you and animal noises, anyway?"

"You not hearing," hands indicated the size of the creature, "Wahoona?"

"From the burning tree? Of course not! By Gol's right arm, you're a figment from some mendicant's tale! Zmee hissy-spit and that fur-beast's grunt-clicks leave me completely baffled! You'll be sharing jokes with Jin-jin next."

A roar echoed from the cave. Perhaps Zakon was not ahead of them after all, but tracking them from behind!

Naama instinctively ducked, thumbing towards the beach. "Go, go, go!"

The river forked. Naama and Enok followed a game trail along the banks of a ferny creek that meandered towards the sea. Dense forest gave way to a more open sun-lit landscape. Spindle-woods, fan palms, and beach almonds draped in passion-flower vines lined the waterway in a familiar and welcoming fashion.

Anywhere on Zoar, red-shafted sugar palms always signaled a treat. And zhaga were gliding amidst the copse, preying on the cloud of insects drawn by their sugary bracts. Hungry eyes searched for some withered-looking drupes that perhaps the zhrat had overlooked. That would certainly make a more civilized banquet than eating snail eggs and crabs!

Naama, on the other hand, had already taken her fill and was unconcerned with food. She moved now with murderous stealth, glancing constantly over her shoulder and into treetops, prepared for any attack.

A twitterling chirped, her signal to rest. She paused, listening for any telltale sound. Even clean-faced, the intensity of her expression gave him the shivers. Head and shoulders taller, her golden skin freshly oiled, sinews rippling with a hard elegance beneath her scanty garments of woven leather, this was Naama at her primal best, poetically magnificent yet positively frightening.

With the wave of a hand, she bid him continue. Then came maledictions formed of poisoned livers and envenomed spittle in her enemy's eyes, followed by the crunch of pop-eyed midge-crabs squashed gleefully underfoot. Even Jin-jin couldn't resist the occasional nibble. But their very presence had muted all birdsong and stilled all the tocking of frogs. An experienced ear would have made them.

A trio of zhrat, those comical jungle scavengers, suddenly burst from a thicket and onto the waterside trail. Each hand of the leading rooster held a scarlet feather from Zakon's helmet. It blinked at him with a pair of charcoal eyes while brandishing the feathers like trophies. It was odd behavior indeed, and curiously intelligent as it appeared to draw a sigil in the air. And what remained of Zakon's tendrils, the hens dragged clumsily between their legs.

So, the Upholder really was dead. And happy riddance too!

"Nokhi!" Jin-jin squawked.

Enok halted. "What?"

The alien rooster dropped a feather, to extend an open wing claw with pleading looks that were surprisingly Ish-like. As Enok was considering if it wanted what he had lifted from its bower, what sprang to mind were the images of the all the charcoal-eyed creatures that had been hovering lately: the gholuj in prison, the mute Scout who had helped them more than once, and now, too, this thieving little zhrat.

Was it possible that they were all somehow connected?

Ignoring Naama's urging to continue, Enok fumbled instead for the dagger-like amulet that she had found by the forest tree-ways. The corpse of Hozny Kitemaker had hidden it from view, there where she and the black-eyed Scout had previously struggled. It seemed poor compensation this, the amulet for the emerald, though both were merely pendants after all. He spared a backward glance as a growling Naama kept beckoning him forward. Returning eyes, however, met only the pair of hens gazing up at two crimson feathers now fluttering high in the air. The dark-eyed rooster and its amulet were gone.

And with extended wing-claws and eyes to sky, Jin-jin seemed to be waving goodbye.

Light was streaming into the glade, and fragments of a great beach sparkled through the trees.

Wookh. Ka-wookh.

The sound of pounding of surf was as welcome as the sight itself. It all looked and smelled so familiar: the creek, the glade, the whir of insects, the mollifying rhythm of the waves. This was new territory, where none had gone before, yet the welling feeling was that of home.

HOME!

Jin-jin raced ahead.

Ga-runt! Ga-runt! Ga-runt!

Yes, even the yash'kh were here.

Fate was on their side. Fragrant Land's Breath was spent, with salty Sea Broom now rising, yet the beasts lay nobly stiff with their heads arched high in their usual morning torpor. They should have made for the water already, in the lull between the winds.

The fugitives were lucky, very lucky indeed.

And when they struck the beach, he understood why.

DRAGON BOAT

Zakon becomes overwhelmed by his most terrifying enemy ever ... Surprised by bestial allies, Enok intercepts the Dragon Boat but hauls aboard a lifeless Naama. Remembering the Reliquary vision, he perceives a way to revive her.

SUBMERGED LIKE A PREYING CAIMAN, and with consummate stealth, Zakon stalked the fugitive downriver to the cave's exit. He was poised to strike — so ready to strike.

No, WAIT!

Something else stirred in the light beyond. Great Zulyi! The ambush! The barbarian female was directly ahead!

Lifted tendrils tasted the air, detecting a musk so reminiscent of Ur-Atu's broody host. Was this Isha carrying an egg? Its coloration was subtly different from the male's. Bands of heat ringed its chest and belly, appearing spectacularly warm precisely where the male was not.

"Kill it! Kill it!" a much younger Zakon had heard a pregnant Isha cry.

Coiled about a great wooden pike like some roast, tormented, humiliated, and steeled against the desecration of his own flesh, he had wept at the sight of his colony burning.

"No," argued a filthy companion. "It's only a youngling."

The grimy female kept holding its belly, protecting its internal egg. Water streamed from its eyes as it howled, "Pay them back!" to which another replied, "Why? What wrong has this little one done?"

Or words to that effect. His grasp of Y'lan was poor.

"It's a male child. It was born guilty," explained an approaching female, also heavy with egg.

Then came the hairy chieftain, tall, red-furred and powerfully muscular. A raised paw bore a long bloodied object, a sharpened saw-toothed bone-blade.

He would never forget the sights of that day, the peculiar tang of those pregnant Isha, or the madness in their eyes.

Ever.

Back in the present, Zakon remembered, and after so many years of forgetting, considered again the redolence that had struck him upon entering Ukhaz's jail barely three days past. There was no uncertainty here. This Isha *was* carrying an egg, and judging by its gravid odor, likely more than one.

The female barbarian was by far the larger and stronger of the pair, more decisive in combat, and thus the primary target. He should attack it now, fell it and its eggs in a swipe, kill the slave, and then that hated bald-headed bird.

But why was he hesitating?

The pair outside were arguing. Much was unclear but some of it was in Zmiysh. They were defenseless. They were unawares. There would never be a better moment. But where was the other posse? They should have been long ago!

He continued to listen. The slave was defending Zakon's life. It was honoring its words. Honoring them!

NOT A WEAPON IN SIGHT. ATTACK THEM NOW!

What a curious sensation it was to be idle, when every muscle was screaming and ready to do to that slave as had been performed upon him. In some unfathomed recess of his being, however, there was that which simply protested the notion, and in the wavering he began to realize that this particular Ish was no devil. It honored its words, and the way it talked to its deity in the cave — surely any creature that wished for its enemies the same good it would have for itself could not be *utterly* evil, could it? Or was religion the ultimate madness?

And now behind his eyes came the lisping sound of its tongue.

'TO BELIEVE WHAT YOU SEE, STOP SEEING WHAT YOU BELIEVE.'

"Stop it!" he hissed, as the voices of Sneak-tail Snei and the High Wisdom replaced it.

Snei: 'PERHAPS MY WAR, YOUR WAR AND HIS WAR ARE NOT THE SAME AT ALL.' The High Wisdom: 'SO, HERE'S THE RESULT OF BOTH OF YOUR PHILOSOPHIES.'

«What's this?» "Who are you?"

EVEN YOUR SPY SNEI WAS PREPARED TO DEFEND HIM, Hrazul Wise-eye's voice added. AND SHE WAS HARDLY SOME FIRST CAUSE ZEALOT.

"Possibly," he grudgingly admitted. Maybe the slave was more like a Zmee than he had realized — than even *it* realized.

Both considering and rebuffing what the voices kept repeating, Zakon's eyes tracked the fugitives as they prepared to make for the beach. He wanted to dwell again on the day of fire, the day the Ish had mutilated him, to work himself into a rage over the injustice and the cruelty of it, that elsewhere on the mainland was still being perpetrated, but the voices would simply not let him be.

It was an intriguing experience, this dark art of paralyzing the body by confusing the mind. Zakon was thinking some invisible agency was behind it when a sparkle of green caught his eye. The Enokhi creature was fingering a jewel behind its back, and out of sight of the Isha.

It could hardly be true. But it was.

THE SLAVE HAS THE RELIQUARY KEY!

«Argh!»

Suddenly, and completely without warning, a massive weight pinned him underwater, and his astonished tendrils writhed in torment as a thousand tiny teeth assaulted Zakon from behind.

THE WAVES OF THIS BEACH seemed wilder than what Enok knew from home, but that's not what had kept the yash'kh from the water. Like a tide of red blood, a great crimson scourge kept trickling from the forest, onto the beach and into the sea, edging and retreating in harmony with the waves like a score of living creatures.

They were tree crabs. By the thousands!

After decades of wondering, here at last was the mystery solved. In a march as majestic as any Zmee Pilgrimage, traversing dunes and hills and swamps, the crabs were converging here from the manifold reaches of Zoar before embarking for the Shine Water.

Enok's delight, however, was extinguished by a new concern. This colony of reef dragons was new to him. They were smaller than their southern cousins, and with stunted dorsal fins. And they seemed bewildered, if not altogether terrified, by this bloody tide. His plan of escape had always hinged on the primal instinct of the dash, but despite Ssla and rising Sea Broom bidding them advance, a contrary instinct had fixed them to the sand.

How easily unhinged this crazy scheme was!

It was Naama who saw it first. At the very water's edge, a magnificent creature strutted, weeping rut-musk, grunting, and flashing its sailfin in a marvelous display of colors.

Ah, these were all females, and a bull was attempting to entice the pod. However, judging by their posture, fear of the red tide had trounced any interest in courtship.

Then, what blessed relief! Two weather-beaten males on the outer formed a pathetic yet welcome sight. Old Zoub and fat Puzo, bleeding from recent wounds, kept watching forlornly as the majestic younger bull strutted.

Puzo blinked in recognition, and Enok responded in kind. They were old acquaintances these reef dragons and he, and he could naught but pity them. Having finally found a vacant niche with this colony of young females, the pair had briefly lived as brother lords until ousted by the newcomer.

"By all that's sacred, may I never grow so aged as to be hopeless," muttered Enok absently. He indicated the aging pair to Naama, who wagged disapprovingly.

"That living carrion? Wounded beasts give no rides, I'll wager. What about that big fellow, or even those smaller ones?"

Enok shook his head. "Them, I know. Them, I ..." Unable to summon the word for trust, the thought was commuted to a single directive: "Them!"

"*¡Tsk.*" Naama was unimpressed. "They're hardly the pick of the litter. We only have this one attempt, Enok. Are you certain?" She fell to her knees when he nodded emphatically, and spared a worried glance at the forest. "Quickly, show me what to do before those Zmee worms track us down."

Crouching, a crooked stick at his command sketched tactics in the sand. Naama smiled approvingly, rose, and followed his lead. Several cows moved warily aside as they approached. These yash'kh had never seen Elim before.

"Hello again, old-timer," he greeted Puzo in Zmiysh. "You and I will have one last ride to the feeding grounds together. What do you say?" Enok smacked his lips as if eating. "*¡Tsum, ¡tsum, ¡tsum.*"

Puzo winked, working his mouth. "*¡Tsum, ¡tsum, ¡tsum.*"

"That's it, old friend. *¡Tsum, ¡tsum, ¡tsum.* Food. Don't worry, Naama will knock out the opposition, then *you* can lead the daily charge. Alright? Consider it a parting gift."

"Great Goddess! Are you kissing it? *Come on,*" Naama urged. "Just one more impossible hurdle and we're quit of this latrine."

His companion was the eternal optimist. Enok, however, was less certain. If the boat was delayed, they would be forced to haven destitute on some rocky outcrop until the pilgrims passed their way. Or perhaps he and Naama had missed the boat already. So many things in this daring plan were uncertain!

Masking his worries in a show of resolve, Enok strode casually through the pod. These were unfamiliar and agitated cows. One sudden swipe of a tail could break his every rib.

"That yash'kh," he marked the swaggering bull.

"Strike the strutter. Now?"

"Yes. When I give shout."

"Sure, sure. Like we rehearsed. Just don't you spook them like last time."

"Me?!"

"Bones of my mother! Wading up a Zmee latrine! Flying through the sky! Choking in the stink-air of a sky-boat! And now this!" Naama was grinning more broadly than ever. "Glorious! What a tale this will make! I just hope I live to tell it."

"Me too," he echoed privately, giving Puzo an encouraging kick. "Come on, old dragon. Destiny for us both."

THE AGING BEAST KNEW WELL the sight, the scent, and the touch of Two-legged-food-giver. Beside his egg-brother, Zoub, Two-legs was the one consistently friendly creature Puzo had ever known. And for every ride he had shared, there always followed a generous reward. He lumbered towards the surf with an eye upon his rival and another on the crabs, but Two-legs kept stroking his flanks reassuringly, saying that everything would turn out well. Two-legs had never yet been wrong. And hunger, that gnawing hunger, kept demanding satisfaction.

MEANWHILE, NAAMA HAD SNUCK UP on the posturing prince from behind. With eyes too intent on the cows, and ignoring the gangly midge creeping by its flanks, the lack of experience proved the prince's undoing. Barely a cubit from her target, she let fly with her infamous trill. Then a vicious punch to an eye and a pummeling of a rut-tender musk hole left the goliath gurgling. Its tongue lolled sideways, and the groggy head — *thump!* — collapsed to the sand exactly as Enok had foretold.

"By Ma'nuna, that hide's thick!" growled Naama, nursing her hand and venting with a heel to its ribs. "Sorry, beastie, but this is hardly the time for niceties."

Old Zoub now sprang after Puzo. The crabs readily parted.

"Follow me now!" Enok cried with bursting lungs. The leader would not stay dazed for long.

Naama bolted across receding waves to mount Zoub's hind-quarters in a single leap, and shouting after Jin-jin. "Come on! Follow me, birdy!"

Grabbing hold of a flap of Zoub's hide, she inched her way to the towering sailfin. With an arm around a jutting spine through a rip in the dorsal membrane, and hand-in-hand as Enok had taught her, she held on for precious life as the great creature followed the old, new, uncontested master of the pod.

With their onetime leader downed, first one cow then another skirted the prince and trailed after Puzo. In fact, Enok had been relying on the pod for camouflage. Two solitary yash'kh, two escapees: how could one not be suspicious? But Jin-jin hesitated, squawking anxiously. The image of hopping from leg to leg amidst the crabs at the very edge of the surf, and with claws raised and wings outstretched, framed a posture Enok had never seen before, and his heart sank when the meaning struck. Jin-jin was waving a final farewell.

The entire pod of yash'kh quickly plowed through the breakers and into steadier waters, following Puzo to his favorite pastures. There, the Chechi islets stood guard over the single deep channel through the reefs. They were famous for their carmine sea lettuce, a delicacy no Zmee could resist. And the plan of escape demanded the pilgrims keep to tradition and pause for replenishment there.

A new gust salted his face. Sea Broom was rising in force.

The yash'kh used their dorsal fins as sails. So long as the boat was still north or upwind, interception would be easy. However, if they overshot, Enok dreaded the thought, their one chance could be lost forever.

A haunting wail came faint on the breeze. Even if it was Naama, he was in no position to help. She would have to cope on her own.

The Greater Light was now rising high in the sky. By Enok's reckoning, it was early into the second watch. To one side lay the narrow peninsula of Zu'u-Shoran. The sight of a pod of yash'kh was common in these parts. Could he be seen at this distance? Probably not.

YES! I'M ON THE WRONG SIDE!

His back was to the island. And if the wrong kind of someone trained a spyglass at the pod — disaster!

Anxious ages later, Enok's heart skipped at the sight of the Chechi Archipelago.

"Ai-yeeee!" Again came the wailing like a night-howler's screech. Old Zoub had caught up, and straddling his wide leathery neck was Naama, yelping and gesturing at the rear horizon where a skinny cloud rose billowing from some large dot on the seascape.

THE BOAT!

In the all too scant glimpses that heaving beast and crashing waves afforded, the boat grew visibly larger, gaining rapidly, but its course seemed tangential to their own. It was headed straight for the channel, and meant to bypass the islets entirely!

Not too far ahead now were the seaweed beds and the craggy outcrops of the archipelago at their center. Many pods of southerly yash'kh were swarming there already, and Puzo meant to lead his troop to join them. However, to intercept the boat they would need to change course.

Right! But how does one persuade a behemoth to act against its instincts, especially when its breakfast lay finally in sight?

THE HOOKS. NAAMA HAS THEM.

He was still thinking of hooks when Zoub came coasting alongside to the sound of piercing squeals from Naama and a waving hand at Zoar. But it was not the boat that concerned her now. With his back to the island, he had been so preoccupied with surviving the sea, he had completely ignored the sky. Low and rapidly sinking, another sky-boat was headed their way!

The amazon kept shouting, indicating she would join him. She had fashioned a grapnel from the cord about her waist and the hooks from the plaza. Almost no time passed between the ululating war cry, snagging the leviathan, and dangling from Puzo's rump. The very same hooks now proved handy as she clawed her way towards him.

"Have ... to catch ... my breath," Naama panted, laying hold of a dorsal spine through a tear in the sailfin. "The sky-boat! Did you see it?"

"Yes! Yes!" Enok exclaimed. "It falls!"

"Blood and bahalazh! If those snakes attack us now ... Think, Enok! We have to do something!"

In an instant, he realized the craft wasn't from Xira's compound. They were too far south now to have been pursued along the same route. Even so, the red-and-black sky-boat unnerved him.

Tense moments passed.

The balloon's flight would intersect their path, or the boat's. Like in zhakh, everything depended on guessing the opponent's strategy, on asking the right questions. So who was in that balloon? And who or what was their target, the pilgrims or the escapees? Daubed in such Zeruhawi colors — clearly, not the pilgrims.

Naama prodded with a finger. "Stop thinking! Just hide!"

They were exposed. The only cover at hand was behind the great sailfin of the yash'kh, but how to swap sides?

"Here, take one!" Naama had rewound the cord about her waist and freed another hook. "Quick!" She let go of Puzo's great sailfin and hook-in-hand began easing her way up the neck.

With unexpected swiftness, Puzo dived, and the resulting wave swept a startled Enok down into a soundless blue world. He gasped, screaming in silence as his lungs partook too deeply of that killing lifeblood. Images of that awful morning on Breakfast Island flashed through his mind: sweet victory over Xira and the bitter memory of his own near death.

But there was no Hrazul to save him now. Enok knew he was drowning. And of all the things to regret at such a time, it was of never having farewelled Jin-jin in return.

ZAKON FOUND HIMSELF FIGHTING FOR his life. It seemed as if some living boulder had attacked him silently from behind. In his weakened condition, he had barely managed to coil his tail about its great bulk and flip it over sideways.

Great Zhmee! It was a snail! But so impossibly huge!

Pain gripped him — such pain as to leave him gasping. The snail's teeth had pierced the delicate hide behind the neck to strike at tender flesh. Like the zhrat, it was attempting to devour him alive! He forced the creature into an upside-down position and yet it still would not let go.

By Ssla above! This thing had octopus tentacles! Using its huge slimy 'foot,' the creature righted itself, pinning him underwater again with its tentacles around his neck. He fumbled wildly with tail and hands for any kind of weapon. The slave's stumbling-stone was on the riverbed here somewhere.

Aha! Sharp edges at his tail-tip!

With a supreme effort of will, he dashed the rock against the creature's great conch.

«Die!» *Crack!* And again. «Die!» *Crack!*

The snail released its grip and Zakon slid bleeding from his assailant. Suddenly, the cavern exploded with the *chit-chit* and wing-beat of a thousand little khrii-like beasts. Startled, Zakon flared his wings. The creatures squealed all the more loudly and sped from the cave.

Enraged by all the events of the day, his inexplicable hesitation, and now the humiliation of being caught unawares, he hammered unrelentingly at the monster — *Crack! Crack!* — smashing through its shell. He tore away without respite until slimed with its innards, and that squid-snail-thing lay unmoving in the stream.

"Khaa! A Zmee cannot be drowned!"

Inside it were eggs. Almost a dozen of them. He ate one, inwardly laughing, and his tendrils dripping with viscera.

"You wanted a piece of me? Now I'm eating you! I am the Lord of Zoar, and you are … Khoza-zhaar!"

The creature's feelers gave a final twitch. It was dead. Perhaps its own kind would devour it, Zakon wondered. Perhaps more sped his way. Such thoughts aside, there were more pressing concerns: to catch the runaways and retrieve the crystal pendant. Even if that Enokhi slave were a being and no mere beast, no god, no cunning, no stratagem could ever save it now.

He lay panting in the stream beside the eviscerated shell. A more noble, more rational aspect of himself felt sickened by what he'd done, yet something more primal remained murderously enraged, intoxicated by the thrill of killing, and even welcoming the bile in his gorge.

NOW WHO'S THE BARBARIAN?

«What?» Zakon spun about, vainly searching for the invisible entity that was still mentally bombarding him, and using Hrazul's voice!

Invisibility: the missing piece to the puzzle! He almost leapt at the revelation. If he could chameleon and make himself 'invisible,' then so could another adult male. Zoia believed she had sighted him in the Reliquary with giants, or so the slave had said. But she was certainly mistaken. Clearly, she had seen another bull, and merely assumed it was he because Zoar had no others. He was Zakon the Invisible, the most feared Upholder ever. His gift made him virtually undetectable, seeing and hearing whatever he wanted, entirely at his pleasure. Small wonder the Shav'yat forbade bulls on the island!

But this gift in males had become increasingly rare, and the effort was exhausting. So, how could Zoar have had another bull like himself, and no one ever suspect?

He examined his own crooked hands, considering. The mutant hand, the lack of female attributes, shipwrecked with the giants — who else but Zaraza! Another chameleon bull, and disguising himself as a female: how perfect the camouflage!

Was *she* the traitor? Had *she* freed the giant on the dais? Of course! He should have suspected it sooner. Zaraza had always been in league with the giants. She — or rather, he — must have helped the Isha escape too, for only she, or rather he, and die-hard Zeruhawi, had been anywhere near the jail. And now that saboteur was on the Dragon Boat! Zakon had trusted her — *him!*

"Barbarian!"

THE TRUTH IS, said Hrazul's disembodied voice, DIG DEEP ENOUGH, AND YOU ARE ALL BARBARIANS — ISH AND ZMEE ALIKE.

"Truth!" He had been surrounded by incompetence and scheming, by deception and betrayal — all lies of one kind or another. "What is truth?"

THE ASKING IS A CONFESSION: YOU ARE UNABLE TO ANSWER.

"Then I admit it. I don't know what truth is any more."

THAT IS AN EXCELLENT BEGINNING.

Spla-ash!

Something large had fallen from a hidden height behind him.

Spla-ash!

Ahead, an object blocked the exit.

«No! No!» More monstrous snails!

And Zakon screamed in silence at the thought of a thousand tiny teeth devouring him again.

ENOK KNEW HE WAS POWERLESS to save himself. As the silent watery domain chilled him to the bones, and the world of light and warmth grew ever distant, everything that defined him cried out soundlessly in a prayer for mercy where none but The El could hear.

Some great finger had long been stirring the bowl of his fate. A part of him had always sensed it. And again, the ever-present, ever-hidden finger stirred. His scalp throbbed from a searing pain, and coarse reptilian hide scraped his cheeks in a sudden return to the world of lungs and air.

It would all become clear in the days ahead as to what had actually happened. For stability, Naama had been bracing herself with hooked thongs to a jutting dorsal spine, unwittingly striking a nerve, hence Puzo's diving reflex and erratic swerve. She too had been drawn underwater and still bound by the unraveling thong. It was 'sheer luck' she would say, that her trawling hand had caught hold of his tatty medicine stick.

Now she held him fast against the sailfin with his face buried in her bosom. Her heart was beating like a drum against his temple.

"Stooge of the gods! Have you stowed rocks in your kit? Else how can one drown with all that buoyancy?"

Enok doubled over as she loosened the medicine stick, coughing up water, desperate to be rid of it, desperate for air. It came in sweet sharp gulps, each stabbing like a knife.

Naama held him by his loincloth. "That's it. Cough it out." She righted him, strapping his wrist to a spine. "This should hold you. Look! The boat is slowing. It's changing course towards us! It may have something to do with that sky-boat! I don't see any basket, so there might not be any Zmee. It's awfully risky — blood of the gods! — but I can't see what else we can do. This is still our best chance, isn't it?"

Enok was in no shape to respond and she knew it.

"Lady of Luck! The sky-boat should strike somewhere between us and the vessel. I'll steer this beast towards it. Will you be alright?"

Enok only nodded weakly. With all his senses dreamy, his only hope was in Naama's resourcefulness. What had she just said?

"The musk ducts between the eyes and ears ... very tender," he remembered plotting. Was it days ago? A moon ago? "A hook in there can goad it any which way."

Time passed slowly in this dream, and Enok was oblivious to almost everything except his own forced breathing and the hiss of some great dragon.

Choof-woosh. Choof-woosh. Choof-woosh.

The mechanical noise grew rapidly louder. Great Zhmee! The boat was nearly upon them!

Then, abruptly, all sound died but for wave-lap.

A muffled voice spoke with urgency.

Whack!

Naama had backhanded him. "Snap out of it, serpent-boy — or, by Gol, I'll be forced to leave you here!"

She made to strike him again but refrained when he gasped, "I fine now."

"The pod followed us and cut across that monster-boat's path. It's now or never. Come on!" she exclaimed, hastily lashing their waists together. "We can do this. We can if we believe!" She freed his hand from Puzo's sailfin. "Alright? Here we go!"

They both took sharp, reaching breaths, but before he was completely ready, Naama plunged headlong into the choppy sea, dragging him after her.

No! Not again!

After his recent ordeal, the sensation of being dragged under Puzo's belly owned as much of terror as helplessness. When they broke the surface, the wooden hull of the Zmee boat was but a short swim distant. Excepting glimpses of copper below the waterline, it struck the eye like some gargantuan primordial yash'kh.

And the sky-boat was now tumbling on the waves, derelict, and without a gondola. It was merely a runaway balloon, and almost certainly Xira's demonstrator from his hometown. But the sight of cobalt stains across it meant that blood had set it free. The Isthmus Gates must have fallen and Zu'u-Shoran with it. Even so, the Vessel Mistress would have no further interest in it. There was no danger here, except —

Enok tensed as a great gelatinous head drifted past.

'*The jellyfish swarm early this year.*'

"Ai!" Naama shrieked from the burn of a trailing tendril. "Great goddess!" she gasped, "I'm on fire!"

In her panic, she made for the nearest object. Together they rested, clinging to one of the vessel's submerged 'legs.' And there, as tremors and ripples told of internal mechanics, Zelen's warning sprang to mind.

The paddles.

"Bad ...stay here!" Enok coughed. "Boat ... swimming feet."

"Enok, I'm burning! I ... I ... have to ..."

"Go! Must go!"

They were in grave danger and had to keep swimming, more so now than ever.

Naama's breathing grew labored and her limbs stiffened as the poison took effect. "Uh ... uh ... alright! Just another br—"

The 'foot' shuddered suddenly to life. Naama barely managed a squeal before disappearing from sight. The tether went sharply taut, then slackened horribly.

She was gone! Naama! Gone!

With what little strength remained, Enok lunged immediately after her, but she was nowhere to be seen. The medicine stick cursed him with buoyancy at the very time he needed it least. He made his choice. Wiggling free of the Healers' tube and its precious cargo, the only tangible connection to his parents, he dove deep after Naama, down until his hands found the severed cord and her lifeless body adrift like seaweed in the remnants of whatever had sucked her below.

Suddenly, a churning blast thrust them backwards and upwards, away from mangled jellyfish, the outrigger's angular paddles, and the great ship itself. He kept kicking madly, wildly, and flailing with his free hand. Sweet relief filled his lungs as he broke the surface. But the sheer muscled bulk of the amazon was so very, very heavy! With a hand under her shoulder, he struggled to keep her face above water as he paddled desperately towards the vessel.

With Sea Broom now strong against their sailfins, the pod were being forced clear of the ship, to continue their breakfast journey. And the paddles were frothing the water more mightily than before. In mere heartbeats, the ship could accelerate and be forever beyond all reach. But his strength was rapidly failing, and despite his best efforts, he knew he could not save them both.

"Hrazul died! Zelen and Zoia died! And Hatan! No more on my account!" he cried to sea and boat and sky. "No more! Do you hear me? I will not abandon her!"

And in that moment at hope's edge, where silence mocked all faith, when all force was spent and neither death nor life seemed important anymore, the vessel swung its stern towards him, catching them both in a thick trailing net.

Hope stirred.

"Oh, El! Give me strength!"

As though plagued with indecision, the sea continued foaming as the great pilgrim's vessel changed course once, twice, and a third time without substantially moving. And in those buoyant moments on the net, step by painful step, Enok hauled both himself and the unconscious Naama onto a rear low-lying deck, into the shelter of an upturned lighter.

Despite his best efforts to work the fluid from her lungs, Naama showed no signs of life.

"Breathe! Breathe!" he urged in Zmiysh. "You saved me, now save yourself!"

No response.

He slapped her face hard. And again. Frantic hands squeezed her lungs like bellows, yet still without response.

It was a desperate moment. So many the heartbeats lost, so ebbed the hope in his hands. What cunning, what skill now against the very maws of death? And yet, fate is a strange thing, turning, as it often can, on a single timely nudge from a black-eyed stranger; inexperience at the helm, hesitant, steering the vessel one way instead of another; or a forgotten fragment of a story quickened, perhaps, by the chemistry of danger — or by Providence.

This fate was not yet through with him.

AND THEY BREATHED INTO HIS NOSTRILS THE VERY BREATH OF LIFE.

The thought — or was it a memory? — from where had it come? The imagery it evoked swirled about him, tempting, pleading, insistent. The vision in the Reliquary! The avatar leaning over the mud-man had breathed up his nose!

He would ponder its meaning some other day, but for now Enok knew what had to be done. With his bellows full of life's sweet breath, and with a hand over her mouth and his lips to her nose ...

He blew.

WOMB OF GODS‡

Eyda is secretly visited by Sess's other wives, who warn of the impending doom. She discovers for herself the ominous nature of Sess's children, one that will change the world forever ... While sharing the pain of a thousand-thousand worlds, Legate Uriel discloses more of deir mission.

SCREE-EE-EE-EECH.

Squawk-honk!

Scree-ee-ee-eech.

Squawk-honk!

Fang-swans had descended noisily with posturing and bonding-calls upon a distal outcrop of the Moud. The thicketed, solitary islet teemed with fish and frogs in its shallows, and made a perfect nesting ground. This territory included a high-domed, ornately thatched hut encircled by flagstone yards that centuries of traffic had polished. Unfortunately for Eyda, this remote edge of the archipelago that now drew these swans had long been her private abode.

Eyes crusty with sad and vivid dreams, a wakening Eyda wondered how anyone could ever sleep through such a racket. Frankly, they couldn't! This was all Sha-Noa's fault. Hadn't she had warned him time and again to never feed the swans?

Judging by the halo around the doorway, dawn had long since broken. It had been years since she had missed the rising of the Greater Light, her time for ablutions and thanksgiving by the river-bank. As she made to rise, a child slid from her breast, mumbling sleepily.

"I hate dragons."

Craning her neck, and rubbing sleep from her eyes, Eyda surveyed the tangle of bodies. Nestled against her were so many children, even more than last night's seven, and she could naught but be warmed at the fond remembrance of bygone days. Her tiny home was once again full of little dreamers, and the sounds of their contented slumber. Mindful of the little ones, she collected her shawl and her prayer mat, parted the curtain, and once outside, kissed her fingers and blessed the tapestry there.

The sight of Sess's token arrested her. Odd that it had fallen so. Perhaps one of the children had plucked it free. As she pocketed it, another ear-splitting hail received an answering *squawk-honk!*

"Sha-Noa!"

An airborne clog and then its twin sent the fang-swans scampering. They were fiercely territorial and would surely become aggressive if they settled here. Well, this was *her* sanctuary, and she was not inclined to share it.

"Shoo! Be gone!"

She hobbled after the intruders to where the youngsters had played last night by the river. Yes, her clogs were wet; yes, she was aggravated. Try as she might, though, it was hard to stay mad at the boy, especially as he had salved her despair with just the right tonic. Truth be told, she had long dismissed any joy of a full and stuffy house. She had equally long convinced herself that such age as hers transcended any caring. Here, she was safe. Here, she had her independence. Here, none could attack her or rule over her again. Surely, this was freedom, wasn't it?

However, the crumpled gift of food from a child last night had struck her like a knock to the elbow. Strange that such kindness should come from a guest and not from one of her own. Actually, the girl *was* family, a far-born granddaughter whose simple offering aroused in her a discontent she couldn't yet define.

Anyhow, her time for ablutions was long overdue, for poking

red now above the giant rushes of the Soud's vast everglades, the Greater Light bathed the river in ruddy browns and greens. Like Enok, this was her favorite time of day. The ever-brightening dawn had always been a harbinger, a metaphor, a promise of a time when the drab of the browns would succumb to shimmering blues — where the sorrows of night would flee before the brilliance of eternal day, and one that brooked no evil.

But the first to be purged were the evils within, yet dawn's pure shafts never quite seemed to lance the slippery source. With eyes closed, tapping her breast in contrition, Eyda knelt on her mat towards those impotent rays. She was a poet at heart, admittedly so, just indulging romantic illusions. And these were all too easily dispelled by the acrid reality of some upstream neighbor's fire.

Her ablutions began with the usual ritual, finishing with "Let my eyes behold no ... evil." She faltered, more hopeful than believing, yet upon a finger lifted from the shallows a world of rising promise hung reflected in a drop. And in that moment, as the trajectory of her life came clear in a new and frightening way, she anointed her eyes with that promise and renounced her bitter words.

"Oh, El. I'd forgotten how easily the gods can twist our speech. And too how readily my own mouth undoes me. I've been cursing everyone and everything because I hate what I've become. I'm ashamed to admit that my Mati sees what I've long kept denying. 'There's no deception like self-deception,' right?" That wasn't really a question. "I can hardly keep blaming others for what I've been doing to myself. Forgive me," Eyda sighed. "Now I have this hunch You're wanting of me what I'm incapable of giving. But how can I regress the years and be what I once was?"

Before her forehead touched the mat in a final act of contrition, a child's hand lightly brushed her back. It was Kalmiya, Eyda realized looking up, the considerate little food-bringer of the night before.

"My cuddle-mommy's coming."

Eyda forced a smile. "Soon, I'm sure. She misses you too."

"No, Old Maa. I mean ..." The little girl cocked her head, listening bird-like. "One, two ... four people. They're here already. Look!"

Almost as if summoned, four hooded figures came tramping barefooted directly through the grove of jute, even though they could easily have traced the causeway on clogs. These were Sess's other two wives, and with them, Sha-Noa's mother Mehet'abel, and Mati's wife Saz'yana. Their arrival was unnerving: they had meant to visit covertly.

"Please," whispered Eyda, with a halting hand towards the hut, "let the children sleep a little longer."

"We've nay come for them," replied the swarthy wife of Sess, "but for ye."

"So early in the morning?"

The wives exchanged knowing looks. "For certs this be the only chance today to meet without incident."

Eyda shook her head. "Excuse me? Incident?"

Saz'yana explained. "Someone severed the head of Surai's idol while everyone slept, then set it alight. Sess's boat caught fire and sunk. It's a wonder no one was injured."

Mehet'abel added, "Surai accuses you."

"*Pshew,*" Eyda snorted, then couldn't help suppress a chuckle. "That's absurd!"

"What's so funny?" the little girl asked.

Saz'yana formally presented Sess's Elim wives to their mother-in-law. By their looks, they saw nothing humorous in the idol's demise. The swarthy, almond-eyed woman of thick ebony hair came introduced as Layla. The exotic dress of twine and colorful beads in geometric patterns beneath a borrowed cloak and shawl were not unlike the fashions of Eyda's childhood. And the lanky, shaven-headed waif with the impossibly blank complexion was Rahel. An intricately embossed dress of dyed buckskins fringed with silver and turquoise clearly marked her as no mere slave. Her feathered robe with a downy hood bore all the hallmarks of royalty. The more Saz'yana explained, however, the more confusing it all became.

"From the Yawning Plains? Daughter of the chief?"

"The wife that is first, *am I*," voiced pale Rahel in the singsong manner of the Plains-folk. "Only a child when given to your son in marriage, I was — barely older than little Kalmiya." She embraced the child and kissed her.

Eyda had sheltered among the Plains-folk once. They were a marvelously generous and spiritual people, though she had never been comfortable with their diet. They were semi-nomadic fell-mongers and — *ugh!* — habitual meat eaters like the Akadians. Judging by her age, this Rahel must have been a child-bride. Why had Sess taken a mere girl for a wife? That wasn't the Sess she knew, or rather, had known in bygone days.

"So you, the elder, are the second wife?"

Almond-eyed Layla nodded. She was smallish compared to her fellow wife, yet with all the airs of a matron.

"The Nor Mayana is ... was me home. Me brothers were lords of the New Towers." Her speech was clipped, her vowels too short, much like her own mother's dialect had been.

Mayana were geyser systems springing from great wounds in the earth. Eyda had grown up around mayana too, and felt an immediate kinship with this petite stranger. Indeed, she had all the looks of some long-lost cousin.

Eyda forced a little levity. "Oh for the steamy springs of home! To luxuriate in hot mud, and death to all the ticks! You and I have much in common," she offered, but was abashed at the rebuttal.

The apprehension of the newcomers was contagious, and while motioning them to take comfort on flagstone stools or recline on bales of straw, she couldn't help but wonder how Sess had taken such cheerless brides, and from beyond the edges of the world besides. Just how far had her son been wandering?

"Me home be gone forever," told Layla with a faraway look. "We be a people of tears now. Reavers swept through Rahel's steppes, over the alpine forests, then descended like a plague upon the Broken Lands, plundering, burning, taking captive whomever they wished. For years they kept to their own realm, but they grow restless again and for certs now head this way."

"Reavers? Akadians!"

"From the river Hidekel," Layla affirmed, "who serve the Anaki, Surai's blood-kin. They make camp at the falls called Twin."

Zhakh's magnificent falls were far, far upriver in wild and dangerous country, beyond even where the Crooked Thumb and the Grand Banks came together at Zakon's Reach. That territory formed the very protection upon which marshland elders had long relied. Nobody lived there. Nobody *could* live there, or at least that's how it had always been.

Pale Rahel concurred with a nod. "Returns downriver does nothing now. No one."

"But Sess did. You too," Eyda countered.

"A trader, my husband is," explained Rahel. "*The* trader, the most shrewd of Ish. The Anaki lords gave the river — all of it — from the Fearful Territories to the Six Fingers, to Gul'shan, of Surai twin brother."

"Naama's pups."

"Yes, but how did —"

"Something Surai herself said. Besides, the resemblance is unmistakable, but that's another story. I still don't see —"

"The only way continue trading, my husband could —"

"*Our* husband," quipped Layla with trenchant eyes upon Rahel.

"— our husband could, take Surai as wife did he. This way is now the world."

"Ye canno' trade anywhere now 'less the gods themselves or the Anaki godlings permit it," Layla explained. "And ye be of no account as an Ish these days till ye espouse ye-self an Anaki. Please, we need ye to understand."

"I don't see how this has anything to do with me. Does your husband know you are here?"

"Husband!" spat Rahel. "Since married Surai did he, became the husband did *she*, and now the wife is *he*."

"And we," Layla shared a poignant look with her fellow wife, "be reduced to slaves. That's all any of us be to the Sons of God."

Eyda paused to reflect on this change of name, and balked at the insinuation. In her day, it was 'Sons of the Fallen,' or 'Sons of the Gods,' but never *the* God. She shuddered and wondered what else had changed in the outside world in all the centuries she'd missed.

"Believe me, they are daughters and sons of *no* gods, and certainly not of The El."

Layla continued. "Ye see, at first, they were welcome. We had trade — jewels, fine cloth, and so many things from the great city that tickle ye senses."

"As she says," Rahel affirmed. "At first, welcome were they. Give, give, and take nothing do they except pledges. 'Sons have you. Sons strength yours are. Sons unto yourself keep you,' say they. Not want war do they, only trade. And come with such fearful weapons do they! So trade do all instead of fight — but when for the pledges returning, return do they in such fearful numbers! And none can pay. So take do they ... and never return do the taken ones." Layla took Rahel's hand when she faltered. "What joy be there?" wept Rahel, "and what hope have we ... when a hundred sons but no daughters? Too weak were we in our hands."

"Nay, too cowardly of heart, all of us" Layla confessed. "Old Maa, ye of all folk should know of what depravities the Anaki be capable. They know neither shame nor mercy."

"Nor kindness," Rahel lamented.

"Sess came to warn ye and tha kin."

"Me?"

"Methinks Lamek in particular," said Layla. "Of ye, he feared ye wouldna understand his choices."

Three wives, and a boat adorned with what she now remembered as the trappings of a brutal Reaver posse — Eyda shook her head with a shiver. "He's right. I don't."

Layla continued. "Surai be blind to his real intentions. He had to trick her. She has —"

"Powers. Yes, I know," Eyda finished for her. She wanted no reminding of those horrific days of her past. Such deeply buried memories they were too, shameful and disturbing, deliberately forgotten — that is, until today. "Truly, I'm sorry for what happened to your tribes. But even with Surai and her brother to lead them, a Reaver posse couldn't possibly prevail against the sheer mass of people here. Right?"

Layla laid a hand on Eyda's. "Old Maa, it be utterly hopeless. Encamped be more than forty giants — Glorious Ones and their half-breed Anaki — and with as many heads to their Akadian Reavers as an endless sea of rushes.[lxvi] They nay have interest in proving themselves, for they be unbeatable already. As for trade, ye have nothing they want, except —"

"Forty giants here, you said? Gods and their godling mules?" Eyda was dumbstruck.

---

lxvi   In descending order, the power elite of the Akadian class system. *Glorious Ones* is the worshipful term for otherworldly *Sons of the Gods,* just as *The Fallen* is a pejorative.

Two giants leading a posse of Reavers had long been the norm: a Striker and his Fist, the captain and his subordinate, the two horns of the charging beast. But forty on a single campaign seemed unimaginable, unless every giant alive was headed this way! There were simply fewer giants than people were led to believe, for the birth of a mongrel godling was about as common as a dark-noon day, particularly since the wombs of mixed-bloods were barren. Having lived with that titan Surai, Rahel and Layla ought to have known that by now.

Oblivious to the fears of the adults, the girl chimed, "Preeminent Mother says that everyone will love me."

"Sweetheart, already they do." Rahel grabbed the child and held her tightly in a wet-eyed embrace. "Precious little baby."

"The girls," moaned Layla. Her almond eyes were wide and dry. She had cried beyond relieving and exhausted all her tears. "How can ye lay hands upon such innocents?"

Eyda looked at each of the four women in turn, seeing their anguish but still not comprehending.

Rahel covered the child's ears as Layla wailed in a whisper, "Oh Maa! They be coming for the girls!"

The tang of hastily prepared festive fires wafting towards the Great Salty Sea was a sore reminder that the feasting at grandson Lamek's continued apace, despite the tragedy of Sess's houseboat burning down. Lamek had always loved to put on a show just as much as he loved to grumble. Three hundred years hadn't changed him.

And when the Greater Light had blued the waters, the children had departed with their mothers for the morning meal leaving their Old Maa to contemplation by the riverbank.

The morning's revelations had jolted her as no news ever had. Rahel and Layla had unburdened themselves, and yet there was something they had withheld, possibly because the children had awoken and were milling about the yard and they didn't want to upset them. And, of course, the sudden arrival of scalding tongues in search of their missing children had hardly been helpful.

Did they think the shock of having to confront the Anaki would overwhelm her? That fleeing the marshlands was unthinkable? What did they have here anyway? Huts of reed and bamboo; nothing she would be loath to abandon. The real treasure was in the schoolyards, in the skipping grounds, and in every mother's bosom.

So how should she respond?

She would tell The El, and They would guide her with that quiet little voice that had steered her through her darkest days. She was anxious but not frightened. The giants had already done their worst to her and yet she had prevailed. Both as the warrior Deina, and as captive slave, she had been terrified of death; as Eyda the devout she had welcomed it. Indeed, she had died a little more each passing year since Enok disappeared. No, she was afraid of neither the giants nor the slavers, not for herself anyway.

Enok had believed that here the Ab-Sethi remnant would lie beyond Anaki clutches. The everglades of the Six Fingers were wide and daunting, so most would escape should the beasts of the cities ever darken the land. 'Wars end the fruit of evil, not the vine,' he had said. 'But one day, one day, The Light will outshine The Dark, and consume it stump and root.'

But this was not that day, for if she had understood rightly, her people were soon to face an enemy skilled in every hideous technique of war. Surely, fleeing was the wiser choice, but here they were already at the very edge of the world. Where could they possibly go?

Yes, the inland Sea of Eloah: it had not crossed her mind in decades, now suddenly it loomed large in her spirit like some fatal premonition. Rumor placed it amidst the Fearful Territories, there where the mightiest of rivers began in awesome fury, a magical, terrifying place that was so far beyond every known horizon, that it had never been much more than myth.

The threads of so many tapestries began there — Elim, Zmee, Wahoona, Jinauq — there where her Enok had gone, across that sea and into legend. The tribe could haven on its shores, perhaps becoming myth themselves beyond the setting of the Greater Light, for here at its rising, evil had sought them out, and she knew her world would never be the same.

The fears and confrontations of the morning had left Eyda utterly spent. Her prayer mat had been resting too long by the riverbank and was for sure now beginning to wick. To hang it to dry and take a nap was as much as she could manage. However, the morning haze had cleared and the day now was as glorious as the morning had been dark. Wouldn't it be a balm just to bask in the sunlight?

In the silt by her feet, and half-mucked by the toe-prints of scoop-bills, the children had illustrated her story. Here, a face streamed with rays. Enok with an aureole? There, a head with a third eye and a serpent's tongue. Ava-Baba speaking Zmiysh? And scattered along the riverbank glistened the imprints of their own feet.

SUCH LARGE FOOTPRINTS TOO, Eyda wondered, FOR MERE CHILDREN.

And she found herself marveling at how an old woman could become absorbed by something so ordinary. Such common things, footprints, yet suddenly more precious than jewelry ever could be: the dear little signatures of her grandsons and granddaughters. Such wonderful children. The future of her people. Of all people. They could journey with her to Eloah's inland sea, far from the corrupting influence of Surai and her kind.

An epic trek, but they would, yes.

Eyda stumbled. *No!*

DEAR EL, MAY IT NOT BE SO!

She studied the imprints more closely, counting in disbelief and tracing them shakily. She checked another, then another.

Five. Six. Clearly six, and six again!

The sight rent her heart in a pain more intense than anything the giants had ever inflicted. She tore at her garments until her knuckles turned white.

OH SESS, WHAT HAVE YOU DONE!

She bowed reflexively, forehead to the mat in a warding against new evils. "Let my hands do no wrong. Let no dark word pass my lips. Let my eyes behold no evil ... do no wrong ... no dark word ... behold no evil." Faster and faster the words tumbled until her daily prayer was a meaningless blur.

"Oh, please. Please," she sobbed. "Oh, El."

So many the footprints with extra toes!

Indeed, there *was* something the women had failed to tell her. Sess's children — her own grandchildren! — were of giant stock. Layla and Rahel were merely nursemaids. The mixed-blood progeny of giant and Isha were rare, and they were always barren. Always. But here now was the rarest thing of all: Surai was a mixed-blood who wasn't. What then of the titan's daughters, Raama, Kalmiya and the others? Or even Sess's other sons?

There had clearly been a misunderstanding. Perhaps the fault had been her own. Times were different now. The Anaki weren't after *all* the girls in the marshlands.

They had brought an army for Surai's.

ELISHAN GRIPPED HIS STAFF INSTINCTIVELY, priming for a fight. Things would never be the same again. The enemy now knew where they were and what they were hiding: thousands of innocent villagers untouched by big-city vices, and knowing little of weapons or war.

In her grief, little Eyda had voiced her inner torment and Legate Yuriyel had recorded it all. "I can see now why The El is concerned," said Yuriyel gravely, "and why They wanted a representative to investigate — to this place, at this time."

Elishan begged an explanation.

"If Surai's children can also beget, it could well spell the end of the Elim as a distinct race. See? They look like quite ordinary. But in a thousand years, or two — who knows? — all the bloodlines will have mixed."

Starion's white brows came together. "That's something of an overstatement, don't you think?"

"It all makes sense now." The Legate massaged deir jowls pensively.[lxvii] "The everglades of The Soud are the perfect hideaway. And the islets themselves are veiled by an intractable sea of reeds. I think that's why Sess returned to the Six Fingers, to hide the children, or have them slain."

Elishan was taken aback. "That's unthinkable!"

Helon gripped him by the shoulder. "Eli, remember what Sess's wife wailed about laying a hand on the children? Yuriyel's right. She was referring not to the slavers but her own spouse."

The Legate elaborated. "To be taken by the slavers, to put it crudely, as breeding stock is ghastly enough, but Sess understands

---

lxvii   See the preface on Genderless Pronouns: *dey / dem / deir* are the epicene
         equivalents of the singulars *they / them / their.*

the greater consequences, and struggles with the responsibility." After a pause, Yuriyel added softly, "We are here to encourage, not to condemn, but I daresay Sess may prove a more noble character than his mother supposes."

"It just cannot be true," Elishan found his own mouth saying. "So what are we to do, just let them be taken by the slavers? We need help. Urgently."

Everyone was silent, tacitly agreeing.

It was Starion who eventually broke the quiet. "I see the dilemma. It's about restoring this world to its rightful custodians, but since the children are part us — the rebel us — we have no jurisdiction over them or any of their descendants." He stabbed the earth with his broadsword in a call to arms. "Me, I'm military; here to fight and help the Elim regain their world. Well, Legate, you now have something meaty to report, but yours is the easy job."

"Easy? *Easy?* You have no idea," voiced the Legate with a slow shake of the head and with eyes widening heavenward. "Thousands of worlds are still wondering what *did* trigger the rebellion, and why The El *didn't* intervene to prevent it. Should the murder of eternal beings carry eternal consequences? Is The El's decree of rebel punishment just? You know of what I speak. What about rehabilitation? Is that even possible? Will there ever be another rebellion, and if so, what will The El do next time?"

Elishan frowned quizzically, wondering about the pains and losses that made the Legate reason so. "Next time?"

"You see, little Watcher," the Legate explained, imbibing of the morning sky and all the worlds beyond, "the heavens resound with a billion-billion doubts and as many cries for justice, for understanding, concerned not for just the war's conclusion but all that follows after. Judgment? Certainly. Healing? How can memories be healed? Restoration? What's gone is gone forever. After all we have endured and all we are yet to witness, how can our relationships and innocence ever be as they once were, knowing the fate of former friends, rebels we once held to bosom?"

Starion agreed they were good questions. Judging by his looks, Helon did too.

"And from what I have seen from afar," said the Legate with the hint of a worried expression, "the rebel leader Bel nurtures here what dey love most in demself: self; for in an obsession with self, kin are made alien, the webs of fellowship are torn, and in the sundering, Bel patterns over and over the image of deir own insurrection.

"Who of us didn't hope for a speedy end so life could return to normal? However, I'm now of the opinion that this conflict will not be so easy to resolve, and a war of bloodlines here will complicate an already tricky situation. Believe me, I would rather be 'up there' fighting with your warriors than be the one in the court of The El to this make public."

Yuriyel crouched to finger the soil underfoot, sifting it like a curious child. "You see, in many ways, The El are on trial just as much as the rebels: Their right to govern, the justice of Their decision making."

Elishan was shocked. "What a notion! Just whose questions might these be?"

"You are more fortunate than I in not having witnessed the rebel leader's accusations. How Bel prances round the bar, demanding the Judge Themself to take the stand! 'Dark, light, polar opposites: if They made the one, did They not also make the other? And if I grow toward that different light that They Themselves have made, how then can the fault be mine? Theirs be the blunder, so then let *Theirs* be the remedy!' Those were Bel's very words."

Silence lingered, deep and anguished.

Then, "Is it a crime to ponder, to ask questions, little Watcher? Think: could an all-knowing El have prevented what we see here today? What we ourselves survived at peril? Given the nature, perhaps even the inevitability of rebellion, and the primacy of The El's own law, is all this" — Yuriyel took in the sky, the river, the dirt, eyes finally resting on Eyda — "some kind of best possible outcome? If so, what are the criteria, and would we even be able to comprehend them?

"As I said, there are innumerable questions, but The El's response is always the same. They stretch fingers at this captive world and say, 'Behold, there is Our answer.' This world is —"

Starion ventured, "A microcosm?"

Elishan shook his head slowly, beginning to understand, though he had always suspected it. "More likely it's a testament."

Yuriyel nodded. "And, I think, a trap. *Here* is the courtroom. *Here* are the witnesses. *Here* are all our questions answered, the rebut to every rebel accusation — here, *here* in the richness of this world and in the future history of its people. And the remedy *will* be The El's. I really do believe that. How? No one has a clue, not really — not the Temple Sarafs, the Kheroub, nor even your even Melakh Seers, that is, the few that yet remain.

"And as for the Dreaming Snails, if they were not in hibernation, I would certainly have asked." Having saluted Elishan's insight, the Legate raised an eyebrow suggestively. "I doubt this concludes Eyda's story."

Though Elishan had been Eyda's Guardian and knew the essentials, Helon had been Enok's, and was more intimately acquainted. He shook his head slowly. "No indeed."

The two giant beings, Yuriyel and Starion, exchanged significant looks. "I have a reasonable idea, Helon, who first fathered the godling race. There aren't that many candidates," said the Legate. "But what of the mothers — or was it mother? Who was —"

"The womb of the gods?" Helon offered.

"If you put it that way, yes."

Elishan watched sympathetically as Helon resigned himself to the inevitable. It would all come out now, how Helon had saved this 'womb of the gods.' It was ironic, really. In a way, this whole world was a kind of 'womb of gods,' a cradle for the amazingly complex race of the Elim, the Ish and Isha they had struggled so hard to nurture.

Though Helon began to dissemble, there was no fooling the Legate. "Naama?"

"Yes, but not quite in the way you think."

"Oh? I should like to know more about this Enok. He and the Havilan obviously succeeded in returning to the mainland. Time and again they saved each other's life without an inkling of your presence. You did your job well."

Helon shrugged, dismissing the compliment. "He made a few ill-considered choices and I made some hasty ones of my own. I think I failed the 'inkling' part. And if I knew then what I know now, I would not have helped him rescue her after that incident with the primitive propellers."

"But you did."

Helon nodded reluctantly.

"To The El, all life is precious," Yuriyel consoled. "The El *are* life, the very life of life. You did what you knew was right; just like you saved that Zmee, Zoia, in the Reliquary. No, wait — it couldn't have been you."

Helon shook his head. "The pyramid was harmonically shielded and completely opaque to the higher realms. Until Enok mentioned it, I would never have guessed a Kheroub lay concealed in its resonator. The only way inside was to assume physical form, but I couldn't risk either being seen or becoming mortally vulnerable. And, for my kind at least, the heady inebriation of physicality here quickly becomes downright debilitating. Actually, I think it was all the doing of the black-eyed Zmee, but at the time, I had no idea of who that really was."

Elishan nudged his colleague. "Keep going."

"Well," Helon explained, "given our altitude, we rarely see into someone's eyes directly. Honesty, back then, I never suspected, never even imagined that my mission could have such far-reaching consequences."

Understanding lit the Legate's birdlike face. "That black-eye was a Shinarn, an undercover changeling, the key to all the mysteries."

"I know! A changeling under my very nose! I only realized it towards the end, when the zhrat that had made off with the Reliquary key caught my attention with the plumes from Zakon's helmet, using them like semaphores. They signed me a message! And all those years I thought I'd been stationed alone on the island," concluded Helon shyly.

"We are never alone," whispered Yuriyel absently. "Never alone. And that four-faced Kheroub must have been secreted long before your arrival, and I daresay since the very institution of this world, and only by The El's command. Which suggests of course, that They had anticipated these very events, doesn't it? Anyhow, I'm curious, what was the rooster's message?"

Helon felt foolish knowing he'd been secretly helped for years. But changelings were like that, or so it was said. Like the Four-faces, the nature of their actions were a mystery to all but The El and themselves.

And so with eyes averted, Helon hesitantly confessed, "'We ... are never ... alone.'"

Chuckles rounded the group. Even Yuriyel let slip a grin before coming to stand beside Elishan to study Eyda's ritual of staring shut-eyed at that hazy orb of the morn.

"Your little charge holds more of this saga, and I daresay I'll not be going anywhere until all of it is told. And, as the tattooed boy phrased it, Eyda needs to 'see her nose.' Can you arrange it?"

Elishan looked to Helon, who nodded. "As with dreams, we can but seed the thought through the Guardians. I'll send the message. Then perhaps she will help you answer all those, ah, *questions*."

The Legate's lips parted slowly in a modest smile.

Bronzed Starion, ever the warrior, wanted more of the bull Zmee Zakon. "So he met his end in that cavern, right?"

Elishan found it amusing how his partner's head wagged slowly with all the airs of some great secret.

"No," said Helon casually. "His beginning."

CROSS-LEGGED ON HER MAT, and shut-eyed towards the rising Greater Light, Eyda enjoyed the patterns sunshine made on her eyelids: oranges, blues, purples, fragmenting, recombining, shifting with every rub of the eye. However soothing the images, meditation was impossible. Everything troubled her: the now, the bygone, and their point of collision.

A single act, a single breath, a single slap to the face and death was brought to life. Enok's actions had been both pivotal and disastrous, yet who can ever predict the harm that comes from good?

WITH A HAND OVER HER MOUTH AND HIS LIPS TO HER NOSE ...
HE BLEW.

That was all of Enok's escape that she knew. What happened afterwards, between saving Naama and reaching the mainland, was something he had always shied from discussing. Had he come to regret the saving? Had something passed between them he wanted kept private? Naama had been incredibly beautiful, and was as much by circumstance as by some strange nuance of Havilan law forced to present a temptation. So, was Surai right? Had there been a brief dalliance after all and with Surai herself the result?

"Burn you, Surai! You and your aspersions! Get out of my head!"

But in venting her anger over that titan's wiliness, and how morally opposed they both were, the children's wheedling of last night echoed in her soul with a poignancy that challenged such conceit.

What did Ab say?

'THAT'S HARDLY FUN IF YOU'RE ALWAYS LONELY, UNLESS YOU CAME HERE TO DIE. DO YOU WANT TO DIE, OLD MAA?'

That little seer had peered behind her veil, and his reverberating question had spawned a dozen others in her mind. In so many, many ways, wasn't she already as good as dead? Wasn't it her self-isolation that had aged her and left her empty? Hadn't the desperate striving after security wrought in her a selfishness that was no less ruinous than some 'divine' Anaki 'right' to the same? Therefore, how was her self-righteousness any better than Surai's?

OH, ENOK! YOU FORETOLD MUCH, BUT DID YOU SEE *THIS* COMING?

Eyda made her way her back to the hut, pausing to reflect at the brocaded tapestry of her life outside its entrance. Story after story she traced with loving fingers, ending at the large yellow token, and with a hint of self-mockery as her fingers groomed wild hair at the mere memory of her husband. What a sight he had been when they first met, dyed yellow to the knees! She had taken an instant dislike to him, and she could only guess what his own first impressions had been; though he had steadfastly claimed he had loved her long before they ever even met. She was his 'dream girl,' he would say.

Oh, men were such liars in love, but what a lovely lie it was.

Lies indeed.

Some made you smile, others had to be challenged.

And if even half were true of all that Sess's wives had shared, then a battle royal loomed against the Anaki and their lackeys — perhaps not yet a war of blades but certainly of words until the peoples of the Gihon left these everglades behind.

She had been Deina once, the Sickle: sharp-tongued, fleet and nimble, feared. Her husband had introduced the water lilies here, not just as a living memorial to love but to forever remind her to curb her violent nature, to drown it out instead with beauty. But hadn't that very splitting of her natures diminished that which makes one whole? Indeed, a burgeoning reality demanded that she reconcile the two halves of her past — of hobbling Eyda, her lover's Lily, the devout; and fearsome Deina, lissome warrior, the Sickle — and of the two make one.

But what power had she against the likes of Surai?

In her bosom sputtered the flame of a sacred trust. She would never be rid of it, this flame, she accepted finally. For the children last night awoke in her so many things a Maa ought never have forgotten, especially that the one strength that never aged was the ceaseless power of the tongue. There truly was both life and death within it.

She had made an exception for her son Mati, told Enok's story, and given those school children her heart. For that brief moment, in that consecrated space, she had become vulnerable again — there, she was forced to acknowledge, where true religion, true humanity, was ever to be found.

"I *am* a storyteller," she accepted wistfully, and vowed ever to continue as long as willing ears remained. However, she would no longer deny that it was the warrior-spirited Deina that she, old Eyda, had pined for these long and lonely years.

But what had she for weapons? Neither spears, nor clubs, nor daggers now but something far more consequential: not just words but stories.

As both Eyda *and* Deina, she was once again the Sickle. And she would reap indeed.

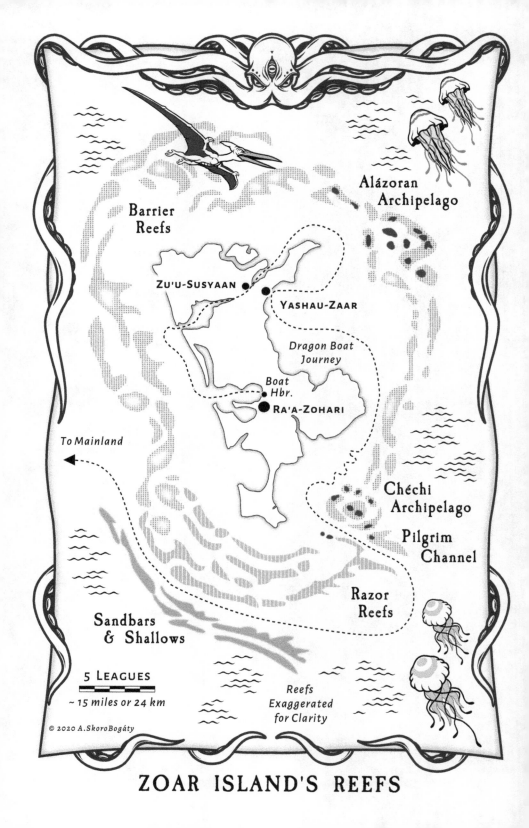

ZOAR ISLAND'S REEFS

SON OF YARED

A board the boat of Zmee pilgrims, Enok contemplates the strangeness of his past, the promise of the future, and the daunting burden of that knowledge.

FROM BENEATH AN UPTURNED LIGHTER at the low-lying stern of the Dragon Boat, there was precious little view of the world that Enok had known. The Greater Light was so high in the sky and out of sight that he could scarcely estimate the time. His best guess is that a watch had passed since he had hauled them both aboard. Luckily, the same kind of webbing that had saved them earlier also secured the barges. Its modest elasticity had allowed for just enough of a gap to crawl to safety, and drag the bulk of Naama after him.

He lay nestled now against her unconscious form with his head propped on an elbow, watching each rise and fall of her breast with grateful eyes. She had been in such a state once before, and he was confident she would recover. Her physical resilience was nothing short of amazing. It was curious, though — wasn't it? — that her journeys to and from the island should be so alike.

And here it was again, he thought, that tantalizing evanescent symmetry of life. Was it the signature of some unseen hand, and possibly of destiny?

He had treated Naama's jellyfish burns with an acetic wash from a medicine stick, and had cut and bled the most severe of her burns to remove every vestige of poison. She had lost an ear in the underwater accident, and had sustained a gash near the shoulder. Maybe that's why she wore such heavy arm bracelets. Without them, she would likely have been gouged beyond all remedy.

That chalky salve of hers proved handy. It had dried both their wounds more quickly than even sulfur did a Zmee's. But even though he had dressed all her wounds with shreds of swaddling, her once flawless golden skin would almost certainly bear scars.

They both would.

Zelen had been true to her word and had provisioned the barges well. The hull-turned-ceiling of the upturned lighter held the promised cache of supplies: a spyglass, two small knives, water bladders, and another medicine stick. The second flatboat was amply stocked with food but it was pilgrims' provender, ascetic, and hardly flavorsome. The nuts were a boon, though.

Above him, a single turquoise feather tipped with gold dangled from a slender chord. It was one of Jin-jin's, and probably salvaged from Hrazul's necklace. Enok reached out, then drew back. It was a hallowed token now, and a souvenir of nothing but loss: of childhood, of Hrazul, and especially of Jin-jin demself. How appropriate now, he thought, savoring the nutmeat, was any thought of that zany fire-bird.

GOODBYE, MY ETERNALLY HUNGRY FRIEND. "Farewell, egg-sisters," he whispered, conjuring those final images of all who had perished on his account. "Hrazul, Zoia, Zelen; you too, Hatan. May I prove worthy of you all. At last, I'm free."

Now that he was safe, and with time to think, he felt bombarded again by so many questions. He studied his own hand. It had five fingers, and so did Naama's. The giant boy Refa, however, had six, like a Zmee.

Oracle Zoia, he was beginning to appreciate, had been wiser than he, and her words rang now more clearly than before:

'IT'S UNLIKELY THOSE GIANTS ARE YOUR PEOPLE.' And even if they were, 'YOU MAY BE OF THE SAME RACE BUT YOU ARE NOT OF THE SAME KIND.'

And what about the giants he had glimpsed yesterday, crossing the dais in the pre-dawn mists? Why, even Zakon, blessed riddance of him, claimed to have seen a giant invisible to everyone else.

So many giants! Was Naama allied with them?

Possibly. Probably. No, definitely.

But if she was truly of the Elim like himself, why then was she so large, as well as a complete stranger to beast-song? Hatan's clicks and grunts had rapidly made sense, except to her. He thought hard. It suggested he was special. But if that were true, then why had his parents surrendered him in Hatan's charge to the Zmee if they and his own kind were supposed to be enemies? The giants had been after something, and his parents had thought nothing of giving their lives to protect it. But what, or who, was the object of the giants' desire? The clay balls Zoia had hidden inside the now battered medicine stick, or a ten-year-old boy? What were the odds of both being true?

Yes, he had recovered Zoia's spheres. In those panic-filled moments of hauling Naama up the landing net, he had found his medicine stick snagged and covered with jellyfish tendrils. In his first relaxing moment, he had checked and they were intact. Each was merely a lump of unglazed pottery, marked in runes similar to the living stones of the dais in Ra'a-Zohari. They were familiar symbols but their message was indecipherable.

Their origin and purpose, why giants had come in search of them, or even why they had been vaulted in the Reliquary for a generation, he was at a complete loss to explain. Were they talismans, or perhaps keys to some ancient magical power like the High Wisdom's emerald?

Oracle Zoia had known the truth. Clearly, others knew too.

All this speculation made the head spin. However, one thing was now clear: the giants had been his parents' enemy, so the giants were his enemy too, and by association, Naama with them. She declared herself Havilan, and yet the Anaki were her people. How could she be both? He beheld her sleeping form with detached admiration. The long legs, the smooth golden skin: such a wondrous and beautiful enemy! Would she ever cut his hair again?

Nevertheless, he silently vowed never to speak of these rune-covered mysteries to this lovely barbarian, or of the green crystal pendant now safely hidden in the new medicine stick.

But Naama had saved him in the end, when she need not have. Whatever her allegiances, there was a spark of good in her. He and the barbarian she were bound now, if not by mutual indebtedness, then bound perhaps by mutual scars. Whether fate would sunder them and pit them against each other, only time itself would tell.

She had spoken of family, a mother.

YARED! AYMA!

Perhaps, with luck, one of his parents might still be alive, or even — what's that word? — a *brother*. He was once again Enokhi-bun-Yared but not quite yet a true child of the Elim. That would be his primary mission: to find his family, to uncover the truths that had shaped him.

Now, what to make of all the black-eyed creatures that appeared when things were at their worst: the zhuk-eyed Zmee, the ebony-eyed gholuj in his cell, and even the zhrat with charcoal eyes that had signaled him with Zakon's helmet feathers?

Weird.

The boat had now left the Chechi Archipelago far behind. Owing to the immense tangle of jellyfish there, the pilgrims had broken with tradition and skipped the traditional feast. The little islands were now mere dots on the seascape, and the verdure of Zoar Island itself just a lonely green bump on the ocean.

A bump. A pyramid. The Reliquary.

Oh, enigma in stone!

What was that mountain's true purpose? Even the Zmee were at a loss to explain it. The 'living stones' were a mystery even to them. There were strange forces at work here, and a forgotten history. His palm still bore its distinctive burn from the Reliquary.

He pondered its vision and what it meant. Six days: in six strangely urgent and increasingly frenzied days, the brighter glory of Ssla born of Oo-Ssla, and everything that grew or breathed, flew, swam, or crawled, whether plant or beast, were made — no, rather born: wonder beyond wonders, all born in a birth that would brook no delay. This world and its peopling was no hasty afterthought, but the fulfillment of a yearning that stretched beyond the most ancient of heavens to before even light itself had a name. And from that primal urge, all the dawns thereafter had sprung.

The primal urge. The First Cause. The El.

Yes, this was all the work of The El. And as a dead world had been granted a soul, Enok had witnessed the first of its days.

Through a gap beneath the barge, he imbibed of a final glimpse of the world he had known: the sea, the island, the birds, the sky. Beyond all that was, this world was special; his people were special. Surely, *that* was the message of the Reliquary.

And yet, something had gone awry. This was no longer the pristine newborn world he had seen in the vision. Something sinister had infected it and soured the amity between the Elim and the Zmee. The germ of it was buried in old Ukhaz's tirade, and surely the strangest accusation:

'THE FIRST CAUSE DROVE THEM OUT ... AND THE INSOLENT BEASTS BLAME US.'

But mistress Zoia's enjoinder before their separation suggested a slender hope:

'TO STAND AGAIN ON THE HOLY MOUNTAIN ...'

And then do what exactly?

The island at the center of the world was the original homeland of his people, just as Zoriyan was the Zmee's. This 'insolent beast' would find that mythical island, he decided, and experience it for himself. For Yared and Ayma, for Hrazul and Zoia and mighty Hatan, he would dedicate his life to unraveling the truth of Hra-Adin, or A'din as Naama had called it. There he would be the tears of the Zmee, and perchance fulfill the hopes of all who had 'died that he might live.'

Hidden too in his kit was the daasht, a Mapmaker's diary in shorthand that read almost as good as a map. It might point to friendly territory once he approached the inland sea. Enok had just assumed that Hatan had stolen it from Zoia, but now, on reflection, it had almost certainly been entrusted. That thought spawned so many others, and it simply ached to ponder any of this too deeply.

And last, though hardly least, were those almond eyes of his midnight girl with her wild billowing hair. She had been visiting in dream for the past several few moons, beckoning wordlessly, with such longing in her gaze. He was convinced now she was not the Isha of the Reliquary vision but a daughter. And she was waiting, tormented, needing him as much as he did her.

Was this ... could this ... be love?

Now far beyond the archipelago, the boat began to wend its way through the channel sands that were drawn like bars across the sea, the furthest limits of the world he had known. In so many ways the island, its vast reefs, and even its weather, had been like some colossal insidious octopus coiling about him, smothering every attempt at escape. Even now the tentacles of Sea Broom were tugging at the edges of the wood-and-rubber barge, stabbing chilling tips at the stowaways beneath; and the once placid turquoise sea had darkened to angrily clap the deck with spray.

You must not leave; you will not leave, they all conspired to say.

But vain such efforts were as the great vessel turned to face the Broom head-on. The very same wind that had long resisted a younger Enok's escapes was now powerless, cleft by a mechanical behemoth that knew nothing of aching limb, the sting of jellyfish, or any terror of the deep. And yet he briefly lamented how the spume of its wake formed a vanishing path to a world he could never revisit.

He had been sheltered by a pacifist sect for nigh on fifty years. Even now Zmee were unwittingly protecting him. At that, he laughed and cried and laughed till both were but a hiccup. Though tempered by so many losses, it felt so good to laugh, and to finally laugh triumphantly at the edge of Zoar's reach.

OH, EL! I'M FREE!

But ahead, too distant to be seen, lay the Gihon river delta. Portrayed like Zakon's crooked reach, maps surely underscored its perils, but with growing confidence Enok knew it for no obstacle to the portal of his fate.

Utterly spent, he collapsed to yield a weary soul to sleep.

Might he dream? Perhaps, but not of today, for Zakon's Reach lay waiting.

There lurked both danger and adventure.

Ahead everything was new.

THE END

INTO THE LIGHT‡

Wheezing to an expected end, a spent and broken Hatan is comforted by a Son of Heaven. But are the images real or merely imagined? And is death to be his fate, or life?

THERE IS A SEASON FOR EVERYTHING under the heavens, and the great cycles that drove the stars and the Lesser Light, and the wind-blown clouds that streaked across them, were witness now to the end of Hatan's season as an exile. And this cycle was surely to be his last, for he would soon be little more than a corpse.

Against knotty roots carpeting the edge of a brook, the mighty Wahoona lay broken and spent, not only unmoving but unable to move, and with eyes fixed helplessly at the stark reflection in the brook of his ruined fortress as dawn brought its remnants to light.

Hatan — Mighty Ceder, as the First Father of the Ish had named him at the dawn of all things — was going the way of all flesh, and the forest had wept him a requiem through the night. The hooting of the night-howlers, the cawing of the zhrat, the croaking of the great canopy toads had seemed all the more melodic than he could ever remember. He had known them all and loved all of them in place of the family he had missed so much.

FAMILY!

However, the cacophony of this family had owed as much to alarm as despair. So rich the memories of that treetop lodge that had been a haven to so many. It had lit the night like a glorious summation of all the mornings of his days, and its reflection had been both beautiful and terrifying — images of crackling, devouring flames with a heat so intense it had killed the neighboring trees and scorched everything but the laughing brook.

BURN, BURN BRIGHT, MY BEACON, Hatan had urged, wheezing painfully. SIGNAL THE LAST OF MY DAYS TO MY KIN. IF THE EL SO WILL, PERHAPS THEY MAY YET APPREHEND MY DEMISE, AND RAISE A LAMENTATION OVER THEIR LONG-LOST KING.

Mesmerized by the dancing images of his own pyre, seeing but not seeing, Hatan had conjured images of home and relived the adventures of his days. He had fulfilled his promise to the Children of The El, to Yared and his Ayma. He had guarded their unsuspecting boy and watched him grow to the cusp of manhood, though sadly, as a beast of burden. A lowly slave!

But that's not what those green-skins had promised! Their tongues were surely as twisted as their bodies. Though he had escaped the serpents, he had kept his word to the end, secretly watching out for the boy, praying and praying and praying that somehow, someday, while the light yet shone in his eyes, that they would meet and flee together. The daasht of that old mother Zmee, their ever-masked Ancient One, pointed the way home. That was the seal of the deal. But a deal with the wind is what it had been, for only a Zmee could interpret its runes!

Strange, that on the very night he had brought up his hard-won incense to light a beacon to The El in a final despairing petition, that the beloved lad crashes into his roost! And on a flying egg! Who but The El could plot such a thing?

His one prayer now was that his own death, and that of so many others, hadn't all been just vain prayers in the smoke. For the wicked Anaki had found the boy at last, and the lad was utterly blind to it.

MIGHTY EL, O LORD OF LIGHTS, GRANT ENOKHI EYES TO SEE!

Hatan wheezed. This cruel dawn that now ascended upon the earth shamefully exposed the great king of the forest Wahoona as crumpled and broken, broken. He could do little but breathe in final gasps and stare at reflections dancing mockingly on the brook.

Despite exhausting his tears upon it, it tormented him now with strange contorted images, flames taking wing like a wondrous fire-bird. Surely, this would bring the ultimate death! And glorious! But a face formed amidst the fierceness, taking shape as a towering Ish-like being. As Hatan feared the Anaki were upon him, a comforting voice formed in his mind.

"N'bwaga, Hatan!" *Don't be afraid,* the being meant. "Hatan *ıts ıts* Wahoona-rosh." *Hatan, truest king of the Wahoona.*

Do YOU KNOW ME? Hatan failed to utter for want of breath.

The great being seemed a Son of Heaven, an emissary of The El. He'd seen many such Eloi in the days before the Great Exodus, when the First Parents of the Elim still ruled in A'din.

YOU NEED NOT DESPAIR, said the being wordlessly, crouching beside him. YOU HAVE DONE EXCEEDINGLY WELL.

The pleading and self-loathing in Hatan's eyes were as eloquent as any speech. LOOK AT ME. MY BEST WAS NOT ENOUGH.

YOU PREPARED ROOSTS FOR THE ISH-CHILD, the being responded, DUG HIM A CAVE-HOME ON THE MOUNTAIN, SAVED HIM MORE THAN ONCE FROM DROWNING ON THE REEFS, SENT YASH'KH HIS WAY WHEN HE NEEDED THEM MOST, USED TREE CRABS TO CLEAR FOREST TRAILS TO SOURCES OF FOOD: NO SMALL FEATS, THESE.

YOU EVEN PLANTED HIM GRAPEVINES AND SUGAR PALMS YEARS AHEAD OF THEIR NEED. AND DIDN'T YOU KEEP TRACK OF THE LAD BY MEANS OF THE ZHRAT AND THEIR SONGS?

THAT PART WAS JIN-JIN'S DOING, Hatan sighed. BUT WHAT'S THE POINT OF ANYTHING NOW? DID YOU NOT SEE THE HALF-BREED ISHA IN THE FLYING EGG? HAVE NOT THE ANAKI TRIUMPHED?

The head of the being shook in Ish-like negation. NAAMA? NO. THE GREAT QUEEN IS A VICTIM OF THE ANAKI AND DESPISES THEM AS MUCH AS YOU. SHE WATCHES OVER THE ISH-CHILD FOR NOW.

Hatan groaned. BUT SHE REEKS OF THE ENEMY! AND SHE IS SET TO BIRTH MORE OF THEM; SURELY, YOU MUST KNOW. ENOKHI HAS NEVER BEEN IN GREATER DANGER!

ALL OF THAT IS TRUE. Even though only a reflection, a look of concern clearly furrowed the being's face, before nodding with an audible sigh. SOMETIMES TO WIN, YOU HAVE TO LOSE. IT WAS THE ONLY WAY TO FREE THE BOY.

AH, Hatan wheezed painfully, beginning to understand what

the Son of Heaven had risked as images formed in his mind. BIRDS EAT THE FRUIT BUT SCATTER THE SEED? Yes, sacrifice makes victory of defeat. The image shifted upon the brook. TELL ME TRULY. IS THIS BUT THE DREAM OF THE DYING?

The being rose and the image upon the water fled. Flames flared upon the brook again, flickering like bird-wing in wonderful colors, and now they settled upon his chest in a form of blue and gold. Vermilion claws pricked his skin. This was no mere image!

JIN-JIN!

The bird-king chirped a greeting.

ARE YOU HERE TO BURY ME? Hatan wondered. I WOULD HATE THE FEAR TO GNAW ON MY BONES.

Like the great being's, Jin-jin's thoughts became clear without speech. SLEEP NOW, OLD FRIEND. AND I WILL DREAM WITH YOU.

IT'S TIME, YOU FIRST FATHERS, the Son of Heaven added. YOUR WORK HERE IS ENDED. I AM HERE TO TAKE YOU HOME.

BEFORE MY END, IF THE EL ALLOW, Hatan inquired of the heavenly being, LET ME GAZE UPON YOUR PERSON, AS ONCE I DID OF YOUR KIND AT THE DAWN OF THIS WORLD.

Slender hands, yet far more powerful than his own, shifted him into a seating position.

"Me? I'm only a Watcher," said the Son of Heaven aloud in the language of the Wahoona and while baring fangs like Enokhi and his Yared often did.

Watcher: the word was wondrously alien, and the being was grinning broadly, Ish-like, marking it as something truly noble. And the resemblance to Enokhi was remarkable, even to the color of the crop.

Hatan was thinking how curious it was that all three of them should have fur hued of sunset, when, suddenly, the brook was gone, the forest too. He could feel his bones and flesh dissolve, being lifted, *lifted*, **lifted** above all sight and sound and touch.

"My name is Helon," said the Watcher.

And then everything was light.

GLOSSARY

Note: stressed vowels are indicated with diacritics. Exotic words are accompanied by an IPA transliteration.

For additional details about races, geographies, lexicons, or simply for a handy on-line "who's who," please visit the mobile-responsive companion glossary at *www.lostworldtributes.media/universe*

A

AB — æb
A god or demigod: Tattooed son of Surai and Sess.

AB-SÉTHI — æb ˈsɛθɪ
Society: An insular and oft-ridiculed tribe devoted to preserving the oral histories of the First Parents. Archaic devotees of The El.

ACOLYTE
Society: A live-in student of a Zmee of the Venerable class.

AKÁD, AKÁDIANS — æˈkæd
Society: A multi-species society of Elim and others who are the pawns of the para-human Anaki, whom they worship as gods.

ÁLAZAR — ˈæləzɑː
A Zmee: 'Gray-face,' First Disciple of the High Wisdom.

ANÁKI — æˈnɑːkɪ
Society: 'Sons of the Gods.' Para-human offspring of The Fallen (gods) and females of the Elim and other terrestrial races.

AVA-BÁBA — ˌʌvʌ ˈbʌbʌ
See: Enok

ÁYMA— ˈeɪmʌ
  An Elim: Enok's mother.
ÁYSHA — ˈeɪʃʌ
  A Zmee: Unusually verdant First Disciple of Hrazul, Zelen's egg.
AZHAKH-NÁ — ˌʌʒʌx ˈnʌ
  Society: A Zmee philosophical and religious sect. Pacifists striving to find their lost homeland, else live peaceably with the Elim.

B

BÁBA — ˈbʌbʌ
  Society: A respectful Marshlander term for any male elder. 'Maa' would the female equivalent.
BEL
  An Ethereal: The invisible, despotic rebel leader of all non-corporeal Elder Gods, the corporeal gods (The Fallen) and hybrid demigods (Anaki). Supreme hater of The El.

C

CHÉCHI — ˈʧɛʧɪ
  Botany: A mildly narcotic carmine seaweed beloved of the Zmee. Usually reserved or occasions of state due to its rarity.
CHIRÚK — ʧəˈɹʊk
  A beast: A forest khwatl, and Enok's pet.

D

DEMIGODS
  See: Anaki.
DÉINA — ˈdeɪnʌ
  An Elim: The young Eyda, known as The Sickle.

E

EL-BENÉI
  Species: Very tall and powerfully built Eloi from another heaven. As Watchers, often take combative posts.

ELDER GODS

>*Society: Enemy ethereals (rebel Watchers of various species) who cannot assume physical form except as apparitions. These are the ultimate rulers of The Fallen (gods)and Anaki (demigods) and Akadian society.*

ÉLIM — 'iːlɪm

>*Species: Humans.*

ÉLISHAN — 'ɛlɪʃaːn

>*An Ethereal: A non-military Watcher. Formerly a guardian of a young Eyda. Species Melakh.*

ÉLOI — 'iːlɔɪ

>*Species: Any kind of intelligent humanoid.*

ÉNOK, ENÓKHI, AVA-BÁBA — 'iːnɒk, ɛ'nɒɣɪ

>*An Elim: The chief protagonist, also termed Ava-Baba (Great Father) by later descendants as a token of veneration.*

ÉYDA — 'eɪdʌ

>*An Elim: The old Deina. Commonly called Old Maa. The prime storyteller and Enok's widow. The aging and reclusive erstwhile matriarch of the Gihon everglades.*

F

FIRST CAUSE

>*Deity: The Zmee designation for the supreme deity whom Elim call The El.*

FOUR-FACES

>*See: Kheroub.*

G

GAYÁN — gʌ'yʌn

>*Geography & Species: The intelligent but inconscient living soul of the world. The biotic life principle.*

GHÓLUJ — 'ɣɔːlʊdʒ

>*Species: A scaly pigeon with a long barbed flexible tail that resembles a rock when curled at rest.*

GODS

>*See: Elder Gods, and The Fallen.*

GOL

>*A god or demigod: One of The Fallen. A prince of the Anaki gods and a ruler of the Akadian horde. Formerly species El-Benei.*

GRAND ORACLE

   A Zmee: The top academic and governmental post held by the High Wisdom. Ruling matriarch of Zoar Island and Enok's former mistress.

GUARDIANS

   Society: A specialized class of Watchers posted by forces loyal to The El to directly prevent otherworldly interference in the self-determination of Elim at the personal or corporate level.

GUARDS

   Society: Zmee guards are militia separated into Reef Scouts (aquatic), Forest Spotters (rural), and Civils (metropolitan). The livery of each is distinctly different.

H

HÁTAN — ˈhætæn

   A beast: Enok's childhood guardian, a powerfully muscled Wahoona chief.

HÁVILANS

   Society: A matriarchal and (mostly) all-female warrior society in the deserts of Havilaa who have fled Anaki abuse. The sworn enemy of the Akadians and the Reavers in particular even though they worship the same gods.

HÉLON — ˈhiːlɒn

   An Ethereal: An ethereal non-military Watcher. Formerly a guardian of a young Enok. Species Melakh.

HIGH WISDOM

   A Zmee: Spiritual head of the Azhakh-Na, office held by the Grand Oracle.

HÓZNY — ˈhɒzniː

   A Zmee: 'Kitemaker,' an associate of Xira. A champion glider and kite-maker.

HRAZÚL — hjʌˈzʊl

   A Zmee: 'Wise-eye,' First Disciple of Zoia, Zelen's eggling, later the Oracle of Ish. Enok's confidant.

I

ISH

   Species: Male Elim. A term often applied to the species as a whole.

ÍSHA

> *Species: Female Elim. An antiquated term but one increasingly used to indicate 'specieal' purity, that the woman is not a hybrid of the Elim and some other Eloi race, and thus all the more precious.*

J

J'ÁTHRA-YA — ʤə ˈʌθɹʌ ˌjɑː

> *Geography: The annual Zmee fertility pilgrimage to the temple of Zul-Al-Kahri on Mount Ur-Atu overlooking the inland sea at the center of the world.*

J'NÁ-ZERU — ʤə ˈnʌ zɛˌɹuː

> *Society: Zakon's personal highly trained Zeruhawi all-female militia who are sworn to die, if required, in order to complete their mission or Zeruhawi objectives generally. Named after the Na-Zeru, the Zeruhawi emblem of a four-legged serpent ring.*

JINAÚQ — ʤɪnˈɔːk, or ʤɪnˈɔːkw

> *Species: Semi-feathered turkey-like dragons with child-like intelligence, limited flying ability, yet with telepathic and amazing powers of mimicry. Playful, comical creatures.*

JÍN-JIN

> *A beast: Enok's comical Jinauq companion.*

K

KÁLMIYA — ˈkælmiˌjʌ

> *A god or demigod: Fair-haired daughter of Surai and Sess.*

KHEROÚB, FOUR-FACES — xɛɹˈuːb

> *Species: Extremely tall four-faced creatures from another heaven who can only exist locally as projections outside their own mobile dimension. They are immensely powerful beings and rarely speak. As Watchers, they generally assume posts as recorders and observers.*

K'HUDÁ — khʊˈdʌ

> *A Zmee: The Vessel Mistress. 'Captain' of the Dragon Boat.*

KHRII — xɹiː

> *Species: Bony crested flying lizards akin to extinct giant pterosaurs. They dwell along seaside cliffs.*

KHWATL — xwɒtl

> *Species: Shy, forest-dwelling, flightless and semi-feathered terror birds akin to the extinct phorusrhacos.*

KUSH — kʊʃ
An Elim: A marshlander scribe. Son of Mati.

L

LÁMEK — ˈlæmɛk
An Elim: 'The Complainer,' business-like son of Mati. Sha-Noa's father. Merchant of tree-sap, pitch and rosin.

LAND'S BREATH
Geographic: See Winds.

LÁYLA — ˈleɪlʌ
An Elim: Second and tawny wife of Sess. A tribal relative of Eyda's.

LONG-HORNS
Species: Ceratopsians.

LONG-NECKS
Species: Sauropods.

M

MA'NÚNA — məˈnuːnʌ
An Ethereal: One of incorporeal Elder Gods, who appears in hermaphroditic form. Sacrificially worshiped by various martial societies as the goddess/god of both fertility and war. Commonly known as the Twain Goddess.

MÁTI, MATÚ-SELAH — ˈmʌti, mʌˈtuːsɛˌlaː
An Elim: High Priest of the marshlands tribe, son of Enok and Eyda, respectfully termed 'Baba' by marshlanders.

MEHÉT'ABEL — mɛˈhɛtˌʌbɛl
An Elim: Wife of Lamek, daughter-in-law to Mati.

MELÁKH — mɛˈlaːx
Species: Very tall and slender Eloi with elongated heads from a watery world in another heaven. As Watchers, they generally non-combative posts.

METHODICISTS
Society: A Zmee bloc adhering to Methodics, that is, scientific rationalism. Though despisers of the Elim, they're not particularly warlike.

N

NAÁMA — ˈnaːmʌ
A god or demigod: The shipwrecked Havilan Battle Queen. Enok's rescuer.

NEWCOMER
  A Zmee: See Zaraza.
NIGHT'S KISS
  Geographic: See Winds.
NÓA — ˈnəʊʌ
  See: Sha-Nóa

O

OLD DAME
  A Zmee: An impolite byname for the deposed High Wisdom and Grand Oracle, who are the same person. While 'High Wisdom' is her ecclesiastical title, 'Grand Oracle' is her academic one. Both her age, intimate name and her moniker are unknown.
OLD MAA, MAA — mɑː
  An Elim: Common and respectful referent to old Eyda.

P

PÚZO — ˈpʊzɒ
  A beast: A fat and aging yashurakh friendly to Enok.

R

RAÁMA — ˈɹɑːmʌ
  A god or demigod: Swarthy daughter of Surai and Sess, and Sha-Noa's look-alike.
RAHÉL — ɹʌˈhɛl
  An Elim: First but youngest wife of Sess. A princess of the Plains-folk.
REAVERS
  Society: Brutal Akadian slaver-traders. The Elim vanguard of any Anaki expedition. They always travel as well organized hordes.
RÉFA — ˈɹɛfʌ
  A god or demigod: Naama's son. An Anaki godling.

S

SÁRAF — ˈsæɹəf
  Species: Extremely tall, fiery, bird-like Elim of the highest heaven with feather-like membranous wings. As Watchers, often take commanding positions.
SAZ'YÁNA — səzˈjɑːnʌ
  An Elim: Mati's wife and generationally younger sister.

SEA BROOM

   Geographic: See Winds.

SESS

   An Elim: Last son of Eyda and Enok. A trader and adventurer.

SHA-NÓA, SHA, NOA — ʃə ˈnəʊʌ, ʃɑ:, ˈnəʊʌ

   An Elim: Last son of Lamek, look-alike great-grandson of Eyda.

SHAV'YAT — ʃʌvˈjʌt

   Society: Zoar's ruling council of twenty four Oracles headed by the Grand Oracle, who enjoys powers of veto.

SHINÁRN — ˌʃɪˈnɑːn

   Species: Mute ethereals who can take the physical form of any species for extended periods. Their eyes are always black.

SHUKHÁI — ʃʊˈxɑːɪ

   A Zmee: The Pilgrim Leader.

SKAZAÁR — skəˈzɑːɹ

   A Zmee: The Chronicler.

SNAKÁSH — snəˈkʌʃ

   A Zmee: Disciple of Skazaar the Chronicler.

SNEI — sneɪ

   A Zmee: 'Sneak-tail,' lyrical and annoying Second Disciple of Oracle Zoia. Co-disciple with Hrazul. One of Zakon's informers.

STÁRION — ˈstɑːɹɪɒn

   An Ethereal: The Princeps. An ethereal military Watcher of the mighty El-Benei species.

STAR WASH

   Geographic: See Winds.

SURAÁZH — sʊˈɹɑːʒ

   A Zmee: Prefect of Zoar's northern Susyaan prefecture.

SURÁI — sʊˈɹaɪ

   A god or demigod: Naama's daughter. Sess's dominant wife. A magus.

T

TERÁS — tɛˈɹæs

   An Elim: Young schoolyard scribe, son of Kush, grandson of Mati.

THE EL

   Deity: An Elim term for the supreme Eternal Creator Spirit.

THE FALLEN

Society: Elder Gods (rebel Watchers) who have irreversibly taken physical form in order to procreate. The masters of the para-human Anaki and the multi-racial Akadian society beneath them.

THAAZH — θɑːʒ

A Zmee: 'One Eye,' the Apothecary / Healer, and Mortician.

TRR-BAHÁL — tr bʌˈhɑːl

Species: Any razor-toothed carnasaur or similar creature. 'Trr' refers to their cooing, and 'bahal' to their unpleasant odor.

U

ÚKHAZ — ˈʊxʌz

A Zmee: 'Old Black Feathers,' 'The Harsh,' the Prime Oracle of Law.

UPHOLDER

See: Zakon.

W

WAHOÓNA — wʌˈhuːnʌ

Species: Powerful and intelligent aquatic yeti-like tree dwellers. Often live in a symbiotic relationship with forest-dwelling Elim.

WATCHERS

Society: Beings from other heavens (dimensions, planes of existence) now defending the Elim against unwanted foreign (alien) exertion. Composed mostly of highly qualified volunteers. Multiple species.

WINDS

Geographic: The four primary summer winds of Zoar — Land's Breath: after dawn, gentle. Sea Broom: early to mid-morning, stronger. Night's Kiss: late after noon till evening, variable. Star Wash: late evening till dawn, variable.

X

XÍRA — ˈksɪJʌ

A Zmee: 'Stargazer,' the Venerable of Sky, former disciple of Zoia. Enok's sworn enemy.

Y

YAHL — jɑːl

Botany: A waterlily from whose root a narcotic is extracted. Used in religious rituals both by worshipers and sacrificial victims.

YARED — ˈjæɹɛd

An Elim: Enok's father.

YÁSHURAKH, YASH'KH — ˈjæʃʊɹæx, jæʃx

Species: Great sailfinned marine dragons akin to a dimetrodon. Hated by the Zmee, whom the yash'kh may attack without provocation. The name itself contains a curse word.

YÉLZA — ˈjɛlzʌ

A Zmee: First Acolyte of Xira. A youngling.

Y'LÁN — jəˈlæn

Language: The lingua franca of the Elim. There are many dialects but the vocabulary is essentially the same.

Y'SHÚR — jəˈʃʊɹ

A Zmee: The Shipwright.

YÚNI — ˈjʊnɪ

A Zmee: 'Little Greeny,' new disciple of the High Wisdom.

YÚRIYEL — ˈjʊɹɪjəl

An Ethereal: An imperial Legate. A towering and fiery ethereal Saraf. A star dweller.

Z

ZÁKON — ˈzʌkɒn

A Zmee: 'The Invisible,' the Upholder, High Sheriff, a Zmee bull, and Enok's nemesis.

ZARÁZA — zəˈɹʌzʌ

A Zmee: 'Newcomer,' the shipwrecked cripple, and presumed slave of Naama.

ZELÉN — zəˈlɛn

A Zmee: 'Ever Curious,' 'Steam-maker,' master boilermaker. Hrazul's egg-bearer.

ZERUHÁWI — zɛɹʊˈhɑːwɪ

Society: A fanatical Zmee cabal who are intent on militaristic action to eliminate all Elim everywhere.

ZHAAL — ʒɑːl

A Zmee: The badly scarred Metal Smith.

ZHAKH — ʒɑːx

Society: A strategy game for two played on a chess-like board. Advanced players play two games at once, each with slightly different rules favoring either attack or defense. One of the games is played to win by losing.

ZHMEE — ʒmiː

A Zmee: The Great Zhmee. Mythical male ancestor of all Zmee.

ZMEE — zmiː

Species: Great large-headed, large-eyed serpents stranded from they know not where. They have six-fingered hands, and two sets of collapsible membranous wings that extend from their ribs.

Females are green; males are red and often have hind legs. Both have facial tendrils that communicate through color and movement. The thicker crown tendrils of adults both signal and detect emotion, act as secondary sensors, and are instrumental in sexual coupling.

ZMÍYA — ˈzmɪjʌ

A Zmee: Mythical female ancestor of all Zmee.

ZMIYSH, ZMEEZH — zmiːʃ, zmiːʒ

Language: The lingua franca of the Zmee. It has a Low form (Zmiysh) for private or common use, and the archaic High form (Zmeezh) employed in public address and by slaves when addressing their superiors. Normally, both are just referred to as Zmiysh.

ZÓAR — ˈzəʊɑɹ

Geography: A grand solitary island distant for the mainland. The last known female Zmee colony.

ZÓIA — ˈzɔjʌ

A Zmee: 'Life-giver' or 'Prime Mapmaker,' the Chief Oracle of Maps. Enok's current mistress.

ZÓRIYAN — ˈzɒɹɪˌjʌn

Geography: The lost homeland of the Zmee. Another planet.

ZOUB — zʊb

A beast: The friendly old one-tusked yashurakh, and sibling of Puzo.

ZÚLYI — ˈzʊlʲɪ

A Zmee: Ancient preserver of Zmee culture. An egg of Zmiya. Founder of the presently scattered Zmee civilization but not especially of Zoar's.

AFTERWORD

Every fantasy world has its magical system that attempts to render the impossible plausible. Mine was inspired by the primordial elements of the Mosaic book of *Genesis*. Several of its early themes are quite exciting as world-building material:

- the tension between the two nigh reciprocal accounts of Creation as seen through earthbound eyes;

- the serpent of Eden, and the fate of its unstated partner and offspring;

- the creeping curse upon the natural world, or what I've termed the Woebegin;

- the para-human Nephilim, the hybrid offspring of humans and those otherworldly 'Sons of God.'

Additionally, I'm indebted to that ancient Jewish apocryphal work, the *Book of Enoch*. It seeded my curiosity in the backstory of antediluvian characters, and in the notion that even Watchers (otherworldly beings) have had their share of troubles.

Now, though inspired by these sources, *Enok* is pure fantasy — as are those very chronicles, some say. Even so, I can't help but wonder whether the reality behind their mythos wasn't even more fantastical than anything I've conjured here.

ACKNOWLEDGMENTS

Many made this book both what it is and what it isn't. To all these folks, this is your book too, and I offer humble thanks:

- to my girls — *bless their beautiful hides!* — for being such obstreperous sources of merriment and stimulation;

- to my wife in particular, who has never let me suffer long under her long-suffering;

- to my editors and critics over the years: Wendy Blaxland, Amy Bursten, Julie McCarthy — who surely laughed *at* me and *with* me but helped sharpen my craft;

- to those talented artisans who realized my vision: James T. Egan of *Bookfly Design* (cover, USA), Graeme Kirby of *KirbyJones* (print interior styling, Oz), and Hilman Hamidi of *99designs* (icons & artwork, Indonesia).

ABOUT THE AUTHOR

While travel and cultural immersion have long been the author's cardinal muses, in the shadow of the viral pandemic he admits only to fingering the ancient classics and anything on cosmology, paleontology, or lost civilizations. He remains at heart, however, that nerdy kid who long devoured a book a week, and all of them science fiction.

His scholastic curiosity spans both science and theology, and he writes from a position where like the tension between the heart and mind, the interplay between the two informs a unified whole.

That inchoate quest for his authentic self has been a meandering across the physical sciences and information technology in various technical and managerial careers. Thus he finds it enormously amusing that this journey has brought him full circle back to that love of challenging story.

Without question, his most satisfying endeavor has been this debut novel. After nearly two decades in the cabinet, he's glad it's finally out.

André may be engaged as *@EnochianFabler* on social media, or via the website *lostworldtributes.media* where he blogs and expands on the story universe.

CPSIA information can be obtained
at www.ICGtesting.com
Printed in the USA
LVHW032029200121
676997LV00004B/87